D1171285

Reflective Wisdom

Reflective Wisdom

Richard Taylor on Issues That Matter

EDITED BY

John Donnelly

PROMETHEUS BOOKS • BUFFALO, NEW YORK

Published 1989 by Prometheus Books
700 East Amherst Street, Buffalo, New York 14215

Library of Congress Cataloging-in-Publication Data

Taylor, Richard, 1919–
Reflective wisdom: Richard Taylor on issues that matter / edited by John Donnelly.
p. cm.
ISBN 0-87975-522-9
1. Philosophy. 2. Political science. 3. Ethics. I. Donnelly, John. II. Title.
B29.T37 1989
191—dc20 89-10303
CIP

Printed in the United States of America

Foreword

I am profoundly grateful to John Donnelly for bringing together this sampling of my writings, some of them from long ago and some very recent, and for the great time and labor he has spent doing it.

When I first learned of his wish to do this I was astonished, for we seem philosophically far apart. Dr. Donnelly is a faithful Roman Catholic, and I am a humanist. We have, nevertheless, a strong intellectual affinity, viewing the same things as problems, though not always arriving at the same answers. Dr. Donnelly is, moreover, the only person I have ever met who understands everything I have written. Some have found my analytical writings of interest, but have been bewildered by my reflections on the mystery and meaning of life. Others, apparently inspired by the latter, have scorned the former. John Donnelly understands it all.

Something should be said here concerning the theism that dwells so comfortably within my humanist philosophy. Many associate humanism with atheism, even considering them inseparable. In fact there is no connection. Spinoza, the father of biblical criticism and an outcast from established religion, considered God's existence a certainty. Socrates, disdainful of the pious pretensions of his contemporaries such as Euthyphro and Anytus, nevertheless had no doubts of the existence of the gods. William James, the leading enemy of absolutisms of every kind, had a strong affinity to the religious temperament. And J. S. Mill, the greatest defender of liberty in the history of philosophy, whose utilitarianism anticipated the situation ethics of most contemporary humanists, was also a theist, though a tepid one.

My own belief in God, without which I would feel inwardly impoverished, springs from my awareness of the profound mystery of nature and of life. I adhere to no church, affirm no creed, and abominate organized religious practice. These things are all merely human, and represent, in my view, the corruption of a religious outlook, not its expression. The history of organized religion is the history of oppression, as real today as ever. This is because religion serves as a convenient instrument for the intolerant. It is not inherent in a religious outlook, or the sense of mystery to which I have alluded, but about which so little can be said. It was David Hume who said that religion rests not on reason, but on faith, and who had one of the characters in his dialogue on this subject say that there are times when the thought of our creator flows in upon us like a sensation. And that, I think, is the end of the matter, beyond which nothing more can be said. It is very much in order for philosophers to criticize religion and expose fallacies here, as elsewhere, but when I see a philosopher undertake to "prove the existence of God" I am reminded of children playing at being stock brokers and bankers: They have not the remotest idea what they are talking about. Nor will I regard it to the point that some arguments of this kind appeared over my name a quarter of a century ago. I was, philosophically, very young then.

The world and life are far less simple than even the best philosophers portray them they as being, and, equally to the point, they are less simple than religious zealots would have us believe. Possibly I have managed to express some of my sense of it in the pieces that follow, and I deeply hope that some readers, whether they agree with what is said here or not, will at least share my bewilderment and that this will nourish in them the spirit of tolerance and the sense of absurdity we all, as human beings, share.

Richard Taylor

Preface

This volume collects a number of Richard Taylor's writings, conveying his thinking on a range of issues that matter such as the philosophical search for wisdom; the meaning of life; reflections on self and world; liberty and the nature of government; the critique of various religious claims; assessing the ethical views of John Stuart Mill and Immanuel Kant; the nature of ethics; the defense of a virtues theory and the search for personal excellence and happiness; the analysis of love and friendship; reflections on the nature of marriage; and metaphysical views on materialism, fatalism, and a critique of polarized thinking.

Throughout the book, Taylor seeks to illuminate perennial questions about human existence. He offers a vision of philosophy as wonder and insight along with conceptual analysis—in short, philosophy as reflective wisdom. Meaningful human existence is ultimately located in human creativity, where persons aspire (despite Taylor's presumption of fatalism) to create their own lives as works of art, acting as veritable novelists of their own existence. The essays included, while by no means exhaustive of Taylor's philosophical work, are designed to convey a sense of the range of Taylor's views on a number of important ethico-religious and socio-political issues.

Richard Taylor and I have become and remained friends in spite of deep philosophical differences. Unlike Taylor, I am neither a fatalist nor a materialist. Instead, my own metaphysical sympathies are for a reasoned defense of human freedom within the framework of what philosophers refer to as "agency," coupled with an attempt to vindicate a form of dualism so that persons might be viewed as psycho-physical wholes. And, unlike Taylor, I have tried to support a philosophical case for postmortem, personal survival along the lines of Christian eschatology.

On the socio-political front, I am not a conservative like Taylor, but a liberal progressive in the classic democratic tradition. Ironically, though

Taylor is a political conservative, he supports a right of choice with respect to abortion, while I wrestle with the seemingly bizarre alliance of being both a liberal and one opposed to such choice.[1]

Taylor and I do seemingly meet philosophically on the matter of belief in God. However, while I am a classic theist, Taylor is more properly classified as a fideist with decided pantheistic proclivities. And, however one chooses to characterize Taylor's rather idiosyncratic religiosity, his basic belief in God seems to have no logical bearing on his moral or socio-political philosophy.[2]

Whereas Taylor appears to supplement his Aristotelian humanism with Nietzsche, I would supplement a humanistic ethics with Jesus. Clearly, any eudaimonistic ethic seeks to foster human flourishing or excellence, but unlike Taylor, I believe that an *imitatio Christi* offers a genuine path to the amelioration of the human condition. And for me, Jesus is more a role model to strive to emulate than an authoritarian figure (as depicted by Taylor) to obey blindly.

I offer these brief autobiographical comments to indicate that, while I admire Taylor's philosophical reflections, I do not always agree with them. My comments on the essays included here are for the purpose of clarifying Taylor's ideas and not necessarily endorsing them.

I have learned much from my study of Taylor's writings over the years. I suspect I have learned much more from my correspondence and conversations with him. Taylor is an excellent philosophical mentor and an esteemed friend.

I am grateful for the secretarial assistance of E. J. McDowell, the Philosophy Department secretary at the University of San Diego, in the preparation of this book.

And much as Taylor rejoices in the existence of his two young sons, Aristotle and Xeno, so, too, do I rejoice in the blessings afforded me by my two children, Colin and Maria Donnelly. May they all flourish in the years ahead.

NOTES

1. Taylor's thoughts on abortion can be found in "Abortion and Morality" (co-authored with Jeanne Caputo), *Free Inquiry* 2 (1982); and "Abortion and Public Policy," *Free Inquiry* 3 (1983).

2. See his latest book, *Ethics, Faith and Reason* (Englewood Cliffs, N.J.: Prentice Hall, 1985).

Contents

PART THREE: POLITICS, RELIGION, AND ETHICS

PART FOUR: LOVE AND SEX

PART FIVE: METAPHYSICAL MATTERS

Introduction

Richard Taylor was born November 5, 1919, in Charlotte, Michigan, one of twin boys born to Marie Louise Taylor that day. He never knew his father, who died quite unexpectedly a few months before his birth, after having minor nose surgery. Taylor confesses that he has never regretted being raised without a father. His mother, who lived to be ninety-eight, died in 1985.

Richard's mother instructed him in the "small virtues," placing great emphasis on the appearance of probity, as might be expected in the Michigan heartland. Of course, he eventually learned to do things his own way. In a privately published book, *My Mother: A Memoir,* Taylor writes: "Eventually I adopted, as my substitute rule, that I should care nothing whatsoever what others might think of me, but only what I think of myself."

Richard Taylor has been thrice married, and his present wife is over forty years his junior. He is the father of two infant sons, Aristotle and Xeno; two grown sons, Christopher and Randall; and a stepdaughter, Molly, whom he helped raise. Taylor writes:

> My mother took the rules concerning the relations of the sexes to be inscribed in stone. Girls—or at least the right ones—were always referred to as "lovely," and I was exhorted to always treat them as I would want my own sister treated. That was perhaps the strangest precept of all, and yet its message was clear and it stuck. Its effect was that I did indeed come to think of female people as angel-like beings, and have ever since. . . . But along with this veneration for the fair sex went also a passionate desire which has been a bane to me as well as a powerful goad and inspiration.[1]

His mother also instructed him in health-management. Her nurturing love was expressed in preparing hot oatmeal, spinach, castor oil, and cod liver oil for her son. His bedroom window was open at night, even in winter, so as to avoid tuberculosis. And for being the obedient son who dutifully ate his oatmeal, Richard would find a wrapped, clean penny at the bottom of his bowl. All early lessons in fortitude.

From his mother, Richard learned that idleness is to be shunned, and that "things worthwhile are not easily won." He learned to value thrift, and to avoid the "trivially frivolous." Overall, "life was not to be thought easy, and there would be no unearned blessings."

> We are what we have made of ourselves, for better or worse. But some parents seem to know how to encourage what may be worthwhile in their children, and to discourage the opposite through discipline and restrained but constant love. Other parents fail abysmally at this, having little awareness of their children's sometimes unexpected strengths. My mother was a paradigm of the former, and I am sure that it was from her that I learned whatever I may know of what it is to genuinely love a child, or indeed any person.[2]

Taylor did his undergraduate study at the University of Illinois, where he majored in zoology. He served several years as a wartime Naval Officer assigned to the Pacific Fleet. In that often lonely and difficult period he was inspired by his off-hours reading of Plato and Schopenhauer and fell in love with philosophy. After his naval service, he took an M.A. in philosophy from Oberlin College and then went on to Brown University for his Ph.D. He joined the faculty at Brown upon graduation and, eventually, became William Herbert Perry Faunce Professor of Philosophy there.

Taylor left Brown in 1963 to join the Philosophy Department at Columbia University. After only two years there, he moved to the University of Rochester where he taught for exactly twenty years. He has held visiting appointments at Princeton, Cornell, and Ohio State University, but his love of undergraduate teaching is shown by his visiting appointments at Swarthmore, Wells, Hamilton, Hobart and William Smith, Hartwick, and Union colleges. He currently serves as Leavitt-Spencer Professor of Philosophy at Union College.

Taylor is probably the most anthologized American philosopher still living. His essays appear not only in the usual expected places, such as innumerable philosophy texts, but also in popular magazines, such as *Cosmopolitan* and *Free Inquiry*. Astonishingly, selections from the "Index" of his widely used *Metaphysics* book have even surfaced in such periodicals as *The Christian Century, Mother Jones,* and *The Country Journal.* Consider these entries from *Metaphysics* as but a sample of his indexical whimsy:

> *Animals,* as metaphysicians; *Ants,* as subjects of divine knowledge, and law of excluded middle; *Bicycles,* their relationship to their parts; *Chisholm,* as cartoonist; *Dentists,* how they cannot see toothaches; *Destiny,* how time carries us thereunto; *Diogenes,* his cup and how it rusted; *Doorknobs,* impersonality of; *Evangelists,* how they stupefy with vain promises; *Frogs,* how they feel; *Graveyards,* how we all sink thereinto; *Head,* how God counts the hairs thereon; *Men of Greatness,* how they are unappreciated by their mothers; *Mice,* difficulty of getting rid of; *Nothing,* its ineluctable approach; *Tourism,* as substitute for metaphysics.[3]

Around the late 1960s, Taylor began to rebel against the mainstream academic tradition of analytic philosophy in which he had made his own reputation. His break with the tradition was not over the "relevance issue," so much as Taylor's displeasure with that tradition's perceived lack of philosophic depth. The first expression of that revolt was probably found in his article "Dare to Be Wise," followed shortly after by his book *Good and Evil* that constituted the transition to a somewhat novel approach to "doing philosophy." A knowledgeable observer of the Zeitgeist of contemporary American philosophy could easily unearth in *Good and Evil* a defense of "virtue ethics," which has now become so much in vogue in professional philosophy.[4] Taylor subtitled the book "a new direction," although its roots firmly rest in ancient philosophy. Mysteriously, Taylor has never been acknowledged, much less applauded, as the harbinger of the "new" turn in moral philosophy.

In *Good and Evil,* Taylor avoided the fastidious puzzles that preoccupied moral philosophy some twenty years ago, such as John Searle's promising derivation, Max Black's analysis of *wants,* or the descriptivist/prescriptivist controversies surrounding the is-ought question. For Taylor, these fact/value issues were all "poor substitutes for what a wise person ought to think about things of human significance." Instead, Taylor sought "to get the problems of good and evil out of the lint-picking into which they have deteriorated and into the world in which we all live." It was an uncommon suggestion back then to claim that philosophy has no small contribution to make to problems involving personal excellence and the meaning of life.

Unlike so-called philosophical "pluralists" who have been rebelling for years in the American Philosophical Association, and in the last decade making significant political gains (substituting a conventionalism of their own making), Taylor has remained an intellectual maverick. Neither pluralist nor analyst, the iconoclastic Taylor subscribes to his own ideology.

Nietzsche spoke of the tasks confronting philosophical laborers and philosophers proper and questioned whether any philosopher could face up to the latter challenge and "apply the knife vivisectionally" to the basic issues affecting the human condition. The early Taylor was a high-caliber philosophical laborer, utilizing the rigorous machinery of logical analysis. But he then turned his considerable dialectical acumen to the search for philosophical wisdom. In short, Taylor became a philosopher proper, even if his sagacious irreverence at times nullified his being a proper philosopher.

Philosophical probity notwithstanding, I dare say that any philosopher would be justifiably proud of Taylor's mainstream philosophical accomplishments. Indeed, in the period 1954–1963, six of Taylor's articles appeared in *The Philosophical Review,* a publication that is often viewed as the epitome of philosophical achievement. And in approximately the same time frame, he had nine articles published in the British journal *Analysis.* Taylor has also had four articles published in both the *American Philosophical Quarterly* and the *Review of Metaphysics,* three in both *The Journal of Philosophy* and *Philosophical Quarterly,* and two in both *Philosophy of Science* and *The Monist.* He has also published in *Mind, Inquiry,* the *Australasian Journal of Philosophy,* and *International Philosophical Quarterly.*

On the occasion of his sixtieth birthday, a Festschrift, edited by Peter Van Inwagen, was presented to Taylor. That book, *Time and Cause: Essays Presented to Richard Taylor,*[5] includes among its sixteen well-known contributors such pillars of the mainstream elite as J. J. C. Smart, Roderick Chisholm, D. M. Armstrong, Hector-Neri Castaneda, Sydney Shoemaker, Myles Brand, Keith Lehrer, and Joel Feinberg.

Taylor's influence, both directly and indirectly, on professional philosophy is considerable. Many of his former graduate students, whose doctoral dissertations he directed, have achieved prominent standing in academe. Some names that immediately come to mind are Keith Lehrer, Myles Brand, Peter Van Inwagen, Eric Mack, and Steven M. Cahn. Of course, incalculable is the extent of the influence his books, articles, and reprinted essays have had on students, especially undergraduates, over the past thirty-five years.

Taylor's books include the bestseller *Metaphysics,* now in its third edition (1983), which has been translated into many languages; *Action and Purpose* (1966); *Good and Evil: A New Direction* (1970); *Freedom, Anarchy, and the Law* (1973); *With Heart and Mind* (1973); *Having Love Affairs* (1982); and *Ethics, Faith and Reason* (1985).

He has edited and written introductory essays to a number of classic historical works in philosophy, for example, *The Empiricists* (1961), *Mill's Theism* (1957), *The Will to Live: Selected Essays of Arthur Schopenhauer* (1961), *The Basis of Morality* by Schopenhauer (1965), and *The Fourfold Root of the Principle of Sufficient Reason* by Schopenhauer (1974). His basic inspiration remains Greek philosophy, as is most evident in his latest book, *Ethics, Faith and Reason.*

Taylor is also a lifelong beekeeper, and author of *The Joys of Bee-*

keeping, The New Comb Honey Book, The How-To-Do-It Book of Beekeeping, and *Beekeeping for Gardeners;* he also has a regular column "Bee Talks" in *Gleanings in Bee Culture.* Indeed, his mother's dying words to him were "How are the bees?"

> Without bees my own existence would be a shadowy thing, like a world without flowers or without stars or without the songs of birds. The world of men is always uncertain, seldom inspiring, often a source of discouragement and dismay. But the keeper of bees, like anyone who has welded his life to the cycles and patterns of nature, can always turn to his tiny creatures and his craft.[6]

Although Taylor is a laureate of the Academy of Humanism and widely known in secular humanist circles, he is also a fideist. He has in his *Metaphysics* offered original and provocative defenses of both the cosmological and teleological arguments for God's existence. Nonetheless, Taylor insists that his belief in God has nothing to do with the enterprise of philosophical theology. He admits to having "a profound and unshakable belief in God," but he adheres to no particular religion or specific denomination. He is quite adamant about his religious convictions having no basis in philosophical argumentation. There is perhaps no philosophical argument about which doubt is impossible, and Taylor's belief in God rests, by his own testimony, on the impossibility of doubt. Ironically, like Hume, the idea of God flows in upon him like a sensation. Moreover, he is decidedly no supporter of organized religion and has some stinging, Nietzsche-like critiques of Christ and The Sermon on the Mount in *Ethics, Faith and Reason.*

His writing style is highly readable, largely jargon-free, and unfettered by footnoting. At times, he seems quite inconsistent (or, more charitably, engaged in philosophic *tours de force*), as witness his famous defense of fatalism in *The Philosophical Review,* coupled with his "I Can" article alongside the former that defends a version of agency-theory or metaphysical libertarianism.

Looking back at his days at Brown University, and offering "A Tribute" to his former mentor and colleague Roderick Chisholm, Taylor wrote:

> . . . I do not think I can now say that I ever actually *learned* one single philosophical truth in all those years of the most painstaking and laborious inquiry, assisted by what is surely one of the finest philosophical minds in the world. I came to know everything there is to know about the problem of free will, but did not learn, and never expect to learn, whether anyone has a free will. I came to know every argument that bears on this question, have never heard a new one since, and never expect to, but I never learned the answer to it. I am certain no one else has either, though many think they have. I came to know everything there is to know about the so-called

> mind-body problem, and about personal identity, but I never learned which of the many philosophical opinions on those matters is correct. Instead, I learned to express with the utmost precision certain commonplace presuppositions and, of course, I learned to detect what was arbitrary, inconsistent and false in the opinions of most philosophers, particularly those contemporary thinkers who deliver their opinions with the most unabashed confidence. And yet I know that it was these philosophical exercises that made me a philosopher, if indeed I can claim that name.[7]

Taylor has never been afraid to take up provocative, controversial topics, as in his oft-misunderstood and maligned book *Having Love Affairs.* He can also be quite adept at indirect communication, as in his sardonic essay "De Anima," where he seeks sarcastically to reject the notion of an incorporeal soul.

Whether he is being the hard-core analyst dissecting the mind-body problem or freedom versus determinism, or verging on the mystical (see the selections from *With Heart and Mind*), Taylor remains (in the words of Peter Van Inwagen) a "master dialectician." Those of us who are familiar with Taylor's philosophical styles, whether in his writings or his conversations, know how indescribably *sui generis* he is as a person.

Taylor is one of the definienda in the seventh edition of the satirical book *The Philosophical Lexicon,* edited by Daniel Dennett and Karel Lambert. There, "taylor" is a verb as in the idiom "to taylor the argument." And "to taylor" is defined as "to defend an absurd position or conclusion by inventing equally absurd premises or inferences, as in 'it's easy to get a proof of fatalism if you know how to taylor the argument.'" And to add acidity to satire, the *Lexicon* goes on to speak of the phrase "Taylor's dummy" as meaning "an absurd principle on which to hang bits of metaphysical nonsense." Of course, inclusion in the *Lexicon* is more or less coveted as a sign of recognition in one's profession; and the humor, while acerbic, is respectful. The distinguished entrants provide fodder for the in-house jokes of their colleagues.

This book will offer some specimens of *tayloring.* As editor, I may have tailored the selections included herein, but the volume remains Taylor-made throughout.

NOTES

1. *My Mother: A Memoir.*
2. Ibid.
3. *Metaphysics*, 3rd edition (Englewood Cliffs, N.J.: Prentice-Hall, 1983).
4. *Good and Evil.* (New York: Macmillan, 1970; Buffalo, N.Y.: Prometheus Books, 1984).
5. Dordrecht: D. Reidel, 1980.

6. *The Joys of Beekeeping* (Interlaken, N.Y.: Linden Books, 1984).
7. *Analysis and Metaphysics; Essays in Honor of R. M. Chisholm*, ed. Keith Lehrer (Dordrecht: D. Reidel, 1975), p. 5.

Part One

Wisdom, Meaning, and Virtue

Introduction

As I noted in my introductory essay, the first fifteen years of Richard Taylor's philosophical career earned him a reputation for being a highly prominent practitioner of analytic philosophy, known for his clever, technical, often sterile dissection of various philosophical puzzles that governed mainstream philosophical activity in the profession. From all of this a more mature Taylor blossomed, and he became a public philosopher of sorts, less interested in intramural academic philosophy and more attuned to the basic philosophical issues that affect the human condition.

Taylor is at heart a metaphysician, anxious to get at the *whys* of human existence. A master dialectician, he often views a philosophical argument as a *tour de force.* His overall aim is not so much knowledge or a strict proof of this or that issue, as it is an illumination or understanding of the issue under discussion. He consistently tries to shed some synoptic light on the difficulties and perplexities inherent in the human condition.

Taylor believes that persons need to philosophize, for all humans need to give some structure to and confer meaning on their lives. However, he doesn't pursue public philosophy with blinders on, for he is well aware that most people live their lives unreflectively, and he isn't about to promise that philosophizing is fun or anxiety-free. He fully recognizes that philosophy offers no tangible rewards other than wisdom itself. But the unexamined life, as Socrates observed, is not worth living.

Taylor can still find a place for philosophy as the analytical study of concepts, provided it also includes the utilization of holistic imagination and the application of practical wisdom. In short, philosophy is to be pursued as a rational, synoptic, and practical discipline. And, when properly conducted, philosophy can free us from dogma, prejudice, and other specious forms of belief.

In the essay "Dare to Be Wise," Taylor defends the classic role of the philosopher as the lover of wisdom. He was motivated to write this essay by his annoyance at the "prattling stuff" that had become the esoteric staple of academic philosophy in the 1950s and 1960s.

Taylor attempts therein to deconstruct the quest for "philosophical knowledge." However, his deflationary critique should not be construed as an attack on philosophy itself. To be sure, people can have knowledge *about* philosophy (e.g., that Plato believed in the existence of universals, that Descartes developed a defense of the ontological argument, that Hume was an empiricist, that Kant developed the categorical imperative, etc.). But, Taylor argues, it is sheer "pretense" for anyone to think there is such a distinctive thing as philosophical knowledge.

But what of the standard items of putative philosophical knowledge generated by deductive argumentation? Don't philosophers begin with true premises, couple them with valid rules of inference, and then draw a true conclusion? And isn't that conclusion an item of philosophical knowledge? Not really, Taylor claims, because, for example, if the conclusion drawn is independently rejected due to its falsity, then this leads to a rejection of the ratiocination that yielded that conclusion.

Taylor writes: "If the plausibility of the premises is supposed to be evidence for the plausibility of the conclusion, then, by the same token, the implausibility of the conclusion is equally evidence for the implausibility of at least one of the premises." In short, one person's *modus ponens* argument is another person's *reductio ad absurdum*.

Taylor feels that a good deal of so-called philosophical knowledge is a result of drawing inferences from ingrained prejudices. For example, a philosopher begins with some datum like "I, sitting here at my desk, am one and the same person as the paper boy in Charlotte, Michigan, back in 1928." This is an assertion of personal identity over time. Then the philosopher draws some metaphysical inference, e.g., that I am a changeless self; and should people question the original datum, they risk being labeled philosophically obtuse.

Taylor maintains that the premises found in philosophical arguments are not known by any distinctly philosophical means. Rather, the truth of such premises can be known by any rational, observant person. It's true that philosophers control the domain of argumentation that involves the use of counterexamples, but all that that type of argumentative technique demonstrates is a refinement of verbal skill and cleverness for refuting error.

For Taylor, wisdom lies at the heart of the Aristotelian notion of *theoria*, and any truth yielded therein cannot be proven but only displayed. The significance of the great classic philosophers rests not in the various propositions or systems of thought they claimed to demonstrate; rather, their importance lies in the enduring vision they imparted in their discussions of the great issues affecting the human condition.

Taylor's caveat to philosophers is that they argue less and look more. There is a need for vision, wonder, and insight if philosophy is to be restored.

In "Time and Life's Meaning," Taylor wrestles with the grand theme "Is there any meaning to life?" Philosophers have traditionally interpreted this question to be posing either the *cosmic* query "Is there any meaning *of* life?" or the more *terrestrial* query "Is there any meaning *in* life?" The former question seeks some grand rhyme and reason for life and offers an answer by postulating a God who by a divine bestowal supplies the rational apotheosis for life from *without.* The latter question seeks an answer from *within,* which is provided by human agents themselves who willfully confer meaning on their lives by their creative activity. Taylor's sympathies lie with the terrestrial approach to the question.

In an earlier essay "The Meaning of Human Existence," dealing with the same classic existentialist theme, Taylor claims that sheer life itself (i.e., mere quantity of life) is "not self-authenticating," that is, sufficient unto itself to confer meaning.[1] Nor does being biologically classified as a member of *Homo sapiens,* with an animalistic instinct for self-preservation, confer meaning on human existence. Meaningfulness is also not conferred on human existence by theological talk that humans are made in the *imago Dei,* or by philosophers who, á la Kant, speak of human autonomy and dignity.

In an attempt to locate what does constitute meaningful human existence, Taylor presents some paradigms of meaningless existence, focusing on the myth of Sisyphus, the case of an innocent prisoner sentenced for life to dig and then refill holes, and some chanting nuns who perpetually pray in a cloister. And by a method of *via negativa,* Taylor tries to locate some clues as to what would, by contrast, constitute a meaningful life.

The various paradigms, beautifully sketched by Taylor in that essay, reveal the essence of meaningless existence to lie in its purposelessness and endless repetition. The toil, suffering, or pain involved in such paradigms, however severe, are really accidental. Indeed, even a life of self-proclaimed satisfaction or contentment can yet be meaningless. Too often, people mistake as meaningful a clockworklike existence, chiefly centered on finding contentment in the avoidance of boredom. Such persons find at best an illusory form of happiness in various outlets of escape, such as the pursuit of honor, fame, wealth, and other external possessions. And phylogeny recapitulates ontogeny here! For a great many people "are born, pass through the several stages of life, indulging, for the most part, only trivial thoughts and feelings, absorbing pleasures and distractions, fleeing boredom, conceiving no significant works, and leaving almost nothing behind them."

Philosophers have long been puzzled by the notion of *time,* some even declaring it illusory. Taylor locates the significance and the reality of time in human creativity. However rare, there are some individuals who create their own historical reality and thereby create meaningful lives.

To be sure, far too many people live Sisyphean existences. That is, they live in a world devoid of history and time, engaged in pointless, eternal recurrence. The actors may change, but the play remains endless, and the acts are constant. Their world is timeless, lacking purpose, achievement, and novelty of any creative sort.

By contrast, "life is truly meaningful only if it is directed to goals of one's own creation and choice and if those goals are genuinely noble, beautiful, or otherwise lastingly worthwhile and attained."[2] In short, by our creative activity we confer meaning on our lives. "Rational beings are the very creators of time itself, in the historical sense, for without them there would be only a meaningless succession of things and no history at all." But creativity involves more than mere ratiocination, or "the capacity for fabrication." The creative person is a novelist of himself or herself, and not a conformist content to accept the reigning ideas, values, and religious views of the day.

In "Ancient Wisdom and Modern Folly" Taylor shows his appreciation for the work of the ancient moralists and attempts to foster both an understanding and a resumption of their virtue ethics. In stark contrast to the classical moralists, Taylor finds contemporary philosophical ethics quite primitive, with its concentration on the notions of moral rightness and wrongness and associated ideas of duty and obligation. Instead, for Taylor, questions like "What is human excellence?" "What are the virtues?" and "What leads to eudaimonia?" are the central issues in ethics, and decidedly not the current mainstream query "What is morally right or wrong?"

By *virtue,* the ancient moralists meant personal excellence, the composite of qualities found in superior, self-possessed, rational individuals—Aristotle's persons of worth. However, when contemporary ethicists talk about happiness, justice, friendship, and the like, these concepts become corrupted and replaced by notions of secular egalitarianism or by Christianity's promulgation of the beatitudes. "The meek and the poor in spirit were never imagined by the Greeks to be among the blessed. They were quite rightly seen as the wretched and the antithesis of any ideal of virtue that the pagan moralists were capable of imagining."

Similar emasculations have occurred today to the concept of happiness. Contemporary moralists regularly associate happiness with feelings of pleasure or contentment, or the avoidance of boredom, and often back it with the utilitarian principle of maximizing happiness. The end result is that contemporary ethicists completely misunderstand the ancient's concept of happiness as a life of virtuous activity, as the fulfillment of one's function as a rational, creative, reflective, knowledgeable person.

Contemporary ethicists speak of actions as morally right or wrong. But such talk requires the invocation of some customary rule, law, or transcendent moral principle. However, much as it is absurd, say, to hold a particular action as a legal obligation in the absence of any legislation that so imposes that obligation (e.g., one can hardly be obligated to pay state taxes in a state that imposes no such obligation), so, too, Taylor argues, it is nonsensical to describe an action as morally wrong in the absence of any moral principle that forbids it. Yet contemporary moral philosophers engage in just such nonsense, providing no apparent source for such putative moral principles allegedly governing right, wrong, or obligatory actions. Rather, contemporary ethicists reject appeals to divine command morality and largely seem content to spin out self-invented principles such as Kant's categorical imperative or Mill's principle of utility. The end result is that contemporary philosophical ethics is groundless.

NOTES

1. Richard Taylor, "The Meaning of Human Existence," in *Values in Conflict: Life, Liberty and the Rule of Law,* ed. Burton Leiser (New York: Macmillan, 1981), pp. 3–26.

2. Ibid. p. 21.

1

Dare to Be Wise[1]

Students of philosophy learn very early—usually the first day of their first course—that philosophy is the love of wisdom. This is often soon forgotten, however, and there are even men who earn their livelihood at philosophy who have not simply forgotten it, but who seem positively to scorn the idea. A philosopher who, disclaiming any philosophical knowledge, dedicates himself to wisdom is likely to be thought of as one who has missed his calling, who belongs in a pulpit, perhaps, or in some barren retreat for sages, but hardly in the halls of academia. For philosophy, it is supposed by vast numbers of students and teachers of the subject, has for its goal philosophical *knowledge,* and indeed even *certain* knowledge. It is presupposed, therefore, that there is such a thing as philosophical knowledge, and there are even men who think themselves the possessors of at least some of it.

I shall maintain that there simply is no such thing as philosophical knowledge, nor any philosophical way of knowing anything, and defend the humble point that philosophy is, indeed, the love of wisdom. I believe the philosopher's claim to philosophical knowledge is a pretense. It is, moreover, precisely this pretense that has tended to make philosophers of today look ridiculous in the eyes of the world. With so much folly abounding, so much unhappiness even in the midst of riches, so many lives seemingly wasted in the pursuit of specious ideals, men have looked hopefully to the philosophers for light upon some of those things that have always been of deep concern to thoughtful man. They have been puzzled and somewhat dismayed at what they have found. The philosophers, in turn, have been surprised to find their work the subject of considerable and unflattering editorial comment, which they

From *The Review of Metaphysics* 21, no. 4 (1968): 615–629. Reprinted with permission from *The Review of Metaphysics.*

have for the most part swept under the rug and out of sight. It has been a matter of genuine concern to those "outside" philosophy to realize, when wise men are sought, that not only do the philosophers not resemble very closely what they would suppose were men of great wisdom, but many do not even seem to profess a love for it. They are instead embarked upon the pursuit of philosophical knowledge—which of course no one wants to find fault with, provided there is any such thing. But what this philosophical knowledge more often than not turns out to be is either knowledge of the meanings of more or less ordinary words, facility in the techniques of logic, adeptness at definition, or felicity in saying what everyone already believes, and none of these is likely to seem to other men of mature judgment very promising of wisdom nor, indeed, even worthy of men of learning.

KNOWLEDGE VERSUS WISDOM

Socrates considered himself the wisest Athenian, precisely because he knew nothing, and was aware that he knew nothing. His advantage over his fellows was just this, that although they similarly knew nothing, they thought they knew much, while he was spared this conceit. A similar thought was expressed by Lao-tse: "To know and yet (think) we do not know is the highest (attainment); not to know (and yet think) we do know is a disease."[2]

Now of course Socrates, in his profession of ignorance, was not disclaiming the kind of knowledge that is the common possession of men—the knowledge that water is wet, that the fire burns, and snow melts, etc. But there is a vast realm about which men cannot know just by observing, which includes such things as the nature of man, the rational life, what is good for man, what is good for the state, and all those things that are so deeply important to religion and bear upon the meaning of life. It was about all these things that Socrates somewhat ironically professed ignorance. But he did not on this account deem them unimportant. On the contrary, he thought they are the only things that are really important at all. Though he *knew* nothing about them, though they could never be known in any way comparable to our knowledge that water is wet and fire burns, he never doubted that there is such a thing as wisdom concerning such things, and through his whole life he sought it. His searching expressed itself, not merely in his curiosity and his paradoxical dialectic, but in his whole manner of life. Indeed, it entirely determined his whole outer and inner life, and even his very death.

Except for the Cynics, Stoics, and Epicureans, who were Socrates' true heirs, many of his successors even to this day have more or less substituted the ideal of philosophical knowledge for philosophical wisdom. They were largely guided to this by the example of mathematics and particularly geometry, which seemed to thinkers even as recently as Kant to be an existing proof of the possibility of purely rational knowledge. St. Thomas "proved" that God exists, and numberless things besides. He "answered" just about every question a thinking man might ask, setting out his philosophy as a seemingly endless series of questions *and answers,* and with a note of finality that seemed to leave no doubt. Very few today would concede that he really proved any of those things, in the sense of producing any knowledge of them at all. Yet who can deny that those who embraced his thinking were infinitely better off than those who scorned thought altogether, or embraced superstition? And the reason is surely that *thought itself,* even though it may yield no knowledge, is something to be prized. Descartes and Spinoza similarly "proved" that God exists, and a great deal more. Indeed, they both thought that we can achieve not only knowledge, but even certainty, concerning the soul, human motivation, free will, and virtually everything under the sun. It is significant that both philosophers, quite unlike Socrates, took geometry as their model. We know now that the profession of knowledge of all these things was a delusion, that they possessed knowledge of none of the things they set forth with such imposing proof. And yet we know too that their writings are among the intellectual treasures of the world. Why? Because we recognize that profound thought, even when it seeks knowledge and yet gives us knowledge of nothing, may nevertheless help us towards something infinitely more precious, which is philosophical wisdom.

THE MYTH OF PHILOSOPHICAL KNOWLEDGE

Philosophers of this generation do not appear to have disabused themselves of the idea that there is such a thing as philosophical knowledge, that the key to such knowledge is found within the discipline of philosophy itself, and indeed, that such knowledge is possessed by at least some of those—very often themselves—who have extensively pursued this inquiry. That this latter supposition is naive should be obvious to anyone who merely looks at the externals of the situation. It is perfectly commonplace to find philosophers who meet and talk daily, customarily read and discuss each other's work, who have abundant time to acquaint each other with the fruits of their inquiries and the foundations upon which these rest, and who yet agree upon absolutely nothing of a philosophical nature. One believes, the other denies, that universals exist; one maintains, the other doubts, that the mind acts upon the body; one shows his students that the ontological argument is sound, and his colleague shows the same students that it is not; one affirms, the other rejects, the doctrine of free will—and so on to every philosophical question on which one may have an opinion. This is perfectly obvious even to philosophical beginners, and yet the pretense persists, even among philosophers, that there is such a thing as philosophical knowledge, and even that philosophers possess it. Now to be sure, there are differences of theory in every area of inquiry, but in the sciences, for example, it is not pretended that the truth is known in those areas of research and speculation where there is in fact controversy and deep division of opinion among those who are learned in the subject. There are differences of view even in physics, certainly. But what if there were a department of physics whose members held different opinions on virtually every question of physics? Suppose some affirmed and others denied the existence of phlogiston, some defended and others attacked the doctrine of the elasticity of air, and some upheld the atomic theory of matter while others preferred a theory of elemental qualities. Would not the suspicion arise that perhaps there was no real *knowledge* of physics in that department in the first place?

Now I am not, of course, denying that there is knowledge about philosophy, or that philosophers can be, and sometimes are, learned men. Some philosophical scholars have, in fact, a vast erudition, which is not only an enviable ornament to themselves but an inestimable credit to their culture. Such knowledge, then, is not denied; for just as there can be knowledge about music but not, strictly, musical knowledge, or knowledge about literature but not literary knowledge, so also there can be knowledge about philosophy. Almost any philosopher knows, for instance, that Socrates died in 399 B.C., that he taught Plato, believed in the immortality of his soul, and so on. Similarly, a philosopher can explain what pragmatism is, is likely to know Santayana's theories of essences, and can usually give some account of Kant's transcendental aesthetic. But none of this is philosophical knowledge; it is purely biographical and historical, and can for the most part be found in any schoolroom encyclopedia. From similiar sources one can derive all sorts of information about music, composers and musicians, or about poets and their work; but just as such knowledge fails to make one a musician or a poet, so likewise the knowledge about philosophy, however great, does not make one a philosopher.

PHILOSOPHICAL ARGUMENT

One might be tempted to say, then, that philosophical inquiry is just very difficult in comparison, for example, to scientific inquiry, and its fruits of knowledge are therefore yielded more slowly and in small bits. Difficult it most certainly is, for one really must think even to understand it, to say nothing of contributing something of one's own. But is it really an *inquiry* at all? Is it a quest that yields knowledge of anything? If so, what is its method? Not, evidently, observation and experiment, for there are no laboratories of philosophy; there are only libraries. And blackboards and chalk.

Well, there *is* alleged to be a method, a procedure for the attainment of philosophical knowledge, and the mention of blackboards suggests what it is. It is the method of the *philosophical argument.* This consists essentially of seeing what is implied by what, typically by writing things all down on paper or blackboard. By this method philosophical knowledge, sometimes even certainty, is supposed to be acquired by a rational mind, and while the device itself is not the unique possession of philosophy—it has always been useful in law, for instance—philosophy is nevertheless its original home, and philosophers the trained experts in the use of it. Now no doubt the latter is true. Philosophers are, in varying degrees, the trained experts in philosophical argument. But what I am maintaining is a pretense, is that any knowledge is obtained by this instrument. Probably no man ever wielded philosophical argument more skillfully than Socrates, or with more devastating effect, and philosophers today possess absolutely not one particle of knowledge that was not equally known to Socrates, excepting that vast knowledge which they, together with those who are not philosophers, have gleaned from *outside* philosophy—from history and science, and generally from seeing what goes on and reading of what others have seen. From philosophical argument itself philosophers have learned nothing that was not known to Socrates, and he honestly and rightly conceded that he had thereby learned nothing at all.

Philosophical argument takes a variety of forms, and I shall not attempt an inventory of them. The simplest conception of such argument is that we write down true statements—statements that are most often taken as true by ordinary commonsense, incidentally, and not by any special philosophical vision—and then see what they *entail.* We know that if the original statements (premises) are true, and the reasoning valid, then lo! the emerging conclusion will have to be true too, and therefore an item of knowledge. The "evidence" for it will be the very statements appearing above it. And it will therefore be an item of *philosophical* knowledge, since it was gained in a purely philosophical way, that is, by a philosophical argument.

But that nothing has ever been *learned* by such a performance is quite readily seen by considering that if the conclusion of such an argument is implausible, if it runs contrary to what jurists sometimes refer to as one's general "knowledge of the world," then there is not the slightest reason left for clinging to the premises. Indeed, if the conclusion appears the least doubtful, then at least one of the premises, indispensible for getting such a conclusion, is automatically infected with the same doubt. In short, unless the conclusion is something one already happens to believe, the argument accomplishes nothing at all. If the plausibility of the premises is supposed to be evidence for the plausibility of the conclusion, then by the same token, the implausibility of the conclusion is equally evidence for the implausibility of at least one of the premises. So far as gaining any knowledge is concerned, then, we end up exactly where we started, with what we already knew having the final say in the matter, and we have obviously *learned* nothing. Philosophical argument may indeed be the child of philosophy, but commonsense or the general, educated knowledge of what is so in the world most assuredly is not, and if the latter, with which we begin, is still what we are obliged to end up with, then the profession of philosophical knowledge is a pretense indeed.

Here it might be thought that we should simply be more fastidious in the choice of our premises. We should not pick them willy-nilly from the common knowledge of mankind. We should, guided by the example of Descartes, start with things known with certainty to be true, so that they will not later become infected with any doubt that may appear in the conclusion drawn from them. But here the difficulty is obvious: By virtue of what we do know those things to be true? Not, surely, by philosophical arguments, for we must first know these things to be true before we can even compose such an argument. By what is self-evident, then? But here again, what seems self-evident ceases to seem so the moment it is seen to entail what is implausible. By the immediate testimony of our senses, then? But philosophers have no special gifts of the senses, and what they are able to infer from this testimony, others who have never heard of philosophy are able to infer just as well. From the sciences, then? But again, scientists themselves are quite as capable as any philosopher of seeing what is implied by their findings and drawing the proper inferences. So long as intelligence is the more or less common possession of man, we shall not need one group of observers to see what is so, and another group of thinkers to draw the appropriate inferences—though some persons unfamiliar with the subject seem to have the quaint notion that this latter role is to some extent filled by philosophers of science.

PHILOSOPHICAL ANALYSIS

Another form of philosophical argument has for its goal the refinement of meanings, and this is much cultivated in philosophical seminars today. Here a typical procedure is to begin with certain words in more or less common use, express them in ordinary or interesting contexts, and then try to enucleate the connotations of those words in such contexts. This is sometimes done by listing, on blackboard or paper, what must be true, in case the given statements in which those words occur are assumed to be true. For instance, what does it *mean* to say that a given man *moved* his hand? That he moved a match *with* his hand? That he did this *freely?* That he thereby *caused* a fire? That he is thus *responsible* for this? And so on. The manner in which this is discovered is quite interesting: it is done intuitively, through the consideration of imaginary cases. And the results obtained are then tested by what might be regarded as still another form of philosophical argument, namely, by the "counter-example." Thus, having listed what must be true in case the original statement is assumed to be true, the task is to try to invent some imaginary situation in which all the listed statements would be true, but the original false! This having been done, the next step is to find still another condition to add to the list which will have the effect of ruling out the counter-example while preserving the assumed truth of that with which we began. This sometimes goes on for weeks.

This sort of exercise is highly invigorating. It also promotes what men have always found to be a most exhilarating pleasure, the pitting of wits one against another, and it is therefore in some ways ideally suited to the philosophical seminar. It does, moreover, produce intellectual benefits whose value I shall not for a moment diminish. It sharpens the mind to an unbelievably keen edge, and it was, in fact, by essentially this method (without blackboard) that Socrates so refined his own intellect and speech, to the rue and resentment of his victims. It is much cultivated today in England and America and fills a mountain of philosophical journals. The late J. L. Austin, from seminars at Oxford bearing such titles as "Puns and Riddles" (in which the only text was a dictionary) sent forth legions of young philosophers into the English-speaking colleges and universities, their minds honed to an edge capable of splitting out the most subtle distinctions of meaning imaginable and with the felicity of discourse that so agreeably reflects such a mind.

But my point surely remains, that through such a procedure no philosophical knowledge ever emerges, but only a type of wit and skill. The statements which are the data for such arguments are not even things that anyone for a moment supposes are true; such statements as, for example, that a certain man (usually "Jones") moved his hand, striking a match, causing the woods to burn down, and whatnot. The question is never whether any such thing actually happened; the question is only what things like that *mean.* And there is a perfectly plain sense in which an illiterate janitor knows quite well what they mean. He knows exactly what is being said if told that someone burned down the woods with a match, and he also knows quite exactly the circumstances under which such a thing would be true. He only lacks the wit and facility of language to spell it all out. A philosopher may not, therefore, on the basis of such exercises as this, pride himself on any knowledge that is denied to the vulgar, nor even, I believe, on any additional power of good judgment or reason. His "knowledge" is only a knowledge of how to put what is known—or rather, generally believed—with fastidious precision.[3]

ETHICS AND ANALYSIS

In contemporary ethics the method of argument is even simpler, and it is significant that here philosophers, with an air of modesty, sometimes seem to vie with each other in disclaiming philosophical wisdom with respect to things good and evil. The typical procedure is to set forth some fictitious situation—such as some professor's imagined neglect to return a borrowed book—and then consider "what we would say" concerning various features of this. Or sometimes questions having a semblance of ultimacy are put forth—such as, whether pleasure is a good, or the only good, whether there are right actions that exceed obligations, whether responsibility attaches to actions arising from ignorance of fact, and so on. But they are "answered" in the same way; namely, by eliciting "what we would say" about them. Now it is obvious that what we (whoever that is supposed to include) *would say* concerning anything under the sun is precisely what we happen already to *believe* about it. What turns out to be the final appeal here, then, is ordinary opinion, and opinion which was, moreover, settled before the inquiry even began. What this or that man would upon reflection *say* about this thing or that might, of course, be utterly foolish; but there is nothing in this type of procedure which would be likely to exhibit this, precisely because what "we would say," or in other words, what "we" happen rightly or wrongly to think, is itself the ultimate test of what ought to be said. The best that can be achieved by this approach is consistency; but of course the silliest discourse imaginable can be perfectly consistent throughout. It appears again, then, that by such argument no knowledge results, except the knowledge of what we already think, and the knowledge of how to put this clearly and consistently. It is almost too obvious to point out that no philosopher, by such a procedure, comes to know anything that is not just as well known by any decent civilized man, nor, even more obviously, does it make the heart any better—but of course it was never meant to do that.

PHILOSOPHICAL REFUTATIONS

While philosophical arguments evidently do not, then, lead to any knowledge of truth, it must nevertheless be conceded that there is one important use for them, and that is the refutation of error. They are thus used, and often used effectively and well, not only in philosophy but in science, law, and every area where reasoning occurs. If, for example, one shows that a given theory, principle or generalization of any sort—philosophical, legal, scientific or whatever—is inconsistent with itself, or with some generally accepted principle, or with some datum that is accepted as true, then the demonstration of this constitutes a philosophical argument. In a similar way it can sometimes be shown that certain positive (enacted) laws, for example, are inconsistent with each other, or with some superior law such as the Constitution, or that their effects are inconsistent with the purposes for which they were framed, and so on, and these demonstrations take the form of philosophical arguments. Again, philosophical arguments are sometimes applied to philosophical theories themselves, to show that such theories are inconsistent with themselves, or more commonly that their implications are inconsistent with certain facts that have been overlooked, and so on.

In this restricted sense, then, it cannot be denied that philosophical arguments sometimes do yield knowledge; namely, the knowledge of error. The discovery of error does not by itself, however, exhibit any positive truth. A man might know that ever so many things are false—and here again, Socrates comes to mind—and still not have the least idea what is the truth of things. And what I have been maintaining is that philosophical argument, so useful, sometimes, for the discovery of intellectual error, is by itself utterly useless for the discovery of truth; it can show what is *not* so, but never what is.[4]

SAPERE AUDE!

There remains, accordingly, wisdom. That not all philosophers possess it, or even love it, is a truism; but from another point of view a philosopher has surely failed, as a philosopher, if he utterly lacks it. The image of a philosopher who is at the same time a fool is in some ways droll, but from another point of view it is appalling.

There is nothing eternal about wisdom, though in a sense it is timeless. What was wisdom for the age of St. Thomas is perhaps not wisdom for us, but at the same time, the question whether this or that man's thought embodies philosophical wisdom is one in which time is usually no factor. Wisdom need not perish with the passage of time, nor does the succession of generations automatically add to it; one age can be as wise or as foolish as another, however far removed from each other they may be.

And what is it? What is this wisdom that philosophers, by their very name, are supposed to prize above every earthly honor or possession? It is, I think, what Aristotle referred to as the exercise of "theoria," which is a unique capacity of men and women which, alas! more or less slumbers throughout the lives of most of these, including even some who are learned. It is something that cannot be taught, cannot be conveyed even by fathers to sons, as Socrates repeatedly observed. It can therefore not be taught in a classroom, nor can one be certified in it by any examination or degree. Essentially it seems to me to be this: the power of seeing those things, great and small, needed for that kind of inner and outer life that Aristotle likened to the life of the gods, to which the eyes of most men seem closed. And philosophers, some of them, have certainly had this. It can, in fact, be claimed to be almost their unique possession, the one thing which they, more than any others, have really offered to the race of men. Story tellers, poets and artists have certainly possessed this perceptiveness, but in a very superficial way in comparison to the philosophers. The truths that are embodied in philosophical wisdom cannot be proved, but only shown or displayed. The idea of evidence is out of place with respect to them, and such wisdom is therefore not ordinary knowledge. But it is something infinitely better, something far more precious than any fact or conclusion that one merely knows.

If one reads Descartes he is rewarded mainly by the instructiveness of his errors. Such works stand as a lasting reminder that an intellect so great can nevertheless get everything so terribly wrong, so utterly out of accordance with what actually exists, so fantastically unbelievable, in spite of the most elaborate precautions against error (immunity to doubt) that it is possible for one to erect. The same type of distortion runs through Spinoza, whose imposing demonstrations have not the strength of a feather. Yet between Spinoza's proofs—in the corollaries, notes and asides—there resides a priceless philosophical wisdom for anyone who can disregard the intellectual window dressing and *see* things as Spinoza saw them. Without this his philosophy would survive, if at all, only as a curiosity. His observations on self-love and the love of man, the bondage of the emotions, freedom, human nature, human well-being and so on, are so clearly independent of his ostensible "proofs" that the connections must be contrived; but they are nevertheless filled with reflections on what we see all the time, but their significance has so eluded us that it is as if we were without eyes. Some philosophers, recognizing the character of wisdom, have disclaimed any pretension to prove what they were saying. Epictetus addressed himself to his pupils in an epigrammatic, oracular style, enunciating how life, death, folly and moral virtue appeared to him, and illustrating with examples from the daily life that is familiar to everyone. Protagoras approached things in much the same way, and when Socrates asked him for an argument, Protagoras delivered instead a long speech, and a speech so wise, so perceptive of the ways of man and the world, that I believe it was partly lost even on Socrates. Protagoras denied, in fact, that there is any truth, and hence any proof of it; there is only better and worse, and it was his self-appointed mission to display what was better, drawing from what he saw going on around him. The same is found in the writings of William James, who similarly had a low view of truth as it is usually conceived in philosophy. He enjoyed jolting his readers by describing truth as "what works" and in terms of "cash value" and so on, and of course his critics found in him an easy target for refutation. It is difficult even now for students of philosophy to read his arguments without feeling pity for their inventor. Still, the thought of William James has endured while the refutations and even the names of his philosophical critics have been all but forgotten. The reason is that James's wisdom was genuine, and the knowledge of his critics was superficial. James looked at the same world we all look at, but he saw in it what most men go to their graves without seeing. He could describe the most commonplace situations, attitudes and feelings in a manner that the reader could see to be true, touching sometimes the deepest meanings of life, but it took the eye and mind of a James to see and record them. The special regard a man has for his own clothing, the act of will in climbing from a warm bed into a cold room, the delight one can derive from a smell that is bad, the concern a man has for the comforts of his home, the love of one's country, the simplest sentiments of piety—things of this sort, some significant and some seemingly banal, were the grist of James's thought. In themselves they are neither rare, profound nor mysterious. We look at them without seeing much; James looked, and saw, and therein lies his incomparable worth as a philosopher.

Such philosophers are not exceptional, nor have I just picked out some few that I happen to admire. Most of the philosophers whose works have endured and have earned the title of "classics" have embodied wisdom in the sense that I have tried to adumbrate. Some philosophies, such as the paradoxes of Zeno, have gained fame primarily as intellectual curiosities and specimens of intriguing dialectic, to be sure, but this is what is exceptional. The greatest philosophical arguments that we still hold up to students to emulate have seldom made their way into posterity by their incisiveness alone. The dialectical acumen of a Hume or a Leibniz was an embellishment, almost a veneer, to the clearest and deepest knowledge of the world and could never have existed without it. The arguments of such thinkers—Hume's arguments for skepticism, for example—are sometimes hardly more than ingenious *tours de force.* They are not really studied with the purpose of deciding whether to embrace their conclusions, for men's opinions on things of importance are in fact never arrived at by that route. But Hume's reflections on morals, religious faith, human sentiments and passions exhibit truths that stand in need of no strained argumentation, and are in fact supported mostly by illustration drawn from the common experience of mankind.

Nor is wisdom just a thing of the past. One must be more than an acute thinker to be a wise man, but the two are not enemies. Wittgenstein's arguments, for instance, are sometimes so curious and puzzling that even his followers dispute what they are, and yet this great man intrigued his students, even wrought a "revolution in thought" according to some, largely by begging them to look at what it was they were saying instead of being obsessed with what followed from what they were saying. It was characteristic of him to say such things as "Don't think about it; *look* at it." *Theoria* of the very same kind is beautifully exhibited in the writings and talks of Gilbert Ryle, whose controversial fame is for this reason most assuredly well earned. Here is a man who adores puzzles, and one is hardly a philosopher who does not, but his thinking does not end in them, and he does not imagine that they settle anything. Indeed, when one occasionally runs across his papers of an earlier decade it is sometimes hard to believe in their authorship, so far has he moved from the mere argument of then to the philosophical wisdom of now. The older things seem like curiosities hardly worth reading. His great work, *The Concept of Mind,* is an extensive description. Philosophical argument appears in it almost entirely destructively, intended to bury old prejudices, and is quite ancillary to the author's positive philosophical purpose. The great insights of the book, like those of James, are supported entirely by observations, mostly upon perfectly commonplace things, piled one upon another until the truth is virtually driven into the reader's skull—illustrating again the capacity of a wise man to see what fools, and even learned and subtle fools, can somehow only look at.

The enemy of wisdom is not so much ignorance as blindness and folly, and wisdom is nourished not by argument, but by curious wonder. It will never perish so long as there are perceptive minds that are deeply bewildered and honest, whatever may be the fates of the schools.

NOTES

1. Originally composed at the request of students of the University of Rochester for circulation among themselves. The title is borrowed from McTaggart.

2. *The Sacred Books of the East,* ed. F. Max Muller, Vol. 39 (Oxford 1927), p. 113.

3. These remarks have been taken to mean that I think such philosophical activity is of trivial value, though in fact I assert the opposite. (The examples are drawn from my own writings, which I do not despise.)

4. The foregoing remarks altogether have been strangely taken by some to mean that I think, in agreement with some of its recent critics, that philosophy is a pretense. I have in fact claimed the opposite, that philosophy is the love of wisdom.

2

Time and Life's Meaning

It has been characteristic of metaphysics, since the beginning of philosophy, to deny the reality of time. The characteristics ascribed to it by unreflective people, particularly that of *passage,* have seemed so puzzling and paradoxical that the metaphysical temperament has preferred to banish time altogether rather than embrace those paradoxes. Thus Parmenides, the earliest metaphysician, denied reality to all time and becoming, leaving his bleak and changeless conception of reality to be perfected by his pupil Zeno. Plato, too, declared that reality can only be the eternal, describing the strange passage of time in which we mortals live as nothing but that eternity's moving image. Among modern philosophers Spinoza sounded the same note, being unable to think of any reality in which time, by itself, could make a difference, while Immanuel Kant reduced it to a mere form of sensibility. Among recent thinkers McTaggart comes at once to mind, with his proofs that the concept of time is simply self-contradictory.

Time, which seems to move, but in only one direction and at no assignable rate, *is* paradoxical, to be sure, but no declaration of its unreality can alter the fact that we feel it. With each setting sun we see our lives shortened, see the events that we felt so lively just moments ago begin receding into a fading past, gone forever. And with each rising sun we see hopes unfold in fulfillment or, perhaps more often, collapse with finality, to be replaced by new ones. These things are too close to us, too keenly felt, to be declared illusory. To suggest that our rejoicings and sorrowings rest upon illusion, out of deference to metaphysical requirements, would seem to rob our lives of all meaning.

A few philosophical thinkers, aware of this, and starting from

From *The Review of Metaphysics* 40, no. 4 (1987): 675–686. Reprinted with the permission of *The Review of Metaphysics.*

experience rather than reason, have found in time and its passage the most basic of realities, real to the point of being unalterable in its course and in its effects. Henri Bergson comes at once to mind, with his notorious declaration that "time eats into things and leaves on them the mark of its tooth." The metaphor is an outrage to reason, but perfectly captures the way time is felt. We feel it eating into things, into ourselves, and its marks are all too visible. We are, it has often been noted, the only beings in creation who can contemplate in thought our own graves, make plans upon that anticipated calamity and, it should be added, can actually sense its approach.

Time, then, it would seem, is very real to contemplative beings. But I am going to go farther than this, by suggesting that time is not merely something to be understood and described, as has been done by numberless philosophers and poets. Time, I shall contend, has little significant reality except in the context of beings who not only think and feel, but who *create*. It is this capacity for creation that not only gives time its most fundamental meaning, but gives our lives whatever meaning they have, as well.

I

To begin to see this let us think of the whole of inanimate reality, that is, the entire world, considered as devoid of life. It is a world without history or meaning. What happens in that world has happened before and, considering any event by itself, it makes no difference when it happens, nor even any sense to assign it a date. Time is here irrelevant. The earth turns, for example, but it makes not the least difference whether a given rotation is the millionth, or hundred millionth. Each turning is the same as the others, and no assigning of a number to this one or that has any significance. And so it is with everything else that happens in that lifeless world. A mountain rises gradually and is gradually eroded, but it makes no difference when this happens. And raindrops fall, but that a given raindrop should fall at one time rather than at another does not matter, nor is it even easy to make such temporal distinctions. Each drop is just like any other, and no newness is introduced by supposing that it falls earlier, or later, or even millions of years earlier or later. Such a world is without novelty. Combinations of events might occur which occur at no other time, to be sure, but they are already contained in what has gone before. What happens is but a consequence of what has already happened. Such a world could not, to any god contemplating it and capable of understanding it, contain any surprises. Nothing, in short, would ever be created in such a world. There would be novelties of sorts—for example, a snowflake that resembled no other—but these would not be creations in any sense. They would be but novel combinations of what already existed and then pointlessly fell into those combinations. That lifeless world, in short, resembles a clockwork, but one from which the moving hands are missing. What interests us about a clock is that it tells time, but the lifeless world we are now imagining tells us nothing of the sort. On the contrary, the very image of it is enough to exclude considerations of time. The god we imagined a moment ago would discover nothing from the prolonged contemplation of such a world other than what he already knew, and what he could anticipate in it would be nothing not already implicit in his memories of it. Time, to be sure, would exist for such a god—otherwise his contemplation could not be prolonged, nor would it make sense to speak of his memories. But then, by introducing such a being we have, of course, abandoned our premise of a lifeless world.

II

Let us next, then, add to this lifeless world, in our imaginations, the whole of living creation, excluding only rational beings, that is to say, beings like ourselves who are in the broadest sense capable not only of understanding, but of creative thought and action. What we have now is still a world without history. Except for the long and gradual changes wrought by biological evolution, nothing new or different occurs in this world. The sun that rises one day illuminates nothing that was not there the day before, or a thousand or million days before. It is simply the same world, age after age. The things in it exactly resemble those that went before. Every sparrow is just like every other, does exactly the same things in the same way without innovation, then to be imitated by every sparrow to follow. The robin or squirrel you see today does nothing different from those you saw as a child, and could be interchanged with them without discernible difference. Each creature arises and lives out its cycle with an invariance that is almost as fixed as the clockwork we imagined a moment ago, and it is, again, a clockwork without hands. That such a creature should live today or a hundred years hence makes no difference. There are days in this world, but no dates. And each such creature then perishes, leaving behind it nothing whatsoever except more of the same kind, which will do the same things again, and beget the same, these unchanging cycles then to be repeated over and over, forever.

III

The introduction of living things into our imaginary world has, however, resulted in one significant difference, and that is, the rudimentary *sense* of time, at least among some creatures. Irrational beings do not, of course, contemplate in thought their own graves, reflectively make provision for their descendants, mark anniversaries and so on, but they must nevertheless sometimes feel time's passage. A trapped animal feels its life ebbing and senses the approach of death, and perhaps birds, however mechanical or instinctive their behavior may be, have some anticipation of what is going to be done with the nests they build. Our pets anticipate their meals and look forward to them, and possibly the hours drag for them when we leave them alone for the day.

So to that extent time has, in a significant sense, been introduced into our world by the addition to it of living things. But there still remains this huge difference, that these creatures have no history. Each does today what was done by those that went before, and will be done by those to come. The world we are imagining thus resembles an endless play in which the acts are all identical. Every stage setting is the same as every other, the lines spoken are the same, the costumes the same, and the things done the same. Only the actors change, but none introduces any innovation. It would make no difference to any audience which act they saw, nor would there be any point in numbering the acts, or noting which followed which.

The world just described is not, of course, an imaginary one. It is the very world we live in, considered independently of ourselves and our place in it. It is a world in which there is a before and after—the sun, for example, must have risen in order to set—and it is one in which the passage of time is felt. Yet it is timeless in another significant sense, that it has neither history nor meaning. Its meaninglessness is precisely the meaninglessness of the play we were just imagining. There is never anything new, no purpose, no goal; in a word, nothing is ever created.

IV

This sense of eternal meaninglessness was perfectly captured by the ancients in the myth of Sisyphus. Sisyphus, it will be recalled, was condemned by the gods to roll a stone to the top of a hill, whereupon it would roll back to the bottom, to be moved to the top once more by Sisyphus, then to roll back again, and so on, over and over, throughout eternity. Here, surely is existence reduced to utter meaninglessness. Nor does that lack of meaning arise from the onerousness of Sisyphus' task. It would not be redeemed if the task were made easier, by representing the stone as a very small one, for example. Nor does that meaninglessness emerge from the sheer boredom of the task. It would still be there even if we imagined Sisyphus to rejoice in it—if we imagined, for example, that he had a compulsive and insatiable desire to roll stones, and considered himself blessed to be able to do this forever.

The meaninglessness exhibited in this myth is precisely the meaninglessness of the world as it has been described up to this point; namely, that of a world without history, a world that is in this significant sense devoid of time. It is, like the cycles of Sisyphus, a world of endless and pointless repetition.

V

If we now modify the story of Sisyphus in certain ways we can take the crucial step needed to transform it from an image of meaninglessness to one of meaning. In so doing, we can finally see what is needed to give the world and human existence, or the life of any individual person, meaning.

Let us first suppose, then, that Sisyphus does not roll the same stone over and over again to the top, but moves a different stone each time, each stone then remaining at the top of the hill. Does this make a difference? Hardly. One stone does not differ from another, so what Sisyphus is now doing is essentially what he was doing before, rolling a stone, over and over, to the top of the hill. The stones, for all we know, merely accumulate there as a huge and growing pile of rubble.

So let us next imagine that this is not so, that the stones, having been moved to the top of the hill, are one by one, over a long period of time, assembled into something beautiful and lasting—a great temple, we might suppose. Has Sisyphus' existence now gained meaning? In a sense it has, for his labor is no longer wasted and pointless. Something important does come of it all. But that existence might still be totally meaningless to Sisyphus, for what we have imagined is consistent with supposing that he is totally ignorant of what is happening, that he is aware only of rolling stones, one after the other endlessly, with no notion at all of what becomes of them, the temple being entirely the work of others and out of his sight and ken. From his point of view, then, nothing has changed at all.

We next imagine, then, that this latter is not so, that Sisyphus sees the fruit of his toil gradually take shape, is aware of its importance and beauty, and thus has at least the satisfaction of understanding what is happening and realizing that what he does is not totally in vain. Something important does come of it all, something that is great and beautiful, and it is something that is understood.

Now have we invested his existence with meaning? In a sense we have, for Sisyphus has been converted from a mere beast of burden to a being who understands. But there is still a lot missing. For what we now have before us is consistent with the idea that Sisyphus is a mere slave, a rational slave up to a point, to be sure, but still one who goes through endless and repetitive motions over which he has no choice, these being entirely dictated by others, and for a result in which he has no hand, but can only passively observe. To revert to our image of the endlessly repetitive stage play, Sisyphus is here like an actor whose luck is to be cast in the leading role, but with this difference:

an actor can at least reject the role. Such an existence is not without fulfillment of a sort, but we must remember that it still corresponds to the meaningless and, in a significant sense, timeless existence into which the whole of animal creation is cast. The vast array of living cycles today resemble those of a thousand years ago, and those of a thousand years hence. Nature, so conceived, is not without grandeur and beauty, just as we can imagine the temple that rises from Sisyphus' labors to have the same qualities. But that image still lacks an essential ingredient of meaningfulness, unless, of course, we are willing to ascribe a fully meaningful existence to a merely productive machine, or to a slave who has no voice whatsoever in his own fate or even his own actions from one moment to the next.

One final modification is needed, then, and that is to imagine that Sisyphus not only moves this prodigious quantity of stones to the top of the hill, but that he does so for the very purpose of seeing them converted to a beautiful and lasting temple. Most important of all, this temple must be something of his own, the product of his own creative mind, of his own conception, something which, but for his own creative thought and imagination, would never have existed at all.

VI

It is at this point, then, that the idea of a fully meaningful existence emerges, for the first time. It is inseparable from the concept of creativity. And it is exactly this that was missing from everything we have imagined up until now. Nature, however beautiful and awesome, exhibits nothing of creative activity until we include in it rational beings, that is, beings who can think, imagine, plan, and execute things of worth, beings who are, in the true sense, originators or creators. Rational beings do not merely foresee what will be; they sometimes determine what will be. They do not, like the rest of creation, merely wait to see what nature will thrust upon them. They sometimes impose upon nature herself their own creations, sometimes creations of great and lasting significance. Rational beings are the very creators of time itself, in the historical sense, for without them there would be only a meaningless succession of things and no history at all. An animal can, perhaps, anticipate its own death, as can a person, and an animal can bring about works, sometimes of considerable beauty and complexity, as can a person. But what the animal thus does has been done in exactly that way millions of times before. One thinks of the complex beauty of the spider's web, the intricate basketry of the oriole's nest, the ingenious construction of the honeycomb—all things of impressive intricacy, sometimes arresting and marvelous, but also things that disclose not the least hint of creative power. They are, like Sisyphus' labors, only endless repetitions. Human beings, or at least some of them, are capable of going a crucial step further. What a creative mind brings forth is never something merely learned or inherited, nor is it merely something novel, like the snowflake that resembles no other. It is what a creative mind intends it to be, something to which the notions of success or failure can apply, and sometimes something of such extraordinary originality that no other man or god, no one but its creator himself, could have foreseen. And if that creative mind possesses, in addition to this, the rare quality of creative genius, then what is wrought is not merely something that others could neither do nor foresee, it is something they could not even imagine. Thus we see the aptness of Schopenhauer's dictum, that while talent is the ability to hit a target that others miss, genius is the ability to hit a target that others do not even see.

The ancients, in their philosophies, were fond of describing their gods as rational. This idea of divine rationality has persisted among metaphysicians, but the concept of rationality has become narrowed. We think of rationality as care and precision in thought, a due regard for evidence and consistency, and sometimes as mere restraint in conduct. But the ancients quite properly associated it with the contemplative life in the broadest sense. The creation of things beautiful, profound, and unprecedented expressed for them the essence of human rationality. Sisyphus displayed his ultimate rationality, not merely in understanding what he was doing—something that would be within the power of a mere slave—but, as we have modified the myth, in the display of strength and genius that took the form of a beautiful and lasting temple, born first in his own imagination. That was something that no mere slave, and indeed no mere human being, and in fact no other being under the sun except this one, could ever have done. The creative genius of a particular person is something that by its very nature cannot be shared. To the extent that it is shared, such that what it brings forth is also brought forth by others, then it is not only not genius, it is not even a creative power. It is but the capacity for fabrication which, however striking it may be, is quite common throughout nature.

VII

Lest the impression be given that the creative thought and work that I am here praising is something rare, the possession of only a few, let it be noted that it exists in degrees and is, in one form or another, far from rare. What is rare is, I think, the proper appreciation of it. We tend to think of creative works as spectacular achievements, particularly in the arts, but in fact the human capacity to create something new is sometimes found in quite mundane things. Thus, for example, the establishment of a brilliant position in a game of chess is a perfect example of creativity, even though the result is of little value. Things as common as gardening, woodworking and the like give scope to the originality of those who have the knack for them, and are probably the most constant source of life's joys. Intelligent, perhaps witty conversation, and the composition of clear and forceful prose are just as good examples of creativity as the making of a poem of great beauty or depth of meaning, however much they may differ in worth. My own favorite example of a creative work, and one whose value as a creation is rarely appreciated, is the raising of a beautiful family, something that is reserved for the relatively few who can, as a natural gift, do it well. Of course the mere begetting of children is no act of creation at all. It is something that can be done by anyone. And other creatures sometimes with great skill convert their young to self-sufficient adults. They succeed, however, only to the extent that these young exactly resemble themselves, whereas rational human parents should measure their success by the degree to which their children become self-sufficient and capable adults who do *not* resemble their parents, but express instead their own individualities. This is an art that is neither common nor easily learned.

VIII

It would be gratifying if, in the light of what I have been saying, we could now rest upon the comfortable conclusion that our lives derive their meaning from the fact that human beings, and they alone, impose a history upon nature, that the world does not merely persist from age to age, nor does it merely change in the manner of the endless recurrences we see throughout the rest of creation, but that changes are imposed upon it by the creative power of humankind. That would be true, but too general, for in truth, creative power is not something particularly sought and prized by most people. Our culture has taught us to regard all persons as of equal worth, and our religion tells us that this is even God's estimate. Indeed, we are taught that we are, each and every one, created in the very image of that God, so that no one can claim for himself more importance than anyone else. Our lives, it is implied, are invested with great meaning just by virtue of our common humanity. We need only to be born, and our worth is once and for all assured. We are, to be sure, set apart from the remainder of creation, according to this tradition, but what sets us apart is not necessarily anything we do. We are set apart by what is merely given to us, so that a human life, and a valuable and meaningful life, are presumed to be one and the same.

That conception of meaningful existence, which is so familiar, is very sadly at variance with the conception of meaningful existence that I have developed. For in truth, creative power is no common possession. Creative genius is in fact rare. The work of the vast majority of persons does not deviate much from what others have already done and from what can be found everywhere. There seems even to be a determination in most people that this should be so, a determination to pattern their lives after others, to seek as little originality and individual self-worth as possible. People tend, like apes, to mimic and imitate what they already find, absorbing the ideas, manners, values, even, indeed, their religions, from those around them, as if by osmosis. They appropriate virtually everything, returning virtually nothing of their own creative power. The lives of most persons are like the clockwork to which I have so often alluded. They are born, pass through the several stages of life, indulging, for the most part, only trivial thoughts and feelings, absorbing pleasures and distractions, fleeing boredom, conceiving no significant works, and leaving almost nothing behind them. It would be sad enough if this were merely so. What is far sadder is that it is thought not really to matter. Religion then reinforces this by proclaiming no one can, in God's sight, rise above others anyway, that the fool is already as blessed as the wise, and that the greatest possible human worth has already been bestowed upon us all by our merely being born. It is a hard notion to overcome, and weighs upon us like lead. It tends to render even the exemplary among us weak and hesitant.

We take much comfort in that part of the Bible, the very first book, which assures us that we are all the veritable images of God. We tend to overlook the first five words with which the Bible begins: "In the beginning, God created . . . ." That the result of that act is heaven and earth may be overwhelming, but the emphasis is wrong if we dwell on that. What is significant is that the original description of God is as a *creator.* And it is this, surely, that endows one with the divine quality. That human beings exist is not, in itself, a significant fact. That this or that being is possessed of human form, or is of that biological species, is likewise of no significance, whatever may be the teaching of religion and custom to the contrary. What *is* significant, what gives any human existence its meaning, is the possibility of creative power that thus arises. But it is no more than a possibility, realized here and there, more or less, and fully realized only in exceptional persons.

IX

One brings to consciousness the indescribable worth of creative power by imagining specific instances. Consider, for example, that on a given day the sun rose, as usual, and that throughout the day most of the world was much as it had been the day before, virtually all of its inhabitants doing more or less what they were accustomed to doing; but, in a minute part of that world, a nocturne of Chopin's came into being, or a sonata of Mozart's. On another day, otherwise much like any other, Lincoln composed his address for the visit to Gettysburg, or, Matthew Arnold wrote the concluding lines of his *Dover Beach,* or

Grey his *Elegy,* or Plato his *Symposium.* That a little-known woman gave birth to an infant in Malaga, Spain, one October day in 1881 means very little, but that the child was to become Picasso means much. And to complete this kind of imaginative exercise, one needs to fix in his thought some significant creation—something, perhaps, as small but priceless as a prelude of Chopin or a poem of Keats—and then realize that, if a particular person had not at just that moment brought forth that utterly unprecedented thing, then it would never have existed at all. The thought of a world altogether devoid of music or literature or art is the thought of a world that is dark indeed, but if one dwells on it, the thought of a world lacking a single one of the fruits of creative genius that our world actually possesses is a depressing one. That such a world would have been so easy, so inevitable, but for a solitary person, at a single moment, is a shattering reflection.

This, I think, is the verdict of philosophy. One wishes it were the theme of religion as well, for the voice of religion is always louder than that of philosophy. That a world should exist is not finally important, nor does it mean much, by itself, that people should inhabit it. But that some of these should, in varying degrees, be capable of creating worlds of their own and history—thereby creating time in its historical sense—is what gives our lives whatever meaning they have.

3

Ancient Wisdom and Modern Folly

The Oxford edition of Aristotle's *Nicomachean Ethics* includes a detailed table of contents wherein every topic touched upon in the work is noted in outline. Nowhere there does one find reference to any distinction between right and wrong, nor to duty or obligation. Certain Athenian practices, moreover, which a modern reader might suppose would have involved ethical issues deserving of a philosopher's attention, such as slavery and infanticide, are likewise not alluded to.

How come? Is it not surprising that this great treatise on ethics which, together with Kant's writings on the subject, stands as one of the most important contributions to moral philosophy that our culture possesses, should entirely disregard concepts that one would think lie at the very foundation of the subject?

The explanation is that the philosophers of antiquity did not think of ethics as having to do with moral right and wrong. It was religion, and the advent of Christianity in particular which, for better or worse, injected that distinction into philosophical ethics. The moral philosophy of the ancients revolved, instead, around the concepts of virtue, happiness, and justice. But to this one must immediately add that their understanding of these three concepts was vastly different and profounder than ours—so different, in fact, that it is difficult for a modern reader to study the ancient moralists without thorough misunderstanding. And this is true not only of philosophical novices. Indeed, I have seen philosophers of standing, who earned their livelihood teaching that subject, who supposed, for example, that Aristotle, in his application of the doctrine of the mean, was trying to draw a distinction between right and wrong!

From *Midwest Studies in Philosophy* 13 (1988): 54-63. Reprinted by permission of the University of Notre Dame Press.

Our misunderstanding of the ancients thus arises from two sources. The first is that we read into their writings our own conceptions of ethics, which have a religious rather than a philosophical origin. We thus suppose them to be addressing themselves to questions which were remote, not only from their interests, but from their comprehension. The profoundly unfortunate result of this is that we tend to think of the writings of the ancient moralists as primitive, as mere adumbrations of a subject that awaited sophisticated development by modern thinkers. I call this profoundly unfortunate because it blinds us not only to the treasures that this classical literature contains, but to the worthlessness of most modern ethics. It is the modern efforts at philosophical ethics that are primitive and vacuous, and we have no chance of improving upon the ancients without at least first understanding them.

The other source of our misunderstanding is, of course, that the basic concepts upon which the moral philosophies of the ancients rested have become so trivialized in our thinking that we have little appreciation of what they were talking about. This is especially true of the concepts of virtue and happiness. Most persons today, for example, even including the philosophers, would find nothing terribly incongruous in saying of some man that, while he might be uneducated and poor, and unable to point to any significant personal achievement, he might nevertheless be a *good* man—a description that would have been totally incomprehensible to Aristotle. Similarly, most persons today, including even philosophers, would probably see nothing inherently funny in describing a child, or even a moron, as *happy*. Indeed, there are even philosophers who speak of happiness as if it were a *feeling*. And so, equipped with no better understanding than this, it is no wonder that the profundity of the ancients should be so largely lost to us.

I shall now undertake three tasks.

First, I shall explain the basic meaning of virtue, happiness, and justice, as these figured in the writings of the ancients, and note how watered down the first two of these ideas have become.

Second, I shall explain the basic meanings of the terms right and wrong, and indicate how the idea of moral right and wrong found its way into philosophy. In doing so, I shall suggest that this distinction is quite worthless and offers no hope for enlightenment in the area of philosophical ethics.

And finally, I shall enter a plea for the ancients, urging that we not merely try to understand and appreciate their moral philosophies, but that we resume what they undertook. More precisely, I shall urge that we once and for all expunge from our thinking the ideas of moral right and wrong, ideas that have led and will continue to lead to nothing but darkness and vain meddling in the affairs of other people and cultures, and turn instead to the ideas of virtue and happiness. The third idea from antiquity, that of justice, I shall leave aside, first because it seems to me, as I think it did to the ancients, the less important one, and second, because people today, including philosophers who are supposed to be wise, seem incapable of talking about justice without infecting the idea with those very moral overtones which I have urged that we get rid of.

THE CONCEPT OF VIRTUE

Virtue to the ancients meant personal excellence, that is, individual strength or superiority. Thus a virtuous man was not, as we tend to think of him, one who merely fits in with or accommodates himself to others, or who poses no kind of threat. He was, on the contrary, someone who stands out as superior to others, someone who is quite literally better than others, uncommon, noble, and therefore deserving of honor in a sense in which others are not. We, unlike the ancients, think of virtue as the expression of a benevolent will, such that a virtuous person is marked by selflessness and kindness. He is one who puts the interests of others equal to his own, great virtue being a devotion to the interests and needs even of strangers or, sometimes, even of enemies. Such personal meekness comes very close to being the antithesis of the virtue of the classical moralists. For them virtue was the expression, not of a good heart, but of a good mind, such that a virtuous man is identified by his resourcefulness, his powers of achievement, his stature as a thinker and planner or, in a word, his rationality in the broadest sense. A man of virtue was to the ancients a man of special worth, and was to be contrasted, not with the vicious, as we would think of them, but with the worthless. Thus while our model of a person bereft of virtue would most likely be a criminal, the type of person most likely to occur to the ancients would be the slave, the "living tool," as Aristotle described him, the worthless person.

Misunderstanding of the ancients is thus especially acute with respect to their concept of a *good man.* These words instantly evoke in us a certain image, together with an automatic approval, but the image is quite the opposite of what would be intended by the writer if he were a Greek. Contemporary people would have no difficulty in pointing to masses of the meek, ignorant, and dispossessed and saying, with sincerity, that each and every one might be just as good as the best of us and every bit as deserving. Indeed, modern moralists are quite capable of declaring that they want nothing for themselves which they do not also want for others, even for the least among them. This would have seemed to the Greeks, if not self-contradictory, then at least sick and perverse. To see this, imagine Aristotle's reaction if someone were to point to his slaves and say, with a straight face, that each and every one of them is as good a human being as Aristotle himself. I believe one has to dwell on this image for awhile in order to appreciate its absurdity.

Aristotle's *Nicomachean Ethics* abounds with illustrations of the points just made, but so do the philosophies of the Stoics and the portrayals exhibited in Plato's *Dialogues.* To cite a small but revealing example from Aristotle,[1] it will be recalled that he reserves his third kind of friendship, friendships of "the good," to men of outstanding virtue, and declares such friendships to be rare, precisely because those capable of it are so few. Common people are incapable of such friendship because, being common, they lack the requisite excellence. When Aristotle says of such friends that each must be "good," the modern reader almost automatically missunderstands him to be speaking of how such men treat each other, which is a total distortion. When we see what Aristotle does mean by "a good man," we see how difficult it was for him to imagine establishing any kind of friendship with a slave or any person who is not, in his sense, *good.*

The same point arises in connection with Aristotle's famous description of the proud man, as one disdainful of common things and contemptuous of ordinary people, a man who believes, correctly, that he is deserving of great honors, but is willing to accept them only from those who are themselves of sufficient worth to render them worthy of such bestowal. Modern readers, infused with the Christian concept of virtue as including humility, tend to look upon Aristotle's description of pride as an aberration, when in fact it is simply a logical consequence of the Greek conception of virtue which seemed to him obvious.

The Stoic philosophy, which had such a profound and enduring impact on the thinking of the ancients, exhibits the same idea of virtue, that is, personal excellence. For the Stoic this virtue was simply the only thing that mattered. Virtue was within the reach of a truly rational man and, once he possessed it, he could not be divested of it, not even by the most calamitous misfortune. The Stoics did, to be sure, speak sometimes of duty, but if you look closely you see that this is always duty to oneself. The Stoic who comes upon the distraught man, weeping over his calamities, comforts him, but not from any prompting of the heart. He does it to prove his own goodness, once more, to himself. The virtuous man was, to the Stoic, a man whose life was so totally rational that feelings had almost no place in it.

Again, when Diogenes, confronted by Alexander the Great, asked the king whether he was "good or bad," and Alexander replied that he was "good, of course," we are tempted to read into this our own watered-down conception of goodness. Alexander certainly did *not* mean that he was benevolent and kindhearted.

The Greek ideal of virtue, so different from our own, is also abundantly exhibited in the Platonic dialogues. When Socrates repeatedly wonders why the sons of virtuous men are not themselves virtuous, it is worth noting what kind of men he is referring to.[2] He is not speaking of the common run of honest and decent Athenians. Similarly, when Callicles identifies virtue with strength, that is, with personal ability and resourcefulness,[3] Socrates never really repudiates that image. Instead, he leads Callicles to the discovery that the description of such virtue is not as simple as he had supposed.

To illustrate this idea further would only be, I think, to belabor it. It is enough to say that this idea inspires virtually every page of the classical moralists' writings that have come down to us. We must not approach these writings having in mind the concept of virtue embodied in the Beatitudes. The meek and the poor in spirit were never imagined by the Greeks to be among the blessed. They were quite rightly seen as the wretched and the antithesis of any ideal of virtue that the pagan moralists were capable of imagining.

THE IDEA OF HAPPINESS

The Greek *eudaimonia* is always translated "happiness," which is unfortunate, for the meaning we attach to the word *happiness* is thin indeed compared to what the ancients meant by *eudaimonia. Fulfillment* might be a better translation, though this, too, fails to capture the richness of the original term. I shall follow custom and use the term *happiness,* noting, however, how this word must be understood if it is to capture the meaning of *eudaimonia.*

The ancient moralists thought of personal happiness as something that is rare, ill-understood, and indescribably precious. It was the aim of every classical moralist to discover what this elusive happiness consists of and to point out the path to its attainment. The different post-Socratic "schools" were distinguished from each other by how they resolved these two issues. Most of the classical moralists simply assumed, quite plausibly, that nothing can be of greater importance to anyone. They further supposed that the path to this goal is a long and difficult one, filled with pitfalls, and the pursuit of it the work of a lifetime. Thus did Aristotle, expressing an attitude characteristic of the classical moralists, raise the question whether any man can really be called happy until he is dead.[4] This did not mean, of course, that the dead might be happier than the living, but that happiness is to be thought of as the blessing of one's whole lifetime. It is not something ephemeral that might be gained one day, lost the next, regained another day, lost once more, and so on. I believe it is no exaggeration to say that one cannot even begin to understand the classical moralists without an appreciation of the place of this idea in their thinking.

The concept of happiness in modern philosophy, as well as in popular thinking, is superficial indeed in comparison. Even J. S. Mill, whose strange, almost grotesque utilitarianism rests so heavily on the concept of happiness, does not bother to explore what it is. At times he even treats it as being nothing but the feeling of pleasure! Having introduced the *word,* he then hastens on, almost childishly, to try to derive from it some rule of moral obligation—a proceeding which would have left even the hedonists of antiquity totally baffled.

Nor is Mill by any means alone in this superficiality. I cannot offhand think of a single philosopher of the modern era who has even attempted what the ancient moralists took to be their paramount responsibility, namely, to ascertain the nature and conditions of personal happiness. It seems to be assumed that, since the word is in such common use, its meaning must be well understood, and hence, that it must be known by all what happiness is and how it is achieved. The fact that most people, including most of those who are envied, live out wasted lives and go to their graves never having known the kind of personal fulfillment sought by the moralists of antiquity should raise doubts whether the knowledge of what happiness is can be considered common. Nor does the fact that most persons would, if asked, probably declare themselves happy, change this. One's own happiness or lack of it is perhaps the easiest thing one can be deluded about.

Thus people speak of happy feelings, or bid each other to have a happy day, with no awareness that a valuable idea is thus trivialized. Similarly, no incongruity is seen in describing a child or even some worthless person as happy. There have even been philosophers who have spoken of happiness as if it were a feeling. Sometimes the same philosophers speak glibly of "maximizing" happiness, and think they have made a meaningful utterance, even without the least hint of what personal happiness might be, or how its achievement in even a single individual is to be ascertained. Along with this superficiality has gone a tendency to deem it presumptuous for anyone to instruct another person in such a subject. Each person, it is sometimes thought, must be the ultimate judge of his own happiness, of what it consists of and how it is attained. It would be difficult to imagine a presupposition more deadening to a spirit of inquiry, for it appears to rule out the very asking of the question most ancient moralists considered to be at the heart of all their reflections. By assuming such a position, a philosopher eliminates in advance the possibility that people might erroneously think they have achieved personal happiness. If someone sincerely declares that he has met his goal of personal happiness, then we are somehow supposed to simply take his word for it. Thus, for example, if we are shown someone who has succeeded overwhelmingly in the honest attainment of power and wealth, and who declares himself totally satisfied with what he has done and judges his life to have been happy, then we are somehow not allowed even to raise the question whether his life has not, unbeknown to him, been badly spent after all, even though this might be quite obvious to anyone of minimal wisdom. The question, "Who's to judge?" comes almost automatically to the lips of those who have not learned to reflect, who have, indeed, been taught that the quest for wisdom in this area is somehow improper. Thus do the opinions of fools come to be vested with the same importance as the profoundest and clearest reflections of the wisest men of the ages.The silliest among us thereby achieves, as if by right, the stature of an Aristotle in the realm of moral philosophy.

The idea of happiness was seldom far from the center of ancient reflections on ethics, even when the topic under consideration would seem only loosely related to it. Thus Plato's *Republic* is concerned with the nature of justice, but Plato regarded it as a potentially fatal flaw in his analysis that the guardians might fail to be happy, or that the state itself might fail in this respect.[5] In meeting that challenge he presented his own, characteristically Greek, conception of happiness as the rule of reason, both in the individual and the state. And, also characteristically, that conception of happiness coincides almost exactly with the Greek conception of virtue, giving clear meaning to the claim that happiness is not after all the reward of virtue, but virtue itself.

Aristotle identified happiness as that which all things seek,[6] but he did not imagine that he had thereby given any real content to the concept of it. To do this he resorted to an illation familiar to us from Socrates; namely, that happiness is a kind of fulfillment and, more precisely, the fulfillment of one's function as a person.[7] Not surprisingly, this again turns out to be the fulfillment of one's function as *rational,* in the Greek sense of the term; that is, as intellectual, contemplative in the ancient sense, capable of thought, reflection, creativity, and knowledge. But once again, Aristotle is not content with abstract description.[8] He describes the state of personal happiness in great detail, notes the role of "externals" in its achievement, describes how it is related to pleasure, and then finally describes at length what a genuinely happy life consists of. To do this he does not, of course, merely record the testimony of those who believe, perhaps erroneously, that they are happy. He instead describes what fulfillment must consist of for a rational being, much as a physician might describe, in terms of the idea of function, what health must consist of.

The Stoic philosophy proceeded in much the same way, but pushed to an extreme the Socratic injunction to perfect one's own soul or inner life. It is hard, Epictetus said, to combine the industry of one who values externals with the apathy of one who does not, but it is not impossible. For otherwise, he adds, it would be impossible to be happy. The Stoic happiness, like the Aristotelian and the Platonic, then turns out to be one and the same as virtue, and once attained it is secure forever quite regardless of fate.

Of course even a brief allusion to the Greek ideal of happiness would be incomplete without reference to the Epicureans. Epicurus' question was the same as that of all the ancient pagan moralists, namely: How can I make myself happy? But he departed from most moralists by identifying happiness with the cultivation of pleasant sensations and the avoidance of painful ones. The perfection of virtue and the cultivation of justice and honor were made subordinate to this. His moral philosophy thus consists of an extensive manual of instruction on how happiness, thus conceived, can be won.

One cannot fail to see that the Epicurean conception of happiness, while having some plausibility, is shallow in comparison with that of the other ancient moralists. But it is also worth noting that this ancient hedonism is not as shallow as its most famous modern version, that of J. S. Mill. Epicurus did at least undertake, through many instructive pages, to tell us how his goal might be achieved. Mill did nothing of this kind at all. He merely made the abstract claim that it is good, said almost nothing about what it consists of beyond declaring it to be pleasant, said almost nothing about how it can be won, but instead simply deduced, as he imagined, an abstract and implausible moral rule that it is our duty to increase it. It is not very clear how he convinced even himself of this strange injunction, other than by a kind of play on words, much less how he thought it would persuade anyone else.

THE CONCEPT OF JUSTICE

The ancient idea of justice is far too complex for adequate discussion here, besides which it is the least important of the three concepts around which the moral philosophies of the ancients revolved. Virtue and happiness were central themes for all the classical moralists, but justice emerges in the thinking of some of them, such as the Cynics and Stoics and even the Epicureans, only as a subordinate or derivative one.

In general, the ancients entertained two quite dissimilar ideas of justice. The first was justice considered as a virtue, and the other, justice considered as custom, particularly the customs governing the sale and exchange of property.

The first idea, that of justice considered as a virtue, is well exhibited in Plato's *Republic,* where justice is identified with a certain harmonious condition of the soul. By extension, it is identified with a similar harmony within the parts of the state, or rather, of a just, good, or virtuous state. Little is said in the *Republic* concerning what the laws should be, other than identifying their source in those persons, the guardians, who embody the virtue of justice most perfectly.

The second idea, of justice considered as customary rules, is perfectly expressed by Gorgias in the Platonic dialogue named for him.[9] Gorgias, it will be recalled, defines rhetoric as the art of persuasion in matters of justice and injustice, and casually notes that the youthful students who come to him for instruction in this art can of course be presumed to know what justice is. That assertion shocked Socrates, as it does us, but probably no other Athenian of that day would have seen anything odd in it. All Gorgias was saying was that young men of good families can be presumed to know the customs of the Athenians. Socrates understood him, or rather pretended to understand him, to be ascribing to callow youth a knowledge of some ultimate and *natural* principle of justice, something which Socrates certainly made no claim to know and which he doubted anyone knew. But that idea of justice, as something fixed, true, binding on all, and having no origin in human fabrication, which is also how we tend to think of justice today, was not very familiar to the Greeks. Eventually it evolved into the idea of natural law, which is still to this day a fond notion in some quarters of philosophy and jurisprudence.

The second idea of justice as custom was also well expressed by Protagoras, who while he rhetorically ascribed its origin to "the gods," described it simply as consisting of those arts and rules, varying from one place to another, which men follow in order to make social life possible or, when the practices are good ones, which enable social life to thrive.

Again, Aristotle perfectly expresses this second idea of justice when he remarks that the gods have no concern for justice, explaining that the gods have no interest in contracts, the exchange of property, and so on.[10]

How very far modern ethical thought has departed from the thinking of the ancient moralists, and how very much it has, in my opinion, degenerated from that of our remote philosophical ancestors, is illustrated by the history of this idea. If one takes the classical Greek view of justice, so perfectly expressed by Protagoras, identifying it with the laws and practices of a given state, then it will immediately follow that justice is as variable and relative as those laws and practices themselves. One will then not be entitled to describe any such laws and practices as *unjust*. The only question that can arise concerning them is how well they work for those who live under them, or in other words, whether the laws and customs of a given society enable it to prosper and thrive. That is a kind of question that admits of a verifiable answer, but it will not enable one to villify the society in question as "unjust." Such a conception of justice, then, provides no excuse for waging war, except in defense. No nation, under this condition, can stand in moral judgment of another. Today, however, people think it perfectly acceptable to villify other nations and to threaten war against them, even when those nations pose no threat to their interests, and for no other reason than that their laws and practices are deemed somehow "unjust." We have, in other words, taken those practices and principles which suit us, and which we identify with justice, and treated them as *natural* principles, to which other nations must bend, whether they suit them or would even work for them or not. The result is nothing but mischief and the prospect of bloodshed.

MODERN ETHICS

Let us finally look briefly at the ideas of right and wrong around which all modern ethical philosophy revolve and which, as we have noted, are so significantly missing from the reflections of the pagan moralists of antiquity.

To speak of an action as *wrong* is to say that it is in some sense or other forbidden—for example, that it violates some rule, law, or moral principle. To say of one that it is *right* is to say that it is not in any such sense forbidden, or in other words, that it is permitted by such rules, laws, or principles. And to say that a given action is *obligatory* is to say something different still; namely, that some rule, law, or principle requires that it be done.[11]

This is, I think, perfectly obvious with respect to actions that are governed by man-made laws and customs. There can be no legal wrong that violates no actual law, nor can one have a legal obligation which no law of man imposes. In the absence of a criminal statute one can commit no crime, no matter what else might be said in condemnation. And in the same way are legal obligations, such as the obligations to pay taxes or to perform covenants, created by laws, whether these are found in the common law or in enacted legislation. In the absence of legal prohibitions one can commit homicide, but not murder; one can enter upon, but not trespass; can occupy, but not own; can take, but not steal. All such pairs of actions differ, it is obvious, *only* with respect to the existence or non-existence of laws prohibiting them.

It is the same with respect to the usually unwritten laws of custom. Mendacity, for example, is wrong even in those instances which cannot be prosecuted, for it violates a rule of custom that is valuable, imposed in non-legal ways, and generally accepted. Similarly, the obligation imposed by a pledge, such as a pledge to a church or a charity, derives from a rule of custom and is considered to be binding even when it is neither enforceable by law nor imposed by any moral rule other than custom.

So long, then, as we confine ourselves to rights, wrongs, and obligations that are merely legal or customary, keeping aside any that might be thought to be moral as well, it does seem fairly obvious that they are intelligible only as the creation of rules of some sort, that is, actual laws, or rules of custom. No sense can be made of the suggestion that someone trespasses in the absence of any law of real property, or that one can be guilty of bigamy in a society whose laws permit plural marriage, or that one can commit murder in taking a human life under conditions that are permitted by law, as in abortion.

No great acumen or philosophical reflection is necessary to see that the same must hold of *moral* right and wrong; namely, that these are relative to rules too, although here we are talking not about mere man-made custom or law, but rather moral law or, as it is more commonly called, moral principle. Even though this should be quite evident to anyone who will reflect upon it, it is probably the commonest error of contemporary ethical philosophy to disregard it. Philosophers are sometimes heard to declare, for instance, that such things as war, or enslavement, or abortion, are somehow morally *wrong,* imagining that they have said something meaningful and significant even in the absence of any reference to any moral principles that forbid them. No one would fail to see the absurdity in someone's asserting the existence of a *legal* obligation in the absence of any actual law that would impose it. Why, then, is the absurdity less apparent when one moves to the level of moral obligations and rules? Suppose, for example, someone claiming to be versed in the law were to suggest that people have an obligation to file income tax returns even in a society, such as Saudi Arabia, whose laws impose no such taxes. Such a suggestion would surely be met by laughter. Without the rule, there can be no corresponding obligation. Why then, one wonders, does a philosopher imagine that he can speak of some *moral* obligation—such as, for instance, some presumed obligation to make other persons happy—without feeling any need to justify or even refer to any moral principle that might yield such an obligation? Yet this does constantly happen. Persons well versed in philosophy are sometimes heard rendering moral judgments upon this and upon that, out of thin air, without hint of any reference to any moral rules. They seem to expect those around them simply to nod agreement, when the appropriate response would again be laughter.

If this is so—that is, if moral judgments are meaningful only in the context of moral rules or principles—then any philosopher approaching ethics in this way has got to tell us what those moral principles are *and* where they come from. We know where laws come from, namely, from human legislators, and there are established ways of discovering what those laws are. Similarly, we know where customs originate. They are human inventions sometimes, but not always, created in response to certain needs. They are then transmitted by acculturation and constitute the foundation of the popular or conventional ethics familiar to all. But with respect to the moral rules and principles that are supposed to transcend both human laws and customs, I believe it is fair to say we do *not* know where they are supposed to come from, or how they are to be known. It was once generally believed that they come from God, conceived as a supreme lawgiver. The classical moralists did not entertain such a view, but the Christians who followed them did, and many religious persons throughout the world still do. Such people have no difficulty giving meaning to the ideas of moral right and wrong. Modern philosophical moralists do not trace such distinctions to divine command, however, and in the absence of any other source it is difficult to see how the moral laws or principles upon which such distinctions must rest can be presumed to exist at all. It is therefore doubtful whether there is or can be any such thing as philosophical ethics, as that subject is understood today. Philosophers can, to be sure, *make up* moral principles, to their hearts' content, and have in fact done so with great abandon. The result is that we have a wide selection from which to choose, ranging from the categorical imperative of Kant to the greatest happiness principle of Mill. Or we can do what these authors have done and fabricate some new rule of our own, one that will enable us to praise as "morally right" those actions we happen to approve of and to condemn as "wrong" those we happen to dislike. But to note this is, I believe, equivalent to saying once more that there is no such thing as philosophical ethics, if that discipline is supposed to be concerned with the ideas of moral right and wrong and moral obligation. A subject matter whose content differs according to what philosophical author one happens to read, who can do no more in the defense of his favorite rule of morality other than to enunciate it, is hardly a discipline worthy of being taken seriously.

Shall we, then, abandon ethics as an area of philosophical inquiry? Hardly. We need only abandon the vain and pointless philosophical ethics that concerns itself with such empty concepts as moral right and wrong and moral obligation. But there still remains the ethics of virtue, which is philosophical ethics in its original form. It is an area of inquiry that is vast and profound. The ancients wrote thoughtfully and incisively on such things as happiness, virtue, honor, pride, friendship, and, in general, the rational life. I suggest that it is way past time to return to themes such as these, with the hope that philosophers might again live up to their name as lovers of wisdom.

NOTES

1. *Nicomachean Ethics* 8.1156b.
2. *Protagoras* 320; *Meno* 93.
3. *Gorgias* 483.
4. *Nicomachean Ethics* 1100a10.
5. *Republic* 419–420.
6. *Nicomachean Ethics* 1097a15–30.
7. Ibid., 1095b15–30, 1098a5–15.

8. Ibid., 1097a20–30.
9. *Gorgias* 460.
10. *Nicomachean Ethics* 1178b10.
11. It is the lasting value of Kantian ethics to have insisted that obligations are derivative from rules, commands, or "imperatives."

Part Two

Personal Reflections

Introduction

In 1969, while on sabbatical leave in New Zealand, Taylor was inspired to begin writing *With Heart and Mind.* While walking on a desolate beach, Taylor was struck by how "sea and sand suddenly appeared as a lovely and awesome theophany." The musings collected here from that book illustrate Taylor as the more visionary, the poet, the mystic, and less the philosophical dialectician. A forceful attempt is made to penetrate the sundry illusions that separate heart and mind from love of God and the world, and to convey the picture "that being is one and identical with God the creator." In the spirit of Spinoza, Taylor remarks: "The world was not made by God. It is made of God."

Taylor believes that love is the animating passion that abolishes the distinction between me and thee, between self and others. "Love is the perception of identity, and one who sees God and the world in this way has no greater need to be loved by other things, than to love them, for these things have ceased to be other and have also ceased to be things." The solitary Cartesian self isolated from the world leads to lovelessness. And ethico-religious pronouncements that seek to create duties or obligations to love, and thereby bridge the void between self and others, however well motivated, only lead to pretense and rectitude, and, as a consequence, make love into a cold, abstract emotion.

Given our egoistic predilections for an autonomous self as the center of the universe, it shouldn't be surprising that the quest for love will often fail. Ploys of self-embellishment may be attempted to make others love me, but love "is not nourished by what sets its object apart, but by what reaches across that apartness." Taylor compares this path of self-ornamentation to a spider that spins its web ever wider, while the center of its domain shrivels in loneliness. And ploys of self-possession also fail, leaving us with the Sartrean divide of the *être-pour-soi* (being-for-itself) and the *être-en-soi* (being-in-itself).

Nonetheless, it is difficult for most people to resist the Cartesian perspective—the egoism of self-consciousness—and to begin to view the world and others as one in "unself-conscious absorption." Unlike children who can approach the world in wonder and without guile, we adults take refuge in our respective egos. The result is that the "stars, the sky, snow-covered meadows and quiet groves, are no longer home, no longer warm and friendly. Home is four walls, and outside is the world." Taylor shares some poignant insights, not unlike Kierkegaard's, on the purity of heart found in children and the double-mindedness of adulthood.

Turning to some metaphysical and Buddhist reflections on the nature of the eternal, Taylor claims that the eternal is not found in any Cartesian disembodied mind, nor in any Platonic world of forms, but rather in nature herself. Taylor suggests that there are two ways of conceiving of reality and human existence, and he employs the similes of seas and rivers and the endless generation and corruption of the waves and bubbles that appear there. He admits that there is no way to determine which perspective is correct, but he seeks to display the view he favors.

From the first perspective, one can imagine the bubbles on the river as self-conscious. The bubbles are viewed as contingent entities and bare particulars that are generable and corruptible, passing into existence and out of it, while the river persists. On the second perspective, there is just the river, which assumes new forms eternally—a bubble, a rapid, a waterfall, or whatever. From this latter viewpoint, it would be illusory to regard the bubbles as separate things distinct from other items in the river. That is, from this second perspective, there are distinctions in space and time, but not in real beings. Paradoxically, from the second perspective that Taylor favors, the bubbles are not contingent, since they have no being of their own to lose. To extend the metaphor to the Cartesian *cogito,* there is thinking but no self, except in form alone. Selves are modes not substances.

Even if we can appreciate the illusion of selfhood, that does not necessarily rid us of the illusion, much as the rainbow appears to us as a real, independent thing despite our knowledge of the physics of refraction. However fictitious, the denial of the self mocks us. We think it's *our* fiction, after all. Even the epitaph on a gravestone seems to declare, pathetically, "Here I am." In this connection, Taylor has some penetrating observations to make on the epigraphs of graveyard monuments and markers. "As a dust mote is infinite in comparison to a boundless vacuum, this too is not nothing."

Given Taylor's vision of reality, and despite his attempt to liberate us from that captivating notion of selfhood, the irony remains of "the almost invincible power of the illusion just when we thought we had abolished it."

Taylor is also an aphorist, and a collection of some sixty-eight of his aphorisms and epigrams is contained herein. These terse precepts, adages, saws, and maxims seek to convey some general truths or insights about human nature in short pithy sentences or succinct paragraphs. (If the term *epigram* denotes a short, often witty poem, then there are no epigrams in this section. However, the term *epigram* sometimes refers to an especially barbed or cynical maxim, in which case there are quite a few epigrams in this book.) They range over a number of topics covered in discursive and narrative depth elsewhere in this book. Often unconventional, they rankle our hearts and minds, but they also goad us into philosophical reflection.

Taylor is also a beekeeper and a well-known writer on apiculture. He observes and laments how people often subconsciously fall into a particular lifestyle that mimics the reigning economic values of our culture that so prizes external possessions. As an alternative to this vulgar posture of acquisitiveness, Taylor proposes that persons strive to create their own lives as works of art, or aim to be novelists of their own existence.

Beekeeping has provided for Taylor such an alternative lifestyle, and he has found creative fulfillment there. "The beekeeper has constantly before him some of the most exquisite of nature's creations . . . and through his own ingenuity and skill he is able to offer to his fellow men the loveliest product of nature." Taylor eloquently and reverentially describes his comb-honeying activities, and the ecology of his beeyards. "We were not given the world to dominate it, to subdue it or exploit it as though it were a kind of warehouse placed at our disposal and for our exclusive benefit. Rather we were given it to make our home in it, to share it, to glorify it, and to glory in it."

In "Universities and the Debasement of Learning," Taylor reflects on the changes that have occurred over the past twenty years during his long teaching career in American universities. He claims that such institutions, which offer doctoral degrees and assorted postbaccalaureate professional programs, are now largely moribund as undergraduate centers of instruction in liberal education. The universities were once centers of learning and culture, genuine communities of scholars devoted to the liberal education of both graduate and undergraduate students. Today, Taylor avers, they no longer incorporate this ideal.

Back in 1971, in an article "Death of the University" that appeared in the *Hamilton Alumni Review,* Taylor compared American mega-universities to large imaginary hospitals, endowed with ever-expanding research facilities and physical plants. His analogy was and remains striking and instructive. In his mythical hospital the patients (undergraduate students) are largely incidental to the operations of the medical facility. To be sure, the patients make up a large part of the hospital's population, but their needs are largely attended to by nurses (untenured teaching assistants, lecturers, or assistant professors), while physicians (senior faculty members) make brief periodic rounds to check on their welfare. Most of the patients (largely faceless except to the business office that keeps an elaborate computerized record of their stay) manage to get well by self-healing.

The physicians spend most of their time attending to their researcn projects. Those deemed the very best physicians rarely have to confront a patient. Professional advancement results from research performance and successful grantsmanship (aided by a cadre of nonmedical managers that engage in fund-raising). The care and treatment of patients rarely enters into the annual salary evaluation.

Despite any appearance to the contrary, the imaginary hospital is really a medical research institute. Ranking adminstrators, aided by public-relations specialists, regularly write or speak (often platitudinously) on some noble goals of medicine but mostly rationalize the high cost of running the hospital.

Anyone familiar with the state of higher education in America cannot fail to see the marked similarity of the actual university to that mythical hospital that Taylor sketched. However noble the goals of medical or educational research, such programs are not the principal function of either the fictional hospital or the nonfictional university.

Much like the fabricated portrayal of medical practice, so too the actual goals and practices of liberal education have been compromised in our universities to serve the research needs of the faculty or the reigning socio-political needs of the government or the private corporation. If there is any hope for higher education today, it lies in the distinctly liberal arts colleges. Yet too often these colleges are financially strapped, and even when not, they are saddled with the inferiority complex generated by the insidious myth of the research university and its educational mission.

Taylor's analogy is not intended as biting commentary on actual hospitals. Rather he is comparing our modern universities to fictionalized hospitals that are only nominally engaged in health care. By so doing, he is trying to illustrate how the actual contemporary university is as absurd an institution as the depicted, make-believe hospital. The comparison does not seem overdrawn.

In "A Fulfillment," Taylor reflects on his changing attitudes toward both life and death, brought about not only by his advancing years, but also by his unlikely marriage to a university student, who is over forty years his junior. His December/May marriage may not have rejuvenated him, but it has replaced his cynicism about the experience of marriage with "gratitude and wonder." Blessed by the births of two young sons, he finds himself dealing as a father with the modern responsibilities of sharing child care.

Intertwined with his renewed vigor for life, family, and marriage was the realization amid this that death is slowly but surely approaching. This has led Taylor to become very practical, as he purchased new life insurance, assessed his net worth, wrote a will, etc. His sleep is now interrupted, not with abstract philosophical concerns, but with nocturnal ruminations about his pension benefits, his survivors' benefits, and the like.

The younger Taylor was caught up in the whirl of an academic career and the various professional aspirations it spawned. Now semi-retired, that's all in the past. His current reality focuses on immediate family. He seems grateful that unlike some older people who combat loneliness with an often obsessive love for a pet animal, he can instead direct his energies to the need to love his family and thus find fulfillment.

4

With Heart and Mind

PROEM

These thoughts, although of a philosophical character, contain no philosophical dialectic. They seek instead to convey a certain vision and so might appropriately be called a collage or a montage, were such words not pretentious. Let us simply say they are a picture.

The picture, if one were to try encapsulating it into a few words, is probably the oldest philosophical and religious idea known to man: That being is one and identical with God the creator. Exactly the same picture is rediscovered in every age and in every corner of the world. It is at once terrifying and completely fulfilling. It will never perish, and nothing will ever finally replace it. Nothing possibly can; its endurance is that of the stars. Wise men, seers, philosophers, prophets, poets, hymnists, mystics, try again and again to paint this picture, in parable, declamation, psalm, poem, fable, dialectic, allegory and song, and I have added my own small effort. I have tried to express in various ways, some grave and some lighthearted, and some whimsical, what it is like to see at last, to penetrate the illusions that encompass us, to be in a certain state of heart and mind that can only be described, however prosaically, as an absolute love for God and the world, a love that banishes all arising and perishing, and reveals an identity of every spirit to the rest of a creation that is precious beyond any possibility of utterance.

From *With Heart and Mind* (New York: St. Martin's Press, 1973), pp. 8-11, 18-22, 23-26, 27-30, 31-34, 55-60, 82-83, 136-138, 140-142.

LOVE AND SEPARATION

Love is a perception of identity. It is only by such a perception that the distinction between the *me* and the *thee* is abolished. The abolishment of this distinction is not merely the necessary condition of loving; it is just what loving is. All those other relationships that men have called loving—cooperating, giving and taking, possessing and, most remarkably of all, copulating—only superficially resemble loving, in one way or another. They at first glance *appear* to be states wherein the interpersonal gulf is bridged, though in fact it is as absolute as ever.

So long as I think of myself as an absolute, so long as, like Descartes, I think of myself as something existing in my own right, ultimately distinct from everything else, then there is only one possible way I can view the rest, and that is as *other,* as something alien. In the presence of this other, which carries with it the possibility of threat to what I think of as mine, my natural response is to withdraw into my shell, into an acknowledged separateness and abandonment.

Lovelessness is thus the perception of difference, of a gulf between me and thee across which we can only communicate, in the sense of sending (or rather offering) and receiving (or acknowledging) messages. From my point of view, which is that of a center of existence, such communication is only a tenuous interaction, very liable to failure, between me, the central existence, and the other, or that which is peripheral. Only with the abolishment of that gulf can there be communication in its true and original sense of "giving to another as partaker."

It is not being suggested that men should pretend not to notice their differences, that they should try to act as though these did not exist, and that they should baptize these attitudes as "love." This is indeed a common conception of love, and one that we are constantly exhorted to cultivate. In no other way could love ever have been represented as a *duty,* as it frequently is. Kant even made this a pivotal point of his ethics. But clearly, I can think of it as a duty to love others only if I do regard them as *other.* It would be silly to speak of my having a duty to love that with which I entirely identify, for I do already love, in that very identification. Thus does a mother truly love her children, just to the extent that she thinks of them as hers—not hers as possessions, the way material things might be hers, but hers as being a part of her very self. It only begins to be her duty to love them—which is really only pretending to love them—when this identification is eroded.

Acting as though the differences between myself and others did not matter is absolutely to acknowledge those differences. It is not love but pretense, a really ugly imitation of love. It is not ugly of itself, since it is only an acknowledgement of difference, separateness, of an interpersonal chasm, and a resolution to act as though it were not there. There is nothing wrong with that, as such. It may even be essential to that type of social life we call (merely) civilized. But it is ugly if it is paraded as something *else,* namely love, for it is in fact a confession of lovelessness, and making the best of it.

The ugliness of such pseudolove is precisely the ugliness of everything specious. Thus, if something were paraded before us as an oracle, as a fountain of wisdom, and closer inspection revealed it to be nothing more than a jackass artfully decked out and dressed up to suggest learning and wisdom, the ugliness of the intended deception would be overwhelming. Again, if one were to approach the holy, only to have it turn out to be not merely profane, but a desecration of the holy, the ugliness would be sickening, and the more so if one were exhorted to pretend not to notice what was going on, to go through every motion of being in the presence of holiness and even roundly to declare it such.

In the same way, if one represents lovelessness, difference, the alienation of one soul from another, as an ultimate fact of existence, and then begs us to pretend not to notice it, to go through every motion of pretending to love, and even to declare that we do, the ugliness of the pretense is sickening. Seeking love, one is carried in the very opposite direction, and a wall is erected between oneself and the rest of creation—a wall that is made the more impenetrable by being rendered all but invisible.

The man who thinks that loving consists of treating others in a certain way, treating others according to certain formulae he has picked up—perhaps from his church, perhaps from his philosophy, it does not matter where—performs a double deception. He deceives not only a good part of the world, but himself as well. *He* thinks he loves the world. In fact he only treats the world in certain ways—as he might treat a pet dog or a child to which he thought he had certain obligations, as master or as father. Others are led also to think of all this as love, when it is nothing but rectitude, and thus do they come to think of love as something cold and even somewhat disagreeable. Because he has already mislabeled his rectitude, his decency, his sense of obligation, by giving these the name "love" and shining this light upon them for all to see, he not only makes it hard for others to love (for they think they have now seen what a cold thing it is), but he makes it impossible for himself.

If my hands are already filled with sand, and I think it is all gold, it is not possible for me to add gold to them, even if it is right at my feet; for I will not let go of what I have, nor can anything be added to it.

EGOISM

The egoist is simply a self-conscious man. Therefore, all are egoists, for no one for a moment forgets who he is, or has the least difficulty picking himself out, even in a crowded room. When one is speaking he is aware that he is speaking, though not perhaps aware how rudely or how foolishly. When one hears his own name, he is under no misconception whose name it is, as he sometimes is when it comes to the names of other people.

All of us are profoundly self-conscious, every one of us being acutely aware of himself at every moment, acutely concerned for himself, how he is faring in relation to the others around him, how he looks to them from moment to moment. It is in fact so natural for one to think of himself as an absolute center of the whole universe, and of everything else as simply the furniture of the world that is all *around* him, that for some it seems impossible ever to think otherwise or even to consider that any other metaphysics is even remotely possible.

The egoist's consciousness of himself is so absorbing that he is seldom able to become aware of other things, except in a derivative way, or in the manner in which they bear upon him, as presenting threat, promise or opportunity. Thus it is wholly impossible for the egoist to see an ant, for example, crawling across his desk without feeling a strong impulse to brush it off, an impulse that excludes any other response, even the response of curiosity, not to mention sympathy or even love. If he finds a nest of fledgings, his impulse is to run for a camera, that he might exploit this otherwise trivial situation for something of some use to himself. It is quite impossible, as impossible as the moon's ever reversing the direction of its orbit, that he should stare in wonder, even become intoxicated with deep, almost pitying love for these small beings, without, just for a moment, one single thought of himself; or (in a truly metaphysical transcendence) that he should discover his own soul in the small bits of wonderment that lie so clearly beyond the surface of his own skin.

Egoism seems characteristic of the transition from child to man, and is therefore childish only in that sense, that it characterizes the emergence from childhood. The child himself is only minimally self-conscious. He is capable of wonder, capable of staring at the most trivial things—at an insect, a fish, a remote star; even, sometimes it seems, at the air itself, or at clouds, or the sky. Men do not do these things; or at least it requires a great deal of piety for a man to think of doing them. The child has not arrived at the stage of fear and grasping, at the stage of manhood, where everything is contemplated through the prisms of question marks. Are these things useful? Is there money in them? What can I do with them? It is not for the child a matter of doing. It is a matter simply of unself-conscious absorption. It would be dangerous for a man to go about things so dreamily. His day would seem almost endless. Very little would get done. It is partly this guilelessness, this innocence, aptly described as wide-eyed wonder, that gives childhood its charm. In their inward yearning for such wonder, such unself-consciousness, men are almost prepared to worshp childishness. No sin seems quite so base as the corruption of a child's innocence, of his very childishness; and while most men seem to assume that this reverence for childishness is merely the desire to protect that which will someday grow to manliness, it is more likely that the gifts of innocence and wonder, of which the years rob us, are secretly envied—and rightly so.

Such innocence badly equips one for survival. Survival requires the shell that more than anything else distinguishes child from man. The world provides its substance, and its accretion is automatic. Things now come to be seen as *out there,* different, other; and as this perspective becomes clearer, so does another idea crystallize and become so firmly entrenched that no man can ever henceforth entirely shake it off, except in rare moments. This is the idea of the self, the ego. For one can hardly view the world as *out there,* except in relation to what is *not* out there, and that can be nothing but the ego. The idea of the *other* presupposes what is *not* other; and the *different,* what is the *same.* The whole thing is of course a myth, nothing more than a viewpoint acquired in the interest of survival, and yet it is so firmly embedded in our thought that even metaphysicians usually regard it as a datum, as something clearly given, rather than a problem, a puzzle, a fiction.

Thus is achieved the transition from childishness to manhood. It is a transition from belief to pretense, from sunlight to shadows, from naive candor to the most fantastically woven garments of make-believe, from faith to animalism—and yet it is thought absolutely necessary to make that transition, to blast the spirit out of everything, leaving brute matter, and to interpose walls throughout creation, precipitating small egos where before there were a god and a soul.

From now on the stars, the sky, snow-covered meadows and quiet groves, are no longer home, no longer warm and friendly. Home is four walls, and outside is the world. Living things—the insects one so patiently watched for hours without the least sense of patience, the minnows and snails that charmed one, that he seemed even to live and die with, the things of the grass and the air and the lake and forest—these are no longer things whose life is shared, but foreign things, other, beyond the self, beyond soul and spirit, things to be dealt with, used, looked at, sometimes hunted, even eaten. For the first object of life is not worship, but survival, and beyond that, the enhancement of what one has now discovered to be the ultimate reality, the basic reality, that to which all else is reduced, in terms of which all else has its meaning—and that is of course the self, the ego.

Now what before were realities, or childishly seemed so, move about one almost like shadows, things of form, but without substance, mere shapes, moving images that merely impinge upon one in various ways. A child is never astonished to see tears on the face of his father; it is quite natural, almost expected. But at the point where childishness has been put behind and self-consciousness has entered, the sight is shattering, almost like seeing a statue shedding real tears. It pierces for a moment that veil which has reduced the whole of otherness to a shadow existence; it momentarily reminds one of a common spirit, a common reality that makes no distinction between oneself and others. And for just this reason it is frightening for it suggests that one of life's certainties, one of the premises of all philosophy and an article of most theology—namely, the ultimate reality of the self or private soul, and its absolute separation from whatever is not oneself—may be less than quite certain.

Reminders of this are of course everywhere: in the heavens at night, in the hills, in the woods and lakes; even in the tiniest things, in a single hair, a leaf or blade of grass. But it sometimes takes something shattering to force one to heed them, something like seeing one's father crying, as though a statue could feel. Then it is not egoism that blasts the spirit out of everything, but sympathy that, in spite of one's efforts, fears and mortification, blasts a hole, a brief hole, in the wall of separateness that has been erected by our own defensive egoism.

THE ETERNAL

We are the creation of God, though nothing but form arose with our birth nor will perish with our death. Our being is not something grasped hazardously, not something rationed, augmented or diminished, according to what we deserve; nor does it belong to an immortal soul we carry within us, as one might, for security, carry a gold-piece in his pocket.

Being is epitomized, not by impenetrable rocks, but by waves spreading themselves over the surface of the sea. These perfectly exemplify change, and the eternally changeless. Our stone edifices and monuments express our wishes, not our perceptions. We raise them skyward as though to remove them from the world of decay, as if to point to the permanence of heaven, as though to establish, here and there, specks of immutability that not even an eternity can corrupt, so deeply do we crave something that will remain. Our monuments are as large as we can make them, though we know they are still only specks, and we make them of granite, though we know that time will reduce them to the elements as inevitably as a raindrop is dispersed.

What captivates the metaphysician in this is not the illusory character of what is sought, for the eternal and changeless is certainly not an illusion; but rather, the inappropriateness of its symbols. A rock, a monolith, a temple, a granite arch, these are transient things. We know this. By what, then, shall we represent the eternal, if not by these imperfect means?

Oddly enough, this very eternity and changelessness, even the unchanging God, are beautifully symbolized by the turbulent sea, ever changing and yet ever the same. Here is our model of being and of creation. In the picture one finds himself, too, as a part of that creation. Here one sees mortality expressed, not in a unique origination *ex nihilo* and a unique extinction, but rather in our perpetual regeneration, shared by the entire creation. A wave, a raindrop, a waterfall, a person, a rock, a star, is at no two instants the same wave, drop or whatever. All existence, excepting God only, is instantaneous. Yet this arising and passing exists only on the surface, like the ocean waves. Beneath it nothing has arisen and nothing has gone.

Plato looked at the world and saw nothing but change, and therefore, he thought, decay, a continuous lapsing from reality. The world of sunrises and sunsets, of seasons, of birth and death, is at no two moments the same. Like the ocean, what it is is constantly changing into what it is not, and every earthly thing partakes of this mutability. Plato saw rocks and mountains, the heavens themselves, drifting constantly from being to nothingness. This world of matter cannot then, he thought, be real. It at best resembles or partakes of reality. The real, he was quite correctly convinced, is the changeless, the same from age to age. Its symbol is no mutable thing, such as a rock, of whatever durability, but rather, the changeless idea, the form, something divorced from everything mundane. Nor, he declared, is our mortality an ultimate fact, for this belongs to our bodies, which lie in the world of sense, and not to our inner souls. If we must have a symbol of reality from the world of sense, Plato suggested, we should look to the sun—something far removed from the earth, and the source of pure and inexhaustible light, in which no darkness, symbolic of nonbeing, is mingled. Even so, it is an imperfect symbol, for like everything grasped by sense, it is subject to change.

Plato should, however, have sought the eternal, not in his own supposed ego, mind or soul, nor in metaphysical abstractions that are sundered from nature, but in nature herself—not, indeed, in nature created, but in nature creating.

That the eternal might be epitomized by the sea, by that very perfection of ceaseless change, could never have been the least credible to Plato. And it is, indeed, at first hard to grasp, really about the last thing that would occur to one. It is no wonder men have invented the myth of heaven and the myth of the soul. Yet once this simile is understood, it can never be surrendered.

A wave moves over the face of the ocean. We can see it, distinguish it from another, even touch it and trace its brief history. It arises at a particular place, a particular time, swells, moves steadfastly, breaks—and is gone forever. But in truth no wave has moved at all. In truth the undulations of the water are vertical, not horizontal. It only seems that something has moved over the surface. A given wave is at one moment so entirely distinct from what it, the "same" wave, was a moment before, that it may share not one common element with its predecessor. All that has arisen, moved over the surface and then perished, is a shape, a modification. We call it a thing, and could even, if there were a point to it, give it a name. If conscious, it could assert "I think; I am." But that which affirmed "I think" would not be what affirmed "I am," except in form only. What there is, is the sea, here and there momentarily modified by waves, and while it is at no two moments the same, it still remains forever the same, changeless, eternal, its transient variations continuing from age to age.

ALIENATION

The illusions of separateness, autonomy and pluralism give rise to the deepest yearning of men and at the same time to incredibly inappropriate efforts to fulfill it. The yearning is to be loved. The means by which men endeavor to attain this love are loaded with the comedy that characterizes all ineptitude, all misguided effort or ill choice of means, and at the same time with the sadness of a seemingly invincible stupidity. One wants to laugh and to cry, as one does watching a clown who fills one's eyes with tears; and one is not quite sure in the end that they were tears of laughter.

Love is the perception of identity, and one who sees God and the world in this way has no greater need to be loved by other things, than to love them, for these things have ceased to be other and have also ceased to be things. Both needs are overwhelming, but both are fulfilled. The perception does not cancel the need to be loved, except by total satiation. Hence instead of rendering the philosopher cold and aloof, self-sufficient and uncaring, the perception fills him with warmth and makes him once more a part of the world instead of a parasite upon it. The craving for self-sufficiency is abolished when the limited and autonomous self disappears from view, and caring ceases to be a passion of desperation. Love is something on which to recline; to the extent that one frantically pursues it, he has already lost it. The man who spans the globe looking for the one true light, losing his way because he is blinded by the light that keeps shining in his eyes, is not likely to find anything that was worth seeking.

If I think of myself as a separate being, I at once become, to myself, a center of existence. "Here" becomes simply where I am, and, without thinking about it, I seem to myself to be the only person, virtually the heart of creation. All else, the universe in its vastness, even God, is "out there," and is an "it," a vast thing, rather than a "thou." The separateness with which I perceive myself produces a gulf between me and all else, between the ego and a vast, cold, uncaring otherness. And of course the gulf is not one I can ever step across, for it is metaphysical, the creation of my own thought.

How, then, will a man's yearning to be loved find expression under such a conception? In two obvious ways, both perfectly familiar and both clearly destined to fail. The first is what may be broadly called self-ornamentation; and the second, the effort to possess. Both are ridiculous, and yet one can hardly help pitying those whose madness devises them.

If I am a separate being and hence entirely other than you, then my only hope for satisfying my yearning will be through some sort of appearance of greatness. I must appear as a kind of wonder, a jewel, a thing of beauty. I must in a word rise above the rest of creation as best I can or, since that is obviously impossible, I must appear to. Thus will I awe all others and, through being awe-inspiring, be loved. But here suddenly the absurdity leaps up. By seeking to be loved, I have established the very conditions that make it impossible, for no one has ever loved that by which he is awed and from which he thus felt far removed. This is in fact the exact description of the defeat of love. Love is not engendered by unique beauty, but by the very plainness that unites everything; it is not nourished by what sets its object apart, but by what reaches across that apartness. The face of love that is felt, that is warm, that abolishes time, space and multiplicity, is a homely face.

Hence failing to impress, one tries to possess. But possession is by nature the acknowledgement of difference and alienation; what I possess, I cannot love, except in a figurative sense. I can only grasp or selfishly hold it. It is not impossible, for example, for a father to love his son; but if he thinks of his son as one of his possessions, or even as his greatest possession, then love for him is impossible. To possess is to use, to subordinate to one's own will, to add on to oneself, to exploit; and nothing like this can even form the smallest part of loving. It entirely rules it out. Therefore, possession of one person by another, even if it should be complete, makes love of that person impossible, by its very success. It is not love, nor a form of love, but a replacement of love, resembling loving only by the presence of concern for the thing possessed. But the concern is misleading; it is really only a concern for oneself, as distinct. "I love you" cannot, under these conditions, ever become "I love thee," for "thee" must denote more than a thing, and what is possessed cannot be more than a thing to its possessor.

SELF-LOVE

An overwhelming love for oneself can be either the most cramping, shrinking and sickening passion one can suffer, or it can, on the contrary, lead to an immeasurable love for the whole of being, which is simply God and creation together. It is odd that one and the same passional state could lead to such utterly antipodal effects, but it is not hard to see how this happens if one considers the possibilities.

The manner in which self-love leads to self-isolation and loneliness is fairly obvious. Consider the tyrant—master of the fates of millions, known and feared by most of the world—who craves the affection of his small daughter and only barely finds any of it. This is certainly a curious image. But we need no such extreme example, particularly if it suggests that there is anything rare and unusual in what it is intended to convey. Simply look about you, at the man who devotes almost his whole energy to increasing his possessions, these growing to a veritable mountain while his inner self shrivels to a nut, totally unloved, totally abandoned by the world he strives so hard to impress. Or think of the scholar, peerless, awesome to the learned world, envied on every side, but nowhere loved, and even resented by his own sons who would rather die than follow in his steps. He has, from self-love, tried to enhance his own being by adding to its ornamentation. He does not differ, inwardly, from the tyrant or the man of boundless possessions.

The image here is familiar, easy to grasp. Its basic element is this: A man is driven by an overwhelming self-love—a state containing, as noted, the potentialities for either heaven or hell. He therefore craves insatiably the love of others, which is absolutely not to be condemned, since this is a craving for what is quite rightly seen to be divinely good. But then he goes about things in the most obvious way, which also turns out to be the most misguided: He seeks to embellish himself by greatly enlarging that part of the world that he can influence, impress, even overpower. By doing this he makes an absolute distinction between himself and that world, so that, as the portion of the latter which he can call *his* increases, the very self he thinks of as at its center becomes reduced to nothing. If anyone were to look for the man anymore, he would immediately find himself in a vast and impenetrable sea of what is not the man, of that with which the man has surrounded himself in the vain hope that he can enlarge his own being by enlarging what he can attach himself to. The result is the exact opposite of what he intended. He is like a spider spinning its web from its own substance, so that as the web gets larger and impenetrable, its source at the center must inevitably shrivel up. The spider becomes no grander as its web increases; it is precisely that which is not the spider that spreads itself out.

Men are not unaware of this danger, and some have responded by condemning self-love itself. One must not, they think, love himself, but should *instead* love everyone and everything else. Some even represent this as a duty. Some even suppose that in fulfilling it one must put on a sad and sober face, as though the love for others is painful, requiring one's own self-rejection. Some even virtually invite the world to urinate on them, thinking that love should be self-sacrificial and needing some dramatic proof of the extent to which self-sacrifice and self-rejection can go.

All this springs from an illusion. Those who, from self-love, seek fulfillment of their craving for love by ornamenting themselves, adding to their possessions, power or status, labor under an illusion. Those who, correctly perceiving that this approach miscarries, seek fulfillment of their craving for love in the opposite way, by self-abasement and self-abnegation, labor under exactly the same illusion.

The illusion is simply that of a self, an ego, at the center of a world, the whole of which is thus seen as something *other*.

There is indeed the self, the ego. If there were not, it could hardly be loved. But paradoxically, that self, that ego, is not distinct from that realm we think of as other. The distinction between the *I* and the *you,* between the *me* and the *it*—between, in short, oneself and the world—is only one of degree. It is not an absolute distinction between two beings. Hence mystics who have thought of themselves as absorbed by the divine were not fools. They have only expressed in a joyous, perhaps melodramatic way, their own liberation from this great illusion.

THE ILLUSION OF SELFHOOD

Appreciating the force of an illusion seldom has any power to abolish the illusion itself. It persists, no matter how clearly and how indubitably the understanding discerns its illusory character. Thus the illusory self, like the face in the mirror, gazes back at one, mimicking his very denials of its reality. Understanding that there is really nothing there does not obliterate the lively appearance. One might even reason, absurdly, that there must be *something* there, for what, otherwise, is it that mocks one? Philosophers have actually said this sort of thing. The realization that an illusion can be *total* is sometimes not easily won.

The stars seem tiny to the child, sparkling grains of silver he can almost grasp by the handful and scatter like sand. They seem no less tiny when he comes to understand that they are in fact immense things. He has lost only the temptation to reach for them. The illusion persists unabated, though it is no longer acted upon. The rainbow, similarly, seems no less definite and no less exactly placed, merely because we have learned the physical principles of refraction. An uninstructed person might seek it out, might even want to touch it. When we say that there is no rainbow there, it is not always convincing, even to ourselves. We do, after all, see it. The understanding of truth does not diminish the illusion's presence and beauty, and we even want to say that in some sense there really is a rainbow there, that it is not a total illusion. But still, it is.

Thus I can declare, and my understanding can accept the truth of it, that this finite and mortal self, for which I have so intense a regard, this existential center of everything, is in fact nothing. I can say it, affirm it, believe it without any doubt whatever—but the illusion has not been diminished at all. It is like the face I see in the mirror. Even as I deny that it exists, it seems to mock my very denial. Yet what I say is true; there is no self there. It only seems to be there.

It was this power of an illusion to make intelligible discourse that so enchanted Descartes. "I doubt that I exist," he said, and having said it, he was captivated by his inability to mean it. The echo always came back, "I exist." Descartes was therefore unable to sustain his doubt. And because the doubt was thus seemingly overwhelmed, he mistook the victor in this contest to be the metaphysical certainty of his self. "I do not exist" *cannot* be true, he thought. So the denial of this negation must be true. Hence certain. But he did not stop to consider that the apparent image in a mirror could have said the same thing, and thereupon could have proceeded through the same strange performance.

Illusions are thus penetrated or seen through, but not banished. When we greet someone in the darkness, only to discover that we are addressing our own reflection in a glass, we stop speaking to it, but it does not leave. The same is true with respect to the evanescent rainbow and the flickering stars overhead, so that the claims of sense and understanding are thrown into a battle in which neither prevails. The same is true with respect to the finite self, which will always seem to its possessor to be the primal reality, more basic even than the world, less doubtful even than God. One can eventually come to see that it is a fiction, but one can never have the least hope of vanquishing it.

One can accordingly not really live as though that inner self, that central contemplator of the world, that ego, were nothing. This would be like expecting the rainbow to vanish at one's command. The nuclear self will always seem to be the thing that really matters. Thus what matters, it seems to me, are *my* thoughts, *my* feelings, *my* consciousness, and even, *my* dreams and illusions—but do not be mistaken about this. What is being talked about in such a declaration are not thoughts, feelings or dreams, but their supposed possessor. There were thoughts and feelings long before I appeared on the scene, and they will continue long after I leave. That does not matter to me. What counts is precisely the "me," the ego, my self. It counts less when seen to be an illusion, certainly, but no metaphysics will ever make it seem the least less real. For this reason the wisest man must act like the fool. Only his thoughts will be different, and these only at those rather rare times when he is able to be philosophical. Otherwise, just as the fool does, he will show off, prefacing everything with the thought, "Here am I." Thus: "Here am I, strong and powerful," and "Here am I, learned," and "Here am I, envied," and "Here am I, a veritable star." Even his gravestone someday will proclaim, "Here am I, take note!" The absurdity now begins to show. It should have been apparent from the beginning.

No illusion can be penetrated if its strength is not first understood. An illusion that is not seen is perfectly secure, for there appears to be nothing from which one needs deliverance. If rainbows were so common as to pass unnoticed, we would not need to be told that they are not there. And so with the illusion of selfhood. We have first to see that it does dominate every thought and act before we can hope to be rid of it. Until then we shall simply take it for granted, probably giving it no thought until confronted with what seems to be the fact of its finiteness and mortality.

Consider, then, the force of this egoism, the manner in which it—as though armed with a whip and inexhaustible in its energy—drives one to any folly and stupidity.

A grown man, roller skating with his children and imparting a certain middling grace to the performance, from time to time scans the periphery of the rink for the reward of the eyes of strangers and even of children, following his movements.

Another, visiting a sick friend, a friend who is, perhaps, at the very portal of death, cannot forgo mention of some recent achievement of his own. The perfect understanding that this could not possibly matter, could not possibly have the slightest significance in these circumstances, does not stay the tongue—the thing has got to be said. At the heart of the story is of course the self, always the central actor.

Another spends his life's energy building a monument to himself—an edifice bearing his name, an institution that will be associated with him, a little empire, something of this sort. It matters not what it is, provided it is ostentatious and its reference to himself is evident. This is so common that it is widely assumed to be a universal need, not subject to question.

The love of this self even extends to its ornaments, which require no excuse at all for thoughtless and vulgar display. "Here am I" then becomes something similarly intoxicating: "Here are things that are mine." And here again of course the crucial reference is not to those things, but to that ego which is imagined to be at their center. Thus are one's children dressed up and displayed, with notices, degrees, stunning connections. It would all be meaningless but for the supposed connection to oneself, the central ego. Exactly the same is often done with pet dogs and of course inanimate things that are considered rare or beautiful, or sometimes, merely expensive, or which can in any way whatever cast a reflection of their worth upon the egos of their possessors. Such things may be utterly trivial, even vulgar; it does not matter, so long as they, like stage lights, can serve to highlight the self which they surround.

Therefore even wise men do not always act wise. The inner self seems to them real, hardly less so than to the unreflective, and they too dread its obliteration, even in the full understanding that it is indestructible. Like any other illusion, this one can be comprehended but not banished. One can see the total stupidity of another's delight at the admiring glances cast his way for some feat of no significance, while nevertheless one pursues delights of exactly the same nature himself. One can feel shame at the display of his own egoism to a total stranger, perhaps even to a child, and his shame makes him wiser; but it does not necessarily induce him to act less foolishly at the next opportunity, perhaps at the very next moment. "Here am I" thus conditions everything he does right to the end, and indeed, beyond, for its power outlasts even the illusion itself, until his gravestone carries the message, "Here am I!" though more soberly expressed. Yet all there was, even from the beginning, and even from the beginning of time, and to its end—which means, without beginning or end—was the reality of God, or that alone which is not an illusion. It is worth something to understand this, however little that understanding will do in diminishing the illusion of the finite and mortal self dwelling for a while at the very center of creation.

NATURA NATURANS

The world was not made by God. It is made of God. God is both the creator of all that is real and that very reality. Believing in God is therefore not believing (or trying to believe) in some farfetched metaphysical hypothesis, nor embracing some all-encompassing theological scheme fabricated by this man or that in a bygone age. Metaphysicians have their own ways of talking. So do theologians. But believing in God is neither a philosophical achievement nor an act of faith, whatever that might be, nor any kind of miracle or gift. It is seeing the world in a certain way. Hence those who do not believe are not simply those who have not studied nor thought, but rather those who have not seen. Becoming religious is thus always felt by the converted to be seeing the world for the first time, whatever may be the symbols in which this theophany is expressed. St. Paul knew what this is like, and had his own way of expressing it, a way that now seems rather quaint. St. Augustine knew too. He thought he heard voices, and from that hour he lived in a different world. St. Thomas knew, and declared his achievements until then to be only straw—achievements that not one man in ten million could match. He had seen dimly until then, but now he saw. Gotama saw it, and from then on was called the Buddha, which means not the learned, but the enlightened. This thought is often and most easily and appropriately expressed as a transition from darkness to light. What makes this mode of expression apt of course is that no one sees in the dark, though there is most certainly a reality to be seen.

God indeed creates the world, but in an act of creating that never began and will never cease. He did not make the world in the sense that reality came into being at his wish, command or gesture, as a magician might produce a rabbit from a hat. Reality can neither start nor cease. Neither can God. That which creates, Spinoza's *natura naturans,* and creation, *natura naturata,* are ontologically one and the same. There are not *two* realities.

Is God thus eliminated? Hardly. One might as well say that such a conception of things abolishes nature—as though anything could do that.

THE INDESTRUCTIBLE EGO

I saw a towering monolith at the edge of a graveyard near my long-accustomed path. It served both as grave marker and as pedestal for an enormous, strange, totally incongruous statue of a fireman. I had never noticed it before, in spite of its extraordinary composition, and not one of my friends who sometimes pass there seems to have noticed it to this day. In graveyards one is only aware of numberless stones of all shapes and sizes. One almost never singles them out or even glances that way. Much less does anyone read the names on them, names inscribed at such cost and labor, in clear, deep, straight characters, made everlasting, ineffaceable, to be read and remembered forever by the living. This seems to be the trusted bond of the dead with the living; the inscriptions of names on rocks. In this way do the buried ones try to reach out to us. It seemed to them, before darkness closed over them, to be the only hold they would have left upon the world of movement and light. They made the most of it then. The stone is there, immovable, imperishable. The name is deeply inscribed; merciless elements will not soon obliterate it. Someone might someday read it; it will be there. Someone may utter the sound, note the dates, count the years, instantly forget—but for just a moment there will be a connection, reaching through the years. At least so it will seem. A name will be mumbled—a name once precious to him who lies there, meaningless to the rest of creation. The dates that will be mumbled mark for him the two most significant moments in the whole of time. To us they are numbers, no different from others.

It isn't much, is it? But it is something. Death takes the rest. The whole of time and space and of earth and sky yield to him. He spares nothing—except traces. We can erect these traces, carve them of stone; they will not soon decay. And why not erect them? It is not much of a victory, but it is something. For one who has nothing else, it is something. It may not be worth a single heartbeat, one breath of air, a touch, a lover's searching look—but it is something. And it lasts.

The gravestone I finally noticed drew my attention because of the enormous statue that surmounted it—the huge spreading hat, boots, ax, courage carved into the expression. This statue stands higher than anything else in that part of the graveyard. Small animals climb about on it in summer. In winter the immovable face stares down the blizzards, day and night, from decade to decade.

The inscription is clear, though unwritten: "I lived, and my existence had meaning that the world must not be permitted to pass over or forget. I was a fireman in this town, and do not fail to note, it is *I* who was a fireman."

It is something. As a dust mote is infinite in comparison to a boundless vacuum, this too is not nothing.

APPEARANCES AND REALITY

Think of a vast river, twisting across a continent, broken at times by waterfalls and rapids, elsewhere broad and gently flowing. Now, disregarding the larger picture, dwell in imagination on one of its least significant aspects, the bubbles that appear from time to time here and there on its surface.

Most of these bubbles vanish almost the moment they appear, while a few cling to existence a bit longer, though none for more than a brief moment. They are terribly perishable, terribly ephemeral.

Now there are two very different ways one can think of this arising and passing away, and these ways mark the division between two distinct metaphysical positions, two ways of conceiving of reality and of human existence. One is filled with meaninglessness and dread, and the other with serenity. Oddly, however, there is no way of showing which is correct. The two metaphysical viewpoints divided the philosophers of antiquity, and they divide thinkers still. All the dialectical machinery, all the wisdom, all the scholarship and science, all the cleverness of man's long history will add not one bit to the balance in weighing these two conceptions. Yet if one fixes his mind on them he can perhaps see which is the fabrication and distortion, the cramp, the entanglement to a peaceful mind, and which is the truth, the scheme that conveys to one a sense similar to that of having come home, tired of pointless struggle, to rest.

There is first of all the viewpoint of the bubbles themselves, if we can for a moment imagine them to be capable of forming a conception of themselves. Such a conception could be expressed thus: Here I am, an individual existent, distinct from others more or less like myself. Like each of these, I came into being at a certain time and at a certain place, and like each of these, I shall utterly perish. The greater river, from which I came, will still go on, perhaps forever, giving rise to ever new existences; but my own tenure of existence is very temporary. I came to the river at one point, as a result of the chance coincidence of numberless chains of events, and I shall inevitably soon depart, never to exist again, the whole river then going on without me, as before, as though I had never been.

That is one way of viewing this arising and passing away. It is realistic and, within the framework that is being presupposed, quite obviously true. A bubble is, within that framework, a separate, discernible existence, having no reality whatever until formed, and ceasing utterly a moment later, without hope of existing again.

But we can also view the whole thing in another way, in a way that is, interestingly, more natural for us who are not bubbles, but detached observers of the changes that unfold before us. For we can say: there does not exist here a plurality of things, the lasting and perhaps everlasting river on the one hand, plus the numberless bubbles that are from time to time superfluously scattered about on it, then haphazardly swept away. There is only the river, which here and there assumes new forms or is modified in this way and that, either briefly or more lastingly. Here it assumes the form of a ripple, there of a waterfall, and numberless other forms in other places. One of the forms is that of bubbles, but these are not things that are added to the river and then taken away; they are nothing but the river itself, as it exists then and there, at that point in time and space. What exists, then, is the vast and everlasting river. It neither comes into being nor ceases. Its bubbles are conceived as separate existences only by a limited imagination. Hence they neither arise nor perish, in any strict sense; we can only say, instead, that the river, the real existence, is ever-changing, presenting the appearance of things being born *de novo* and perishing *in ultimo*. Nor could an individual bubble, if it were a conscious being, truly represent itself as *distinct* from all else or truly make any distinction between itself and others. The only distinctions here are distinctions of points in time and space, not distinctions of real beings. The river, as modified in the form of a bubble here, is one and the same as the river similarly modified there.

The births of the bubbles, as in imagination we watch them arise and float by, are therefore illusions, as well as their perishings; they are neither mortal nor ephemeral, for they have no being of their own either to gain or to lose. The separateness we imagine—indeed, even see—is the separateness of illusion, of failing to see what is in fact before us.

If we could imagine such a bubble forming a conception of itself, or what it would refer to as "I," and of all the others, or what it would refer to as "they," and perhaps cherishing the desire to outlast one or more of them, then *we* could see at once that these conceptions are fictions, mistaking forms for things. But it is when we have seen this and are then seized with the urge to convey our liberating point of view *to others* that we realize, once again, the almost invincible power of the illusion just when we thought we had abolished it.

5

Aphorisms and Epigrams

Plato was wrong when he said that philosophy begins in wonder. Philosophy begins in arrogance and ends in wonder.

Petty cruelties flow from pettiness, large ones from principles.

No one condemns infidelity with more eloquence than the faithless.

Vain people eventually come to believe the praises they so insincerely heap upon themselves.

These who are needed have the delicious sense of being loved.

We appeal to moral principles when we need to justify what we have decided to do.

Men admire fidelity in their partners, infidelity in themselves.

Those who speak much of principles consider themselves thereby relieved of the need to heed them.

We hate not being believed, especially when we are lying.

Religion is thought to be an incentive to virtue, but is rather a means of appearing virtuous to oneself.

As fear is sometimes mistaken for restraint, so is lovelessness mistaken for fidelity.

Few people read in order to learn, but rather, to seek confirmation of their errors.

We despise, not what is evil, but what frightens.

Benevolence does not stir gratitude, but resentment, and if our benefactor happens to be good and noble then we can hardly wait to avenge our belittlement.

A wedding band is, for the giver, a no-trespassing sign, and for the wearer, a boast of virtue.

Morality insulates us against the sight of suffering.

Once you have expressed a fact of life in a formula you need no longer be troubled by its being a fact of life.

Noble persons are least aware of their nobility, which is why they are rare.

Those who lack strength in themselves seek it in God or, if they lack faith, in whatever vulgar group happens to include themselves.

None is so vindictive as one who speaks much of mercy and kindness.

People see their own faults magnified in others. The ignorant hold forth on the general ignorance, the selfish on the prevailing selfishness, and the greedy feel themselves surrounded by greed.

One who tries to impress others loses twice over. They see him for what he is, and as someone who tries to impress others.

That people have no natural sense of right and wrong is proved by the fact that they accept any abomination on the part of their government, without protest and even with praise, so long as they are themselves not threatened.

A slave is one who must do as another bids, and a willing slave one who does so without compulsion. Thus are most persons slaves to conventional morality, but willing ones.

Those who lose because of their own stupidity make much of their moral goodness, especially in love and marriage.

How strange that it should be thought inappropriate to regard with contempt persons who are contemptible.

Nobility of aim and intention is usually a smokescreen for something base, and thus obscures the real motive from the agent but rarely from others.

As beauty is in the beholder's eye, so is obscenity.

No one covets a love affair more than those who so vehemently condemn them.

Most people view each other the way a car salesman appraises the approaching stranger.

Philosophers genuflect to reason as a way of being safe.

The innocent adhere to morality because they literally do not know better.

People without pride seek self-worth in externals, while the proud seek it only in themselves.

You improve your reputation for veracity only slightly by uttering a truth, even a noble one, but be discovered in one deliberate lie, even a small one, and you will never quite be believed again.

A marriage should be judged, not by its duration, but by whether its partners can divorce in friendship.

We sometimes respect the past best, not by preserving the memory of it, but by giving it a proper burial.

When great evils befall us we say "Why?" and emphatically, "Why me?" We never speak thus of unexpected blessings. This is because we regard the former as undeserved punishments, the latter as entitlements.

Moral principles enable us to indulge our natural cruelty without remorse.

Stupid people who have managed a little learning think the world is stupid. This is why professors withdraw from the world.

Those who are filled with Christian charity seem capable of no other kind.

A conventional person bows and conforms for no other reason than to be bowing and conforming.

We see ourselves in the old and dying, and we weep.

People praise morality but envy successful wickedness.

Those who judge others see in them their own worst side. This is why no one speaks more ill of the greedy than one who is frustrated in his greed.

Lasting marriages are based less upon love than upon truce.

There could be no more exquisite punishment for the contemptible, nor sweeter reward for the proud, than to know oneself.

Every moral judgment is an oversimplification.

If one's days are all alike he has little need to live more than one of them.

No happiness is as sweet as the happiness that is undeserved.

Those who are most certain of truth invariably know the least of it.

Philosophers think their beliefs rest upon arguments, but what arguments appeal to them depends upon what they believe.

It is because Socrates took virtue seriously that they called him subversive and killed him. Diogenes took virtue even more seriously, and they thought he was only being a clown.

These who most deplore the passions have the least hope of indulging them.

A perfectly moral person is, like a simple machine, perfectly predictable, and distributes kindnesses and cruelties with precise regularity.

We are told that the world began with an act of creation, but the nobler truth is that it exists for such. Creation does not cause the world, but redeems it.

We listen, as the price of speaking.

Custom spares simple people the need to know what to do.

Morality, in the minds of the vulgar, consists less of doing the right things than of saying the right things.

Every vulgarian is like every other, but the gifted are never alike.

Because we cling to life we think we love it, yet we watch the clock as evening advances, hoping soon to briefly share the state of the dead.

A wretched past is totally redeemed by a good present, but all the past happiness in the world adds nothing to a miserable present.

Cunning people who say the right things at the right times are admired, even by the victims of their cunning.

Innocent boys pull the wings from flies without remorse because they are ignorant of moral principles. Grownups are able to express their cruelty against each other because they have mastered moral principles.

These who endure a cold and loveless marriage to the end praise themselves for their constancy.

What more perfect dying words, from the greatest philosopher who ever lived, than to ask his friends to repay Asclepius the chicken he owed him.

Socrates' greatness was that his life was a kind of joke, of which he alone knew the punch line.

Husbands and wives who find their only great happiness in each other take delight, not in their luck, but in their virtue. Those who find no such happiness in each other but remain companions for life because they fear the alternatives congratulate themselves, not for their prudence, but for their virtue. In either case, virtue turns out to be what is most easy.

6

The Joys of Beekeeping

Everyone, unless he waits too long to exercise it, has a fundamental choice that he can make with respect to his own life. This is the choice, not so much with respect to what he will do for his living, but rather, with respect to what, as a person, he aspires to be. Many people, and probably even most, never really make that choice. Instead, they simply fall into a certain lifestyle, most often the one they find exemplified in their parents and others around them, without considering, or even being really aware, of alternatives. And more often than not, following the most thoroughly established value of our commercial and industrial culture, that way of life turns out to be one of accumulation, that is, the quest for possessions.

But, as people have now become increasingly aware, there are alternatives. Not only is the sheer power to produce goods no longer looked upon as the measure of the greatness of a nation, the ownership of goods is no longer considered the measure of the worth of a person, except in the eyes of a diminishing and vulgar class. One can, if he but takes a moment to reflect upon it, actually choose between these two basic alternatives, and then abide by his choice; namely, shall he spend his life in the indulgence of greed, having for himself no more significant aspiration than owning things and pursuing pleasures? Or shall he instead try to make his life itself, especially with respect to the inner person, a work of art? When put in those stark terms one can indeed wonder why that choice is so often so casually made, or why, indeed, so many simply allow it to be made for them by others, in favor of the first alternative.

From *The New Comb Honey Book* (Interlaken: Linden Books, 1981), pp. 3–5, and *The Joys of Beekeeping* (Interlaken: Linden Books, 1984), pp. 67–72. Reprinted by permission of the author.

Is it not time we thought of our lives as things to fashion in the light of ideals, rather than literally *spending* them in the pursuit of purely mundane and ultimately worthless things, such as riches? Who is more to be envied, someone who has succeeded in surrounding himself with beautiful things? Or one who has somehow succeeded in making his own life beautiful? A person can quite consciously make himself sensitive to nature and to living things, and to thoughts and feelings of people, someone capable of the passions that animate the poet rather than those that drive lovers of gold, someone, in short, who excels by the quality of his own life, to which he has imparted his own reflective values, rather than one whose worth must always be measured by things totally other than himself. There have always been people who have made this choice, the decision to reflectively fashion, rather than merely spend, the life that nature has given them. Thoreau was such a person. So was C. C. Miller, the great American beekeeper who gave up a career in medicine in favor of the beekeeper's craft. What is astonishing is that, considering what is at stake, there have always been so relatively few of these people. It may be that the fundamental drive in each of us is for security. But when that drive claims our very lives and souls then we have, in our desperate struggle for freedom from want, become slaves after all. Everyone, certainly, must clothe his nakedness, nourish his body, and lie down in the comfort of safe shelter; but the thing becomes grotesque when, having achieved these elementary satisfactions, he then tries to indulge them ten times over. This is not, by an enlightened standard, a measure of success, but the purest bondage to the world.

That somewhat philosophical disquisition is meant as a preamble to the very modest suggestion I wish now to offer; namely, that the way of life available to a serious beekeeper offers a special kind of fulfillment. It is no path to power or riches, but it does offer, or at least makes possible, rewards that are vastly more precious. A beekeeper's work can be not merely a means of production, but an art that has its place within the total scheme of his life, which is itself an art in the sense I have tried to convey. It challenges both body and mind, demanding not only endurance and strength but the cultivation of great skill, and at the same time calls forth from within one the inventor, the artist, the poet, and the worshipper. The beekeeper has constantly before him some of the most exquisite of nature's creations, often the beauty of nature that no gallery or temple can rival, and through his own ingenuity and skill he is able to offer to his fellow men the loveliest product of nature.

By these remarks I do not mean to suggest anything so childishly romantic as that a beekeeper's life can itself be completely fulfilling. Of course it cannot, and anyone who was simply a beekeeper, and no more, would have a very narrow and trivial existence indeed. If, however, one aspires to an orderly, simple and disciplined life whose rewards are intangible but nevertheless immeasurable, rather than those that are measured by bank accounts and possessions, then he can become a beekeeper with complete fidelity to his ideals. With only a few apiaries, on land that he need not own, and with very little else in the way of tools and equipment, he can be a comb honey beekeeper and by that means alone earn a very substantial part of his livelihood. If his demands on the physical world are truly modest, he can earn all of his livelihood this way, incorporating his work into the total deliberate scheme that is his life. Or, depending on his circumstances, location and needs, he can treat this as a considerable sideline to other endeavors, whether this be teaching, carpentry, or whatever. Indeed, his larger livelihood, of which comb honey beekeeping is a substantial part, can be beekeeping itself, that is to say, raising and selling honey of all kinds, and perhaps raising queen bees, and making and selling beekeeping equipment. This whole approach to gainful work is highly flexible, easily enlarged or reduced, and at no point need it violate even the most fastidious ideals of the mind and spirit. It is possible in this world to live a life that is modest in its demands on the world and on others, non-exploitive either of people or of nature, a life that eschews bigness and greed and every assault upon the environment, and it is one of the beauties of beekeeping that it can totally blend with such a life. Other things can too, of course, but still, nothing does so better than beekeeping.

A beekeeper has a chance to make lots of friends. I am not speaking now only of the human kind, who are not always the most constant, but of the countless others that relieve what could otherwise be an awful loneliness in the bee yards, woods, and fields. We tend to take the song of birds, the squeak of the chipmunk and the scurrying of the red squirrel for granted. We may go hours without noticing them. But how desolate our world would be without them, and how desolate our lives! The hum of the bees lifts the spirits, but it is not enough. We need the whole of nature, and we need to be reminded that we are a part of it. The same life that pulsates in us, the same yearning and striving, the same love of existence fills everything around us. These things are not foreign, they belong to us and we to them. It is not our role as human beings to conquer, exploit, and destroy, but to build up, protect, and love in the spirit of acceptance the natural order into which we have been placed.

These thoughts are never far from me, and I was forcibly reminded of them one day when I began making preparations to move one of my yards to a more promising location. Beneath the old boards and odds and ends that I throw in front of the hives to keep the weeds down, and under many of the hives themselves, I found numerous snakes, curled up in what they thought was the inviolable safety of those retreats. They were not attracted there by the bees, for I have never heard of any snakes having the slightest interest in a beehive. They were simply secure and, I suppose, warm places. It gave me a good feeling to discover them there, to learn that some of my hives and stands were serving this unintended purpose, and to know that, whatever may have been the snakes' terror at being so suddenly exposed to the light and impending destruction, they were perfectly safe from me. After a moment of that fixed stare and flagellating tongue, inimitable by any other animal, they slid casually into the surrounding weeds. I was sorry to carry off their roofs, but I needed them too.

Once, years ago, I was astonished to find a hen nesting beneath one of my hives. She had found a place safe from the entire world, protected as it was by legions of bees who would have no interest in harming her chicks. I managed to do my bee work there without disturbing her, and I have no doubt her chicks were hatched and brought into the world in good shape, although I was not at hand to witness this.

The kingbirds come around to my home yard, and these are officially described in beekeeping literature as enemies of bees. I suppose they are, in the strictest sense, for they eat them—they drop down and pluck them right from the air, near the hives. But are they not entitled to? As we rob the hives of their honey, the kingbirds rob them of a bee now and then, and the right to do either seems hardly less violable than the other. I do not know how many bees one of the birds may eat. Perhaps quite a few if one were to number them singly. But certainly the number is insignificant in terms of the teeming population that a hive of bees supports. In any case, it is quite certain that the kingbird takes no more than he needs. Can we always say the same for ourselves? I have no objection to the kingbirds, and if my hives, in addition to the bounty they yield to their keeper, give up also a bit of nourishment to these graceful birds, then I have one more reason to be glad that I have them. Certainly, the kingbirds have never reduced my honey crop so much as a pound. They perch along the utility wire that runs across my front yard, spending much more time there than in the pursuit of bees, and in the few minutes they are perched there, far more bees are emerging from the brood combs in the hives than all these birds could catch in an entire afternoon. They follow their ancient patterns, as nature prompts them.

Of course the thought crosses my mind: would a kingbird hesitate to snatch a queen bee departing or returning on her nuptial flight, thus imperiling an entire colony? But then I realize that the likelihood of such an event is so infinitesimal as to be hardly worth the moment it takes to consider it. One could probably keep bees for a thousand years before it would happen.

Skunks visit the hives at night, scratch at the entrances, then snatch the bees that appear in the darkness in response to the disturbance.

I find the image of this droll. I have never seen it happen, and probably never will, but more than once my dogs have gone boldly forth in the night to investigate and then returned to throw the household into shocked dismay, the skunk having known exactly how to deal with that threat. Still, I do not know what it would be like to live in the country without that singular odor of the skunk in the air from time to time, so I count its source among my friends. I can get on with him, and he with me; we simply keep our distances. Anyway, I have always thought that the Almighty was waxing whimsical when He created this remarkable animal and its extraordinary defense. The skunk can have a few bees and I shall not mind. I induced the bees to make their home in my hives, but I did not create them. As things are reckoned by men I own them, but in the order of nature I own them no more than the skunk does. The man whose thought would here turn to traps is still infinitely far from that sense of nature and spirit of acceptance I have spoken of.

Mice are a different story, and it would not be hard to learn to hate them if it were not such a perfectly simple matter to avoid their depredations. Various species of mice, a few of them quite beautiful, find an empty beehive a perfect haven. An occupied hive suits them in late fall, after the bees have clustered and become too torpid to put up a defense. The mouse chews out a hollow, ruining many valuable combs in the process, and stuffs it with the sort of trash it considers appropriate for a nest. A beekeeper should blame himself for this, however, and not the mouse, for it takes nothing more than a wedge of wire screening in the entrance to protect the hive completely. The mesh is large enough for the bees to pass through easily but too small for the mouse. Unless they become trapped inside and have no other way to escape, mice never, as far as I have been able to discover, chew holes in the hive. Nor do they ever climb up the side of the hive to take advantage of openings higher up. Of course, if, as in my yards, unused covers and bottom boards are kept in the apiary, to be at hand when needed, then mouse nests will frequently be found in them, often with baby mice. There is no harm in this. The worst that can happen is delay in the use of the equipment until the tenants have abandoned it. There is no need to dump the tiny creatures out to perish. Whatever task required the use of that equipment can usually wait until the next trip around.

Toads appear once in a while. It is impossible to think of them as enemies, although I have seen them included in that extensive list of "enemies of bees" in one of the leading treatises on apiculture. They may menace hives in tropical climates wherever hives are not raised from the ground, but certainly they pose no threat in more temperate areas. If they ever catch bees, which I doubt, they must get only a few of them. The toad squats Buddhalike, with boundless patience, certain that some sort of insect will come within reach of his tongue before starvation approaches. He impresses my own less trusting mind. I usually move him to my garden and hope he will stay there, but if he prefers to lumber back to the apiary I do not mind.

My friends are beyond numbering. At one yard, but only at one, the indigo buntings come around year after year. I have singled out these finches as special friends because of the indelible impression one of them made upon me when I was a boy. It was the first I had ever seen. Its beauty was exquisite, and I treated it as a messenger of hope.

A woodchuck, too, comes around. He once squared off against my dog, who fortunately had the good sense not to draw too close. The 'chuck gets fatter and fatter until, by late summer, his sleek and portly bulk seems more to roll over the ground than to walk. I believe he is the champion hibernator, far exceeding the bear in his capacity for sleep. By the time he has sunk into his deepest torpor and begun the slow consumption of that great layer of fat his pulse will have slowed, I am told, to only four beats per minute. Then, according to quaint legend, as spring enters, he will rouse himself for the sole purpose of examining his shadow.

Even the crickets fit into the cycle, filling the meadow with their stridence at harvest time. It is hard to disassociate them in my imagination from heavy combs of bright new honey. They are drawn inside to the warmth of my potbelly stove when October's chill puts a frost on the grass, and there they add their singing to the otherwise somber autumn days. The stove seems to affect them in much the same way it does me. It holds the winter's sleep at bay just a bit longer and rekindles fading life. As winter begins to replace the fall I sometimes move a few of the crickets from my honey house stove to my cottage, there to make their home in a tiny bamboo box, sing by my bedside, and gain a further reprieve from winter.

I shall never understand nature, this earth, the bees, the buntings—all the myriad forms. No one ever will. I have no need to. I gaze in unuttered reverence, and I am fulfilled.

7

Universities and the Debasement of Learning

Liberal education has, over the last twenty-five years, passed almost entirely from our rich and prestigious universities to small colleges. There is little public awareness of this change, even in the minds of those who bear the enormous costs of education, but it is nevertheless a change of enormous importance. Parents, shopping around for the "right" college or university, still assume that their children will receive a good education in the best-known universities. They further assume that the quality of a university education will bear some relationship to its gargantuan cost.

Both assumptions are now almost totally wrong. Most undergraduate students emerge today from our best-known universities with virtually no education, in the sense in which that term was once understood. They are, to be sure, haphazardly exposed to various more or less educative experiences, to the stimulus of exchanges of ideas with other students and, sometimes, to a highly cosmopolitan environment. They thus gain a certain sophistication. And they are also likely to become skilled in certain arts valuable to commerce and the professions. But these universities, with few exceptions, do very little for them with respect to worthwhile instruction in areas associated with liberal education. Students are graduated virtually unchanged intellectually, having much the same immature and unexamined ideas and values with which they began. A bizarre result of this is that we now see, with increasing frequency, men and women with university degrees subscribing to the same kind of religious, social, and political hokum that were once associated with ignorance. They seem to have gained nothing in the areas of critical thought and judgment and no understanding of intellectual history and the evolution of thought. Their universities have failed them and, sadly, they do not even know that.

A long and eclectic teaching career has made me aware of this profound and baneful change for some time, but I became aware of it anew when I was recently invited to teach at Hartwick College, in upstate New York, under the flattering title of Resident Distinguished Philosopher. It was my thirteenth academic appointment. My tenured professorships over thirty-five years were in four large universities—Brown, Ohio State, Columbia, and Rochester—but I held many visiting appointments in small liberal arts colleges like Hartwick, among them Swarthmore, Wells College, Hobart-William Smith, Hamilton, and Union, and these were my true love. I have always had a certain ideal of liberal education, and I often found it honored in small colleges but rarely, since the nineteen fifties, in large universities dedicated to graduate instruction and research. I had reasons for staying in the university system, but they had only to do with my own fortunes. They had nothing to do with education.

In most small and well-established colleges such as Hartwick liberal education is still considered to be the college's main mission, even though the forces that have undermined education in the universities make themselves felt there too. A student's education is not left to the outside chance of his encountering an inspired and cultured teacher who takes seriously the role of teaching. It is instead the concern of the college itself, its president and deans, and the faculty as a whole. During my first term at Hartwick I participated in informal faculty luncheons where the President and other administrative officers joined the discussions of the educational goals of the college. The President himself teaches a course in the great books of our civilization. In a typical university, on the other hand, the concerns of its administrative officers have primarily to do with the prestige of the institution itself, with buildings, wealth, influence, and what is called the "visibility" of the faculty, something that has absolutely nothing to do with dedication to teaching. At one of my universities the president found nothing strange in coining for himself the title "President and Chief Executive Officer."

Our largest, richest, and most famous universities boast faculty-student ratios of one to ten or twenty, the implication being that this is about the average class size. But included in these computations are all the graduate students who ever have anything to do with students, though it may be nothing more than periodically reading examination booklets by the bushel. Included also are "teachers" who have not taught an undergraduate course for years, being involved entirely in administrative tasks, and numberless others occupied mainly or entirely with research and graduate instruction.

Some universities still have a "Parents' Weekend" when those who groan under the heavy cost of "higher education" receive a free chicken box lunch and free talks by the officers of administration extolling the fame of the university, the scope of its ever-expanding research projects, and the good fortune of their sons and daughters to be there, "at the cutting edge" of that ongoing research. There are also reminders that only part of the cost of their children's education—that is, the total university budget—is covered by tuition charges, which increase every other year in order, it is said, to further enhance the already strong educational programs that are offered.

The parents then find their sons and daughters being "taught" in vast hordes, often two or three hundred per class, by lecturers to whom their children are wholly unknown. If this is a large private university, which encourages research from its faculty, then a simple computation will remind these parents that they are paying in tuition alone thirty to fifty dollars for each such dreary class meeting of approximately one hour, though it may be held in an auditorium so filled that students must find seats on the floor. If it is one of the larger state universities, where tuition charges are much less, the cost may be half that, but class sizes are apt to be even larger, so that the lecturer may be speaking into a microphone. It thus becomes obvious that the main effort and chief resources of our large universities are not directed toward undergraduate education at all. Their faculties, still quaintly referred to as "teachers," are in fact primarily researchers and project directors whose occasional teaching is hardly more than a gesture to a declining tradition.

Admirable as research may be, it is not what is definitive of an educational institution, and its connection with undergraduate education is tenuous at best. Our richest universities are still thought of as communities of students and teachers, and the illusion is perpetuated. Indeed, a considerable effort of "public relations" is directed to this, with pictures of students busily learning and deeply involved teachers busily teaching. One thus gets the impression that a student fares best at the hands of "teachers" who for the most part do not teach, that the best education will be obtained where it is least prized, that vast classroom audiences attest, not to the monumental neglect and indifference of the university to the educational needs of the students, but to the renown of its lecturers.

Research institutes are not new. The Institute for Advanced Study at Princeton has an illustrious history. The Center for the Behavioral Sciences at Stanford and the Rockefeller Institute in New York are similarly well known, although the latter, significantly, has for some time been calling itself Rockefeller University, in spite of the fact that it has never engaged in undergraduate instruction. What is new, however, is that virtually all of our large and wealthy universities should have evolved to a similar end without there being much public awareness that such a profound change has occurred.

The explanation is not hard to find. The change in the role of universities began with the enormous influx of support for research, from governmental and other sources, following certain alarming scientific achievements in the Soviet Union in the 'fifties, particularly the launching of the Sputniks in 1957. The National Defense Education Act soon followed, then the Higher Education Act of 1965, plus other legislation making loans and grants available to students. University enrollments increased rapidly, as did funding for research, particularly in the sciences. This led to an intense competition for faculty, and one inducement that was always offered was the promise of minimal teaching. Professors, in turn, began perfecting a new art, which came to be known as "grantsmanship." This consisted of getting ever greater funding for research. Much of this money flowed directly to the university, to meet the highly inflated cost estimates for maintaining research facilities. Professors thus came to be rewarded, not for their teaching, and sometimes not even for the value of their research, but simply for their ability to bring in money, an ability that was sometimes perfected to an art and applied to what very much resembled a game. One thus finds today, not just in the sciences but even in such fields as philosophy, professors whose salaries stagger credulity, but who do virtually no teaching whatsoever. They are, of course, listed as teaching "full time," and lists of "course offerings" carry their names, though these "courses" may have only two or three graduate students whom the professor may see, more or less informally, from time to time.

Professors' "lists of publications," upon which their "visibility" entirely depends, meanwhile keep growing, sometimes including papers researched and written almost entirely by graduate students, the professor disingenuously claiming, as the director of their research, joint authorship. A single doctoral dissertation can sometimes yield many such "publishable papers." The graduate student thus gets a fine beginning for his own list of publications, together with joint listing with a name well established, placing himself in position for jobs and promotions; the professor pads his own growing list, positioning himself for new and larger grants; and the university enjoys the influx of large amounts of money, duly noting who won them. So everyone comes out ahead—except, of course, the undergraduate students who, in this greedy rush, are left very far behind and largely unnoticed. They are noticed by the bursar's office, which will see that no degree is granted until every lab fee and library fine has been paid, and by the office of public relations, when stories and pictures of students are needed to keep up appearances. Then on their final day these students will, as bidden, all rise together and at a stroke receive, several hundred at a time, their degrees. These are, when they bear the name of a great university, valuable documents, useful in opening the doors of opportunity, though few realize how little they may represent in terms of actual educational achievement.

It costs about twenty thousand dollars a year to attend some universities, more than half of which is tuition alone, and tuition is increased regularly, usually every other year, by seven to ten percent, enough to make it double every decade. This has become policy even for universities whose vast endowments would suggest a reduction of tuition costs rather than increases. These enormous costs, far from strengthening the quality of university education, as claimed, have the effect of debasing it still further as students, often forced deeply into debt, gravitate to courses from which they can expect some cash pay-back. Thus courses in accounting and business management proliferate, and competition increases to get into pre-medical and other pre-professional programs. Courses that have always been at the heart of a liberal education, on the other hand—the classics, literature, philosophy, and so on—correspondingly decline. The whole emphasis thus becomes misdirected, and universities, once rightly thought of as fostering culture, understanding, and the disinterested pursuit of truth, have become instead training grounds for the pursuit of power and wealth.

During my last twenty-five years of "full time" university appointment I rarely spent more than five hours a week in a classroom. This was the standard course load. I spent almost no time at all on committees or other service. Typically I taught two undergraduate courses which met on Tuesday afternoon, then again on Thursday, a total of two and a half hours each of those days. At one university my teaching was at one time all done on Tuesday—an undergraduate seminar in the afternoon and a graduate seminar in the evening. The rest of the week I could be, and sometimes was, hundreds of miles away. Usually, however, my undergraduate courses were lectures to classes of from one hundred to three hundred students, virtually all of them unknown to me. When, as a gesture to the liberal arts, one of these was a required course, then there were always a few rows of students in the back paying very little attention and some of them sleeping. I ruefully reflected at times that they were paying about forty dollars each, just in tuition, to hear me lecture that day. All grading of papers and exams and computation of grades were done by graduate students or, sometimes, undergraduate seniors who were minimally paid by the university to be my teaching assistants, though they did no teaching at all. They were happy to claim this title in their own resumes. Sometimes a course had as few as forty or fifty students, and this was considered a small class. And sometimes, by my own choice, one of my two courses was a graduate seminar, which met once weekly, and for which the students were expected to do most of the work. There was no special preparation on my part for any of these courses. I had taught the undergraduate course so many times over the years that I needed only to remind myself, on my way to class, what I was going to talk about that afternoon. The graduate seminars, which typically had from two to six students, were mostly involved with whatever I happened to be doing at the time—writing a book, perhaps, or some papers I was hoping to publish. This was my "research," which I thoroughly enjoyed, all of which was done at my leisure at home. When published it gave me "visibility" and occasional job offers from other universities, something that is immensely helpful in negotiating salary increases every year. The books, which grew out of my teaching, usually earned me royalties, sometimes handsomely. So again, everyone came out ahead—except, again, the undergraduate students, and their parents who were paying the cost of this.

If we consider that there are about sixteen weeks in a semester, and allow for holidays, for class meetings I missed because of scheduled examinations (proctored by graduate students) or to attend conferences or whatever, it averages out that I could not have spent more than 150 hours *per year* in teaching. To this should be added that I received paid sabbatic leaves every few years (to do "research") when I usually went off to New Zealand or some place and did no teaching at all. And for this I not only received a bountiful salary but a lifetime income into retirement, most of this paid for by the universities as one of the many fringe benefits. Nor is my case unusual. Indeed, I had a reputation for being one of the more dedicated and conscientious teachers. There were many known to me whose contributions to the education of students were less, but who were sometimes rewarded even more handsomely.

The goals of a large university work with dreadful effect to reduce the role and significance of the undergraduate student to near zero, particularly the ever-present goals of national prestige and wealth. The universities pay lip service to the enlightenment of the mind but jettison such concern the instant the enticement of money is seen. This, together with student demand, accounts for the proliferation of schools of management in the past several years, whose faculties contribute only minimally to the education of undergraduates in any traditional sense of that term. The universities honor, in word, intellectual honesty but utilize every gimmick of advertising to present themselves as something quite different from what they are, combining this with appeals for gifts "to education." In return for a substantial gift they sometimes offer to attach the donor's name to a library cubicle, or for a larger gift, to a room, and for a truly magnificent gift, to a laboratory, or even, perhaps, to a building. Praising the ideals of the mind, they unabashedly pursue the ideals of the market place. Professing to honor the teacher and his role, they promise him the very minimum of teaching, reward him when he does not teach, and offer at most words of praise, and seldom even that, for professors who survive these blandishments with a genuine concern for the minds of their students.

An educated person cannot be neatly defined, but it is not someone who is merely knowledgeable and skilled. One can be ever so expert at accounting, or dentistry, or marketing, or doing symbolic logic, and still be quite uneducated in any significant sense. An educated person knows the culture of which he is a part, knows its past, its promise and its limitations; he has an appreciation and love for great achievements in literature and the arts; he has a refined understanding of human nature and is able to assess both the merit and the occasional worthlessness of his own ideas, to create new and better values for himself; and above all he has a hatred for the specious and tawdry and a love for truth, including useless truth, and truth that is unpleasant. Someone of this description is not the product of chance. What is needed, for there to be such people, are educators who prize this ideal and who do not subordinate it to anything else.

Until the nineteen-fifties university presidents often wrote and gave speeches on the nature and problems of liberal education. Such opinions were often highly original, perceptive and valuable, and were heard with respect. It is difficult to think of a university president today offering such a performance without raising smiles. There are writings and speeches, of course, but they are about the organization of the university, its staggering costs, and, always, its future greatness—concerned, indeed, with everything *except* the life of the mind and the ideals of liberal education. When these are referred to at all it is in platitudes. An aura of unreality surrounds the whole business.

Again, until the nineteen-fifties universities were seriously concerned with curriculum, the roles of the sciences and the humanities in a liberal education, the emphasis that should be placed on great books, and so on. The august committee of the curriculum at a good university was often presided over, and largely guided, by its president, and the educational needs of the students were the first concern. Somehow the ideal of an educated man, in a sense akin to Aristotle's use of that honorific term, was in the minds of those to whom the education of young adults was entrusted. What has, since then, come to distinguish the curriculums of most universities is that they hardly exist. The problems of education are more and more met by simple neglect, as individual professors put into play their own idiosyncrasies and fond notions. Problems of course requirements are met by abolishing requirements, problems of grades are met by virtually abolishing any grade below C, and reserving this for cases of utter failure. Problems of comprehensive exams are met by abolishing comprehensive exams. Universities, in short, bereft of educational leadership and drawn to more worldly goals, allow matters to take their own course in whatever way seems effortless. The loss is very great, and it can surely be wondered whether all the vast research activities that are preserved are, taking everything into account, really worth it.

Thirty years ago a professor who assigned to sophomores Machiavelli's *Prince,* Plato's *Republic,* or Mill's essay *On Liberty* was likely to find that many of them had already been required to read them. Today, on the other hand, it is perfectly possible for a student to be graduated from an American university without having seen such works, without having read Hobbes' *Leviathan,* Locke's *Civil Government,* the Declaration of Independence, the Constitution of the United States, the Bible—indeed, without having read much of any of those classic works upon which Western culture and American democracy largely rest. Great and powerful universities exist in which there cannot even be found a department of classics, where political science has become totally analytical and empirical, reflecting the research interests of the faculty rather than the demands of liberal education, and where such hitherto liberalizing forces as philosophy have degenerated into analysis, mathematical logic and semantics. Quantification is what counts, and what is susceptible to it flourishes, no matter how arid and devoid of intellectual significance it may be. What can be measured is publishable, whereas what is merely ennobling often is not.

Does all this mean that higher education, conceived in terms of the growth of the mind, is disappearing from the American scene? Fortunately not, for the universities in which it once flourished never monopolized it. Liberal learning still thrives in our many liberal arts colleges, where the intellectual needs of undergraduate students still receive first consideration. In these colleges students are likely actually to be known not only by their teachers, but sometimes by their presidents. Such teachers are usually teachers in fact, and such presidents are often educators in fact. Perhaps it will come to be recognized that large and wealthy universities are primarily centers for research and training grounds for advanced technicians and specialists, while our liberal arts colleges will receive overdue recognition as the primary source of that special breed of human being who will always be essential to any society deserving to be called civilized, the educated men and women.

8

A Fulfillment

My oldest son is 39 years old, my youngest barely 1. The nearly four decades that separate them include my entire professional career, from graduate school into retirement. They include, too, the births of my grandchildren, two failed marriages and then marriage, once again, to someone too young to remember the Beatles. I, at 67, remember silent movies.

A man in his 60's does not expect to fall in love with a woman of 18, and much less does he expect her to fall in love with him. Past failures had, in any case, left me cynical. But this beautiful student, whom I would so unpredictably marry five years later, never had any doubts almost from our first accidental encounter. She had, I eventually learned, seen me sometimes from her dormitory window and pronounced me ridiculous, but our lives were changed by our meeting and by the letters back and forth that soon followed. The constancy of her feelings, which made irrelevant to her our difference of age, finally replaced my cynicism with gratitude and wonder.

I was not much aware of the passage of the years until my infant son, who will rejoice under the name Aristotle Eli, made his existence deeply felt in my life. I had always mingled easily with students and was surprised whenever they referred to some of my colleagues as the younger professors. Even the start of my Social Security and annuity checks had little impact on my feelings. I got the senior-citizen discount on movie tickets, sometimes on dinners too. Such benefits extend to spouses, so my wife was entitled to them too, but we never claimed them. She was too young for that part of the senior citizens' world. Even I felt out of place there.

I have raised children of my own before, as well as a little stepdaughter who now has her Ph.D., but fatherhood this time is totally different. I had no role with my other children until they came home from the hospital with their mother. This time my wife and I went several weeks to baby classes in joint preparation for birth, and I saw my son lifted from her womb. My wife, expecting me to draw from experience, sometimes raises elementary questions of infant care which I cannot answer at all.

There are two other big differences, both psychological. One is readily understood and was almost predictable. The other is profound and touches upon the meaning of life.

Death had always seemed to me 100 years away until my new son was born. Now I began to feel the passing of every precious day. My thinking had always been given over to abstractions. Now mundane concerns began to press in on me. I immediately felt the need for life insurance, lots of it. Until the baby came, I had no clear idea what insurance I had. This was quickly attended to, and I passed the required physical exam easily enough. Then I composed a will. I looked at my investments, which had been casual, few, and long neglected. I urgently found out what they might be worth—not much, but rather more than I would have guessed. I found out I could safely die any time and my wife and baby would not be thrown onto welfare. But youth is gone forever. I now make little, periodic investments in Government securities carefully chosen to mature when my infant Aristotle is ready for college. I get up at night, not to fuss with philosophical manuscripts, but to examine once again my modest investment position, life insurance contracts, retirement benefits, medical insurance and survivors' benefits. The evening news brings the report that Benny Goodman died. So did Cary Grant. And Desi Arnaz. And Horace Heidt. My wife never heard of some of these people. I wonder whether she noted how old they were. I did.

A profounder effect of late fatherhood has been a new awareness of something in myself, and apparently in others, that I had never thought much about. The first time I held my new son in my arms I felt as though I were dreaming. I still feel that way every night as I rock him to sleep in my arms, lulled by the nocturnes of Chopin, then gently lower him into his crib. Sometimes I doze myself, his head against my chest, and the reality becomes the dream. I have loved children before, but other things competed for my thoughts—my manuscripts, my standing in the university, my friends, my future. Now I stand outside the university. Challenges there are all past. I know where I shall always live and what my income will be. My thoughts are free to focus entirely on my wife and baby.

When I was a graduate student, I had a professor, nearing retirement, whose two marriages had been childless. He had an obsessive love for a cat. His unabashed devotion to his cat was regular conversational fare even beyond the university. It seemed a quaint idiosyncrasy, but I understand it now. I have since noticed many instances of older couples, past hope for children, whose emotional lives have come to center upon some dog or cat.

At another university, one of my associates found himself suddenly with unsought custody of his infant grandchild. He did not need this. He was a towering figure in his field. Yet that infant reshaped his life and, while his custody lasted, overwhelmed every other interest he had. This baffled me at the time.

This sort of thing is familiar, but who has tried to understand it? Loneliness does not explain it. The way old people dote on their grandchildren is legendary, too. I used to assume it was because they had nothing better to do.

Psychologists have written much about the need to be loved. Less has been said about the need to love. Your love becomes overwhelming when its object is helpless and dependent and your own hold on life seems uncertain. Perhaps Plato was right when he said that our love for our children springs from the soul's yearning for immortality.

I lower my sleeping son into his crib. The Chopin record will shut off automatically after a while, and the house will be still until the baby's first importunate cry in the morning. One more precious, irreplaceable day is ending, and I am fulfilled.

Part Three

Politics, Religion, and Ethics

Introduction

Richard Taylor describes himself as a political conservative in the American tradition. By the term *conservative,* Taylor means someone who wishes to keep (conserve) the values embodied in the United States Constitution. Unlike liberals, Taylor believes in a limited form of government, "not one that tries to determine for free citizens what is best for them and to deliver them from all evil." If not quite a political libertarian, Taylor is surely a minimal state theorist. As a conservative, he believes the American form of government rests upon the Constitution, which provides both a charter of government and a declaration of rights.[1]

Taylor laments the fact that a number of people and groups, often labeled "conservative," are currently attempting to "trash" or undermine the Constitution and replace it with other values. For Taylor, this amounts to subversion. However well motivated, superior, noble, or true their alternative values might prove, the fact remains that they are subversives. Those substituted values might take the form of religious creeds or political manifestoes. Oliver North, Jesse Helms, and assorted religious fundamentalists are really political subversives, while ironically (despite its popular perception), the ACLU is conservative.

Turning to the topic of *liberty,* Taylor reflects on John Stuart Mill's classic defense of the principle of liberty. He contends that Mill's various formulations of the liberty principle, which are designed to demarcate the proper role of governmental interference in individual lives, are prescriptively incoherent. Specifically, Taylor maintains that Mill's views on liberty are so open-textured that they support in principle any type of criminal legislation whatsoever and, consequently, fail to protect our basic liberties.

Mill claimed that societal or governmental legislation can be rightfully exercised involuntarily over members of the community "to prevent harm to others." Clearly *harm* here refers to more than bodily injury or else people would have no legal protection from theft and fraud. However, to broaden the notion of harm so that it includes injuring a person's deep interests (whatever they might be) is to forsake the protections normally afforded by a liberty principle. For virtually all actions would be legally prohibited employing this wide sense of *harm,* inasmuch as people have deep interests in all sorts of religious, patriotic, moral, and esthetic issues, the frustration of which would harm them.

The dilemma, then, is as follows: Mill's expressions "hurting others," "doing evil to others," "affecting others," etc., can be interpreted either in a restrictive or nonrestrictive way. If interpreted narrowly, then our liberties remain considerable, provided the exercise of such liberty causes no physical harm to others, but as a result, legal protections against theft and fraud remain tenuous. However, if interpreted broadly, and given the fact that many people's sensibilities are easily offended, then there will likely be considerable legal restraints placed on individual liberty.

To avoid the horns of the Millian dilemma, Taylor attempts to develop a genuine principle of liberty wherein any restrictions placed on individual exercises of liberty can be justified by avoidance of even greater evil. Taylor believes that coercive legislation can be warranted if it prevents injury, and we injure each other by various forms of assault, theft, and fraud. These sorts of injuries are bad-in-themselves, and not merely conventional harms. Genuine *natural* injuries cause harm and evoke resentment from the injured victims by virtue of their humanity, unlike *conventional* injuries that cause harm and evoke resentment that is learned or conditioned. "One learns to despise the eating of pork, the desecration of a flag, the practice of polygamy, but no instruction or conditioning by society is needed to render a man resentful of a threat to his life or limb."

But, *pace* Taylor, isn't stealing someone's property a mere conventional injury? Taylor responds that, yes, ownership or possession is a conventional notion, but the felt injury caused by the destruction of what is otherwise artificially created is natural. Taylor proceeds to claim that any natural injuries can be justifiably prohibited by law, but not purely conventional injuries. So there can be laws against assault, theft, and fraud for natural injuries and resentments result therefrom.

Turning to the role of liberty in the pursuit of various forms of sexual behavior, Taylor writes:

> . . . Society may not properly interfere with any sexual practices whatever involving adults, except in cases of assault (e.g., rape) or fraud (e.g., seduction of the young). Similarly, the traditional institution of lifelong monogamous marriage, however good, inspiring, and desirable, deserves no protection of law, nor has the State, for that matter, any business meddling in this relationship at all, except indirectly where the safety of

> children is involved and where the protection of society against contagious disease is implicated.

However, Taylor is not prepared to place restrictions on individual freedom or allow for any paternalistic legislation against *self*-assault, theft, or fraud. Moral and religious advice is here appropriate, but not the sanctions of the criminal law. Limits remain to the legislation of morality.

Since it is good to fulfill an aim or desire, human beings need the freedom to do so, and any restraint placed on their liberty must be designed to prevent an even greater evil from resulting.

> Concerning any practice the lawmaker may ask only: Is it injurious to anyone but the agent? And if he is able to answer "yes" to that question, then he needs to ask still another: Is the injury thus wrought of a kind that would be felt by all or most men, independently of their training, customs, and conventions? And only if *that* question, which is a question of sociology rather than one of jurisprudence, can yield no answer but "yes" does that lawmaker have any concern with the practice at all.

In "The Basis of Political Authority," Taylor argues that *fear* and *deference* are the cornerstones of political authority, irrespective of what form a government may take. Deference is the more appealing basis of the two, and can easily lull people into thinking that they are free and can choose to govern themselves through elected representatives. However, Taylor believes the vaunted will of the governed is either mythical or pernicious.

Taylor seeks to reconstruct the rise of political authority. He begins with the most miniscule form of government, namely, a situation where two people join in some common endeavor, say, fishing, and by drawing straws (or some such random method) elect a leader. Suppose the elected leader relies on a sacred book for his governance, generates deference by it, and is prepared if necessary to strike fear (in the lone person governed) by the sword. Should the governor make his decisions by consulting the will of the lone person governed here, and the latter not obey, then the governed's veto amounts to a condition of anarchy. The governor's reputed laws or commands turn out to be mere requests for voluntary cooperation and compliance.

Enlarging this society a bit, so that it now consists of some six members, can help us understand how no democratic form of government is realizable. Suppose the governor now requires the consent of the other five persons to rule. If any one of them decides not to obey, the system becomes potentially anarchic, or reverts to a form of despotism of the majority. And of course a system of majoritarian despotism can cause havoc to the minority's wishes and interests, likely resulting in the anarchy of rebellion.

To bolster the reigning political authority, much larger and sophisticated societies resort to a *charter* that describes the rights of the governed and the limitations on governmental power. There is a felt need to develop a sense of community and foster the idea of national allegiance to that government. Deference and fear are introduced to bolster an allegiance to the laws and institutions of the country. Myths are cultivated, and priestly symbols abound. Elaborate rituals, garish costumes, and impressive edifices aid the governing bureaucracy, who interpret the sacred texts in which the laws of the land are enunciated. These sacred texts need not be religious *per se,* except in the fervor in which they are interpreted and the deferential attitude they arouse. The sacred texts can be quite secular, offering an ideology of economic and political "truths," which grandly interpret history and purport to offer a path to human amelioration. And, always available to back up the sacred texts, rituals, and priestly class, when necessary, is the standing militia.

Taylor is boldly seeking to expose the myth of the democratic government. Indeed, he alleges that it is highly "doubtful whether any form of government is more hostile to freedom than an actual democracy." Paradoxically, any traces of democracy being operative and the guaranteeing of human rights being realized are largely brought about by a nonelected, venerated, independent judiciary, which can restrain the majority will when needed. In the United States, for instance, it is the Supreme Court "which protects the freedoms, property, and well-being of individuals and minorities, such as the poor, the racially outcast, the criminals, including those that would elsewhere be deemed enemies of the state—persons who would have precious little chance if left to the tender mercies of democratic forces."

These nine jurists rule in their impressive chambers, presiding as modern-day archons robed in priestly garb, surrounded by various symbols and rituals of the Republic. They are sometimes divided over their fundamentalist or constructionist readings of the sacred text that is the Constitution. And our attitude toward this quasi-religious hierarchy remains one of deference.

In his essay "The American Judiciary as a Secular Priesthood," Taylor develops his previous thoughts about the basis of political authority. He states and attempts to defend the seemingly paradoxical thesis that our basic political liberties derive not from any representative democratic form of government, but instead stem from the secular priesthood of the judiciary that serves as "a despotic bulwark of liberty." The judiciary not only interprets law; it often creates a number of civil liberties and human rights, with the paradoxical result that the personal freedoms Americans have come to enjoy are the result of an authoritarian elite in a pluralistic society. To bolster his thesis, Taylor cites several Supreme Court decisions such as *Brown* v. *Board of Education* in 1954 that conferred previously nonexistent rights on blacks in the area of educational opportunity.

Taylor traces the similarity between religion and law to two traits of human nature that seem essential to a well-functioning society, namely, imitation and the servility of esteem and deference. The institutions of religion and the law are both hierarchical, being invested with ultimate authority at the highest levels. And both at the highest levels are infallible in their respective declarations on faith and morals and the law. Both institutions rely on sacred texts as the basis of their authority, supplemented when needed, by tradition and a body of interpretative literature. Not surprisingly, both institutions often make their respective appeals to the church fathers and the founding fathers.

Both institutions are also beset with liberal/fundamentalist debates. Religious conservatives appeal to the inerrancy of Scripture, while their judicial counterparts invoke the strict constructionism of the Constitution. Religious liberals favor the spirit of religious dogma, not its letter; while judicial liberals opt for the "emanations" of the law's spirit. Just as conservative religious or legal decrees can prove intolerable, so too can liberal religious or legal pronouncements prove imperialistic. Both institutions offer elaborate rituals, codes of dress, honorific titles, and prescribed demeanor to foster their respective priesthoods. Not surprisingly, they conduct their major functions in sacred places—temples, churches, or mosques for the religious; courts or halls of justice for the judiciary.

In his essay "Is Man a Creation in God's Image?" Taylor reflects on the book of Genesis, where human beings are described as having dominion over all of creation, inasmuch as they are made in the *imago Dei.* Taylor attempts to expose this metaphorical "conceit," and thereby to undercut the uniqueness of humanity.

Taylor claims it is creation itself that is the *imago Dei.* He dialectically tries to avoid a pantheism that would make God and the world the same, maintaining instead that the world is God's mode of appearing to us. In short, the visible world is a theophany "related to its creator as a rainbow is related to the diffusion of water that underlies it, namely, as the visible appearance of its invisible foundation."

As a materialist, Taylor is convinced that the soul is not an incorporeal substance. Of the some 436 references to the soul in the Old Testament (the Hebrew term being *nephesh*), Taylor claims the consistently uniform sense of nephesh is "life" or a "living thing." He attempts to reinterpret four troublesome passages that would seemingly postulate persons as having or being souls or discarnate personalities. And, while the New Testament uses the term *psyche* 57 times, only a few such passages indicate that the soul is capable of existing apart from the body.

Taylor historically traces the modern usage of the term *soul,* denoting some sort of disembodied mind, to the Orphics, who divorced the human psyche from all material forms. Matter was regarded as base, and the body viewed as a prison that the soul seeks to escape from via moral purification. Ironically, then, the elevation of human beings above the rest of creation because of their possession of a soul is more of a pagan notion than a biblical idea. Socrates, Plato, St. Augustine, and Descartes all refined the concept, so that it became through the influence of neo-Platonism part of orthodox Christian teaching. Human beings are not just a part of nature, but apart from nature.

Like Schopenhauer, Taylor views all living things as part of a continuum. Human beings share with nonhuman animals the will to live. Anything else is anthropocentrism or speciesism. The machine has no ghost.

In "Religion and the Debasement of Goodness," Taylor formulates his "law of epigony." An epigone is someone who inherits a noble and good set of values and ideas and then, while presumably preserving and protecting them, actually corrupts such values, substituting instead the relatively worthless and in turn extolling it. The very defender becomes the enemy, and the resultant debasement "becomes enshrined in custom and in popular religion."

To illustrate his thesis, Taylor begins with the concept of *patriotism,* which is the love for one's country based on its goodness. The epigone eventually debases such love into the love for the symbols and ceremonial rituals of that country. A patriot comes to mean someone who venerates the country's flag and scrupulously obeys the various rules on how it is to be handled and displayed. During the bicentennial, Americans grotesquely venerated the Statue of Liberty, seemingly oblivious to any thoughtful reflection on the meaning of *liberty.* The symbols became the object of adoration, and the very mark of patriotism.

The same phenomenon has happened to the notion of *marriage.* Originally, marriage was based on the mutual love of the couples who so bound each other. But the conjugal union has now been replaced by the legalistic. Marriage is regarded as a contract, binding even when the couple no longer love each other. Infidelity is no longer associated with the loss of love, but regarded as a breach of contract. Constancy of love has degenerated into the longevity of the marriage itself.

Similar debasement has occurred to *religion.* Religion means love of God. But, consistent with the law of epigony, the symbols of religion have come to be venerated and not what they supposedly symbolize. The religious person owes his or her loyalties to a church or religious authority, so that religious values become fused with cultural values. Even now, one can easily be a religious atheist!

It is important to underscore that Taylor is not criticizing patriotism, marriage, or religion. Indeed, in their original meanings, he considers them unqualified goods. But he is pointing out how they have become corrupted by their very upholders, who substitute things of lesser value, or of no value at all.

The same law of epigony occurs in *ethics*. For instance: the notion of virtue has been debased. Taylor's Nietzsche-like reflections about virtue are clearly controversial. Basically, he claims that we have debased the Greek model of a virtuous person as the superior individual who through training makes himself or herself inherently better than others. Instead, we have substituted a kind of ethico-religious egalitarianism. Like Callicles in Plato's *Gorgias,* Taylor believes that debasement of virtue arises from "a kind of herd morality, wherein the same words continue to be used—words like *virtue, goodness,* and *worth*—but are given meanings that are very nearly the opposite of what they originally had."

In "Action and Responsibility," Taylor analyzes the notion of *moral responsibility,* focusing not on the associated concept of human agency and immanent causation, but instead on the widely held view that there are morally right and wrong acts that agents are responsible for and accordingly subject to praise or blame for performing.

To build his case for the thesis that there are no moral rights or wrongs, Taylor begins with some nonmoral rights and wrongs. In games, institutions, or societies, rights and wrongs (unlike goods or evils, which are relative to ends or purposes) are created by rules. Such conventional rules literally create the distinction between right and wrong, determining what is obligatory, permitted, or forbidden performance. The same situation holds for the law, where legal rights and wrongs are not "part of the metaphysical fabric of the universe," simply awaiting discovery by rational inquiry.

Taylor claims that similarly in ethics, rules and laws also create the very distinction between right and wrong. Such laws are not descriptive of some antecedently existing right or wrong, unlike goods and evils that are discoverable in experience, however "relative" they may be to human needs, desires, and purposes.

Taylor is raising a question familiar to readers of Plato's *Euthyphro*: Are certain things required (forbidden) because they are right (wrong), or are they right (wrong) because they are required (forbidden)? Given Taylor's views on polarity, the choices are not that clear-cut. The truth seems to be that human beings discover it is advantageous to behave in a certain manner, and these useful behavioral patterns become customary. Any deviation from such patterns is considered blameworthy and censurable. Soon, positive rules are formulated to insure compliance. These positive rules are often backed by appeals to God, sacred texts, or the moral law. But ultimately the behavior enjoined by the rules is adopted because it is to the mutual advantage of people. If the rules prove no longer feasible, having no practical point, then the actions enjoined are no longer right or wrong.

Since human nature is an amalgam of reason and will, there is bound to be tension between a perspective of *moral rationalism* where reason apprehends the good and our conative appetites seek it, and *moral voluntarism,* where the will seeks an object of desire and cognition discerns the means to it. Taylor favors the voluntarist approach. Persons as conative beings have certain basic needs, wants, desires, and aims in life, and therein resides the genesis of good and evil. Good and evil, in short, are supervenient upon human nature.

In brief, Taylor claims that we do not desire the good because it's good (intrinsically), but rather things or actions are good because we desire them. As conative beings, we have various needs, desires, interests, etc., and given that fact about the human condition, certain things are valuable such as health, knowledge, leisure, beauty, etc.

By contrast, rights and wrongs stem from conventional rules or customs (often bolstered by appeals to God, the authority of some legislator, or a priori practical reason). Indeed, if every person's needs, desires, purposes, etc., could be satisfied or attained without any frustration or hindrance to others, then there would be no need of rules, and hence no created distinction between right and wrong.

The grammar of a law or rule is that of a command or imperative. Moral laws are not, despite appearances, assertions or predictions. And commands presuppose a commander, who is able by appropriate sanctions to compel people to obedience. However, contemporary philosophers have largely abandoned belief in God as the source of the moral law, leaving them in their typical moral discourse with commander-less commands, sourceless moral principles, and sanctionless injunctions. Immanuel Kant was even forced to try to replace God as the source of morality with vaunted human reason, suitably deified as an end-in-itself. But Taylor tries to show how the alleged empire of moral responsibility and the moral laws governing right and wrong have no emperor (human or divine). The result is that philosophical ethics is "devoid of intellectual content."

Taylor proceeds to outline how current conventional morality and its slavish rule-following mentality has undercut the practical ends of ethics. He briefly describes four representative types of conventional morality. The *prude* seeks to master important natural feelings and inclinations by sacrosanct, trivialized rule-worship. The *pedant* has just a few rules that are viewed as inflexible, and when various dilemmas result therefrom, resorts to hair-splitting casuistry (e.g., the principle of double effect). The *formalist* is so "absorbed in the visible conventions of social life" that he or she worships etiquette, so complete is the conflation of ethics with esthetics. Such formalists are dull, unimaginative, and predictable persons, so mindlessly attuned to fixed rules that they may be fastidious about speech and dress, yet conscienceless on more significant moral matters. Finally, the *zealot,* equipped with similar inflexible rules as the three other conventional moralists, seeks to impose such conduct on others. Zealots would ban cigarette smoking, outlaw certain school textbooks not in conformity with the values of their inflexible rules, etc. The four ideal types need not be mutually exclusive, and all are alike in clinging to certain inflexible rules, even when the application of such principles defeats the very human needs and purposes on which ethics rests.

Taylor notes that even those persons who still believe in God as the source of moral obligation actually belie this belief in practice. That is, such persons are constantly rendering these commands (encapsulated in their ethico-religious principles) defeasible by their own feelings and inclinations. They seem prepared to abide by the inflexible moral law "Thou shalt not kill any person," but they quickly resort to their own needs and goals and are quick to make allowance for abortion, capital punishment, self-defense, the waging of war, etc.

In "A Modern Version of Hedonism," Taylor takes up J. S. Mill's version of hedonism. Mill held that *pleasure* is the ultimate intrinsic good, and he identified it with *happiness*. From this presupposition, Mill derived a principle of moral obligation, namely, that one ought to maximize pleasure and minimize pain for the greatest number of people. Mill's hedonism was thoroughly altruistic, unlike the Cyrenic or Epicurean forms that preceded his view.

Taylor critiques the consequentialism of Mill's position, for such utilitarianism is often earned at the expense of a virtue of character. He finds Mill's emphasis on the *quality* and not the mere quantity of pleasure not only *ad hoc* but incoherent, akin to claiming that some twelve-inch rulers are longer than others.

Taylor then turns to an analysis of the basic supposition of hedonism, namely, that pleasure is the only thing good for its own sake and pain the only thing bad. He draws a distinction between two meanings of *pleasure* and *pain* and two meanings of their cognates *pleasant* and *painful*. The first sense of pleasure (hereafter pleasure 1) serves as a name or description of various sensations, feelings, or experiences. The same holds for pain (hereafter pain 1). The second sense of pleasure (hereafter pleasure 2) serves as a term of appraisal for any feeling, sensation, or experience one happens to like or regard as good. Pain in this second sense (hereafter pain 2) is a term of displeasure or disapproval for any feeling, sensation, or experience one happens to dislike or regard as bad.

Given this distinction, something can be pleasant 2 without involving a pleasure 1. And so, too, can something be painful 2 without involving any pain 1. Taylor claims that when the hedonist claims that "pleasure 2 is always good," or that "pain 2 is always bad," such statements are trivially true, being tautologies.

If the hedonist claims (intending to make a true and informative statement) that pleasure 1 is the only intrinsic good, or pain 1 the only intrinsic evil, then the hedonist is maintaining what is false. For one can be happy even when experiencing painful 1 sensations, and unhappy even when experiencing pleasant 1 sensations.

As we have seen earlier, Taylor is a critic of rule-following morality. Instead he favors a somewhat modified Protagorean ethic based on humanity's conative nature, consisting of such un-Kantian needs, wants, and aims as the desire for life and love. What Kant termed "pathological" is for Taylor the very basis of moral incentive, namely, love and compassion, which as passions cannot be commanded. For Taylor, the ideal or ultimate moral aspiration is "to be a warm-hearted and loving human being."

Unlike Kant, Taylor tries to show how the quest for the "true morality" has so rarefied philosophical ethics to a level of abstraction that it becomes utterly removed from the practical needs of human beings. Pragmatic, conventional rules of behavior that have previously enabled people to engage in cooperative pursuits and tame their basic egocentric urges have now been replaced by Duty writ large. Kant held that we are obligated to act out of respect for the moral law, and not out of any personal feelings or inclinations. His categorical imperative dictated that a person "Act only according to that maxim by which you can at the same time will that it should become a universal law." But, Taylor alleges, Kant's glorious imperative is a command minus a commander, being promulgated by abstract reason itself.

And despite the vaunted Kantian language of persons as ends in themselves, whose dignity stems from their rational nature ("Act so that you treat humanity, whether in your own person or in that of another, always as an end and never as a means only"), Taylor claims that Kantian morality is subversive of any strictly humanistic ethic.

Because of the allegorical nature of fables or parables, it would be rash to interpret Taylor's fable on the governance of the kingdom of darkness in any decisive way. It can be noted that Taylor's polemical storytelling here is clearly against the grain of mainstream philosophical writing. This genre of fictitious narrative seeks to engage the reader in a state of intensified self-awareness, as the reader attempts to undo the various dialectical knots and in the process heightens the reader's ethical sensitivity to the issues being raised. Taylor's fable seems designed to jolt the reader out of any ingrained, conventional mode of thought.

The fable relates how Lucifer and his immediate successor have been restored to Heaven, by divine grace, for their various acts of kindness in Hell. Such beatific elevations mandated a new gubernatorial election in Hell, and the Council of Evil, armed with its inflexible criterion of complete moral depravity, must decide who will govern Hell from among the four promising finalists.

Consistent with the genre of parable, Taylor never tells us who won the election, but I suspect he favors the seemingly least likely candidate, Deprov. The dark-horse candidate, Deprov, has led a very self-righteous, law-abiding, premortem life and, given his Kantian-like moral character, could never fathom why he had been consigned to Hell. Of course he enjoyed tormenting others in the service of law and conventional morality and was the very banal incarnation of bourgeois evil. But, in modest humility, he couldn't conceive himself as qualified for the very incarnation of evil compared to his three rivals, all of whom were mass murderers.

Like the ancient Greek moralists he so admires, Taylor contends that virtue is a skill, a personal excellence. Genuine happiness, or a life lived in accordance with the virtues, involves a basic fulfillment, a perfection of the rational capacities of a person.

Taylor includes the virtue of pride as a component of his ethics of aspiration. Such a claim is in direct opposition to Christianity, which regards pride as the primary vicious trait of the denizens of Hell. Pride is the justified love of oneself, and far from thinking it a vice, Taylor regards pride as "a kind of summation of the virtues." Genuine pride rests on excellence of moral personality. It is not to be confused with conceit, nor any unwarranted sense of self-esteem.

Proud people regard themselves as superior to others and so do not seek the approbation of others for their conduct. Instead, they find their self-worth within themselves. Taylor concedes that pride "cannot be proved to be worth having." That is, in the area of virtue-ethics, individual moral sensibility is the final authority, for an ethics of aspiration deals with matters of goodness and not of truth.

Pride is also not arrogance nor self-affectation. The proud person's delight rests on self-esteem and the virtues upon which it supervenes, and is not equatable with the vain person's self-worth that is dependent on possessions, power, prestige, and assorted externals. Nor is pride equatable with the excessive self-absorption of egoism. Proud persons "compare themselves only with the best. They are properly ashamed if others are wiser than they, or if others conduct their lives with better order and rationality, or if others have greater courage and self-discipline."

The proud person is wise, often erudite, creative, and courageous. Such a person doesn't easily engage in "small-talk," and avoids the prattling conventional wisdom that promulgates a kind of mindless conformity to reigning socio-moral values.

In this section's concluding essay, Taylor reflects on *happiness* as the "basic concern of all ethics." It consists in the proper functioning of the whole person, who is fulfilled in achieving the highest personal good. The Greeks termed it *eudaimonia,* often translated as human flourishing or personal excellence.

It is difficult to pursue happiness when we are so often ignorant about its nature. Pop psychology often suggests that happiness is more a euphoric feeling than a state of achievement. Yet, despite self-avowals of exultation, genuine happiness often eludes the merely self-satisfied who otherwise rejoice in gregarious domestication or self-righteousness. Reminiscent of his earlier remarks on the meaning of life, Taylor speaks of people "without personal biographies except for the events which the mere passage of time thrusts upon them." They do not create any personal values, but contentedly absorb the values of the *status quo*. "Such persons are not fulfilled but merely satisfied."

Nor is happiness, a state of being, equatable with pleasure. As mere feelings, pleasures prove fleeting, unlike the stability afforded by happiness. As we saw in the fable on Hell, pleasures can result from acts of sheer depravity, but happiness could never result from vicious conduct.

Nor is happiness equatable with the absence of pain or suffering (indeed it is compatible with moments of dejection or frustration) or the avoidance of boredom. Sadly, many people settle for such specious forms of contentment, much as many people mistakenly identify genuine peace with the absence of warfare or the cessation of hostility. And happines is not to be found in a life of busyness, whose frenzy conceals the lack of self-fulfillment.

Taylor maintains it is also sheer folly to seek happiness in externals, such as honor, power, beauty, wealth, or even health. Happiness may often be accompanied by such external goods (and couldn't ever be entirely devoid of them), but even the sum of such externals doesn't guarantee happiness.

Instead of all these false starts, Taylor believes the proper path to happiness resides in a life of virtuous activity. Human flourishing is the byproduct of reason, reflection, and creativity. It cannot be conferred upon persons, like wealth, beauty, or fame, and one can fail to attain happiness by mistaking it with its specious rivals. Taylor has attempted to cast light on what genuine happiness is, by showing what it is not.

NOTE

1. In correspondence, Taylor maintains that he is not taking sides on the current controversy in jurisprudence about the use of an activist reading of the Constitution versus a strict constructionist or "original intent" interpretation of that document.

9

What a Conservative Really Is. And Isn't.

I am a political conservative, of the traditional kind, who enthusiastically voted for and supports President Reagan, in spite of his occasionally distressing pronouncements. But I protest the increasing use of the label "conservative" by people who have no idea what it really means. Indeed, it is sometimes associated with sheer narrowness of outlook.

A political conservative, within the framework of United States politics, tries to conserve something quite specific—namely, the values embedded in the Constitution.

These values were eloquently articulated in the President's Inaugural Address, when he reminded us that our government is supposed to be one of limited powers, not one that tries to determine for free citizens what is best for them and to deliver them from all evil.

More precisely, a conservative recognizes the Constitution as a statute, a charter of government, and a definition of rights.

Political subversion, on the other hand, is the attempt to subordinate that Constitution to some other philosophy or creed, believed by its adherents to be nobler, wiser, or better.

It would be subversion, for example, to subordinate the Constitution to the Communist Manifesto, even if done without violence and from a sincere conviction of the superior justice of a Communist state. Similarly, if anyone were to try to replace the Constitution by, say, the Koran, then no one would doubt that this would be an act of subversion.

The extreme improbability of anyone's attempting this does not, of course, affect my point. Similarly, for anyone to subordinate the prin-

---

ciples embodied in the Constitution to those of the Bible, or to those of one of the various churches or creeds claiming scripture as its source, is political subversion.

Nor is subversion made less so by the good and sincere intentions of its advocates, or by their great numbers, or by the nobility of the alternatives advocated. An act of subversion would be no less subversive if carried out by a bishop, by an army general, or by a political party, than if done by agents of a foreign government.

Subversion is not defined in terms of the means by which the basic principles of the Constitution are undermined, nor by whom this is attempted, nor in terms of the truth or falsity of the doctrine by which one seeks to replace those principles. The attempt itself is subversion.

Nor is it a question of what is really noble or ultimately true or good. The question concerns instead the historical and traditional foundation of our political society, which is the United States Constitution, and whether it should be conserved.

Religions may be based upon holy books, economic policies upon the doctrines of learned theorists, and morality upon creeds or the promptings of this or that conscience, but none of these things constitute the foundation of government in our beautiful country, however common elsewhere. Nor will they ever be, without subverting the real foundation, which is law—that is, an actual Constitution.

It is sad indeed, then, to a conservative to see such spokesmen for higher morality as Jerry Falwell, Jesse Helms, Phyllis Schlafly, and the chorus of others, all with their notions of what is best, usurp and misuse the name "conservative."

They are right, of course, in saying it is not the function of the government to pour blessings upon us in the forms of art, health, and education, however desirable these things may be. But it is likewise no proper business of government, as envisioned in our Constitution, to convert schoolrooms into places for prayer meetings for our children, or to compel impoverished and unmarried girls, or anyone else, to bear misbegotten and unwanted children, or to make pronouncements on the theory of evolution, or to instruct law-abiding citizens on what is and what is not allowable with respect to family values, or to determine which books can and which cannot be put in our libraries or placed within reach of our children.

Perhaps there is a religion, or a political philosophy, whose truths are nobler than those held by our Founding Fathers.

Perhaps there are persons who have a clearer vision than our judiciary, guided by our Constitution, of what is right and wrong.

But it can never, in the eyes of the genuine conservative, be the role of government to force such claims upon us.

The Constitution explicitly denies to government any such power, and a conservative is simply someone who thinks the provisions of that document are worth conserving.

10

The Classical Defense of Liberty

The problem of liberty is first of all a problem concerning the creation of criminal law—the prohibitory part of the law that attaches penalties to certain behavior. Civil law is related to liberty in a quite different way, generally providing the means to the ends people seek, rather than restricting them through the definition of crimes.

Thus, legislation involves many things, some of overwhelming importance. It is through legislation that agents of government spread poisons over our land, killing insects and, of course, birds and fish; that they despoil our fields and forests to build big highways; they also build and equip universities, care for the poor, regulate industry, communications, and so on, endlessly. But legislation of this kind, important as it is, does not bear directly on the problem of liberty. We shall instead be concerned with legislation, the explicit (and not the incidental) object of which is to regulate conduct. This is law that defines felonies, misdemeanors, and offenses.

Our first question, then, comes to this: To what extent is such legislation justified? Is it justified at all? Since all such law delimits the natural freedom of the individual, is any such law proper? If so, then by what principle, if any? Is there any conduct which may *not* properly be forbidden by law? If, for example, assault may properly be forbidden under threat by the state, may not also the wearing of strange dress, the desecration of symbols, the eating of shellfish or insects, and so on? At what line, if any, may we draw the reasonable limits of social freedom and those of criminal legislation?

It is widely thought that this question was answered once and for all by John Stuart Mill, and that all that is needed henceforth is an

From *Freedom, Anarchy, and the Law* (Buffalo, N.Y: Prometheus Books, 1982), pp. 55–60.

appreciation of his grand principle of liberty and an understanding of the invincible arguments by which he defended it. Even men of such sophisticated legal and philosophical thought as H. L. A. Hart suppose that Mill had defined the principle of liberty, and that his successors need only to expound and defend it.* Hardly any students pass through college without having read the famous essay *On Liberty,* and the prevailing view is that it leaves little more to be said.

This is not so. Mill's essay is a declamation and not a cogent philosophical treatise. As an ideological tract it is, perhaps, inspiring. Some can perhaps derive from it a certain attitude, a certain partisan feeling for freedom, an appreciation of philosophy in the service of a noble cause but one does not in fact find there a coherent principle of liberty. Our first task will be to establish that point and then try to supply the answer for which Mill was groping.

THE FAILURE OF MILL'S PRINCIPLE

It will not be necessary to review the whole of Mill's *On Liberty* because the error in it is central and can be exhibited at once. Essentially it is this: That the principle of liberty, as Mill formulates it, can be used in support of *any* criminal legislation whatsoever. No law, however oppressive or frivolous, really violates it. And clearly, a "principle" of liberty that is not violated by *any* legislation or practice is not a principle at all. It is only a vague and meaningless exhortation.

Mill's Formulation

Mill expressed his central thesis in these words:

> . . . the sole end for which mankind are warranted, individually or collectively, in interfering with the liberty of action of any of their number, is self-protection (p. 956).**

The principle is expressed by Mill in other ways, which he evidently took to be simply alternative ways of saying the same thing, but which in fact render the thing totally ambiguous. Thus, to the foregoing he immediately adds:

---

* See H. L. A. Hart, *Law, Liberty and Morality* (New York: Vintage Books, Random House & Alfred A. Knopf, Inc., 1963).

** All quotations are from *English Philosophers from Bacon to Mill,* ed. E. A. Burtt (New York: Random House, Inc., 1939).

> . . . the only purpose for which power can be rightfully exercised over any member of a civilized community, against his will, is to prevent harm to others (Ibid.).

and then further, that to justify applying compulsion to anyone

> the conduct from which it is desired to deter him must be calculated to produce evil to someone else (Ibid.).

And on the next page Mill expresses his principle one more way by saying

> there is a sphere of action in which society, as distinguished from the individual, has, if any, only an indirect interest; comprehending all that portion of a person's life and conduct which affects only himself, or if it also affects others, only with their free, voluntary, and undeceived consent and participation (p. 957).

Elsewhere in his essay Mill offers still other formulations of this basic idea, but none, I think, which removes the defect contained in these.

That defect is not the falsity of the principle as variously formulated. Certainly the upholder of freedom nods approval of the sentiment expressed in these declarations. The defect is rather that no coherent principle has been formulated. That is to say, if one is seeking a philosophical principle that defines the proper line of governmental and societal interference in the life of the individual, then he does not find it there, for no such line has been drawn at all. A government, however free or despotic, could draw that line in any manner it might choose, and then in complete consistency cite Mill's principle to justify the result.

The Narrow Interpretation of "Harm"

To see this, consider the crucial expressions "self-protection," "harm to others," and "evil to someone else." What, for instance, does *harm to another* consist in? Shall we construe this narrowly, limiting it, say, to bodily injury? Of course not, for the principle would then not allow for protection from such things as theft and fraud. A man could walk off with all his neighbor's livestock and, if charged with overstepping the bounds of liberty, point out in complete truth that he had inflicted no bodily injury on anyone and had, therefore, on Mill's principle as thus construed, harmed no one. Construing the notion of *harm* in this narrow way has the immediate consequence of expanding individual liberty far beyond any reasonable limit and leaves us free to commit any offense to others that falls short of bodily injuring them. *Harming* and *injuring* must accordingly encompass much more than just *wounding.*

The Wider Interpretation of "Harm"

If, to overcome the difficulty just cited, we construe the idea of harm more broadly, we find that the principle becomes so restrictive as to permit no real freedom whatever. If we say, for example, that *harming* a man consists not merely of injury to his body, but to any of his deepest interests, then of course we bring such things as theft and fraud within its meaning. Men do have a deep interest in the security of their property as well as of their persons. But unfortunately, men have *other* deep interests as well which no believer in freedom supposes for a minute should never be foiled.

Thus, there are men who have a deep interest in such things as religion, patriotism, public manners, the preservation of wildlife, and so on, without end. Now if we say that no one shall be permitted to do anything that would foil, frustrate, or damage any such interest held by anyone, this will be about equivalent to saying that no one may do anything at all. The whole of the criminal law would be summed up in saying that all actions are prohibited. And a principle having that consequence can hardly be called a principle of liberty.

An Example

Consider a village whose life centers about the practice of religion. Such villages can still be found in the remoter reaches of Quebec. And now let us suppose that someone settles himself down in that village with the avowed and determined mission of doing all he can, through spoken and written persuasion, to unsettle the religion of these villagers, undermine their faith, and break the grip of the Church upon them. Concerning such a state of affairs we can certainly say, *first,* that if this village is in fact a free society, then this iconoclast can by no means be prevented from pursuing his destructive mission with all industry and vigor, assuming, of course, that his instruments are those of persuasion and not physical violence; and *second,* that such activity on his part nevertheless *hurts* the villagers, in the sense of "hurts" that is now before us. That is, it does most manifestly frustrate and damage a deep interest of its members, or is at least calculated to. Indeed, it is not hard to imagine that their resentment of such activity might be greater than if this outsider undertook to steal all their cattle.

Mill's principle, as thus literally interpreted, does not work, for if it is applied to such a society, with a broad interpretation placed upon the crucial concept of "hurting others," the immediate result is the destruction of the most elementary liberties anyone could claim, such as freedom in the expression of theological opinion. When we consider that there are narrow-minded people (and in fact whole societies of them) who have a deep interest in such things as uniformity of manners and dress, sabbatarian observances, respect for traditional cultural values, and so on, and feel deeply injured by deviations from these, we see how little protection of individual liberty is provided by Mill's principle.

Alternative Formulations of the Principle

In none of his formulations does Mill ever appear to overcome this difficulty. It seems inherent in the principle itself. Thus, when he insists that the liberty of the individual encompasses "all that portion of a person's life and conduct which affects only himself" (p. 957), and that within that realm an individual should be left alone, the obvious response is that no such portion of one's life and conduct exists. *Everything* one does, though it may be no more than the expression of an opinion sincerely held or the display of eccentric manners or dress, affects others. Nor does it do any good to add, as Mill does, that in case one's conduct affects others, this must be "only with their free, voluntary, and undeceived consent and participation." Reverting to our example of the pious village, it is no principle of liberty that the villagers must freely and voluntarily *consent* to the expression of offensive opinions as a condition of their being enunciated. This is exactly equivalent to saying that every opinion to which anyone objects may be legitimately silenced, without in any way infringing the freedom of the speaker. And this is absurd.

The difficulty is clearly insuperable. Either such expressions as "hurting others," "protection," "affecting others," or "evil to others" are given a narrow interpretation, or they are not. If interpreted narrowly, then men must, in the name of freedom, be permitted to do whatever they please, short of physically assaulting their fellows. But if not interpreted narrowly, then men may, in accordance with Mill's principle, be restrained in the most elementary expressions of freedom such as the expression of opinion or even the display of manners or the pursuit of life-styles offensive to others. So however the principle is understood, the result is absurd.

Effects of Mill's Formulation upon His Own Philosophy

This difficulty sometimes infects Mill's development of his own ideas, occasionally with serious result. For example, he decides, in the light of his principle, that a man who chooses a life of idleness may be judicially punished in case his idleness affects others adversely—his family, for example. Should we not observe that there are very few men whose idleness, were they to choose it, would not adversely affect someone, perhaps seriously? Mill draws the same conclusion with respect to such things as drunkenness and extravagance. One is free to be a drunk provided this does not adversely affect others. What others? And how adversely? Mill specifically mentions one's children and one's creditors—but having mentioned these, at what point shall we stop? Shall we include representatives of the Christian Temperance League? If not, why not? Indeed, the whole principle virtually explodes in its author's face when he finds that it permits the judicial restraint of those whose styles of conduct are "offenses against decency" and "violations of good manners," and draws the appropriate inference (p. 1027) that such behavior should indeed be suppressed! Clearly, this is no principle of liberty at all, but an instrument for grinding men down to conform to someone's conception of "decency" and "good manners."

At one point Mill declares that every man should observe a certain line of conduct toward others, such conduct consisting, he says, of "not injuring the interests of one another" (p. 1008). What interests? The interests these others may have in such things as decency and good manners? As if detecting the difficulty here, Mill adds the qualification, "or rather, certain interests, which, either by express legal provision or by tacit understanding, ought to be considered as rights." At the beginning of his essay, however, Mill had forsworn any appeal to the idea of an abstract right (p. 957). But quite apart from this, the qualification hardly helps, for "express legal provision" can be made for the prohibition of any practice whatever, and "tacit understanding" can similarly extend to anything—to bad manners, for example. Nor is the difficulty overcome by Mill's appeal, elsewhere (p. 1023), to the opinion of society concerning what it considers requisite for its protection. Uniformity of theological opinions, for example, as well as obeisance to the flag and other trappings of the state, have been and in fact still are thought by some societies to be requisite for their protection. Again we have, then, no principle of liberty here at all, but a slogan that can be put to any use one wishes, either for the expansion or the abolishment of individual freedom.

The Need for a Clear Principle

Still, the problem Mill dealt with—which is nothing less than the age-old problem of liberty—is one of overwhelming importance. What Mill tried and failed to do is still desperately in need of being done. We do need a philosophical principle of liberty, one that is coherent and meaningful and, above all, one that does not merely presuppose the very distinctions it is intended to make. It is no principle of liberty, for example, to say that every man should have the right to do what he wishes, provided he does not infringe on the rights of others—for that only defines the idea of an individual right by presupposing it and leaves us with absolutely nothing. What is needed is a statement of what men's rights ought to be in a free society, and such a statement is not going to tell us much if it assumes the concept of a right, undefined and unexplained.

THE TRUE PRINCIPLE OF LIBERTY

If, as we have suggested, anarchy is the ideal societal state, but one that is impossible except on a relatively minute scale and under special circumstances of the kind considered earlier, it follows that the corruption of this ideal must be minimal if the maximum goodness possible is to be obtained. Or in other words, since the restriction of any man's freedom by coercive law is an unqualified evil, then no man's freedom should be restricted more than is necessary for the avoidance of even greater evil. On what principle, then, is it permissible to thus restrict human freedom—that is, to generate coercive criminal laws?

There can, properly, be only one such principle, the very one formulated by Mill—namely, the prevention of injury. The almost universal practice of mingling other principles with this one—such as that of fostering what is right or moral and suppressing what is wicked or immoral, or even that of promoting what is good, and generally acknowledged to be good, for everyone—is utterly improper and hateful to anyone who has a sense of the precious nature of freedom.

But of course what is needed at this point is a more precise account of *injury* than Mill ever undertook, for as we have seen, *any* act that anyone has ever had the slightest inclination to legislate against can be represented as injurious in some sense to someone.

The Precise Nature of Injury

There appear to be only three ways in which men can properly be said to injure each other, and these are: (1) assault, (2), theft, and (3) fraud. Actions of these kinds can be called, borrowing from the terminology of law, *mala in se,* or actions that are bad in themselves. This is not, of course, the meaning the expression has in law, but it is useful in suggesting that nothing that is not an assault, theft, or fraud can be bad by its very nature. The expression thus helps to focus our attention upon real evils, and not things that are evil only because conventionally declared to be so. No man, for example, needs to be taught that an assault upon himself is something bad, nor does anyone suppose that the evil of such an action is a mere consequence of some edict, declaration, or law. It is bad in itself, and the same is true of theft and fraud.

All three terms should be construed fairly broadly, but not so broadly as to include everything that anyone happens to dislike. Thus a violent blow to a man is, of course, an assault—but so is deliberately driving him mad by forcing him to swallow a dangerous drug or something of that sort. Similarly, depriving a man of his property by spreading lies about him can be thought of as a species of theft, being essentially no different from physical divestment or seizure of his goods. Or again, seduction by means of false promises appears to be a form of fraud, though it might not ordinarily be so described. Among the things that are *not* to be counted as injuries are mere offenses to taste or sensibility. The use of unconventional and even offensive language, for example, is not by itself an assault, theft, or fraud, nor are eccentric styles of dress and grooming, however much some of these may be detested. Injury must mean something fairly definite and cannot be expanded to include everything under the sun that this or that man may wish to abolish. Otherwise there will really be no principle of legislation at all, other than that of prohibiting what someone happens not to like, which is really the abandonment of principle altogether.

It is not enough, as we have seen, to say with Mill that men may properly be restrained from acting in ways likely to injure others, unless one then spells out what is to be regarded as *injury*. If we limit the notion to personal injury, then we find that a free society must tolerate theft under Mill's principle, so that a man could walk off with his neighbor's cattle and burn all his buildings and still escape any charge of having injured him. If, on the other hand, we expand the notion of injury to include theft, should we not expand it still further to include eccentricity of life-style, the use of offensive language, disrespect for cherished symbols, irreligion, and so on, ad infinitum? Surely there are people who would, for example, be more injured by having their theological beliefs shattered by arguments than by having their very buildings shattered by bombs; and the very sight and sound of unconventional dress and language has more than once moved men to fierce retaliation and bloodshed, which indicates in the clearest way possible the existence of felt injury. How, then, can we declare some such injuries to be innocent actions and properly protected by law, in the name of liberty, and others not? Having decided that no man is entitled to assault, steal, or defraud, why shall we not then add: Nor to offend, distress, and upset?

Natural and Conventional Injury

The answer to this serious problem lies, it is suggested, in a distinction between what may be called *natural* as opposed to *conventional* injury. The basic distinction between nature (*physis*) and convention (*nomos*) was drawn by the Greeks at about the time of Socrates, but the notion of injury has probably never been thus divided. It is a readily understood distinction, enormously useful to philosophy and jurisprudence, and it appears to be just the one that is needed here.

A *natural* injury is something that evokes more or less deep resentment on the part of him who is injured, by virtue of his very nature as a man. A *conventional* injury, on the other hand, is what one resents, not just by virtue of his humanity but because of what he has learned, or how he has been conditioned by his culture. Ordinarily, those actions that are resented by rather few, and disregarded or even positively welcomed by others, are merely conventional injuries, whereas actions that are everywhere resented, at least by most men, are likely to be natural injuries.

The eating of pork, for example, or the disregard of certain sabbatarian observances, or the desecration of religious or patriotic symbols such as rosary beads, flags, and the like, are conventional injuries. That there are men who deeply resent such acts, men who are, in fact, very clearly injured by them, shows only that these acts are injurious. It does not show that they are more than conventionally such. There are doubtless men who would, for instance, more deeply resent seeing their flag spat upon than being spat upon themselves, and who would even risk their safety to prevent it. But such an injury, however deep, is still no more than conventional. The same may of course be said of all injuries arising from eccentric life-styles, uncommon and thus "offensive" language, unorthodox habits of diet, dress, and so on.

On the other hand, injuries resulting from blows or other physical assaults with weapons, poisons, or whatnot, or from the destruction or theft of one's property, or from deceptions, are not mere conventional injuries. For there are no men, or at least very few, who do not resent actions of this sort. One *learns* to despise the eating of pork, the desecration of a flag, the practice of polygamy, but no instruction or conditioning by society is needed to render a man resentful of a threat to his life or limb. Such resentment results simply from his nature as a man. The same may be said of his resentment of the seizure by stealth or the destruction by violence of things he has come to regard as his own, and of deceptions practiced upon him with the view to exploiting and taking advantage of him. Men everywhere resent actions like these, and not because they have been taught to, or so conditioned by their tribes, but just because they are men.

Property Injuries

It might be thought that damage to property, in contrast to damage to one's person, cannot be considered natural injury for the fairly obvious reason that the very concept of property is conventional. *Possession,* to be sure, is no conventional concept, inasmuch as it means simply the having of something within one's power (Lat. *possidere*)—that is, the physical occupancy or grasp of something, together with the ability to hold it. No man-made rules or conventions are needed to determine whether a man does, for example, thus possess a field or building. This can be decided only by trying to dislodge him. But that such a field, building, or anything else should be a man's *property* cannot thus be determined, for the concept of property or ownership is entirely the creation of rules. A man may own a field or building he does not possess, or may similarly possess something he does not really own. One owns something to which he has a valid title, or which he can in other ways declare to be his, by virtue of and in entire dependence upon certain rules and customs.

Can we, then, regard a violation of one's property as a natural and not merely a conventional injury? The answer appears to be that while ownership is the creation of convention, resentment arising from the violation of it is not. That a given building is my property is a fact of convention, a relationship that is entirely the creation of men; but that I should feel injured by someone's destruction of what is thus artificially created is in no similar way conventional. I may learn what, by rule and convention, may be thought of as mine, but I do not similarly learn how to react to its despoilment by others. Or to cite an analogy: The bond of marriage is entirely the creation of custom and law, though it may be based upon needs and desires that are not merely conventional. Thus, to affirm of a certain person that that person is my wife is to affirm the existence of a relationship that is the creation of custom or rule. But it is no mere convention that I should feel resentment if that person is assaulted. Such resentment is not something that is learned, is not something governed by rules, in the sense that it would not exist if it were not for such rules. The rules create the relationship, but not the sense of injury that can arise from it.

In the light of this we can say that while some facts and relationships are the creations of conventions and rules, not all the feelings associated with such facts and relationships are themselves conventional. Some, at least, have their foundation in human nature itself.

Conventional Injuries Not Crimes

This seems to afford the answer to the question that has been raised—the question, namely, of what kind of injury may properly be prohibited by society through the coercion of law. *Any natural injury may thus be prohibited, but merely conventional injuries may not.* This rule is simple in its formulation, but the consequences of applying it would be momentous indeed.

A man may properly and by all means be prevented from assaulting, stealing from, or defrauding another, for the injuries of such actions are natural ones, and the resentment of such injuries natural resentment—not reactions that are learned and thus susceptible to becoming unlearned. No man, on the other hand, may be properly restrained from living in whatever manner he chooses, doing with himself (or with his mind or body) what he will, speaking as he pleases so long as his speech is no part of a fraud upon others, doing as he pleases with whatever is his own, short of using it (e.g., a gun) to inflict injury upon others even though this may, as in the case of a flag or religious artifact, be symbolic of values that are profoundly cherished by others.

No man can assault, steal from, or defraud himself; and accordingly, there can be no natural injury to oneself for which any protection of the law is needed. If a normal man injures himself—as, for example, by taking poison or wounding himself inadvertently or carelessly—then he is in the same position as one to whom has befallen a natural evil or catastrophe, like someone who has been struck by a falling boulder. Such possibilities of self-injury call for no curtailment of a man's freedom, any more than does the possibility of ordinary mishap.

If a man injures another but the injury is not a natural one (of the kind just described), then he does, indeed, injure him. A merely conventional injury is no less an injury than a natural one, and sometimes no less injurious, or even far more so. But if *every* injury, including every conventional one, were a fit object of legal prohibition, then there would be no course of conduct that might not quite legitimately be outlawed. For authority to restrain a man in his actions, it would be sufficient that someone complain about them; and since anything whatever is a perfectly appropriate object of resentment and complaint by someone else, then anything whatever could be properly forbidden.

But this is not the whole of the answer, for one might take just that position. That is, it might be maintained, and indeed often has been, that no man has any right to do anything except what his society more or less generously permits. It would, for example, be perfectly intelligible that in a given society no man could do anything at all to which any man whatsoever raised even the slightest objection; that a sufficient basis for restraint would be the simple objection on the part of another. In such a society there would, to be sure, be no freedom at all, or at least the very minimum, but it would nevertheless have one genuine advantage—the possibility of injury of any kind by others would be reduced to the absolute minimum.

Injury and the Balancing of Evils

The rest of the answer, then, appears to be this: That while a conventional injury is indeed an injury, and therefore something that, abstractly considered, ought not to be inflicted, the evil of such injury can rarely equal that of its prohibition. Such injury (like any other) can be prevented only by placing restraints upon someone's conduct.

Now we have already noted that, the fulfillment of aim or desire being an absolute good, then freedom, with respect to such fulfillment, is an unqualified good. This does not mean that it may never be curtailed, but only that its curtailment must absolutely be justified in terms of the greater evil of the injury resulting from its exercise. Put more tersely, we can say that restraint is always an evil by its nature, but it is sometimes less so than indulgence.

What has been learned can be unlearned. No man, therefore, should be permitted to appeal to a merely learned and conditioned reaction to another's behavior as a basis for curtailing it. We cannot expect men to learn not to resent assault, theft, and fraud, for such resentment was never learned to begin with, and is thus not susceptible to being unlearned. We can, however, expect men to learn not to resent mere conventional offenses, for such resentment has been learned, exists only because it was learned, and can hence be unlearned. Better, therefore, that men should be permitted to burn flags, revile religion, use strong liquors and drugs, indulge in deviant sexual behavior, and all such things, even at the price of evoking deep resentment and thus real injury in their fellows—better all this than that such actions should be curtailed by the coercion of law. It is better because we can at least hope that such learned resentments are not invincible, that they can at least be overcome. Freedom being unqualifiedly good, its abolishment is unqualifiedly evil; and such abolishment cannot ever be justified except in terms of an even greater evil resulting from its exercise.

Applications

Mill concluded his essay with a section entitled "Applications," offering a preview of the new age of liberty that would be ushered in when legislators, magistrates, and mankind generally had grasped and begun to apply his grand principle. We need not follow Mill's example with any similar pleas, but it will be worthwhile to indicate in a general way the consequences of applying the principle that has been enunciated.

Victimless Offenses

Criminologists have lately been propounding the principle that there can be no crime without a victim. In the light of this they have been opposing the practice, particularly prevalent in America, of trying to "legislate morals." Actions which, according to this view, should not be treated judicially as crimes or legal offenses of any kind include such things as drunkenness, obscenity, homosexuality, and so on. Partly their motivation has been, like Mill's, a simple concern for human freedom, but they have also been motivated by considerations of economy. A vast amount of the resources of the police and the entire judicial system is consumed in the attempted suppression of what should be considered, from the standpoint of law (if not from the standpoint of morality), innocent activity.

One can hardly fail to recognize that this formula, "there is no crime where there is no victim," expresses an obvious truth and is indeed hardly more than the expression of common sense. A philosopher is likely to recognize in the term "victim," however, the same fatal ambiguity that was involved in Mill's term "injury." Just what is it to be the "victim" of another man's action? Obviously, it is to suffer *injury* by that man. But here we have to insist that the patriot who sees the flag of his country desecrated by persons he can only regard as cowards is in the fullest sense *injured.* That it does not hurt *him* to see this done is simply untrue. It does not wound his body, but the wound is no less painful for that.

It is hoped that the modification and elaboration of Mill's principle, involving the qualifications of natural and conventional wrong, have removed this difficulty. If so, then the actual workings of that principle are almost too obvious to belabor. We need only to consider a bare sketch of its applications, which will be enough to show that it holds up at those points where Mill's principle, together with certain contemporary formulations from the area of criminology, does not.

Sexual Behavior and Criminality

One of the more obvious consequences of our principle is that society may not properly interfere with any sexual practices whatever involving adults, except in cases of assault (e.g., rape) or fraud (e.g., seduction of the young). Similarly, the traditional institution of lifelong monogamous marriage, however good, inspiring, and desirable, deserves no protection of law, nor has the state, for that matter, any business meddling in this relationship at all, except indirectly where the safety of children is involved and where the protection of society against contagious disease is implicated. No civil authority may presume to insist upon anyone obtaining its *permission,* either for the creation or for the dissolution of this relationship, nor may the state set forth conditions for entering into it or leaving it, except, again, in those rare cases where public safety may be involved or the safety of children somehow jeopardized. Whether a man has one wife, two, or whatever number he may choose; whether a woman has a plurality of spouses to whom she is formally ("legally") married—these things are no business whatever of any legislator. Such matters are fit subjects for guidance and remonstrance from the church (in the case of those who adhere to any church), but not for the compulsive coercion of the secular state. Similarly, it is no business of any magistrate whether anyone has any spouse at all, or if so, for how long, and under what terms or arrangements, nor is it a concern of his whether anyone chooses to cohabit with others of the same or different sex. These things are all matters of convention, posing threat of injury to no one, or at least, to no one except free agents.

Eccentricity and Criminal Behavior

Again, the life-styles one chooses, his manners, his appearance, his personal preferences and practices, what he does with his time, and whether he uses his resources well or ill—all such matters are clearly beyond the proper concern of any lawmaker. What one does with his own body and mind, whether he uses drugs, intoxicants, poisons, stimulants, or whatnot, whether he engages in activities dangerous to his own well-being, whether he takes certain obvious precautions for his own safety, such as wearing certain safety devices on the public highways or locking up his belongings, are beyond any concern of any legislator. Failure to abide by certain standards in all such things involves danger, to be sure, but it is a danger only to oneself, and only indirectly and remotely to others; and any man has an absolute right to court danger, assuming he knows the nature and degree of his risks. So long as his activity poses no clear threat to others of assault, fraud, or theft, then it is wanton meddling for the state to restrain it or to send police officers against those caught up in it.

It is one thing to point out, however wisely, however incontestably, that a certain type of behavior poses dangers to the agent. It is quite another thing to impose criminal liability upon one for pursuing such activity, in full knowledge of the personal danger to himself. Thus, if a man should wish to experiment with dangerous drugs, then this is a proper occasion to educate him to their danger. It is not an occasion for waiting until he does experiment with them and then arresting him. If someone wishes to get from place to place by soliciting rides from passing motorists, and if such motorists wish to pick up such strangers, knowing the occasional danger of such accommodation, then it is appropriate to publicize the facts and perhaps post reminders of them along the highway. It is not appropriate—and is a serious invasion of liberty—to penalize either those who solicit or those who provide such rides. No driver is obligated to pick up hitchhikers. The choice is his. And the danger, to the rather small extent that it exists at all, is his too.

The Principle of Criminal Legislation

In general, then, a legislator may ask concerning any practice whatever: *Not* whether it is in keeping with morality; *not* whether it accords with the ordinary standards of decency; *not* whether it reflects civilized manners; *not* whether it is offensive to the sensibilities of law-abiding citizens; *not* whether it clashes with the cultural and religious heritage of his society; *not* whether it is perhaps pointless, foolish, and profitless; *not* whether it is in keeping with the minimum standards of personal conduct; and *not* (even) whether it is perhaps extremely dangerous (to him, alone, who undertakes it). Such questions as these are perfectly appropriate for moralists bent upon improving men's character and perhaps even raising the general level of civilized life, for clergymen concerned with men's salvation, for parents and teachers concerned with the well-being of children, and no doubt for others. They are of no legitimate concern whatever for any lawmaker.

Concerning any practice the lawmaker may ask only: Is it injurious to anyone but the agent? And if he is able to answer "yes" to that question, then he needs to ask still another: Is the injury thus wrought of a kind that would be felt by all or most men, independently of their training, customs, and conventions? And only if *that* question, which is a question of sociology rather than one of jurisprudence, can yield no answer but "yes" does the lawmaker have any concern with the practice at all. The morality of citizens, whether what they are doing is right or wrong, or whether they even know the difference between right and wrong, is of no more concern to him than to any ignorant and idle meddler. The liberty of citizens—and in particular their freedom from pointless and coercive meddling by the agents of the state—is on the other hand a thing of overwhelming importance to those whose freedom the state can almost whimsically jeopardize. Liberty, if not an absolute good, is at any rate an unqualified one, quite regardless of how this or that person may feel about its mode of expression.

11

The Basis of Political Authority

Fear and deference, and very little else, are the basis of political authority everywhere, in democracies and despotisms alike. The symbol of the first is the sword, and its actual instrument armed men. The symbol of the second is the clerical gown, and its actual instrument a priestly class or, more common now, a judicial class retaining the trappings of a priesthood.

In some states fear is the main pillar, and officially armed persons are constantly in evidence. In others, deference constitutes the larger foundation and in these the police are less conspicuous but always known to be there. In some states both deference and fear are evoked to the maximum by a real and awesome priesthood having immediate control of the police and its firing squads, sometimes with earth-shaking results.

How a people actually fares under this or that political authority depends very much on which of these two foundations is relied upon more, and very little on how, for example, its public officials are chosen. Fear is negative and galling, while deference is positive and sometimes exhilarating. Hence people at least *feel* more free when they bow than when cowed, and may then even speak of governing *themselves*.

Both fear and deference appear natural to human beings. Fear produced by threat, is of course universal, and deference, typically elicited by persons presented as awesome, is hardly less so. It is expressed by bowing, saluting and yielding. Thus a Pope or an Ayatollah or a Grand Lama attracts a vast throng, including numbers of the faithless, even though he offers them no more than gestures and nods. People have at all times invented religions in order to have gods to bow to, and such exalted persons, having the visible trappings of religion, fulfill this same deep and universal need.

First published in *The Monist* 66 (1983): 457–471. Reprinted by permission of *The Monist*.

Fear and deference were originally the foundation for the *existence* of political states, as well as for their authority. Thus a people's bodies and possessions were won by the sword, and their minds conquered by the charisma of some holy man. Today states sometimes arise from more rational foundations—from the promulgation of charters, for instance—and public officials are likewise put in place by more orderly means—by election, for example. But once there, the political authority to be effective must rest upon fear and deference.

AUTHORITY AND POWER

Political authority carries with it certain supreme powers—the power to tax, to adjudicate disputes with finality, allocate public revenues, seize land for public use, raise armies by conscription and wage war, establish schools, regulate commerce, enact criminal legislation and impose criminal sanctions, and so on. Whether these things are in a given state done wisely or not is one question, on which opinions will differ. How the laws under which they are done are enacted is still another question, and not a very interesting one. And how the people who administer such laws are placed in power is still another, of less importance than is usually supposed. Answers to questions like these do not, however, supply the answer to the still further question: What is the basis of political authority in a given state? And the answer to that one is always: Fear and deference.

Because governments wield such overwhelming power over the lives and property of people, and so largely determine their general happiness or misery, it has seemed a problem in our cultural tradition to somehow *justify* that power. In most other parts of the world, where western traditions have been least felt, it has not seemed a problem. There even despotic governments are often just taken for granted, along with the air that is breathed.

The most common approach to such justification has been to portray legitimate governmental authority as expressing, not the will of some person or group, but the will of the governed themselves. If, for example, it is I who voluntarily invest government with powers, then I am only governing myself, and the authority to do so is made obvious. One hardly needs more than to state such a formula to see its mythical character, but it is a myth that has nourished a great deal of philosophy.

A SIMPLE MODEL

To see the real foundations of political authority we need a model, and we shall begin with the simplest imaginable. We shall then invent modifications to this model, making it somewhat more complex and also much more closely resembling what we actually find in the world. In these models we shall see very clearly the real basis of authority, as well as the mythical character of the democratic model.

Imagine, then, a plurality of persons living in physical proximity to each other but without government or, in fact, cooperation of any kind. Each goes his own way, ignoring the others. And now suppose that just two of these join in some common pursuit—fishing, we shall suppose. We can imagine them to agree that one will be entirely in charge, and the other will simply obey, these respective roles being decided, let us suppose, by drawing straws. The boss of this twosome will decide which shall row, which cast nets, where they will fish, for how long, how the catch will be divided, everything. Of course he can do this benevolently, sharing the work and the catch, or democratically, by consultation with the other, or despotically, by doing nothing and then taking all, and so on.

Here we have, in miniscule form, the elements of government. It has a rational origin, namely contract, and no matter how galling the role of the governed may turn out to be, he has no rational basis for complaint. He knew what he was agreeing to, and got what he bargained for.

But while we have before us the basis of this minute government's *existence,* we find as yet no basis for its *authority.* As the two parties to this arrangement came together each by his own choice, so either can abandon it, at will. The governed, for example, having fared badly after the first day of the joint fishing effort, can simply walk away and be done with it.

So now we introduce our first modification. We suppose that the ruling member of this pair bases his every order and decision upon a book, claimed to come from a god, which prescribes in detail how, when, and where fish are to be caught. He takes no action without consulting The Book, and none that is at variance with what it prescribes. It is claimed, though not in fact borne out, that more fish are caught by heeding the esoteric procedures described there. But apart from that, the governed member of the pair is persuaded that so long as the prescriptions of The Book are faithfully adhered to, then at least things will be done in ways that are "right." And the governing member reinforces this conviction by donning strange garb and adopting a solemn demeanor whenever The Book is consulted, uttering esoteric incantations, and fostering a sense of mystery.

At this point a semblance of governmental authority can be seen, as well as its foundation, which is deference. The governed bows to the governor, and obeys.

That foundation is still imperfect, however, because there is no assurance that the governed will not, at any moment, lose his faith and then just walk away. This might indeed happen in case adherence to the procedures set forth in The Book results in consistently poor catches, thus nourishing skepticism. In that case this minute society of fishermen will lapse back into the anarchy from which it had briefly emerged.

The remedy for this defect is obvious. In addition to arming himself with The Book, the priestly gown and the mysteries, the governor arms himself with a sword, placing the other totally at his mercy. Now, as deference perhaps fades, fear takes it place, and the government begins to have a foundation that is real and secure.

AUTHORITY AND DEMOCRACY

Let us now elaborate this model to see whether we cannot perhaps substitute the consent of the governed for fear and deference as the basis of political authority in this minute political arrangement.

Thus, we suppose that the ruling member of the pair bases his orders and decisions, not on some holy book, but on consultation with the other member. While the orders and decisions are in fact enunciated by him, he issues none without the other's concurrence. Hence the governed is obliged to obey no command which does not express his own will. His refusal to go along amounts to formal veto. No force will be threatened to compel his obedience, for there will in that case be no command for him to heed.

Now, for the first time, this tiny government appears to have a rational basis. Its orders are no longer plucked from Scripture, nor do they express a perhaps arbitrary and capricious will of a ruler. We can see *why* they should be heeded, even when they may turn out to be stupid, pointless, and profitless. And the obligations arising from them turn out, by a kind of sleight of hand, to be perfect ones, that is, obligations that will never fail to be met—since any such obligation is abolished simply by declining to heed it! No sword, therefore, is needed to gain compliance.

But it can also be seen that, by thus making governmental authority rational, we have at the same time abolished government itself. One of this pair has ceased to govern, and the other to be governed, and their arrangement has collapsed back into anarchy, the very condition that prevailed before they got together. For before they entered into this relationship, each could do exactly as he wanted, any cooperation with the other being merely voluntary, to be undertaken or abandoned as either saw fit. And now that is again so. If the governed receives any order he does not like, his mere refusal to heed it nullifies the order. This means that no orders exist, and no laws, but only requests and exhortations. Nor should we think of the other, the governor, as subject to the will of the governed; for it is still he, it will be recalled, who initiates orders.

He will of course issue none which he does not wish to see carried into effect. He too, then, is under no obligation to do anything he does not want to do, and is in no way subject to the will of the other.

Thus in trying to supply this kind of a foundation to political authority we do indeed produce something that is superficially rational, but at the expense of the very thing, government, for whose powers we were seeking authority.

RULE BY CONSENT

Now our task is, in our imaginations, to enlarge this miniscule society, to see whether we can preserve in it the political authority that is essential to the existence of any government, at the same time devising some way to insure that its laws and policies somehow express the will of the governed. We shall find that these two cannot be combined. This means that actual democratic government is impossible. If there is such a thing as a free people—and, indeed, there do exist societies whose members are politically free, at least in some significant sense—then this results from something other than a democratic foundation. And we will in fact find that such freedom, where it exists, is a blessing wrought almost entirely by the least democratic of our institutions and, not surprisingly, by a quasi-priestly class.

Returning to our imaginative constructions, then, we now think of our minute society as consisting of, say, six persons, one (only) of whom emerges a foreman or governor by some such means as before, such as drawing straws. And we suppose, as before, that this society has some common enterprise, such as fishing.

We can now make the same suppositions as before. Thus we can suppose the foreman rules either benignly or despotically, holding the allegiance of his people by convincing them that he governs in the name of some god and by the authority of some holy book or, more realistically, by having a gun always at hand.

The foundation of this society's existence, namely contract, is as obvious as before. And the foundation of its political authority, deference and fear, is no less apparent. And the basis of its benign or despotic character, whichever it turns out to be, is also clear—namely, the benign or despotic will of the foreman.

But suppose it is somewhere—perhaps in his holy book—prescribed that this governor shall issue no command and initiate no policy without the concurrence of the other five. Where, when and how to fish will, we suppose, always be matters of group decision.

If we take this at face value, it will mean that any of those five can nullify any order of the governor, merely by declaring his distaste for it, just as before. And the result of this, obviously, will be exactly as before. Government will rest on the will of the people, but the price of that will be the abolishment of government itself. By introducing the requirement of literal consent of the governed, we have thrown these people back into the very condition of anarchy with which we began. Each person is again entirely on his own, to do as he wills, unable to count on cooperation from anyone, even the ruler. For he, too, need not initiate anything which he personally dislikes. No laws or commands exist here, but only counsels and request, and it is not even clear where they come from or to whom they are directed.

MARJORITARIAN DESPOTISM

The next step is, of course, obvious—to suppose that the foreman acts only with the concurrence of the governed, but that a simple majority is considered sufficient. Something is proposed, three concur—and the other two must comply. Such compliance, we must suppose, is ensured by the existence, not merely of a nominal ruler, but a real one, that is, one who can somehow evoke deference or fear. We can suppose, for example, that he is robed, and armed, as before.

This is of course the basic model of democratic government, as it actually exists in the world. Government "by the people" has never meant, and could never mean, by all the people. Rule by some kind of majority is considered an acceptable compromise—imperfect, to be sure, but at least approaching an ideal.

Actually, unless we introduce some very large modification of this scheme, it does not represent government resting on the will of the people at all, but another form of despotism, pure and simple, except that now the despotic will is shared. In the small society we have created, any three of the governed can do, and get, whatever they want, in spite of the other two. Everyone there is exposed to the risk of being compelled to do the very opposite of what he wills. For the perhaps arbitrary, capricious, and greedy will of one person we have simply substituted the combined will of three, perhaps no less arbitrary, capricious, and greedy. For example, with no violation whatever of the democratic principle before us, the foreman might, upon completion of a fishing expedition, propose that the entire catch go to three whom he designates, with the understanding that each will share with him. Thus the ruler ends up with half, these three with the other half, and the other two with nothing—all in perfect accordance with rule "by and for the people," as here conceived. And it is a paradigm of despotic and capricious rule. Nor can we fail to note a certain resemblance to the kind of arrangement common in modern democracies.

CONSTITUTIONAL GOVERNMENT

Of course if things to this way in the little society we imagine, then it will be an unstable one. The two who are victimized will begin to lose their faith in the god, the book, and so on, by which their deference was obtained, and they will decline to join in further fishing expeditions. If they fear the foreman's gun, then they will arm themselves, and their reversion to anarchy will be by the costly route of civil war. They having left, then the next victim of majority rule will soon join them, and a condition of general anarchy will prevail once more.

About the only way this difficulty can be overcome is to introduce the idea of a *charter* which will set forth the aim and purpose of the society (cooperative fishing, we are supposing for now), the general manner in which this is to be done, how the foreman is to be chosen (by popular vote, for instance) and the manner in which his orders and commands come into being (the concurrence of the majority). So far, all the charter does is formalize what already exists; it does nothing to mitigate the evil which was the natural result of what already exists. So it must contain another part, namely, a list of *rights* of the governed that the ruler will be bound to respect, and of *limitations* on the exercise of his powers.

That, however, will be only the beginning of the story, for no such charter can by itself constitute the basis of political authority, for reasons that ought to be apparent. However well conceived such a charter may be, however noble in its ideals and inspired in its content, it will be nothing but poetry unless adhered to by an actual government with authority over its people. And the political authority of every government, whether constitutional, democratic, authoritarian or whatever, will still turn out to be deference and fear.

DEFERENCE TO A PRIESTLY CLASS

To elicit these somewhat complex points, we shall now enlarge our small society of fishermen and the number and nature of its purposes. In doing so we shall see that it can go in various directions, closely resembling actual governments that exist, of which the democratic form is only one. What will be found to remain constant is the basis of political authority in each.

Thus, suppose our minute society grows, to several hundreds of thousands or more, that it acquires such diverse goals as the cooperative development of industry, agriculture, the conditions of leisure, along with the traditional fishing. The single ruler is replaced by several and, eventually, by a large bureaucracy. How these are chosen, what they do, for what purposes, and by what means, are all described in a charter.

They might, for example, be chosen by a spiritual leader, by a priesthood, by some ruling and self-perpetuating council, by vote of the people or some large or small class of these—whatever. However these things are actually done, there will *always* be this problem: That some persons will be disadvantaged by whatever laws or policies are adopted. These will have no incentive to comply, and a strong incentive either to disobey, or to withdraw from the arrangement altogether. One way of avoiding that problem, by getting unanimous consent, amounts, as we have seen, to a reversion to anarchy.

So we have to devise a scheme of actual government, accepting the fact that some and perhaps many persons will sometimes and perhaps much of the time be actually obligated to do what violates their will, their reason, or perhaps even their conscience. There is no way a people can actually be free. The most that can be hoped for is that some, perhaps many, will be free sometimes, that is, acting in accordance with their own reason and will, and, perhaps, that even more can somehow be made to *feel* free.

The most obvious means of securing obedience to an unpalatable command or law is, of course, through fear. But fear is dreadful, and reliance upon it utterly negative. If someone can be induced to obey because he wants to, rather than because he dreads the consequences of refusing, then the whole of life is enhanced, and social life, which might otherwise seem to resemble a prison camp, comes instead to resemble a great brotherhood, at least to its members. Ideally, the people should be welded into a powerful nation, its members willing to do anything that is necessary for the "common good," that is, the goals favored by the majority. They will, for example, be willing to give up, without significant threat, property gained by their own industry, to be used sometimes for purposes that frustrate their own wishes and violate their reason. They will even be willing, sometimes, to expose themselves to great dangers or death.

The way this is achieved is by the cultivation of the second of the two bases of political authority, namely, deference, or unthinking respect for the laws and institutions and the people who administer them. A person always can be induced to obey from fear, but his compliance is reluctant, resented and therefore unreliable. But if he can be induced by deference and respect, then he will obey willingly, sometimes joyously, and irrationally.

What is now needed is the cultivation of deference, partly through the dissemination of myths, or what Plato aptly called a "noble lie," and partly through symbolism, preferably the symbolism associated with a priesthood.

One obvious possibility, for example, is the establishment of an actual priesthood holding the powers of government directly or indirectly in its hands. This is in one respect the best way of all, for respect for the priests of an inherited religion, often rising to reverence, has always been one of the easiest things to cultivate in the minds of the masses, who eagerly turn to religion for appropriate objects of their seemingly natural servility. It is perhaps the only kind of thing for which popular deference can be taken for granted. Sometimes people will voluntarily risk death from no other motivation, sincerely declaring their belief in the enviable status of martyrs. Countless masses will swarm around a Pope, or any other person represented as the exemplar of the priestly class, sometimes falling to their knees, and always gazing up with rapturous expression—even though, significantly, he promises nothing, and his utterances are of the utmost banality. His *person,* robed in strange vestments never otherwise seen, is enough to evoke this response.

It should be stressed that what is essential here is not the mere *fact* of high priestly office, but the *appearance,* for it is this that evokes deference, instantly and without thought. It is not enough that a priest—or chief magistrate or king or whatever—*be* that person. He must present the appropriate striking appearance. This becomes evident if we imagine the Pope, for instance, stepping before a waiting throng garbed, not in the usual strange and garish robes and headgear, but in sweatshirt, baggy trousers, and sneakers, with a cigar in one hand and a bottle of beer in the other. It is similarly absurd to imagine any judge presenting such an appearance while presiding over a litigation. In some jurisdictions the judges even wear outlandish wigs, never seen elsewhere.

This predilection to servility on the part of the people can be utilized, with overwhelming effect, by declaring that there are unseen gods, or better, one such god, that his will has been made known through certain writings, and that the priesthood is uniquely privileged to interpret those writings. The members of this brotherhood are in turn divided by rank, the highest among them then either holding in his hands the powers of government or, no less effectively, blessing whoever does. Associated with this priesthood are the symbols of authority and mystery—strange vestments, for example, and bizarre headgear; temples or mosques, and complex symbolism unique to these; ceremonious behavior on the part of the priests, having no clear practical purpose, involving rising, kneeling, or dancing, and the uttering of arcane words and chants, and so forth.

There have always been political societies based largely upon this special and paradigmatic type of deference, and there still are. So effective are the twin foundations of their political authority, fear and deference, that great nations have grown up around them and achieved such power as to unsettle, more or less, the institutions and the economies of half the globe, all without the slightest trace of rational foundation. Such political authority appears to the rest of the world as reflecting little more than the caprice and lust for power of a priesthood.

But to the people it appears correct, even rational. They believe that behind it lie the correct distinctions of right and wrong. They obey, willingly and eagerly, and they even think of the commands laid upon them as the expressions of their own wills. They are therefore never troubled by questions of self-government, or how to deal with dissent.

What has just been described is, with significant but nonessential variations, the model for every government on the face of the earth, both east and west, despotic or democratic, and the basis of political authority is likewise the same everywhere, fear and deference. The differences have only to do with what is to be considered as sacred doctrine, what is to be regarded in this or that political society as its sacred writings, where those writings come from, what group is to be considered its priesthood, and by what ceremonious means governmental control over individuals is to be achieved.

SECULAR PRIESTHOODS AND POWER

The sacred doctrine of a political order can consist, for example, of ideological, economic, and political tracts and manifestos, defining the classes of people and their conflicting relationships, offering, as do all religions, an interpretation of history and a general prediction concerning the future, and a pathway to salvation. In this case the sacred literature is declared to come, not from a god, but from some man of profound insight together with his disciples. Their writings are deemed orthodoxy, doctrinal departures are condemned and their authors silenced or punished as heretics or revisionists. Saints and martyrs are venerated, their portraits emblazoned everywhere, particularly on holy days, and the actual physical remains of one of them preserved in a crypt, to be viewed by solemn processions of the faithful. The inner circle of the priesthood responsible for interpreting this doctrine consists of a central committee, whose pronouncements are final. This priesthood gains the deference of the masses by staging immense parades on certain holy days, displaying gigantic portraits of the saints and the symbolism of the worldly triumph of the faith, mostly consisting of huge guns and rockets. In addition to these ostentatious exhibitions there is a more subtle cultivation of mysteries. The priesthood itself, for example, operates in secrecy, making known its interpretations of doctrine but not how those interpretations are arrived at. Its members live behind a screen and are, except for their names and priestly status, virtually unknown to the outside world. From time to time individuals from the ranks of the masses are elevated to a kind of minor sainthood for their special demonstrations of zeal, and given the official name "heroes."

That picture, too, is familiar, and the twin bases of political authority in such a society, fear and respect, are conspicuous. Fear is constantly nourished by the omnipresence of armed and ruthless men, empowered to seize anyone at any hour of the day or night, search his household, and remove him to secret proceedings, then banish him to exile. And these two factors, fear and respect, work hand in hand with dreadful effectiveness, for even to cast doubt upon the integrity of the priesthood and the truth and purity of its doctrine is known by all to risk a visit by these armed men, followed by probable exile. Such is, indeed, the chief source of the thousands of the damned who fill the dreary prison camps far away.

The system is essentially religious in every respect except the familiar claim of divine authority for its doctrine and power. And of course whole nations have gravitated to this quasi-religious ideology, achieving such might as to not only unsettle the political and social arrangements of the whole earth, but to totally dominate a great part of it, often with the willing, even slavish, acceptance of the people.

Such is the power of deference, conjoined with fear, and such, too, is the power of religion, or quasi-religious doctrine, to evoke that respect. There are, to be sure, as in every religion, assurances of great rewards to be enjoyed someday, a withering away of oppression, and visions of a great kingdom that will triumph over the forces of evil. These ideals and expectations are represented as the real basis of political authority. But that is a patent myth, and no one really believes it at all. The actual basis of political authority is fear and deference.

The Judiciary as a Priestly Class

And now finally, to see how unexceptionable these two bases of political authority seem to be, let us imagine this possibility.

We suppose that the society we are about to construct, like the one just considered, officially repudiates religion as the foundation of political authority, substituting quasi-religious means and myths to gain the deference necessary, along with fear, for the maintenance of that authority. But as the last relied more upon fear, this one will rely more upon deference, to the great benefit of the people.

Thus, a myth is assiduously cultivated among these people that they govern themselves; that unlike less fortunate members of other political communities, they are a "free" people; that political powers are wielded only with their consent; and that they even choose who shall hold those powers. Stories like this are particularly impressed upon the young, who ceremoniously begin each school day by bowing to the symbols associated with these myths and solemnly pledging devotion to them.

Of course this society has a rich sacred literature, inspiring in tone, proclaiming certain doctrines concerning human nature, government, and the rights and blessings that have been conferred on its members.

Children are made to recite the more basic passages from this literature. The most important such document is called The Charter. It outlines the structure and functions of government and defines certain rights of the people. It is claimed to have come from a sagacious group of historical figures referred to as "The Fathers," and is actually referred to as the "supreme law."

The Charter of course establishes a priesthood, hierarchically organized into various levels of archons. Those at the summit somewhat resemble the "philosopher kings" of Plato's *Republic,* except that instead of being guided by a metaphysical vision of goodness, they are guided by the sacred literature, that is, by The Charter and the rich literature of interpretation and commentary that has grown up around this, particularly from the hands of their predecessors. The main function of the archons high in the hierarchy is the rendition of the true meanings to be found in The Charter whenever these come into dispute. In this they are, as with any priesthood, deemed infallible, and their pronouncements on these matters are in fact final and cannot be overturned by any power of heaven or earth except, of course, by themselves. Even the official Head of State must yield to their claim of authority here, and can be reduced to a common petitioner and even ignominiously forced from his supposedly supreme office when their rulings go against him.

Every subordinate level of the hierarchy follows, of course, the word of the higher archons in resolving matters of dispute among the people. Its members are, like any priesthood, robed, and they follow an austere mode of life, quite aloof from ordinary people, at least at the higher levels. They perform their functions in chambers made to resemble temples. They are addressed in honorific terms suggestive of unique virtue, and when one of them presides over one of the ceremonies within one of the special halls, he is elevated above the rest, so that no one's head can at any time be higher than his.

The halls in which the archons preside are decorated with the symbols of the republic, which all citizens have been taught to venerate, and with epigrams from the sacred texts. The ceremonies conducted in them are highly ritualized, beginning with the loud incantation "Aye yea, aye yea" on the part of a functionary who has no other occupation, signifying that the ceremony is about to start, whereupon all rise as the archon ascends to his place, Elaborate rules, most of them understood only by the archon and the lower functionaries, many of them alluded to in Latin, govern every step of the ritual that follows, which then eventually results without fail in the authoritative settlement of a dispute. Any further consideration of the matters arising from it is undertaken only at the higher levels of the hierarchy, and turns entirely upon the interpretation of the literature and the manner in which the initial ceremony was conducted. Eventually, if the questions of doctrine raised are sufficiently important, the matter will be resolved by the supreme archons, from whom no appeal is possible.

As in the case of any priesthood possessed of a sacred literature, there are within this one both fundamentalists and modernists. The fundamentalists, or strict constructionists, declare their faith that The Charter is to be heeded, word for word and literally, nothing being added or subtracted through interpretation, even by themselves. The modernists or liberals, on the other hand, hold that its true meaning lies in its spirit and emanations, and that it is their special function to discern and interpret these.

The feeling of the people with respect to this priestly class is, of course, as everywhere, one of profound deference, and this constitutes the main pillar of political authority within that state. The great bureaucracy in charge of the day to day governance of the republic defers to it, for in fact nothing can be done without at least its tacit concurrence. By a stroke of a pen the archons alter public policy or overturn practices that have been unchallenged for a century, and they can do this without consultation with anyone but themselves—always, of course, in the name and spirit of The Charter.

This last imaginary society has, of course, easily recognizable counterparts in the real world. The political authority of the western democracies rests, as everywhere, upon fear and deference. In the United States that deference is directed primarily to the judiciary and to the Constitution which this class is charged with interpreting. The power of a court of appeals, not merely to review a proceeding, but to strike down a validly enacted law, or to terminate, at a stroke, practices and policies that have held for generations and which are fervently approved by the majority of citizens, is an awesome one. Yet it is, paradoxically, this power, in the hands of a totally undemocratic and quasi-religious hierarchy, that makes us a free people, and hardly at all the manner in which our official lawmakers are chosen. More strangely still, the Constitution, under which we are supposedly governed, nowhere empowers the Supreme Court or the Joint Chiefs of Staff or any other body whatsoever to review or strike down any law enacted by the representatives of the people. It is a power which the Court has been able to arrogate to itself, solely because of its quasi-religious character and the resulting deference it is able to inspire in the people.

The judiciary is in the United States for the most part not elected but appointed, and all federal judges are appointed. They are responsible to no one, and hold their positions for life. Even where ostensibly elected they are, for all practical purposes, appointed, and usually sit for life if they choose to. The Supreme Court, entirely appointed from a small list supplied by the bar, is answerable to no one at all, conducts its work in profound secrecy, and in this respect resembles a military junta as well as a high priesthood, the crucial difference being that no member of it can, for all practical purposes, ever be removed. Their individual lives are as impeccable, in terms of integrity and virtue, as they are expected to be. It is quite impossible to imagine a member of this court arrested for public drunkenness, for instance. And they are in fact guided by an inspired and semi-sacred document, vouchsafed by the Founding Fathers, whose provisions are indeed noble, particularly when interpreted in the "spirit" that is claimed by liberal justices to be found in it.

THE DESPOTIC CHARACTER OF ELECTED GOVERNMENT

These reflections give rise to this final, important observation. We tend to imagine that our liberties, and the countless other blessings we more or less take for granted, are the result of democratic government. That is our myth. We actually imagine ourselves to choose our public officials, who thereupon govern in our name, and in accordance with our will. Of course nothing could be more absurd. At the highest level of the administrative branch, only two persons are elected, and one of these is a figurehead, who waits in the wings to step in in case the other is disabled or dies. The thousands of other administrators, constituting a vast bureaucracy that promulgates most of the actual law under which we live from day to day, are not only not elected; once in office it is virtually impossible to remove any of them, due to the protections of the Civil Service.

With respect to the legislative bodies themselves, these are elected, usually, by thin majorities, sometimes hair thin ones, and, once in office, their legislative acts are validated by simple majorities again. Thus in both instances huge minorities are left with their wills and preferences not only not carried into effect, but in reality frustrated. They, at least, do not "govern themselves," nor are they governed by *their* representatives; they are governed in spite of themselves, compelled to do what they sometimes deeply detest by laws enacted by representatives of other interests—laws which, however, can still be nullified by judges.

It is doubtful whether any form of government is more hostile to freedom than an actual democracy. This becomes very evident wherever we see such democratic government attempted in the *absence* of a venerable, powerful, independent and non-elected judiciary responsible to no one, somehow able to restrain majorities within a legislative body. In many parts of the world government office is assumed to carry with it a simple right to exploit and abuse. Where tribal associations have traditionally been strong, then members of tribes who find themselves in the minority come quickly to know democratic oppression in its fullest, most brutal form. And if there happens to be a prosperous and easily identifiable minority, such as the Asians in Kenya, then it is but a matter of time before they are virtually driven from the country and their property and business expropriated—by the official threats of a legislature which correctly claims to "represent" the people, and thus express the dreadful will of the majority. We view outrages like this as corruption. We fail to see that it is simply democracy, unrestrained by anything like a powerful and independent priesthood that is responsible, not to any persons, but to a hallowed tradition that has been reduced to written and semi-sacred texts.

It is the judiciary, and certainly not elected lawmakers, that has in the United States enabled hitherto persecuted minorities to emerge into full citizenship, always in opposition to the otherwise immovable will and determination of popularly elected legislatures. It is, every time, the judiciary, usually the relatively tiny Supreme Court, which protects the freedoms, property, and well-being of individuals and minorities, such as the poor, the racially outcast, the criminals, including those that would elsewhere be deemed enemies of the state—persons who would have precious little chance if left to the tender mercies of democratic forces. It should not be surprising that this branch of government should be the least democratic of any. It is the blessing of a free people, not that they live under democratic government, but that they do not.

12

The American Judiciary as a Secular Priesthood

INTRODUCTION

The recent long and acrimonious battle over the nomination of Judge Robert Bork to the Supreme Court forced thoughtful people to confront questions that have long been kept in the background. The issues raised by this extraordinarily able jurist and his sometimes merciless interrogators went to the heart of the question of the role of the judiciary and the constitutional status of certain rights and freedoms we have come to take for granted. Some of these, such as the presumed right of privacy and a whole spectrum of freedoms associated with private morality, are nowhere mentioned in the Constitution, yet they are thought of as constitutional rights. Judge Bork, in casting doubt upon the constitutional basis of those freedoms, sent a chill into the hearts of those for whom such freedoms are deeply precious. The fact that his position appeared unasssailable on purely rational and legalistic grounds made it the more frightening. But the most valuable result of all this was finally to focus on the role of judges, to see that the function of the judiciary is not simply to interpret written enactments, but is instead, in our democracy, to defend and even, to a large extent, to *create* our liberties.

This is highly paradoxical, for the judiciary is the least democratic branch of our government. Its members often exercise power that reaches beyond that of any other institution of government, seeming sometimes to approach the very power of God, and yet, once appointed, they have no responsibility or accountability to anyone but themselves, often conduct

From *Free Inquiry* 9, no. 4 (Winter/Spring 1990).

their basic business in utter secrecy, and usually serve for life. And therein lies the paradox: That this relatively obscure institution, the judiciary, the names of whose members are unknown to most of those whose lives they so deeply affect, possessed of all the trappings of despotism, nevertheless constitutes the bulwark of those freedoms that we associate with democracy.

How come? How is this possible, in light of the almost universal assumption that democractic freedom must be grounded in the will of the people, as this is expressed by vote, representation and accountability?

The answer is that the American judiciary is a kind of priesthood, albeit a secular one. It rests its power on the elements that are found in every priesthood, and draws its inspiration from essentially similar sources.

We all know that judges wear priestly robes, are members of an authoritarian hierarchy, and conduct their functions in places that resemble temples, but few persons have ever reflected about why the judiciary looks so much like a priesthood. The resemblances are no accident. A religious priesthood and this secular one, the judiciary, draw their power from precisely the same element in human psychology, which I shall call the habit of deference. The interesting difference between the two is how that power is used—to stifle freedom, in the case of a religious priesthood, and to foster it, in the case of the secular one.

THE UNIQUE AND THE ESSENTIAL ELEMENTS OF A PRIESTHOOD

Let us consider, then, the features distinctive of a priesthood, and note how exactly they are duplicated in our judiciary. Six such features, some of them important and some less so, come readily to mind.

Priestly Hierarchies

The first is that every priesthood is divided into ascending classes with respect to both prestige and authority, with few persons or sometimes only one at the top, many at the bottom, and lesser numbers at the intermediary levels. The authoritarian character of a priesthood thus distinguishes it significantly from other formal hierarchies, such as, for example, the hierarchy of a titled nobility or of recognized chess experts throughout the world. The degrees of *prestige* are preserved in hierarchies such as these but not the degree of *authority*. There is, for example, only one world chess champion, and he stands above the more numerous masters, grand masters and so on, but he imposes nothing upon them. A pope, on the other hand, or an ayatollah, is not merely elevated above the other levels of priestly hierarchy in prestige; he has also the authority to impose on them what is to be held and taught as doctrine. He declares to the rest what the teachings are. They do not declare it to him. And once authoritatively enunciated, then the rest of the hierarchy, down to its vast foundations, falls into step. What is promulgated from above is received below, not merely as something interesting, learned, inspired, or possibly profound. It is received as something to be heeded, not because of its rational content, for it is likely to have none, but solely because of its source.

That our judiciary has also this sacerdotal character is almost too obvious to belabor. Our court structure is thoroughly hierarchical, its ascending classes differing with respect to both prestige and authority, with a very few—nine, in fact—at the top, many at the lowest levels and lesser numbers at intermediate levels. And these courts are unabashedly and correctly referred to as higher and lower. Nor do the higher members of this hierarchy merely enjoy greater honor and prestige, as do the different levels of an archaic nobility or of chess experts. It is, as with any priesthood, a hierarchy of authority as well. Thus the Supreme Court declares to all what the law is, and the rest, down to the justices of the smallest jurisdictions, fall into step. What is promulgated from above is received below, not merely as something interesting, perhaps profound, learned or even inspired. It is received as what is to be heeded, solely because of its source. And, as the vast laity of the church is expected to fall into step with the priesthood with respect to the content of the faith, the vast citizenry of the nation is expected to heed the orders of the judiciary with respect to the law of the land—though of course not all do, in either case.

Papal and Judicial Infallibility

This immediately suggests the second point of resemblance. The Pope cannot err in any declaration he makes *ex cathedra* in the realm of faith and morals, nor can the United States Supreme Court err in any declaration from the bench concerning the content and scope of the law. Neither of these is really a very far-reaching claim, and both are quite incontestably true, in spite of the antagonism they arouse in the minds of those who do not understand them.

Thus, if the Pope declares something to be a part of the faith, and perhaps cites scriptural authority for his declaration, then it simply follows that what is thus declared *is* a part of the faith. His declaration is quite sufficient to make it such, and this is not open to challenge even by those who stand outside that faith. Similarly, if the Supreme Court declares something to be a matter of law, and perhaps cites constitutional authority for that declaration, then it simply follows that what is thus declared to be a part of the law *is* a part of the law. The law as thus enunciated is not open to challenge even by those who stand outside that law, that is to say, beyond its jurisdiction. The members of this court, it has been often noted, are not made members because they are infallible, but rather, they are infallible because they are the Supreme Court, an authority beyond which there is no appeal. The corresponding description of the pope is, of course, also correct. There is no way the Supreme Court can be mistaken in case five of its members declare, from the bench, something to be law, even though what is thus enunciated may appear entirely novel and heretofore unheard of, even by other judges who stand lower in the hierarchy. The promulgation of the exclusionary rule of evidence, which has no constitutional basis whatever, is a typical case in point. Of course this court can modify its own previous declarations, as can the Papacy, but until this happens what was first enunciated holds as law, in the case of the court, or as doctrine, in the case of the church. Indeed, the court need not even cite the Constitution, or any enacted law, or any other text for its determination, though it usually does. Similarly, the pope need not cite Scripture nor any other text for his pronouncements, though he usually does. The declaration by itself, emanating from the apex of either hierarchy, is sufficient to guarantee its theological or legal correctness. To this it should perhaps be added, even though it should be obvious, that such infallibility holds, in either case, only within defined areas. Neither the pope nor the Supreme Court speaks with the least authority in matters of history, science or art, for example. They also sometimes contradict each other. The church and the court do not speak with one voice on such matters as the legitimacy of divorce, abortion, and so on. But each is powerless to overrule the other.

Sacred Texts as the Basis of Authority

The third and, strangely, least noticed point of resemblance between the two priesthoods is that each rests its authority in part upon a body of literature, the central part of which is deemed somehow sacred or inspired. This central part is, of course, the Bible in the case of the church, and the Constitution in the case of the judiciary. Each is deemed to be the official foundation of these respective institutions, the source to which either type of priesthood reverts, whenever possible, in resolving some matter of the faith or of the law. The qualification "whenever possible" is made here because both canons are in some respects incomplete and obscure, and as a priest must sometimes look beyond the mere letter of Scripture to find its "true meaning," so also must a judge look beyond the letter of the Constitution. Note further, however, that in neither case is the sacred text considered to be the whole of the inspired literature from which the faith or the law is to be drawn. Laid upon Holy Writ are layer upon layer of commentary and interpretation, most of it emanating from the priesthood itself over a long period of time and now deemed authoritative in its own right and beyond serious question. And similarly, laid upon the Constitution are layer upon layer of wise commentary and judicial interpretation, most of this, too, emanating from this secular priesthood itself over a long period of time. Even the same terminology is, suggestively, to some extent the same within both hierarchies. Thus, as the earliest authors of the texts and commentaries upon which much of the faith of the church has been built are called the "fathers," so is the same term applied to the earliest authors of the texts and commentaries upon our original Constitution—the "Church Fathers" in the one case, and the "founding fathers" in the other. Indeed, whenever one sees this word "father" used as a term of veneration and not in its literal sense, he can be fairly sure that he is confronted with some kind of priesthood.

Of course no established priesthood of long standing rests its doctrinal teaching on one primitive text, such as the Bible or the Koran, nor does the judiciary rest its legal doctrine on any one similarly primitive text, such as the Constitution. As the church appeals to the much richer source, referred to as "the tradition," which includes even the opinions of unordained theologians, so does the judiciary, the source in this case comprising the common law and a vast quantity of adjudicative law, as well as the opinions of unsworn laymen and jurisconsults, venerable for their learning and judicial temperament.

The similarity in the roles of the Bible and the Constitution within the religious and the secular priesthoods is worth stressing. Priests, for example, as well as lesser functionaries in the church, swear their belief in and fidelity to the Bible, treating it as sacred, not just for its content, but in its own right. Similarly, officers of government declare their fidelity to the Constitution and swear to uphold it, even being required by law to do so. The Bible is thus much more than an important book to a priest, and the same veneration for the Constitution is nourished in the hearts of judges. Thus no one is surprised to learn that a judge arranges to have his Constitution accompany him into his grave, as Justice Hugo Black and doubtless many others have.

Again, the church feels most secure when its teaching can be clearly rooted in Scripture. This is sometimes impossible, however, either because Scripture is silent on the matter at issue, or because absurd results would follow from certain of the more bizarre things to be found there. In this case recourse is had to the tradition. There is, for example, virtually nothing to be found in the Bible concerning the human "soul," but much to be found in the tradition, going back to St. Augustine and St. Gregory of Nyssa and the other fathers, so here venerable tradition is made to suffice. At the same time, certain arcane biblical references, important to ancient culture but of no importance any more, are more or less treated as if they were not contained in Scripture at all. The legends surrounding the Ark of the Covenant are a case in point.

We should not, then, be surprised to find the same problems presented by the quasi-sacred texts upon which the judicial system rests. The Supreme Court, as well as lower appellate courts, feel most secure when they can point to an explicit provision in the Constitution for a ruling on a point of law. The constitutional prohibition of bills of attainder, *ex post facto* laws and double jeopardy are examples. This is not always possible, however, for that text may contain nothing whatsoever bearing upon a matter of law that must somehow be adjudicated or, as sometimes also happens, what is said in the Constitution might produce an awkward result if taken at face value. Thus, for example, the Constitution is lamentably silent concerning any supposed right of privacy. So the Court discovers such a right in our traditions, although a thin and immensely implausible hint of such a right is triumphantly extracted from the basic writ. How often, on the other hand, does one find judicial decisions pointing to such things as letters of marque and reprisal, twice mentioned in the Constitution, and how many people, including even judges, even know what this means? Certain other parts of the Constitution are perfectly clear and meaningful, but are treated as though they did not exist, simply because it would be awkward to take them seriously any more. Thus this "supreme law of the land" prohibits state legislatures from impairing the obligations of contracts, yet states quite regularly do so by prohibiting foreclosures, exempting beleaguered banks from certain obligations to depositors, and so on. The Constitution prohibits any member of Congress from holding any other office under government, yet some are officers in military reserves. The explicit prohibition of involuntary servitude is not allowed by the courts as a basis for challenging conscription, and the constitutional provision that no states may enter into any agreements or compacts with each other without the consent of Congress is at times simply disregarded, as when Maine and New Hampshire, for example, enter into an agreement to settle a boundary dispute. Thus as the Bible is interpreted by priests to mean more or less what they want it to mean, so also is the Constitution similarly interpreted by judges, its gaps being filled in by their wisdom, and the more bizarre of its explicit provisions being treated as though they were not there.

Fundamentalists versus Liberals

The fourth point of resemblance between the two priesthoods is significant and important in its implications; namely, that both contain highly zealous and vocal groups dedicated to the literal interpretation of their respective sacred texts. Thus the "fundamentalists," as they call themselves, attempt to extract the entire doctrine of religion from *one* primitive and uninterpreted text, the Bible, which they declare to be complete and true in every part. Some of its stories and allegories, including those that are of a mystical character and profoundly meaningful to those who understand and appreciate them, are reduced to absurdity by the fundamentalists, who imagine them to be literal descriptions of past events. They think that they have elevated religion by such simplifications. To treat Scripture otherwise, they say, amounts to rewriting it, inserting into the revealed truth one's own fond notions of what should be there. They thus take comfort in what they call the "inerrant," that is, literal, truth of the Bible. Religious liberals, on the other hand, appeal to the spirit of these texts which, with support from Scripture itself, they say gives life, while the letter or literal interpretation kills. This liberal reading of the texts enables them, of course, to find there precisely the lofty and noble principles which they happen to favor, and which they assume must somehow be lodged there, however obscurely.

Precisely the same is found within the judiciary with respect to the mode of interpreting its own sacred text, which is the Constitution. The judicial "strict constructionist" or advocate of "original intent" corresponds exactly to the religious fundamentalist in approach, aim, and conservative temperament. He sees a danger in any kind of interpretation or mode of construing the Constitution other than a literal one. He claims that a judge who goes beyond the actual wording of this text, as it has been delivered to us by "the founding fathers," risks incorporating into it his own private notions of what the law should be.

The opposite or liberal school of jurists, on the other hand, who correspond exactly with the religious liberals of the other priesthood, fervently declare that the "true" meaning of this venerable text is to be found behind its literal meaning, in its spirit or, as the great jurist William O. Douglas sometimes expressed it, in its "emanations" and "penumbras."

The difficulties and dangers of either approach are of course precisely the same both in the church and in the judiciary. A literal reading even of the sacred Bill of Rights, for example, can lead to absurdities and to an intolerable grinding of the gears of tradition against the exigencies of modern life. On the other hand, the tempting appeal to the "spirit" of this text or to its "emanations" has the effect that as few as five mortal judges of finite wisdom can, on this insubstantial basis, foist upon the entire nation, as part of the supreme law of the land, novel ideas of which they happen to be fond, a precedure which Judge Bork aptly describes as "judicial imperialism." This has in fact happened, many times, as we shall illustrate shortly, and it represents a power as awesome as any that has ever been claimed even by the most exalted of priests.

It is worth noting in passing that, of these two tendencies—the "fundamentalist" and "strict constructionist" on the one hand versus the "liberal" on the other—it is the former which has lately been on the ascendancy, the more so since the conservative wings of both the religious and the secular priesthoods tend to ally themselves with each other to achieve their generally oppressive political goals. The appeal to the masses of this simple and narrow approach is very strong, and the political and social effects upon our culture have been both baneful and profound.

There remain two other points of comparison between the two priesthoods, perhaps less sweeping than those already considered but in some ways more suggestive of the true nature of the judiciary.

The Distinctive Appearance of Priests

The first of these is that a sacerdotal hierarchy is always characterized by distinctive garb and demeanor, and by titles suggestive of unique virtue, beginning with "reverend" or "father" and culminating, of course, in "holiness." These features become more elaborate and outrageous as one ascends the scale of the hierarchy. Thus the lowest members of the hierarchy have little to distinguish them in appearance except somber attire and the clerical collar. A pope, an ayatollah, or a dalai lama, on the other hand, *has* to look instantly and radically different, *has* to be addressed in a manner suggestive of supremacy, and even his motions, gestures, and countenance are stylized. The pope, for example, appears in striking robes, of scarlet and white or gold, and under an outlandish headgear never seen elsewhere. He cannot wave excitedly to the crowds that surround him, even though the occasion would call for precisely that response from any other public figure, nor can he be imagined clasping his hands above his head in victorious acknowledgement of the tumult that greets his appearance before the masses. His hand is instead limited to a slow kind of wobble and gentle fanning motion, only barely extended, and his head and eyes generally remain steadfastly forward, with but occasional nods, his face graced with saintly smile. It may be tempting to suppose that all this is but the more or less random and meaningless product of ancient inherited custom, but this would be a great mistake. Something of the sort here described is absolutely essential to any priesthood, but the reasons for this are reserved for later comment.

Now note that the secular priesthood, the judiciary, is similarly distinguished by a special garb and demeanor which, though less garish than, for example, that of the Roman Catholic hierarchy, is nonetheless distinctive. And like all priests, these too are addressed by titles suggestive of special virtue or honor, "honorable" being, in fact, the commonest such form of address. Judges, like clergymen, appear in robes, and they are the only public officials who do. In certain foreign jurisdictions such robes are complemented by strange wigs. In the early days of our republic one of our own Supreme Court judges, William Cushing, appeared on the bench under a wig—a practice which was not, somehow, destined to be carried on, although it is easy to imagine that it could have been. Nor should judges, especially those high in the hierarchy, be thought of merely as politicians who happen to wear robes. The dignity of their role is carried over into their demeanor, as in the case of any priest. Thus an august senator, for example, can emerge from a committee vote or a vote on the floor with his hands clasped over his head and an immense grin plastered over his face, all connoting joyous victory over the other side. But no judge can do this, even after a close decision from the bench when the circumstances would seem to be exactly similar. Supreme Court judges cannot even talk to newspaper reporters without stirring comment, and can never appeal to the masses for support for their ideas, any more than a bishop could. Supreme Court judges are even reluctant to be caught in the eye of a television camera, the Chief Justice, for the most part, absolutely forbidding such encounters. No such restraints are felt even by the most exalted of other public officials, such as the president. Nor is all this, as one might think, the mere arbitrary product of tradition. There is a reason for it all, as we shall see, and it is the same reason that operates upon the priests of the church.

Courtrooms and Temples

Finally, as our sixth point of comparison, note how similar are the settings in which both priestly and judicial functions are carried out, the highly ritualistic character of those that are public and the solemn secrecy that surrounds those that are not public. Halls of justice are set off from all other public buildings by their resemblance to temples, and one steps into a courtroom, as one would into a church, with a certain hush and quiet. Symbolism is essential to both, such that it is as hard to imagine a courtroom without an American flag near the bench as to imagine a church without the cross of Christ near the pulpit. Bits of Scripture adorn the walls and windows of churches, just as bits of text from the Constitution or from illustrious jurists of the past decorate a courtroom. A priest ascends to the pulpit to the accompaniment of fixed ritual in the same manner that a judge ascends to the bench, the latter's arrival being heralded by a ritualistic "hear ye, hear ye" of ancient origin. Everyone forthwith rises, to resume sitting only when the judge has become ensconced at the bench, his head, like that of any priest, higher than all the others so that all look up to him, this being probably the oldest expression of deference known to mankind. What then transpires is formal and ritualized in both cases, called "liturgy" in the one case and "procedure" in the other, both being arcane to the layman.

The deliberations of appellate courts, on the other hand, are conducted in the innermost chambers of these temples with the same secrecy that surrounds ecclesiastical councils, and their conclusions or "orders," sometimes of profound and far-reaching significance, are then announced to the world as a formality—always, it should be noted, as if what is then proclaimed, as doctrine in one case, or as law in the other, has in fact been there from the very start and is thus by no means the creation of the clergy or of the judiciary. The judiciary even has a wonderful term to foster precisely that fiction. It always speaks of "finding" this or that principle of justice or law, and even of "finding" *for* one of the litigants. Thus the notion is perpetuated that law, like dogma, has been right there all along, complete, needing only to be found, ferreted out and brought to view.

THE BASIS OF RELIGION AND LAW

It would not be hard to find other striking resemblances between ecclesiastical and judicial structures, but let us now go to the important question that these resemblances raise; namely, *why* are these two so much alike?

I believe the answer can be found in two traits of human nature which seem somehow necessary for any well-ordered society, and these are the need of imitation and the predilection of the masses to a kind of servility. People have a deep need to be like those around them, to embrace the same mores, to be, in this sense, a part of the same culture—in a word, to imitate. Religion encourages this, by calling upon people to copy each other in ways that have no practical significance, by uttering the same meaningless formulas, for instance, going through the same pointless motions, bowing, kneeling, singing and chanting together with no other apparent object than to be doing these things all together, and to be doing what has always been done. Hence the veneration that is cultivated for old things—for old music, ancient texts, and so on. The imitation is thereby extended, not merely to those present, but to the vaster circle of those past, inculcating a sense of tradition. There are, no doubt, many explanations for this strange orientation of the human mind, many needs that are thus fulfilled, but one practical result is perfectly obvious. People are thus knit together as one culture, thereby providing, to some extent, the conditions for peace, personal safety, and cooperation. This is surely the basic reason why all are encouraged to be like this, to imitate, even in ways that seem on the surface not to matter, and why even harmless eccentric departures are viewed with a certain distrust and hostility.

The same is also true, of course, with respect to the law. It is not enough that we have law. There must also be a profound respect for it, as being, at its foundation, quasi-sacred. And here, too, the human tendency to imitate must be nourished, using precisely the means for this that have been perfected by the church. The law bears upon all those aspects of human behavior that are absolutely essential to peace, security, and cooperation, and it is not enough that compliance should be achieved through fear. The deep need in people to be just like those around them must be cultivated and its strength enlisted, through pledges, ritualized observances, and so on.

I also referred, however, to another trait of people which goes far in explaining the correspondences I have described, and that is the almost universal tendency to servility. People have a need, not only to imitate, but to bow down to persons and things. Churches, I believe, draw most of their strength from this fact, and the judicial system takes advantage of the same deep-seated trait. In Iran the religious and judicial priesthoods are one and the same, and the servility of the people is sometimes exploited to the point of their willful self-destruction or martyrdom. Even their supreme judicial court or, as they call it, their "Council of Guardians" is composed of twelve priests. In the west the two priesthoods are kept separate, but their foundations in human nature are similar.

Thus, when people are presented with some person or thing which they recognize as venerable, usually by its striking appearance, they have a spontaneous impulse to abase themselves—to bow, salute, kneel, to do something symbolic of servility. When the pope appeared on the plains of Iowa large numbers of the awestruck throng surrounding and facing him fell to their knees—including, apparently, some who were not even a part of the faith. His striking presence was enough to elicit that effect. Nothing of this sort would have happened had he appeared in ordinary garb or, as is almost impossible to imagine, in baggy trousers and sweatshirt. Similarly, when a robed judge suddenly enters a crowded courtroom, heralded by the ceremonious and archaic "hear ye, hear ye," there is already an impulse to rise, so that the order to do so is almost superfluous. The other correspondences between the church and the judicial system that we have noted—the veneration of ancient and inspiring texts, the hierarchical structure of both, the honorific titles, and so on—all have much the same effect of bringing the masses of the people into line, inducing them to copy each other and to heed, by a natural servility, the precepts and commands of the hierarchy.

The further underlying reason for this we need not dwell upon, for it is well known. The courts, like the church, rest their authority not so much on fear as on deference. The church cannot compel its adherents to obedience. It can only elicit it in the manner described, which is often quite sufficient. Similarly, although the judiciary, which I have described as a secular priesthood, can often compel obedience to its rulings, it nevertheless must, like the church, rest in the last analysis on the awe and esteem in which it is held. The courts can convict even the highest public officials of felonies, remove them from office, and ignominiously imprison them. The President of the United States can be forced from office by the very justices he has appointed to the bench, notwithstanding his command of the entire armed forces of the nation, and this is due almost entirely to the conviction on the part of the people in the integrity, venerability, and, indeed, the semi-sacred status of that court. And, more astoundingly still, the same Supreme Court can, and often does, promulgate an entirely new and far-reaching principle that overturns the settled and established laws, customs, and practices of an entire nation, without preliminary public hearings or warning, without any need to answer to anyone but themselves and, most astoundingly, without any actual basis for doing so in the charter to which it owes its existence! How is that possible? It is just because the judiciary is, in the sense I have described, a secular priesthood which can rely on the deference of the people to its august character.

Thus the judiciary, though not a religious priesthood, has nevertheless the essential marks of a secular one and, what is more significant, it is a priesthood that *governs,* and, moreover, rules and governs from secret chambers. The highest archons of this hierarchy, the Supreme Court, alone decide what questions to address themselves to, from among the four thousand or so that are presented each year. Indeed, only four of the Court's members are needed for a positive decision at this point. No public hearings are then held, but only arguments for the various sides, and these are strictly timed and can, at the Court's pleasure, be dispensed with altogether. Then follows secret deliberation, sometimes over the course of weeks or months, and finally, the promulgation of entirely new law, valid across the entire nation and virtually immune to repeal, sometimes law that upsets the established customs and practices of an entire culture, sometimes law that abruptly makes what has been criminal conduct no longer so, or conversely, renders criminal what has heretofore been innocent, or sometimes forces upon lower jurisdictions policies radically at odds with those that have the support of the people and with what has been long established there—and all this without warning. Just as, in the most rigid of despotisms, the people sometimes learn with surprise from their newspapers what has without warning come to be law overnight, so also do we.

Here one is tempted to ask: How is this possible? And the answer is that our judiciary is a secular priesthood.

My mode of description thus far might be taken to suggest that I find all this deplorable, that any kind of priesthood enjoying the protection of government should have no place in a free society. In fact, however, the very opposite is true. Personal freedom, in a heterogeneous society such as ours, is possible *only* under a certain kind of authoritarian rule, of precisely the kind I have described. What makes us a free people is emphatically *not* the manner in which the offices of government are filled, through popular vote, as is so widely supposed, but rather, the sacred texts from which our judiciary draws its inspiration, and the final, ultimate, and exclusive power of that secular priesthood to interpret those texts. Viewed this way, it turns out that the idea of a free and democratic society is quite incoherent. We enjoy the blessings of personal freedom, not because we live in a democracy, but precisely because in a most significant sense we do not. Our Supreme Court is in some ways like a governing junta, responsible to no one, tenured for life, and exercising vast powers over the lives of all. It differs from a junta in that its power, like that of the church, rests upon deference and esteem rather than fear, and the sacred text which guides its rulings and enlightens its deliberations, embodying the noblest ideals of freedom, really *is* an inspiring document. The Court does not *have* to heed the ideals embodied in that sacred text, and sometimes does not, but there, nevertheless, it is, thrust upon this secular priesthood as its official foundation and guide. The Supreme Court thus, in addition to resembling a junta, also resembles Plato's council of philosopher kings, except that while they were guided only by their own metaphysical vision of goodness, our archons are, again, guided by an actual text, in places obscure and in need of interpretation but, on any interpretation, an inspiring one.

SOME RECENT JUDICIAL HISTORY

The proof of this theory of the nature of our judiciary is easily found in many of its more far-reaching decisions. Here we will cite only three of the more recent ones, together with one entire specific area of litigation wherein personal freedoms have been won, bit by bit.

The first such landmark decision is that of *Brown* v. *Board of Education,* 1954, which conferred hitherto non-existent educational opportunities on blacks throughout the public school system of the nation and which certainly laid the foundation for the immense strides in civil rights which were to follow.

On a fine summer morning that year the nation awakened to learn with astonishment that a brand new law had suddenly come into being, one that would create vast dislocations and readjustments in the lives of millions, and one which had not only not existed until that moment, but in fact contradicted and overturned what had been settled law for generations. It was a law which, in its final implementation, was going to confer a precious new personal freedom upon millions of people, living and yet to come. And this new law, made valid by nothing more than the concurrence of nine unelected archons, resulted from no popular clamor but was, on the contrary, resented and resisted by vast segments of the population. What is even more to the point, however, is that the new freedom created by this law would not in a thousand years have emerged from the popularly elected legislatures in those jurisdictions most immediately affected, consisting of the former confederacy of states. The entire judiciary, which had until then enforced laws and principles contradictory to this one, fell fairly quickly into line, and democratic institutions throughout the land, most notably the popularly elected legislatures and school boards of the south, had a new ideal thrust upon them, one that had been plucked, certainly not from the letter of the Constitution, but from its spirit. And no outcry of public opinion would be strong enough to reverse or seriously weaken this new law, for it had emerged from the most venerated institution of government, the surpeme level of the judiciary.

The second case in point is the *Roe* v. *Wade* decision of nearly twenty years later, conferring upon women the right to terminate unwanted pregnancies without any other consideration beyond their own choice in the matter, a decision which emerged from a deeply divided court. Here, again, a new law came suddenly into being, leaving the nation briefly dazed with astonishment, and it was a law rendering what had hitherto been criminal, in almost every corner of the land, suddenly innocent and, indeed, the expression of a hitherto unknown basic constitutional right. In this case we see with special clarity how it is the spirit rather than the letter of the Constitution that sometimes inspires the secular priesthood, for one searches in vain through that document for anything that can, without extreme contrivance, be seen as a right to abort pregnancy. And again we ask how long it would have taken democratically elected legislatures to have created such a right. New York, Colorado, and the District of Columbia had already done so, to be sure, but of the remaining forty-eight states it is hard to imagine even half of them following suit within any finite time. So emotionally laden is the issue, and so bitterly opposed by the religious counterpart to the secular priesthood, that even legislators who favor the right are often unwilling to express themselves upon it except in the most banal terms and with an air of apology. What it took, for this revolutionary new freedom to come into being, was a powerful secular priesthood, totally undemocratic in its procedures, responsible to no one and guided only by its own wisdom and what it took to be the spirit of its sacred texts. And the overwhelming result of that decision is that today nearly one-third of all pregnancies are in fact aborted with no legal consquences.

Our third exhibit is the *Baker* v. *Carr* decision of 1962, supplemented by the *Reynolds* v. *Sims* ruling two years later, requiring both branches of all bicameral state legislatures to be chosen by equally weighted votes of the people rather than by geographically drawn districts. This is, in its long-term political consequences, one of the most far-reaching laws ever to emerge from the Supreme Court, even though most of the people do not even know what that ruling is and thus have no idea of how it is going to affect their lives and the lives of the generations to come. What is remarkable about this Court-created law is that, while the U.S.

House of Representatives is thus chosen, the U.S. Senate of course is not. Hence an arrangement deemed suitable for the federal legislature, and even *mandated* by the specific provisions of the Constitution, was deemed by the Court unconstitutional as applied to the states. The basis for that decision was thus, obviously, not the Constitution, and certainly not any enacted law at all, but considerations of fairness and right, pure and simple. Under the system prevailing until then, which had never been seriously questioned by anyone, urban voters in many jurisdictions were in effect disenfranchised and values associated with rural life were given priority, a result considered desirable by many in preserving the values loosely associated with "middle America." But now let us ask what possibility there would have been in bringing about this revolutionary change through democratic process. We see at once that it would have been a virtual logical impossibility. It would have amounted to petitioning legislators to abandon and destroy the very foundations upon which they themselves held office, to surrender the power they securely and quite legally held. What was needed then was, once more, a powerful secular priesthood responsible to no one and not bound even to the letter of its own charter, to create a new and revolutionary law at a single stroke, guided only by its own wisdom and what it took to be the spirit of its sacred text.

Finally, as the fourth exhibit, consider the reform of the criminal justice system wrought by a long series of decisions beginning in the nineteen thirties and culminating in the *Miranda* and the *Gideon* v. *Wainwright* decisions of the sixties. It was the Supreme Court, *and that minute council alone,* that imposed on all state and lesser jurisdictions the requirements that no persons may be exposed to double jeopardy, that judges may not make prejudicial remarks to juries based on the refusal of a defendant to be a witness at his own trial, that defendants in felony cases are entitled to attorneys paid for, if necessary, from public funds, that police officers must remind persons of certain rights before asking them any questions, and so on. What is particularly remarkable about this gradual but extensive revolution, wherein certain rights were created that are found no place else on the globe, is that rather few of them are mandated by the Constitution. There is, for example, no hint of an exclusionary rule in that document, even for federal courts, and many judges of lower jurisdictions had in fact never heard of it when suddenly they found it imposed upon them. And once again we should ask what chance any of these rights would ever have had, were it not for this secular priesthood. The entire criminal class is by its nature excluded from the political process. There never has been, and never will be, an organization or lobbying force dedicated to representing the rights of thieves, rapists, and muggers, nor would any legislator heed such an organization if it did come into being. For such rights to exist, then, they have to be secured and, in the present case, for the most part created, by a priesthood responsible to no one, tenured for life, and guided by nothing more than its own wisdom, enlightened by the sacred texts and traditions of the republic.

It is, then, our blessing, as free people, not that we live in a democracy, but rather, that we do not, for it is a powerful and utterly undemocratic judiciary—a secular priesthood, as I have claimed—that is the ultimate guardian of our freedoms. Representative democracy, in which a sometimes tyrannical majority always prevails, is by its very nature despotic with respect to those freedoms cherished by the minority. One can well imagine, for example, how little separation there would be between church and state if this were left to the majorities elected to state legislatures, particularly within those jurisdictions where religious fundamentalism prevails. Freedom requires powerful judges, beholden to no one and at the highest echelons responsible to no one, who can speak with finality and impose heavy and sometimes unbearable sanctions on anyone who opposes their rulings. The judiciary is, paradoxically, a despotic bulwark of liberty, and, even more paradoxically, it owes this role to its being a kind of priesthood, albeit a secular one.

13

Is Man a Creation in God's Image?

The Judeo-Christian tradition, which is generally thought to rest upon a common conception of God, rests even more, I believe, on a common conception of man, and man's relationship to God. That conception is perfectly expressed in the first and ninth chapters of the first book of the Bible. In the first of these we are told that God said "Let us make man in our image, after our likeness; and let them have dominion over the fish of the sea, and over the birds of the air, and over the cattle, and over all the earth, and over every creeping thing that creeps upon the earth." Further, God is supposed to have bade men to "fill the earth and subdue it, and have dominion over the fish of the sea and over the birds of the air and over every living thing that moves upon the earth."

The second reference, that is, the ninth chapter of the same first book, seems to go even farther in defining man's relationship to the rest of living creation, for there God is represented as saying to Noah and his sons, and by implication to mankind, that "the fear of you and the dread of you shall be upon every beast of the earth, and upon every bird of the air, upon everything that creeps on the ground and all the fish of the sea; into your hand they are delivered." .

These famous passages are almost never singled out for attack. On the contrary, they are so generally admired and universally assented to that it seems only necessary to quote them to obtain immediate acceptance. Discussion sometimes revolves around their *meaning,* and in particular upon the metaphor of an *image* that is crucial to them, but it is almost never doubted that they express an idea that is obviously worthy, noble, and even inspiring. Religious apologists sometimes feel called upon to defend belief in God, in the goodness of His creation, and other things that sometimes kindle doubt, but they never, so far as I am aware, have felt any need to convince anyone of the uniqueness of man that is implied in these passages. The idea needs only to be enunciated, in the biblical metaphor of a divine image, to win approval. The faithless may doubt the reality of God, but even they, if they have been acculturated by the Judeo-Christian tradition, almost invariably uphold the idea of the unique worth of human nature that the Bible here declares.

I do, however, not only question that idea of unique worth, I want to repudiate it. The emphasis of these biblical passages is entirely wrong, and the idea they plant in our minds is surely a false one. Far from being noble and inspiring, these passages are, I believe, utterly pernicious and corrupting, turning our minds away from any proper conception either of God or of creation. What they inspire is no religious devotion, but rather conceit, and the moral repercussions are constantly arising to bedevil not only human relationships, but our feelings and relationships towards the rest of creation.

What I shall suggest in what follows is that it is not man, but rather creation itself, which is quite clearly and literally the image of God. The idea is not new, of course. Greek philosophy tended to represent the world in this fashion, and of course in Spinoza's philosophy the claim is quite explicit, though not expressed in the biblical metaphor. Modern philosophy, however, and especially Christian philosophy, generally takes for granted, uncritically, the view of man and his relation to creation implied in the biblical passages cited.

What I shall now do is, *first,* elicit the fundamental meaning of the *imago Dei* metaphor; then *second,* show that it is not actually the conception of man that is expressed in the Bible taken as a whole, particularly the Old Testament, but is instead an invention of theology, much influenced by pagan thought and religion; then *third,* briefly sketch that pagan tradition, which culminated in Platonism; *fourth,* indicate how that tradition was absorbed by the church; and finally, *fifth,* present an alternative way of interpreting the *imago Dei* metaphor, somewhat after the fashion of Spinoza's philosophy.

These five undertakings will divide my discussion into five distinct parts.

PART I

The Concept of an Image

It is not likely that the author of Genesis supposed man to have been created in the *visible* image of God, in view of the inherent absurdity of that idea, even though in the same book the same word is used to describe Seth's resemblance to Adam, his father. But whatever may be meant by this metaphor, its minimal meaning has always been generally supposed to be (a) that human nature shares some special attribute with the divine nature; (b) that this relationship to God is unique, in that no other thing in creation possesses it, and (c) that the nobility or unique worth thus bestowed upon man gives him a proper *domination* over all other living things. All other creatures are bereft of it, and are thus made worthless except in terms of the value they may have to men. This is, in fact, not merely implied but declared: "Into your hand they are delivered," and "I give you everything." The immediate ethical implication is, indeed, more or less taken for granted by most moralists.

PART II

The Biblical Conception of Man

Apart from the book of Genesis little is said in the Bible about the divine quality in man that is supposed to render him unique within creation, but of course the religious tradition has abundantly filled in this gap. Man, it is said, is uniquely possessed of a divine *soul,* which is the special creation of God. Here, then, is what distinguishes us from the brutes, and confers upon us the uniqueness and nobility implied in Genesis. The matter of our bodies we obviously share with other living things. Hence our special relationship to our creator cannot lie on that side of our natures. But there is this other, non-material side, in terms of which human nature can, indeed, be understood as an image of the divine nature.

What needs to be noted, however, is that this conception of man is not at all contained in the Old Testament. There are, to be sure, many references there to the soul of man, but nowhere does this have the meaning required by the interpretation we are considering.

As Thomas Hobbes pointed out,[1] the word "soul," in Scripture, means simply "life" or a "living creature," and there is nothing, at least in the Old Testament, to suggest that it is anything distinctively human. To "have a soul" is simply to be *alive,* and when, in the Old Testament, the expression does not carry this meaning, then it is merely used rhetorically, as referring simply to *oneself,* or to a person generally.

Hence, while it is indeed the Bible, and the very first book of the Bible, which declares man to have been created in the divine image, it is *not* the Bible which supports the commonest and indeed now universal interpretation of that metaphor. In fact, the metaphor is never explained, and it is perfectly plausible to suppose that it was merely poetic in the first place, or perhaps a simple recognition of man's natural dominion over other living things.

There are, I believe, four hundred and thirty-six references to the soul in the Old Testament, the Hebrew term thus translated being "*nephesh.*" But "*nephesh,*" while it has more than one meaning there, never has the meaning that would be required by this interpretation of the divine image. In other words, the "*nephesh*" of the Bible is *not* a spiritual part of man, unique to human nature and distinct from the body. It is not a thing at all, except in some extended sense. It is simply *life,* or the life of a living thing, and hence no unique possession of man at all. Thus, when in the book of Proverbs (12:10) we are told that "A just man takes care of his beast," the original reads, "the *nephesh* of his beast"—meaning simply, that such a man guards the *life* of his beast or, quite simply, takes care of his livestock. And this is not an aberrant use of the term. It is quite typical.

There are four apparent exceptions to this, that is, four passages in which one might be tempted to think that reference is being made to the human soul, in its more modern sense, but these are merely apparent. Thus it is said that "it came to pass, as her soul was in departing" (Gen. 35:18), and one might take this to imply a distinct soul, capable of separation from the body, but the actual meaning seems to be, simply, that "it came to pass, when she died." Again, where we read "Let this child's soul come into him again" (1 Kings 17:21), we might again imagine a distinct soul, but the passage apparently means only that the child was revived. Or once again, we find the passage "When God taketh away his soul" (Job 27:8), but this only means "taketh away his life." And finally, the expression to "To bring back his soul from the pit" (Job 33:20) evidently means simply, "to bring *him* back."

In many passages the completely non-theological sense of "*nephesh*" is perfectly apparent. Sometimes it refers simply to the *breath* of a person or animal, breath having for the ancients a close association with life. Thus what is translated as "waters threaten my life" (Ps. 68) has the literal meaning "waters come up to *nephesh,*" or in other words, threaten suffocation. Similarly for the passage "His breath sets coals afire" (Job 41:13). The word for "breath" there is, of course, "*nephesh.*" Or "God breathed into his nostrils the breath of life" (Gen. 2:7), wherein the association of *nephesh* with both breath *and* life is made quite explicit. Often in the Old Testament, where such expressions as "says my soul" occur, they are but rhetorical references to the first person, meaning simply "say I."

If we turn to the New Testament we are led to the same conclusion, though of course the New Testament is far more difficult to interpret. Here the word in question is "*Psyche,*" usually translated "soul," but in fact usually meaning simply "life," corresponding to the Hebrew "*nephesh.*" Thus where it is said that "The Son of man has come to give his life as a ransom for many" (Matt. 20:28), the word for "life" is "*psyche,*" and the passage would make theological nonsense if this were translated as "soul." Of the fifty-seven references to "*psyche*" in the New Testament, only one appears to *contrast* it with the body, namely,

"Do not be afraid of those who kill the body but cannot kill the soul (psyche), but rather be afraid of him who is able to destroy both . . . in hell" (Matt. 10:28), but even this does not necessarily imply the conception of a soul capable of existing in separation from the body. The only two references which *do* imply this also imply that the soul is a visible thing, having human form (Rev. 6:9, 20:4).

However, then, one may wish to interpret the metaphor of the image of God, there is rather little scriptural basis for the view that man uniquely possesses a separable, spiritual soul, or that any such soul elevates him above the rest of material creation. It is possible that man is possessed of some unique worth, deriving from his special relationship to God, as has been the teaching of the church, but if so, then there is little basis in Scripture for supposing that such worth attaches to a divine soul.

PART III

The Philosophical Tradition

Western philosophy has for the most part assumed an *obvious* distinction between the soul or mind and the body of a man. This assumption reached its clearest expression in Descartes, who identified the human soul with the mind, and explicitly denied that it was possessed by any other living thing. This seems to philosophers no longer obvious, but many, perhaps even most, still find it difficult to reject every distinction between the mind and the body, although very little is ever said about the minds or souls of animals. Thus has human uniqueness and supremacy, a supremacy that makes human worth quite incommensurable with that of any other thing, been kept alive in philosophy.

This tradition evidently began with the Orphics, or perhaps the Cult of Dionysius which preceded them. The Orphics, whose influence upon Western thought, through Socrates and Plato, is seldom much appreciated, affirmed a dual nature of man, much as the Christian churches do today. They taught that the soul has a divine origin and destiny, is but a sojourner on earth, and really does not belong in the world of matter at all. It can be released from matter, that is, from the body, through moral purity and various ritualistic observances. The body, on the other hand, together with all matter, was represented as base, a veritable prison of the soul—a simile made much use of by Plato. The soul, because of its divine nature, is what is important to any man, and as both Socrates and Plato affirmed, the chief consideration of any wise man must be the "tendance" of his soul, and the constant concern for its purity. The body, on the other hand, being base, defiles the soul by association, and is the source, through its appetites and desires, of the soul's corruption. Some of the words we use today are echoes of this ancient Orphic (and Platonic) view of man—such as "ecstasy," which means literally a stepping out of the body (*extasis*), or "enthusiasm,"which originally meant having a God within (*enthusiasmos*), etc. And the Titans, according to ancient mythology, were sons of the earth who, by devouring the infant Dionysius, came to have mingled in their earthly natures the divine element—a tradition that enabled Plato to refer to the human body as the "old Titanic nature" (*Laws* 3.701c).

This way of viewing the body and soul is still familiar to the Christian tradition, but not, interestingly, to the Jewish tradition. Thus Christians are still taught that the body is something base, the word "carnal" carrying both connotations at once, and bodily desire, particularly sexual appetite, is always thought of as tainted with evil, in spite of occasional official protestations to the contrary. This attitude is not the expression of the Old Testament. There the emphasis is more on what is unlawful, rather than upon what is sinful. Sin has traditionally been thought of by Christians as a veritable *quality* and sometimes, almost, as a substance, after the Manichean conception of evil.

Thus is man elevated, not merely above animal creation, as in the passages from Genesis with which we began, but above matter itself, including, of course, the matter of his own body. But the source of this is less biblical than philosophical, that is to say, pagan. Socrates took over the Orphic conception of human nature and made it the cornerstone of his entire philosophy. And Plato, of course, appropriated the Socratic (Orphic) conception, modifying it in the light of the Pythagorean conceptions derived from his acquaintance with the Pythagorean monasteries of Sicily. In particular, Plato added to the idea of *moral purity,* as the way to salvation, which was the invention of the Orphics, and *wisdom,* which was Socrates' addition, the idea of *rational knowledge,* or *theory* (*theorein*), which he took from the Pythagoreans. The Christian church, inheriting this great tradition through Neo-Platonism, that is to say, through St. Augustine and others, did not at all repudiate it, but instead added one more basis for salvation; to wit, *faith.*

I have sketched this interesting and overwhelmingly important development in our religious and philosophical tradition in order to make two points. The first is that the kind of uniqueness we ascribe to human nature is not really of biblical origin, in spite of its being clearly implied in the metaphor of the divine image, with which the Bible begins. It is of pagan origin, its roots being very clearly in the conception of human nature that characterized Orphism. It is not merely that this conception is very old, but rather, that its growth, from that source, is so easily traceable through Socrates, Plato, Neo-Platonism, and the early Church Fathers.

And the second point is to suggest that this assumption of uniqueness, and with it of specal worth, is quite groundless. The Bible, at least the Old Testament, hardly supports it, and its philosophical foundation is so weak as to make it hardly more than an arbitrary fiction. What seemed true in Socrates' moral and metaphysical vision still seems true, or at least plausible, to people today, even to sophisticated philosophers, but that is not because it was ever shown to be correct. It is, rather, because we have inherited that notion from a very long tradition, so that it has become part of our intellectual heritage, fortified by a strong religious tradition. It is as familiar as the air we breathe and, for that reason alone, it seems as real.

The pagan tradition to which I have alluded culminated, in antiquity, in the Platonism which became so pervasive in the thinking of many of the Church Fathers, most notably St. Augustine. Plato's conception of the soul is fully articulated in his *Phaedo,* wherein the basic Orphic tradition familiar to his contemporaries is given a rather formidable intellectual foundation. What is novel about this dialogue is therefore not the doctrine of the human soul which is found in it—for that was very old and familiar even to Plato's predecessors—but rather, the written intellectual defense of that doctrine.

Let us remind ourselves of what that doctrine was.

Plato maintained, it will be recalled, that (i) the human soul is a distinct but incorporeal substance, capable of existing entirely independently of the body; (ii) that it has so existed, and after the death of the body will exist independently again; (iii) that the soul is a person's true self, his body being a mere appendage or, more aptly, a container or prison of the soul; (iv) that the soul has a divine origin and destiny, and is therefore elevated far above the body in terms of dignity and worth; (v) that the body is accordingly something base and ignoble, a thing of clay that the wise man will gladly be rid of; (vi) that, even more strongly, the body is something worse than worthless, being the source, through its appetites and desires, of the corruption of the soul; and finally (vii) that the soul of a man, provided it can shake off the fetters of the body and all its temptations, is immortal.

When we read the *Phaedo* today we are likely to find Plato's dialectic obscure, but the doctrine of the soul which it is utilized to defend is nevertheless quite plausible, or at least intelligible. We are apt to forget that we have heard it all before, as Christian doctrine.

PART IV

The Absorption of Pagan Thought by the Church

The early church had the model of Roman law together, of course, with the Jewish legal traditions in terms of which it could formulate what then emerged as Christian ethics, but it had little upon which to construct a view of nature and of man's place within nature, other than the great metaphysical constructions of Greek philosophy, particularly Platonism. The early Church Fathers, or at least those of them who had been heavily influenced by neo-Platonism, accordingly took over the Platonic theory of the soul sketched above and forthwith presented it as Christian teaching, in spite of the almost total absence of anything like it in the scriptural tradition.

Origen, for example, identified the soul of man with the mind, thus being perhaps the first to transmit this Hellenistic concept to the newly emerging Christian church. St. Gregory of Nyssa reinforced this idea, and was apparently the first of the Church Fathers to offer a formal definition of the soul, as "a produced, living, rational substance, which imparts of itself to an organic body capable of sensation the power of life and sensation." The very terminology of St. Gregory's definition is in the philosophical vocabulary of the Greeks, and quite foreign to the scriptural tradition. St. Augustine, although he did not, so far as I know, offer any formal definition of the soul, conceived of it in the same manner as St. Gregory, or in other words, in the manner of the Platonists and neo-Platonists who had given the initial direction to his philosophical and theological reflections.[2]

The importance of this idea outside the church, in the purely philosophical tradition, is familiar to all educated persons. It culminated in the metaphysics of Descartes who, first trained by the clergy, went back to St. Augustine, not only for his theory of the soul, but for his arguments as well, his famous "cogito" argument, for which he claimed great originality, being taken directly from the great Church Father. It is not an exaggeration to say that the dual nature of man, conceived as some sort of amalgam of both body and soul (or mind), has been almost a presupposition of the whole of modern philosophy. Even today philosophers are capable of deep perplexity concerning the relationship between the "physical" and what they like to call the "mental." They simply assume that such a distinction is meaningful, never pausing to consider that it seems so only because of a long pervasive religious tradition, which was itself the product of an even older philosophical tradition. If a person merely *hears* certain words often enough, especially during his formative years, then he is likely to assume, forever after, that those words are meaningful, however difficult it might be to define them in clear terms.

And what has this tradition to do with the concept of man, as the image of God, with which we began? The answer to this should by now be quite clear. Invited, almost in the very first words of the Bible, to think of man as having a unique relationship to God, philosophers have preserved this claim of uniqueness by imagining that man alone is possessed of a rational soul. Thus, even without reference to God, the philosophical tradition has fueled human conceit and justified the human race in its arrogance no less effectively than the book of Genesis.

Most philosophers, in fact, simply take for granted that man possesses a special worth or dignity, not found elsewhere in nature, and from these ideas they have derived sweeping systems of morality which, whatever may be their differences, are agreed in reserving to man a special place, and consigning all other living things beyond the pale of ethics. Thus, when philosophers speak of justice, of rights and wrongs, of duties, and so on, one can be almost certain that they are applying these ideas only to human relationships. The ethics of Christendom is a human ethic, and interest in the rest of creation is invariably a concern for these things, only in relation to us. Thus, when people express concern for "the environment," they are thinking of an environment that will be salubrious *for man,* so that concern for things other than human turn out, after all, to be just human concerns all over again. Philosophers have accordingly not questioned the pronouncement of Genesis, that man is created in the image of God, and is accordingly given "dominion" over everything that flies or creeps or swims. They have, instead, given it intellectual content, by inventing the idea of a rational soul and, with that, human uniqueness and special worth or dignity. So fixed have these ideas become in our minds that there are philosophers who deem it only necessary to enunciate them in order for them to be accepted, and the tragedy of the matter is, that in this way, they are almost always right.

PART V

The World and the Image of God

The Bible opens with the declaration that in the beginning, God created heaven and earth, and I want to urge the idea that this very heaven and earth are quite literally the image of God. The world, on this view, becomes, not one and the same as God, which seems to me in every way an absurdity, but rather, God, as God appears to us. The visible world, the world that we know and make our homes in, the world that includes mankind but holds no unique place for him, is thus, on this view, a theophany in the strictest sense. It is related to its creator as a rainbow is related to the diffusion of water that underlies it, namely, as the visible appearance of its invisible foundation.

There is, of course, no proof of this, other than to say that everything we know seems to point to it, and declarations to the contrary, such as the one we have been concerned with—to wit, that *man* is uniquely created in the image of God—seem arbitrary and primitive when we reflect on them.

Thus our race does quite obviously belong to the rest of creation as part of a continuum. What we find in ourselves we find, in greater or lesser degree, elsewhere. And whatever may be the teachings of theologians, and of philosophers, to the contrary, we still feel our kinship with other living things. We suffer and rejoice as they do, and we suffer and rejoice with them. We are begotten as they are, and perish as they do. The very life, and will to live, that pulsates in us, we share with them. All such observations, which could be drawn out to great length, are surely quite obvious, and in their light we can see the arbitrariness of all the familiar claims of unique worth and dignity attaching to human personality. That the distinctions of good and evil apply to man is obvious enough, but the slightest reflection, or even simple observation, makes obvious that this distinction applies in exactly the same way to everything that lives.

Thus when we find Cardinal Newman proclaiming that "we have no duties towards the brute creation," that "there is no relation of justice between us," we can surely see a total myopic view of nature at work. And when the same Christian writer continues that the rest of living creation "can claim nothing at our hands," that "into our hands they are absolutely delivered," such that "we may use them" and "we may destroy them at our pleasure," we see the fruit of the most pernicious interpretation of the metaphor of the *imago Dei.*[3] Father Joseph Rickaby, viewing the world from the same narrow and all too human viewpoint, says exactly the same thing. "In all that conduces to the sustenance of man," he writes, "we may give pain to animals, and we are not bound to any anxious care to make this pain as little as may be." "Brutes," he continues, "are as *things* in our regard: So far as they are useful to us, they exist for us."[4] It would be difficult to imagine the traditional doctrine of man, as the image of God, carried forth with such vengeance to what would seem to be its logical conclusion, and difficult, too, to conceive a doctrine more odious.

But while this authropocentrism seems characteristic of those cultures that have incorporated the Judeo-Christian tradition, it is by no means unique to theologians. Philosophers, too, including those who profess to have freed themselves from theological influence, say much the same thing. The professed basis for their opinion is not biblical, but rather philosophical, which means, in this case, Hellenistic. Thus they say that man is alone *rational,* and that this somehow confers on him precisely that special worth that Christian thinkers have found implied in the metaphor of the *imago Dei.* Indeed, it is here that philosophers and theologians have, with dreadful effect, joined forces, for the Church Fathers, interpreting the metaphor of the *imago Dei* in the light of the Hellenism that so conditioned their thought, declared, in chorus with Socrates, Plato, and Aristotle, that it is precisely the power of rational thought that man shares with God! Thus, however removed we may imagine Kant to have been from St. Augustine, in terms of time, thought, and culture, their conceptions of man are essentially the same. It is rational nature, Kant says, that is to be treated as an end in itself and possessed of that unique worth which he called "transcendent." And in alluding to "rational nature" Kant intended to include not only man, but God, excluding everything else. Indeed, the whole of Kantian ethics can be treated as the logical unfolding of the ethical implications of the metaphor of the *imago Dei.* He all but says so. That this ethic should so closely correspond to St. Augustine's should not be taken to illustrate how truth can be approached from diverse and distant points, but rather, how a single idea, metaphysically pernicious as it is, can gain a foothold and win virtually universal assent, merely by its capacity to reinforce human arrogance and conceit.

CONCLUSION

What I have presented here is not so much a philosophical theory as a way of looking at creation, God, life, and, by implication, morality and life's meaning. It is a way of viewing these that is, I believe, inherently plausible and reasonable, the only barrier to it being a very old but arbitrary tradition, together with our human capacity for arrogance. It is, however, once clearly grasped, vast in its implications and, I believe, overwhelmingly good and liberating with respect to ethics and life's meaning.

NOTES

1. *Leviathan,* XLII.
2. Some of the information here concerning the biblical references to the soul is derived from an article by W. E. Lynch, *New Catholic Encyclopedia,* vol. 13, pp. 449–450 (New York: McGraw Hill Book Co., 1967).
3. St. Gregory's definition is quoted by I. C. Brady, *New Catholic Encyclopedia, op. cit.,* pp. 449–450.
4. Cardinal Newman's statement is given in *New Catholic Encyclopedia, op. cit.,* vol. 4, p. 498. Fr. Rickaby's statement is from his *Moral Philosophy,* "Ethics and Natural Law" (1910).

14

Religion and the Debasement of Goodness

Most humanists who share my aversion to the Christian religion are atheists, but they nevertheless praise the ethical ideals they associate with Christianity, particularly those that attach great value to being human. Christians declare every human being to be precious, to have been created in the very image of God, the lowest among us thus being every bit as good as the greatest and noblest. And humanists, while avoiding the theological language of this declaration, nevertheless affirm the same thing. Indeed, it is common for humanists to criticize Christians, not for their ethical ideals, but for their failure to live up to them. We humanists, they say in effect, carry the ideals of Christianity into our practice better than Christians themselves. There is sometimes much truth in this, but the point I am making is that those ethical ideals themselves are not subjected to doubt or serious criticism. It is, rather, the theological claims that are scorned and, most emphatically, belief in any god.

Let it be clear at the outset, then, that my position is rather opposite to that of humanists on both points. I do, most emphatically, believe in God, and I just as emphatically reject the ethics of Christianity, which appears to me to be the corruption and debasement of what is truly noble. By God I mean the creator of heaven and earth, and of all things visible and invisible, and God's reality is to me as obvious as my own. This is the language of the creeds, and on this point I have no quarrel with Christians. I consider the details of Christian theology, particularly those concerning the nature and role of its founder, to be laughably

---

From *Biblical v. Secular Ethics: The Conflict*, ed. R. Joseph Hoffmann and Gerald A. Larue (Buffalo, N.Y.: Prometheus Books, 1988), pp. 163–173.

absurd, to be sure, but it is not part of my purpose to go into that. I want, instead, to cast doubt on the ethical ideas embodied in Christianity. Though these ideas are almost universally praised in our democratic culture, and even sometimes thought of as its very foundation, I believe that they are not merely wretched and stupid, but are the perversion of what a genuinely noble ethical ideal should be.

Let me, then, begin by introducing a principle that seems so general that I shall call it a law and give it a name. I shall call it the *law of epigony.* The term derives from Greek mythology, the Epigones having been a group of rulers who, in trying to carry out the greatest principles of their predecessors, managed to debase and corrupt them. An epigone is thus an inferior imitator, an heir to something noble who, in his defense of it, corrupts it. And what I have in mind by what I call the *law* of epigony is this: That *everything* that is originally truly noble and good comes to be corrupted by the very human beings whose mission is to protect and preserve it, and, that this corruption takes the form of substituting, for what is noble and good, something worthless, which is then extolled in its place.

What the principle asserts, then, and what it is important to note, is that things noble and good tend to be weakened and debased, not by those who attack them, but rather, by their very defenders. The great destroyer is not he who is bent on destroying. It is the human touch itself that corrupts.

That is the first idea that my law is intended to express. And the second part of my law expresses the manner of such corruption, namely, the substitution of some worthless thing, and the veneration of it.

I believe that religions all over the world exemplify this law as soon as they become settled and accepted and anything resembling a priesthood arises within them. But before leaping to that point it will be useful to illustrate my law with commonplace examples. Many things would serve for this, but I shall illustrate the law first with the concepts of patriotism and marriage. Then I shall consider religion and, finally, the effect of popular religion upon ethics.

Epigony and the Debasement of Patriotism

Patriotism, as we all know, means the love for one's country. This is quite a simple idea, easily grasped. And since the love for anything good is itself something good it is easy to see why it is considered an imperative to nourish such patriotism, especially in the hearts of the young—always provided, of course, that one's country, its institutions and ideals are truly noble. That is the original meaning of patriotism. But what does it come to mean in fact? It comes to mean the love, not for one's country, but for the symbols of one's country, symbols that are in themselves worthless and even, sometimes, pernicious. Thus our image of the patriot is of someone who venerates a *flag,* which is in itself nothing but a garish piece of cloth and the paradigm of a mere symbol. The patriot's treatment of this symbolic object becomes ritualized to the extreme. Rules govern the times and manner in which it is displayed, how it is to be treated when not in use, even the manner of folding it up and, eventually, disposing of it when it has become tattered. He is incensed if the flag is flown upside down, used as a mop, or otherwise defiled. It is as though it were *itself* the object of the patriot's love—which, indeed, it has become.

Other mere symbols of the love of country come to fill the same surrogate role, such as, for example, certain recitals, anthems and pledges, certain dates, particularly those marking the anniversaries of great military victories, certain garb, especially that associated with soldiering, and certain monuments, such as those erected to illustrious military figures, or the colossal Liberty statue that stands in the New York harbor, and so on. And what needs to be emphasized is that the thing all such symbols stand for recedes to invisibility, the symbols themselves taking its place as objects of veneration. Thus things which are indeed totally worthless, except as symbolizing some truly noble thing, come to be invested with an imagined worth of their own. This might be harmless enough, except for the fact that what *is* truly noble and good, the great thing or idea originally symbolized, is lost sight of altogether. And all this is done in the very name of what has, in effect, been cast aside.

The working of my law was quite dramatically illustrated recently in connection with the celebrations surrounding the Liberty statue. Much was made of the statue itself, millions of dollars being spent in polishing it up, throngs gathering to behold it, and so on. But virtually no thought was given to what it was originally supposed to symbolize. Some of the efforts of the news media in this direction were grotesque in their vulgarity. For example, people watching these celebrations on television were at one point shown a gathering of the wealthy who had paid five thousand dollars each for a choice spot to dine and look at the statue. Some of these were interviewed, as somehow fulfilling the statue's symbolic meaning, the astonishing supposition being that it represented the freedom to come to these shores and make money. Indeed, the expression "the American dream" was repeatedly used to mean precisely that.

Similarly, in connection with these same celebrations, the word "liberty" was much used, was in fact woven into every speech and exultation, but at no point did anyone actually stop to consider what that word is supposed to mean. The word itself, which is but a symbol of a precious and noble idea, came to be the thing that was prized, rather than the fairly clear and definite idea that it once symbolized. And what is so sad about all this is that virtually no one noticed the immense perversion that had been wrought. Imagining themselves to be giving expression to the sense and feelings of patriotism, that is, the love for one's country and certain of its noble ideas and institutions, people instead indulged gross and vulgar sentiments for the mere symbols of these, without any awareness of the corruption they were thus fostering.

Epigony and the Debasement of Marriage

The second familiar thing I will use to illustrate my law is the institution of marriage, something as familiar and commonplace as patriotism. The marriage of a man and woman is supposed to rest for its foundation upon their love for each other. Such love being genuine and overwhelming, it is rightly assumed that it will endure, and that the marriage built upon it will also endure. The perfectly human act of "getting" married is thus supposed to be a symbolic recognition of what already exists, namely intense, indestructible, and binding love. It is accordingly this love that is supposed to unite its partners, not the man-made and symbolic recognition of such love. This is, indeed, more or less recognized in the Roman Catholic Church, where marriage is treated as a sacrament whose vehicle is considered to be, not a priest, but the lovers themselves. It is they who formally marry each other. Yet in popular thinking the very opposite is thought to be true, for everyone imagines that it is some clerk, religious or secular—that is, some priest or judge—who thus brings two people together in marriage—who "makes" them, as it is imagined, "really married."

This debasement of marriage at the hands of its most solemn defenders is particularly illustrative of my law. They substitute a legalistic form for the conjugal love which the form symbolizes. Thus they find no absurdity in the supposition that a man and woman might be married even though they have come to detest each other, their marital state having been established once and for all at a stroke. Not surprisingly, they have great difficulty in seeing how a real marriage can exist without the legalistic act, no matter how overwhelming and indestructible might be the love that unites its partners. That, in other words, which one would have supposed was merely symbolic of something inexpressibly precious has preempted the thing symbolized. There are, doubtless, important practical reasons for this, but the fact remains that something good and noble is thereby debased by the very persons who imagine that they are upholding it. The defenders of what is good become, again, insidious destroyers, quite unwittingly.

Similarly, one sometimes finds the institution of marriage described as a form of *contract*, and, amazingly, those who put forth this wretched notion imagine that they are expressing a high standard. Indeed, they are apt to express this idea with moralistic fervor. Infidelity is thus represented as a kind of breach of contract, an act of promise breaking, and is regarded as wrong for *that* reason. The bond of marriage, which was originally precious love, is thus replaced by the most vulgar kind of bond imaginable, upon which business transactions are supposed to rest. And note once again that this substitution of the worthless for that which was truly good is made by the very defenders of marriage. Having lost sight of what it really is, they uphold instead a worthless symbol of what it is supposed to be.

Of course the marriage of a man and a woman does involve a basic promise, namely, the promise to love. But the evil of the failure to love, or of the erosion of that love over time, is not that some promise has been broken. It is, rather, that something precious beyond words—that love itself—has been lost. It is doubtless important that lovers should not lie to each other. But no ultimate good is attained merely by heeding that precept, important as it may be. The ultimate good is that they should love each other, and for that reason have no incentive to lie or betray, or even to contemplate it. Yet it is common to find partners in a marriage, whose bond of love has long since diminished almost to zero, taking satisfaction in themselves, and being praised by others, for having kept to their vows, stuck it out, and made it last. Perhaps there is something admirable in this, as a feat of endurance, but it is not any worthwhile concept of marriage that has been sustained. The very opposite has happened, and in perfect accordance with my law.

Epigony and the Debasement of Religion

The third illustration of my law is found in the course that religions everywhere take as soon as any kind of priesthood is established, or in other words, as soon as human defenders of any religion come forward. The priests themselves become the epigones, the vulgarizers of what was noble and good, and this corruption of the good is wrought, again, in the very name of that good. And my law seems to hold no matter whether we are referring to religion as it is expressed in Islam, Buddhism, Christianity, or whatever.

Thus, as patriotism is originally the love for one's country, and marriage is originally the love of its partners for each other, so religion is originally the love for God. This surely is its underlying meaning. It is this which inspires the Bible, for instance, and from this that we draw our own inspiration in the study of sacred writings. It is what is absolutely essential to the mind and heart of a religious person. Mere belief in the *existence* of gods can have no more significance to religion than belief in the existence of anything else. Thus, to draw again from my two earlier examples, one is not made a patriot by merely believing that his country exists, but by his love for it. And a marriage is not made by each partner acknowledging that the other exists, but by their love for each other. And so, too, for our creator. And this is why the Greeks of antiquity, despite their robust belief in the gods, were nevertheless hardly religious at all. The gods inspired in them fear and awe, but not the love that is inseparable from religion. On the other hand, every expression of a profound love for God, whether in word or deed, is instantly seen as religious, no matter what beliefs or speculations may or may not accompany it. Belief *in* God involves a great deal more than an ontological hypothesis, however firmly held, that there *is* a god.

But what happens when human beings organize to uphold and defend religion? Exactly what, by my law of epigony, we should expect; namely, the *symbols* of religion come to be the things venerated, to the extent that our creator, who was the original object of love in the heart of the religious, is entirely eclipsed by them. And, since religions are always rich in symbolism, the possibilities, and the temptations, for such substitution are quite overwhelming.

Thus, persons are thought of as religious if they exhibit great devotion to a *church*—attend its services regularly, give to it, and make it more or less central to their life's activities. Indeed, in the minds of the extremely vulgar, being religious is virtually equated with "going" to church. Religion, however, is the love for God, not the love for an institution, no matter how old, venerable, and powerful that institution may be. Hence, devotion to a church, instead of being the mark of a religious person, is the mark of one who is not religious at all, except in a debased and popular sense.

Similarly, many persons imagine themselves to express profound religiosity by their submission to a priesthood, or to certain of its exalted members, such as a bishop, an ayatollah, or a grand lama. Indeed, this is, for reasons not hard to understand, fostered by the priesthood itself, apparently with no awareness that religion is thereby debased. The epigones whose very role is the defense of religion become its most insidious destroyers, setting before the faithful such things as holy books, holy personages, various objects and vestments, ceremonious behavior, sometimes on a grand scale, and sometimes, even, meaningless relics and bonds of holy personages and things, and encouraging the veneration of these. In reducing what may once have been a believer in God, possessed with a heart and mind of love for God, to one who submits to a church and its priesthood, bowing to these, embracing their teachings and submitting to their laws, a priesthood replaces religion with something quite different and quite vulgar, and all too unwittingly. So again, the destroyers of what was truly noble and good turn out to be, not its avowed enemies, but its most dedicated human defenders. It is, as in the case of all things good, the human touch itself that corrupts, and corrupts in the very act of trying to foster and preserve. And what makes the process more pathetic is the lack of realization that something very precious has been lost and something commonplace has been exalted. The destroyers of religion actually think of themselves as its upholders and defenders, and in this there is very often no insincerity. Thus a bishop who ceaselessly dedicates himself to his church and its role in human affairs certainly does not think of himself as a foe of religion, but the very opposite, and in this he is perfectly sincere. The illusion is completed when his followers, heeding his exhortations, think of themselves, and of him, as religious. It is the final irony, and a profoundly sad one.

It is the working of this law which seems to me to explain many commonplace things having to do with the church and the clergy. For example, the only president of the United States who was driven from office by his own venality and corruption had, shortly before, been named Churchman of the Year. It was devotion to *church* that was thought to matter or, worse, the mere appearance of this, without even any thought concerning what may or may not lie behind it. The symbol had replaced the thing symbolized. Similarly, I once heard a Roman Catholic priest express concern that one of his parishioners might marry a Protestant, saying to her: "You see, we (*sic*) might lose not only you, but your children as well." This is one of those common and even banal examples of how, in keeping with my law, the corruption of something good is wrought, as in this case, by one of its official defenders. Or again, when Pope John Paul appeared, of all places, on the plains of Iowa a few years ago, he was surrounded by a vast sea of people who had come to see *him*. His very vestments—which, it might be noted, always come to clothe anyone deemed somehow "holy" in the public imagination—bespeak the power of symbolism, and also its destructiveness.

The workings of my law are found no less in the sometimes grotesque behavior of evangelical clergymen, their influence over the masses and their power to extract from them staggering amounts of money for the furtherance of purely temporal causes. Here the debasement of what is sacred achieves a new dimension as these epigones convert the love of God to, of all things, the love of *self*, and religion is reduced to narcissism. Their followers, bathing themselves in self-glorification, declare *themselves* to be, above all, moral, patriotic, and blessed. Their faces radiant with happiness, they go forth, Bibles in hand, to make everyone else like themselves—in the cause, as they believe, of religion.

How far the love of God is driven from religion by the human touch is indicated by the fact that what passes for religion is sometimes compatible with no belief in God at all. Thus a Jewish friend of mine, planning to marry a gentile, tried to reassure his mother by saying that it was in no sense a "mixed" marriage because they were in total agreement on all theological matters, both being atheists; to which his mother responded, "Well, I don't see why you couldn't marry a Jewish atheist." One cannot fail to see that this woman's remark, though mildly amusing, has a point. Modern Judaism, though still considered one of the world's religions, is in fact little more than a culture. What is required, in order to be a Jew, is not a love for God, or even belief that any gods exist. All that is required is Jewish parentage, or in other words, a certain cultural identity.

It would not be so easy to speak, without a sense of contradiction, of a *Christian atheist,* and yet something like this is not uncommon. Thus, for example, a person born of Roman Catholic parents and baptized in that church might go his entire life giving no real thought whatever to his creator. So long as he called himself a Roman Catholic, however, and went to Mass and to confession with a certain minimum regularity—perhaps once a year—then his claim to be a Roman Catholic would not be challenged. Here what counts is not cultural identity but allegiance to a church, and even this need not be strong. In cases where the allegiance is very strong one hears applied the expression, "a good Catholic." What is meant here is that the person so described heeds the practices and laws of the church, particularly those requiring participation in its rituals. It does *not* mean that his heart is filled with a love for God, though this is somehow assumed to be implied. Of course it need not even be implied, for it would be perfectly possible for one to be a very "good Catholic" indeed with only the minimal thought, from one day to another, of God, and with no genuine love for God at all.

Indeed, to make my point in still another way, it is customary to think of children, and even infants, as possessed of religion. This idea is absurd in its very nature, and yet it is absolutely insisted upon and even enforced by law. Thus an infant born of a Jewish woman must be adopted by persons "of the same religion," and the same holds for Catholic and Protestant babies—as if there were any theological sense in which an infant could, for example, be a Protestant. Religion is here considered a cultural identity and nothing more.

It will perhaps be said, very plausibly, that this humanization of things noble and good is necessary, given the inherent limitation of human beings, and that it is not therefore to be condemned. We cannot all of us be like St. Francis of Assisi. We are imperfect people living in an imperfect world, but live there we must, making the best we can of what we have.

This is of course true, but it misses the point. I have not said that everything should be perfect. I have not said that if such things as patriotism, marriage, and religion cannot be what they should be, then they should be abolished altogether. What I have said is that such things, which are in their true nature noble and good, always come to be corrupted by their upholders, and that this corruption consists of replacing them with something else without realizing what has happened. If someone, believing himself to be the pillar of religion, debases the very religion he defends, and does this in the name of religion, then that, it seems to me, is a point worth making. The fact that nothing can be done about it is quite irrelevant.

Epigony and the Debasement of Ethics

Finally, I want to say something about ethics and the manner in which it, too, is debased, in accordance with my law of epigony. This is a large subject, but I shall try to make my basic point briefly.

We can see this debasement, first of all, in the evolution of basic ethical terms, such as charity, goodness, and virtue. "Charity," for example, is derived from *caritas,* the Latinization of the *agape* or Christian love of the New Testament. This was, originally, the most important ethical concept of the Christian religion. *Charity,* however, has come to mean little more than giving to the poor. Indeed, it is even common to speak of giving *to charity,* illustrating an ultimate and final corruption of a precious concept.

Similarly, goodness was originally, by the Greeks, contrasted with what is simply bad, that is, base, and therefore by all means to be avoided in the quest for happiness or fulfillment. At the hands of moralists, however, it has come to be more or less equated with morality, such that human goodness, for example, is thought of as mere benevolence. This is, doubtless, an important human attribute, but hardly the equivalent of the idea it displaced.

The working of my law is perhaps best seen in the evolution of the concept of virtue, however. A virtuous man was, for the Greeks, an exceptional man, one who stood out from others by his superiority over them. Not everyone, they thought, has the capacity for virtue, and rather few ever actually achieve it. Virtue is reserved for those who are inherently better, and it must be cultivated through long training and education.

This ancient ideal of virtue, conceived as personal excellence, of rising above others by one's superiority to them as a person, was an inspiring one. It underlay every treatise of the ancient classical moralists, culminating in Aristotle's writings. But that ideal has by now become so denatured that even educated people can hardly read these great treatises from antiquity without misunderstanding. Aristotle's *Nichomachean Ethics,* which is primarily concerned with the nature of virtue or individual excellence, was readily understandable to any educated Greek of his day, but not by many who undertake to read it today. Readers now suppose that, since it is a treatise on ethics, its author must be dealing with matters of right and wrong, even though those concepts do not even enter into his discussion. The concept of virtue, meanwhile, has become so trivialized that it is sometimes equated with nothing more significant than chastity. And similarly, when Aristotle refers to the *good man* we suppose him to be describing someone who respects the rights of others, who is perhaps generous, kind, and truthful in his dealings with them, and so on. Of course Aristotle meant nothing of the sort. He was thinking of the rare individual who rises above the common herd by the power of his mind, by his strength, resourcefulness and courage, and who is therefore worth something and, in the true sense of the word, contemptuous of common people.

The manner in which this ancient ideal of human goodness came to be corrupted by those very moralists whose chief mission was to defend it was well understood by Plato. In his *Gorgias* he analyzes this decay, using Socrates' interlocutor, Callicles, as the vehicle for his analysis. The common people, Callicles notes, are a weak and mindless herd, and are very numerous. Discerning that they have no genuine virtue, that is, that they are inferior to those exceptional few individuals who are strong and resourceful, they declare such strength and superiority not to be the marks of virtue at all. All men, they declare, are equal—and, as Callicles sagaciously notes, it makes these mindless masses feel very good indeed to be able to believe that they are equal to the best, and hence, just as good as they. Weakness, they declare, is not really weakness at all, but strength. Thus, Callicles notes, there arises a kind of herd morality, wherein the same words continue to be used—words like *virtue, goodness,* and *worth*—but are given meanings that are very nearly the opposite of what they originally had. And we can add to Callicles' observations that it is then only a matter of time before some religious leader will rise to strike a chord in the hearts of these wretched masses by declaring this popular ethic to be ordained by the gods themselves. It is not those who are great and noble who are blessed, he will say, but on the contrary, those who are meek, poor and downtrodden, and it is they, he will say, whom the gods love, who are the very salt of the earth, and who will someday inherit the earth.

The cycle is thus completed, and something that is morally noble and good becomes almost totally lost sight of, replaced by something relatively worthless, this debasement being wrought, once again, by those who imagine themselves to be the upholders of morality. And so great and thoroughgoing is this change that even the most thoughtful and reflective philosophers are likely to be unaware that it has even occurred. The degenerate morality becomes enshrined in custom and in popular religion, and thus comes to be taken for granted as being the true morality after all. It is very sad and, sadly, very human.

15

Action and Responsibility

"Since God is dead, nothing is forbidden."
—DOSTOYEVSKI

The title of my remarks confronts me with two imponderables. The first, the concept of agency, has for the past decade or so been at the center of attention in philosophy. The analytical literature of action theory has accordingly grown very large, and I shall not add to it here except indirectly. I shall only say that the strangeness of this concept has not, as a result of all this attention, been reduced in the least, so far as I can see. It still contains two mysterious ingredients, namely, the idea of a *self* as a unique kind of being, and of *causation* by that self which amounts to absolute creation.

I shall, then, devote my attention to the second idea, that of responsibility. It is this idea, I believe, which is largely responsible for the philosophical concept of agency to begin with. Had people never conceived of themselves as responsible beings then it is doubtful whether they would ever have thought of themselves as agents either, in the philosophical sense of that term. The reason for this is that responsibility presupposes freedom. If anyone is responsible for what he has done, then he must have been free to do otherwise. But in that case he could not have been caused to do what he did, in the usual sense of causation. Nor must his behavior have been simply uncaused. The only description left, then, would seem to be that he, if he was responsible for what he did, must have been the originating cause of his behavior, and must, moreover, have been such that he could have

---

From *Action Theory,* M. Brand and D. Walton, eds. (Dordrecht: D. Reidel, 1976), pp. 293-310.

behaved entirely differently. Or in other words, he must have been an *agent* in the philosophical, or indeed the metaphysical, sense of that term.

That illation, briefly and crudely sketched here, is of course very familiar. From it one can at once see two things, one being the strangeness of the concept of agency, of which we need little reminder, and the other being how much the acceptance of that concept seems to rest upon the belief that people are sometimes responsible for what they do. If this latter were false, then there would seem to be little reason for saying that people are ever agents, in the sense described.

I shall, then, concentrate on the idea of responsibility, with the aim of nourishing skepticism concerning its usefulness.

RESPONSIBILITY AND LAW

What we are ultimately concerned with here is, of course, *moral responsibility,* and not responsibility in its purely empirical sense. Thus both the terms *action* and *responsibility* have an ordinary and unproblematical meaning having nothing to do with either metaphysics or ethics. This meaning of each appears in the remark, "Salt acted corrosively with respect to this iron and is responsible for its deterioration." All this means is that salt corroded the iron, which is not a metaphysical statement, and has nothing to do with ethics. The verbally similar remark, that "This man acted maliciously with respect to his rival and is responsible for his blindness," on the other hand, seems to express a totally different idea of acting and a totally different idea of responsibility. It is the concept of *responsibility* that is embodied in that second statement that I shall discuss, and not the equally strange and interesting concept of *agency* that is found there.

Generally, the idea of *moral responsibility* does not seem terribly mysterious to philosophers. They usually use the term confidently, even glibly. The apparent fact that this kind of responsibility, like the associated concept of agency, applies only to persons and is evidently, like agency, non-empirical, has not deterred philosophers from offering judgments of responsibility with utter confidence. What I want to show, however, is that this idea is not only very strange, like the idea of agency, but is really not a useful one to begin with. It has become a fond thing of philosophy, shedding darkness on our thinking rather than illuminating it, and even causing mischief in the relationships of people to each other.

The Presuppositions of Moral Responsibility

A typical procedure for a philosopher addressing himself to this concept of responsibility would be to set forth, in an *a priori* way, its presuppositions and then, perhaps, delineate the implications of these presuppositions—implications with respect to the concept of personality, for example, or with respect to agency. And I think it is fair to say that such a procedure would receive the approval of almost any group of professional philosophers. Thus one could declare, on the basis of no empirical facts whatsoever, that for someone to be morally responsible for an act, then (i) that act must be caused by him, and not by another person or thing, (ii) that it must be free, that is to say, avoidable by him, and (iii) it must have the quality of moral wrongness, and be such that the agent knows this.[1] All of which implies a uniqueness of persons among all the other things in the world, a unique kind of free causation not found elsewhere in nature, and a unique kind of knowledge, the knowledge of right and wrong. These extraordinary implications should be sufficient to induce skepticism with respect to the whole idea of responsibility, in this sense. They also seem to nourish skepticism with respect to the idea of agency, but I shall not pursue that.

In the past philosophers who have cast doubt upon the idea of moral responsibility have usually done so by attacking the first two of the three presuppositions set out above, that is, by undermining the idea of a free cause. For me to do the same thing would involve an excursus into the concept of agency, and I have said I am not going to do that. Instead I propose to question the third of those presuppositions, which has hitherto seemed least questionable; namely, the distinction between moral right and wrong itself, and the correlative possibility of knowing what that distinction is. And I am going to do this by first showing how the basic distinction between right and wrong arises at various levels, that is, at levels having no necessary connection with moral right and wrong, and then show that a fundamental condition for drawing such a distinction is lacking in the special case of moral right and wrong. Since, moreover, moral responsibility is supposed to be the responsibility that an agent has for his morally wrong acts, then it follows that a necessary condition for applying that concept to anyone is similarly lacking.

The Nature of Right and Wrong at the Level of Games

The first thing to note, then, is that the distinction between right and wrong is created by rules or laws of some sort, whether these be man-made or whether they be considered a part of the order of nature. The similar distinction between *good* and *bad*, on the other hand, is not thus relative to rule.

Thus, to begin at a very elementary level, a *right* move in chess is simply one that is permitted or (sometimes) required by rule, and a *wrong* move one that is forbidden. No sense whatever can be made of describing some chess move as wrong, even though no rule forbids it. There is nothing in the least wrong with moving a bishop from one color to another, for example, except that the rule defining the *permissible* moves of a bishop disallows this kind of movement. Right and wrong are at this level so clearly relative to rule that no one would be tempted to dispute it. The rules do not merely describe that distinction; they *create* it.

The Distinction between Good and Bad

Good and bad, however, are at this level not relative to rules, not even to implicit ones. Chess moves are good or bad according to the purposes of the players, the ultimate purpose or end here being, normally, to deliver a checkmate. Sometimes the best move is one that is contrary to what virtually every player would do under the circumstances, and in that sense contrary to rule—for example, a brilliant sacrifice of the queen. And sometimes a good move can be one that promotes defeat rather than victory. Thus a player might, for example, skillfully render himself vulnerable to checkmate, and receive a checkmate, in order to advance his opponent's instruction in chess (as in the case of a mother teaching chess to her daughter), which illustrates that good and bad are, at this level, relative to purposes or ends, and not to rules.

Here one other peculiarity of right and wrong, which seems to have no analogue in good and bad, should be noted, and that is that while there is only one sense in which an action can be wrong, namely, that of being forbidden by rule, there are two ways in which it can be right, namely, either by being *required* by rule, in which case it is obligatory, or by being merely *permitted* by rule, in which case it is innocent. Thus a chess player acts rightly, upon opening a game, whether he moves his king's pawn one square or two. Either move is permitted, neither is required. It is, however, required, and not merely permitted, that such a move be made with a white piece, not a black one. This distinction between right acts that are merely permitted and those that are required holds, I believe, with respect to every level of right and wrong.

Conventional Right and Wrong

If we now move to another area of right and wrong, which some might consider more significant than game rules, namely, to the area of the unwritten conventional rules of etiquette and social intercourse, we find exactly the same thing. Most of these have little or nothing to do with right and wrong in any distinctly moral sense, and philosophers have therefore bestowed little attention on them. They do nevertheless define quite clearly a distinction between right and wrong, and indeed, they create that distinction at this level, which Thomas Hobbes aptly called the level of "small morals."[2] What is conventionally right is what is permitted or required by some conventional rule, and what is wrong at this level is what is thus forbidden. Thus it is right, or permitted, to co-habitate with one's spouse, but not with the spouse of another person, even when this is not contrary to law. And it is right, or conventionally required, to take an oath of high office with one's hands on a Bible, even though not required by law. And it is in this sense wrong to giggle at a funeral or during public prayers, to use the flag as a mop, to utter vulgarisms in parlor conversation, particularly those associated with sexual behavior, to enter a holy place without a hat if one is a Jew, or with a hat if one is not, and so on. And so it is with respect to that whole body of conventional behavior: right and wrong are at this level quite clearly the creation of rules.

Such rules do not, however, any more than the rules of game, create any distinction between good and bad. More often than not they arise from such a distinction, that is to say, from practical considerations, but they certainly do not create these. It is better, for example, for children to have parents, that is, to belong to families, than not. No rule, conventional or other, is needed to see that. And it is because it is true that many of the conventional rules governing the relations of the sexes have arisen and are so assiduously upheld.

Legal Right and Wrong

Consider next still another level of right and wrong, which some would want to call a still "higher" level, namely, that of the positive laws of a governed society. Again we find exactly the same thing. What is legally right is that which is permitted or required by the criminal law, and wrong is whatever is thus forbidden. The distinction between legal right and wrong is thus the creation of rules, that is, of enacted laws, and of nothing else. No sense can be made of describing some action as legally wrong, even though no law forbids it. There is, for example, nothing in the least wrong with filing one's income tax return on May 15, rather than on April 15, except that this is forbidden by law. So it is with respect to the movement of vehicular traffic, the possession and use of firearms, and indeed, the entire scope of the criminal law. The body of law does not merely *describe* the distinction between what is and what is not legally wrong, it creates it.

A Common Confusion

Here it is not unusual for someone, imagining himself to be very perceptive, to say something to the effect that, for example, such things as assault, homicide, theft, and fraud, all of which are forbidden by law, would still be wrong even if they were *not* unlawful. But this is only to confuse two senses of right and wrong, namely, the legal sense and the so-called moral sense, which we have yet to consider. True enough, most persons would detest and condemn assault, for example, even if it were not forbidden by law, but this is not to the point. Our detestation of the act does not render it wrong in any legal sense. Only a law can do that. When someone is assaulted under the legal institution of slavery, then his assailant acts with total innocence, at the level of the law, whatever others may think or feel, and in no way can he be charged with a crime or tried in any court of law. For that to be possible an actual or positive law must be created.

It is worth noting that this same confusion can arise at the levels of right and wrong with which we began, namely, at the level of what is right or wrong in a game as well as at the level of conventional morality. Thus, one might assert that it would be *wrong,* while playing chess with the valuable pieces belonging to your opponent, to move your rook in such a manner that it ends up in your pocket, even though such a move is not, in fact, prohibited by the rules of chess; or that bigamous marriage is wrong even among those whose conventional rules permit or even enjoin it. But all that is meant by such remarks as these is that such acts violate the criminal law even when they do not violate any rules of games or convention. What is involved here, as in the preceding case, is simply a confusion of different levels of right and wrong.

The Irrelevancy of Law to What Is Good and Bad

Again we find, however, that while legal right and wrong are the creation of rules, good and bad are at this level not thus created, but are, like chess moves, relative to people's ends and purposes. Thus one might manage his affairs—his business, for example—in a perfectly innocent way, and yet very badly. This would be the case if, for example, you squandered your capital on frivolous ventures and thus led yourself into ruin. Bad as this is, no law forbids it. The badness of such an outcome would thus be relative to no rule or law, but only to the presumed purpose of the agent. If, on the other hand, one's purpose in a given enterprise was not his own betterment but that of another person, or perhaps the strengthening of some cause, then behavior that would otherwise appear stupid and foolish might in fact be very good, by virtue of the fact that its purpose was achieved even at the expense of the agent's ruin. Examples of this come very easily to mind—the father who neglects his own affairs in saving his son from perdition, and that sort of thing.

Moral Distinctions

Exactly the same things can now be said of *moral right and wrong,* and of *moral good and evil,* namely, that the former distinction is, and the latter one is not, the creation of rule or law. The difference here is only that, in this case, we are speaking not of the rules of games, rules of custom, nor the positive laws enacted by human legislators, but of the moral law, as it is called. Thus, an action is morally *right* in case it is either permitted by moral law (morally innocent) or *enjoined* by that law (obligatory), and a morally *wrong* (or wicked) act is one that is forbidden by that law. No sense can be made of describing some action as wrong, even though it violates no moral law. It cannot, for example, be morally wrong to remove a living fetus from its mother's womb, or to dispose of excess female infants, or of the aged, unless such actions should turn out to be inconsistent with some moral law—the prohibition of homicide, for example. Such a moral rule or law does not merely describe or give expression to some antecedent wrongness that is discovered to reside in a wide variety of actions; it creates it. People do, to be sure, have an abhorrence of certain actions, and there is no doubt that this abhorrence serves as a powerful inducement to honor the moral law. But feelings such as these can hardly *create* moral right and wrong.[3] This is the work of the moral law, and of nothing else.

Again, however, we find that *good and evil* are, at this moral level, not the creation of any rule or law, but exist antecedently to law and are discoverable in experience. It is a distinction of nature, as philosophers belonging to the age of Socrates would have expressed it. Thus no rule or law is needed to know that hunger and thirst are bad. Similarly, a wound is bad, whether inflicted or accidental; and while a law may render its infliction wrong, no law is needed to render the suffering of it bad. And just as one can innocently make a bad move in chess, or with both conventional and legal innocence bring ruin upon himself or others, so also someone holding great power might, in violation neither of any human law nor of any moral law, and in fact in response to the clearest perception of his duty, bring sorrow and misery to a whole nation through the sheer miscarriage of his efforts. Similarly, one might, in response to no moral incentive whatever, but simply pursuit of personal glory, bring great and lasting blessings to a nation, and at the expense of no one.[4] As at the other levels considered, then, we can see that good and bad, unlike right and wrong, are relative, not to rules or laws, but to ends or purposes. Indeed it is not easy to distinguish *moral* good and bad from other varieties except by considering these to be the fulfillment or defeat of peoples' *highest* aims and purposes; happiness, for example, or peace and security.

Laws as Imperatives

We need next to note that laws, from the relatively unimportant sort that govern the conduct of games up to the highest laws of morality and religion, are appropriately expressed as commands or imperatives, not as statements, predictions, queries, or any other grammatical form.

"Thou shalt not kill" and "Honor thy father and mother" are perfect modes for the expression of law. Often, to be sure, positive laws, as well as game rules, have the apparent form of mere assertions and sometimes predictions, but they are not assertions or predictions. Thus, the formulation "Whoever shall take the life of another shall be punished by death" is not a prediction about what is going to happen to anyone, though it has that form. It is instead a prohibition of homicide, conjoined with a criminal sanction. Similarly, the formulation "Each player makes one move in alternation with the other, white moving first" is not a statement, though it has that form. It is instead a directive or simple command, and could be so expressed without the least change of sense.

And so it is with all laws and rules. Indeed it could hardly be otherwise, because all rules and laws are directives having to do with what actions are and what ones are not forbidden, permitted, and required. Their clearest and most straightforward expression, therefore, is as commands, and they remain commands even when expressed obliquely.

The Sources of Laws

Any command, however, presupposes a source, that is, a commander, and in order to have the force of a command, as distinguished from mere request or exhortation, it must rest also upon some sanction, some externally supplied incentive to heed and obey it. Without such a sanction or threat of penalty a law degenerates to a mere "rule of imperfect obligation," as it is aptly described in the literature of jurisprudence. And in fact the kinds of rules and laws we have been considering do all have these two characteristics, or at least once did.

Thus, the rules of a game, which are commands addressed to players, originate with certain human beings, namely, those who have created those games, and who from time to time introduce modifications into them. No one has ever pretended, for example, that the rules of chess were discovered as some part of the metaphysical fabric of the universe, by some process of reason or inquiry. They are the fabrications of human beings, enforced by human beings,[5] and subject to human revision. So likewise with respect to the criminal law of any political society. This is nothing but the commands of whoever holds sovereign power within such a society. No one ever supposes that the laws governing the movement of vehicular traffic are traceable to any higher source. Some commands of civil authority are, to be sure, thought to have some source higher than human, namely, Scripture, the Ten Commandments of God, or some similar revelation; but this only means that the positive laws of human society are sometimes formulated in accordance with what are thought to be the commands of God. So long as human authority with the power to command prohibits certain practices, and threatens with pains and penalties any who do not heed those prohibitions, then those prohibitions stand as laws of that society, whether or not they are thought to be also laws of God; and they would still be laws even if they were in fact *contradicted* by a divine law—not good laws, perhaps, but laws, all the same.

The Sources of Conventional Morality

Who, then, fabricates the rules of conventional morality? Where is the commander who has declared them, and who are their enforcers? These rules define no game—or at least, no *mere* game—nor do they have the force of criminal law, for no one can be prosecuted for their violation.

The answer to this question was perfectly given by Protagoras, who said, in effect: Everyone commands them, and everyone enforces them. He was clearly right, and his celebrated dispute with Socrates on this question was nothing but the product of a confusion between different levels of law like those already noted.

Thus, Socrates was deeply perplexed by the question: Who are the teachers of virtue? What he had in mind, of course, was a kind of virtue that is not merely man-made, something that is higher than the laws and conventions of human beings. So construed, his question was indeed a good one, and one which, as we shall shortly see, still appears to be unanswered independently of certain theological assumptions. But Protagoras had long since decided, not only that there is no natural or true law of morality, but that, in fact, nothing whatever is true "by nature," in this way or any other realm. Virtue, therefore, could for Protagoras be nothing more than the conventional practices of human beings, which admittedly differ from one time and place to another. So construed, it is quite obviously true that "everyone" is the teacher of virtue or, in the terms in which I have been expressing it, "everyone" (persons generally) is the source and the enforcer of the commands in which conventional virtue is expressed. No particular person commands us not to giggle at funerals or during public prayers, yet we do learn this, from those around us. And violations of all such rules bring a swift and certain imposition of sanctions, in the form of disapprobation from every side, a kind of sanction having dreadful effect in keeping all persons, herd-like, from straying from the path. That Socrates was left speechless by Protagoras' lengthy disquisition to the effect was not the result of his not knowing all those things, for they are quite obvious to anyone possessed of any sense. Socrates' puzzlement resulted from the fact that, while he and Protagoras expressed themselves in much the same terminology, they simply were not talking about the same thing.

Four Varieties of Conventional Morality

Before applying the considerations thus far elicited to the special case of moral law, it is worth remarking that Protagoras was far from unique in identifying morality with mere rules of custom. Indeed, it is characteristic of small minds everywhere to do exactly that, and Protagoras' greatness lay in the fact that he created a brilliant philosophy of ethics and politics around this narrow identification.

Thus we can find four quite distinct types of person who base their conduct and their lives largely upon this strange identification. Let us call them, respectively, the *prude,* the *pedant,* the *formalist,* and the *zealot.*

The first of these, the *prude,* takes for granted that the moral law is expressed in the conventional rules of his culture, particularly through his church, and then, consistently with this, measures his own moral goodness by the sheer *number* of such rules that he is able to uphold. The extreme expression of such prudery is: Everything to which one inclines as a natural good, particularly by the solicitations of pleasure, is forbidden. Such rules, then, need not be of great significance, need not advance any good or reduce any evil, and can indeed defeat felt goods without being abandoned for that reason. All that is required, for the style of life called prudery, is that such rules be numerous, hence largely trivial, and that they be entirely identified with the moral law. The latter ensures that they will be heeded, and the former that the path of such a life will be exceedingly narrow.

The *moral pedant,* on the other hand, euphemistically called the person of fixed principles, is characterized, not by the numerousness of the purely conventional rules he honors, but by his uncompromising adherence to them. Unlike the prude, whose rules are beyond counting, the pedant's are usually reduced to just two or three, usually those prohibiting lying, stealing, and sometimes infidelity. Mendacity, for example, is a conventional wrong, the prohibition of which has quite clearly arisen from the evils that it normally spawns. The moral pedant treats this human fabrication as a moral law, and does not lie even on those occasions when veracity is nasty and petty. So likewise with the conventional rule of marital fidelity. The moral pedant, instead of identifying this with faith in the sense of trust and constancy of feeling, construes it narrowly as inflexible adherence to a rule of sexual conduct, and from exclusive devotion to this loses sight of its larger meaning. So likewise with the prohibition of theft, which the pedant congratulates himself for honoring even when it is plainly stupid to do so.

The third type to identify moral law with convention is the *formalist* who, without the moral fervor exhibited by the other two, is absorbed in the visible conventions of social life, or what are aptly called "externals," such as mode of dress, speech, and manners. These are precisely what are conventional, that is customary. The formalist is neither innovative, spontaneous, nor creative, but instead totally imitates what he finds around him. It is a characteristic of politicians, and indeed of all whose fortunes depend upon the opinion of many. Such a person dresses much as others do, restricts himself to a vocabulary that offends no one, conducts himself unobtrusively everywhere, and is genuinely shocked by deviations from such norms. It is this latter that makes the formalist of some ethical significance, for, inasmuch as his capacity for shock is reserved for morally insignificant deviations, he is, like both the pedant and the prude, quite likely to be insensitive to larger concerns. This is sometimes forcibly brought home to us when it is discovered that some politician, conventional right down to the polish on his shoes, has without apparent feeling of guilt engaged in extortion, the exploitation of the weak, the obstruction of justice, or some one or more of the other arts at which persons in public life are often so skilled, and which the external conventionalism of their lives serves so effectively to mask, even sometimes, from themselves.

And finally, the moral *zealot* is one who identifies the moral law with some *one* purely conventional rule and then, exceeding the pedant, is not content with the inflexible observance of that rule on his own part, but strives to impose it on everyone else too. The rule forbidding the use of spiritous beverages, for example, born of evangelical enthusiasms of the previous century, lacks even a scriptural basis. The zeal of those whose mission is to impose it on the world blinds them even to the fact that Jesus' first miracle was the conversion of water to wine. Other examples of moral zealotry come easily to mind, such as the fanatical opposition to abortion, patriotic chauvinism, and so on.

The Source of Moral Law

If, then, the three levels of law—the laws of games, of custom, and of political societies—are so easily traceable to their sources, where shall we look to find the source of the highest law, that is, the moral law? If the moral law is a command or imperative, as it surely is if it is a law, who has commanded it? Or is this law just a command that is laid upon human beings by no one at all, or that has issued from no commander, from sheer nothingness, or from thin air?

Actually, wherever human beings have upheld moral law, they have, at least originally, assumed a source of it, and that source has been some god. The commandments of God, the moral law, and the law of nature, as it has sometimes been quaintly called, were once all assumed to be one and the same.[6] And this, of course, made perfectly good sense, for it preserved the presuppositions of law, and thus the presuppositions of moral law. That law is a command, and its commander is no human or other created being, but God. And that is what distinguishes it as the *moral* law, namely, that it is commanded by the highest authority, higher than any king, priest, or other merely human authority. The clearest way to think of that moral law is to identify it with explicit commands, explicitly enunciated by God—for example, the Ten Commandments. Here it is not at all to be supposed that these were fabricated by Moses and delivered by *him* to the Israelites, even if we should assume him to have been the wisest man in the history of the race, or assume his purposes to have been noble beyond comparison. Or if anyone *does* make such a supposition, then he is reducing those commandments to the level of mere legality, at best, on a par with other human enactments, such as those governing vehicular traffic, and not expressions of any moral law at all.

No, these commandments were enunciated by God, and laid upon all persons, and the distinction between moral right and wrong was the result of that fact alone. Furthermore, those commands were implicitly conjoined with a sanction, that is, an externally supplied incentive to obedience, for it was believed that their author could reward with the sweetest blessings, and punish with dreadful pains, those who did and those who did not heed and obey. They were not, then, mere exhortations to virtue or wise prescriptions for life, but laws in the full and complete sense.

The Historical Deterioration of the Moral Law

It is very much worth noting what has happened to this moral law, its historical metamorphosis from a genuine moral law to a mere philosophical abstraction that is still called "moral law" even after the preconditions for such a law have been forgotten and even assumed nonexistent. Briefly, what happened is that philosophers abandoned the belief in a divine source of this law, and imagined that they were still making sense in discoursing about it! That there should be a god, having the power to punish and reward, who has laid down commands for his creatures, makes perfectly good sense, whether one believes it or not. And that those commands should be considered higher and more compelling than the commands or laws of any human being also makes perfectly good sense, given their supposed source. And that it should be considered the height of folly to disregard them, for whatever reason, and the clearest wisdom to heed them, considering salvation to depend on this, also makes perfectly good sense. What happens, however, when the very presuppositions on which all this rests are swept aside or disregarded? What happens is that what was hitherto reasonably regarded as the moral law becomes instead an abstraction, a toy of philosophy having not the slightest claim to reverence or respect from anyone, a command that lacks any commander, a law that lacks any source, an injunction or prohibition without any hint of a sanction and one that therefore supplies not the slightest incentive to obedience. What happens, in short, is that the moral law becomes a non-entity, a verbal formulation in the mouths of philosophers which signifies nothing.

The Attempt to Replace God with Things Human

Philosophers have, of course, not been entirely oblivious to this strange development, and some have accordingly tried to replace the original source of this law with something having at least some semblance to a commander, and something which, without too much violence to intelligence, might be viewed as exalted, or even divine. The most heroic attempt was made by Kant, who replaced God's will with human reason, then deified this as something of transcendent worth or as an "end in itself." Thus Kant clearly recognized that the moral law is a command or, which means the same thing, an imperative. Who, then, issues that command, if not God? If its source is some human being, such as Moses or the king or some wise philosopher, then how can it claim to be anything more than the positive law of a political society? How indeed can it pretend to be more than wise counsel, which one may disregard as he pleases? How can the sagacity of even the wisest of men, or even, as Plato fondly dreamed, of a host of these, having the power of kings, convert a command from a mere human edict, however laudable, to something having the grandeur of the moral law?

Kant's answer was that this law emanates, not from some person, but from *every* person, or better, from that in every person which is of more than mundane worth, namely, from *reason.* And Kant even went a considerable direction in supplying this moral law with a more than human sanction, replacing the blessings of heaven and the pains of hell with what he imagined was the practical impossibility of disobedience. One must not with impunity disregard the moral law because, to the extent that he is rational, he cannot.

It is a pleasant fable, and one that human beings will probably always cherish. It appears to restore to ethics some semblance of what philosophers, by their rejection of revelation, took from it. We still have before us something having the appearance of a command, which the moral law must be, and something which can, with a bit of artifice, be made to look like a commander, that is, a source for this law. It has also the great strength of feeding human conceit, in two ways; first, by giving to mankind at least one ingredient of religion that was precious, namely, a foundation of morality that is not merely a conventional or more or less arbitrary human fabrication; and second, by professing to find some purely human faculty having the authority, hitherto possessed only by God, to command every human being, and worthy of a respect that supersedes even the commands of a king. Kant himself, in one of his more fervid exultations, compared the supposed awesomeness of this moral law, and implicitly its source, with the very heavens above.

THE GROUNDLESSNESS OF MORAL RIGHT AND WRONG

Now I come to my final point, and the real point of these remarks, which is, that there evidently is no moral law, and hence, no moral right and wrong at all. The distinction between right and wrong at any level, we saw, requires rules or laws, and moral right and wrong is no exception. One can, of course, as most people do, have strong feelings about certain kinds of action, such as the use of spiritous beverages, the practice of polygamy, the abortion of the unborn or the destruction of infants, and so on, and we have become accustomed to expressing these feelings in utterances having the form of moral judgment. I am of course not denying this. But I do wish to make the important point that there really is no moral law, that there can therefore be no real distinction between right and wrong at this level, and that most of the literature belonging to the genre of philosophical ethics is therefore devoid of intellectual content—something that has, in fact, often been suspected by philosophers themselves. Such books, which have been produced in great profusion throughout the period of modern philosophy, and are still being written and placed before students to read, should all be removed from the libraries, as books in the areas of witchcraft and phrenology long since were, for like these they are devoid of a real subject matter. Exceptions are, of course, such books as rest explicitly upon divine revelation, as well as books that deal only with the history of ethical practices and opinions, and also ethical treatises, if there are any such, that do not presuppose any distinction between moral right and wrong, plus those relatively few classics in this area that charm by their quaint prose and sometimes poetic quality. Apart from these, such books are without content and serve more to muddle and confuse than to edify.

My argument for this conclusion consists of two parts. The first is, that God has evidently issued no commands, and there is no other source adequate to the creation of a genuinely moral law, or a law higher or more authoritative than the expression of a human will. My own reason for believing that God has issued no such command is that no god, as thus conceived, exists. (This is not intended as a declaration of atheism, but rather, as a divorcement of religion from the totally human ethics with which it has become entangled.) Of course, this consideration is conclusive for anyone who happens to share that theological skepticism. A supposed moral law that is not a command is no law to begin with; and a command that issues from no commander, but is instead plucked from thin air by a philosopher, is no "command" even deserving that name, much less deserving the slightest respect of anyone.

But—and this is the second part of my argument—the case is actually much stronger than this, for we can now see that even those who profess to believe that God has commanded his creatures, and who therefore at least appear to possess the preconditions of belief in a moral law, do not in fact believe in any such law, for they do in fact without hesitation substitute their own feelings for this supposed law, without realizing that they have thereby abrogated it. These who profess to believe in the moral law and its divine source, and who accordingly believe they can draw the distinction between moral right and wrong, thus have no more than the rest of us have, namely, strong feelings about certain kinds of behavior which they imagine to be the expression of that moral law in their hearts, even though their own procedure amounts to a disclaimer of that conviction.

The Defeasibility of Moral Rules

This follows from the fact there is no rule of conduct, or no moral law, which is not in fact abandoned in favor of their own feelings by those who unreservedly honor that law. At least I have never met any person, of whatever moral conviction, about whom this did not turn out to be so.

Consider, for example, a perfectly clear-cut case of what purports to be a moral law, the injunction against killing. It is exactly expressed in the command: Thou shalt not kill. This is probably the most widely honored of any moral precept, even by those who disbelieve its divine origin. Even those, however, who most sincerely profess to believe that it is a commandment of God, and that it can never be violated without guilt, do not in fact believe this, for even they treat that law as "defeasible," or in other words, they feel free to make exceptions to it that were never enunciated by any god and are in no way implied in the command.

Thus there is no one who does not immediately qualify that terse law by adding the words, "any person," such that it is taken as a prohibition of homicide only, not of killing as such. We can, perhaps, treat this as the intended meaning and not quibble. But having done that, note now how extensively subject to exception that law is, not just by this or that morally obdurate person, but by those who deem the law an absolute, who even imagine that it expresses the very will of God. Even these readily substitute their own will for God's whenever their feelings sufficently prompt them to.

To illustrate this, let us begin with the straightforward imperative, "Thou shalt not kill any person." Do we have here what expresses a moral law? Hardly, for even those who suppose we have such a law before us are willing to say that you may innocently kill sometimes. Thus, it is said to be morally wrong to kill any person *except,* of course, in the case of:

(a) self defense.

(b) infant females.

(c) a just war.

(d) an unquickened fetus.

(e) a Jew who has had carnal contact with a gentile woman.

(f) the terminally ill.

(g) the avenging of the murder of a kinsman.

(h) the aged and infirm.

(i) a criminal deserving of a death penalty.

(j) idiots, imbeciles, morons, and nitwits.

(k) sparing the lives of others.

(l) obviating great and irreparable suffering.

And so on. It is not hard to see that the list could be easily extended to a considerable length.

The usual response of anyone presented with such a list is to examine it, to see which exceptions are, and which are not really allowable. But that is wholly to miss the point! The command itself is inconsistent with *any* exception, and the moment one begins to make these exceptions, he substitutes for the moral law, upon which the original distinction between moral right and wrong was supposed to rest, something entirely different—namely, his own feelings on the matter. But if *that* is how things are in the last analysis decided, why was there this ceremonious bowing in the direction of a so-called moral law to begin with? And if that moral law was supposed to emanate from God—as I think one must suppose, if it is a moral law or command to begin with—then where has God made these amendments?

The Law of God and Human Feeling

Actually, that last question raises a curious point which seems to strengthen the very point I am trying to make. For one can, in fact, find scriptural sources for some of these exceptions—for innocently taking the life to avenge the death of a kinsman, for example, or to punish a Jew's carnal contact with a gentile woman.[6] But here what we actually find is that those who profess to uphold this law consult their feelings once again, in order to decide whether exceptions which appear to have been explicitly granted by God are really to be allowed as exceptions! Where, then, is the moral law to which we are supposed to yield? And why was it not formulated, at the outset, as: Thou shalt not kill, except on those occasions when you find you can do so with the feeling of innocence!

Of course, there remains one other possibility, and that is to treat this supposed moral law (or any other such command that one might come up with) as being in truth a moral law, and decline to permit of *any* exceptions whatever. Many have in fact tried this. But no one, I think, has ever succeeded, which amounts to saying that no one appears to consider this or any other command to express a genuine moral law. Even those, for example, who have most vigorously upheld the right of the unborn fetus to its life have found it necessary, out of deference to their own feelings in the matter, to allow an exception for ectopic pregnancy, and cases of the murder of the terminally ill can be described which meet with no objection whatever from any quarter.

And this does, I think, sufficiently show that, whether or not there is any moral law, and hence any real distinction between moral right and wrong, at least there is no one who actually believes this, in spite of what they profess. Or if such a person does exist anywhere, I at least have not seen him.

NOTES

1. Of course one may be morally responsible for his exemplary acts, too, but I have limited myself to wrong acts for simplicity.
2. *Leviathan,* Chapter XI.
3. This is one of the enduring points of Kantian ethics.
4. I believe Winston Churchill once conceded this to have been the chief incentive of his great career.
5. One should have in mind here tournament chess, not parlor chess.
6. See, for example, Deuteronomy 19.

16

A Modern Version of Hedonism

I have defined hedonism as any philosophy according to which pleasure is always good for its own sake, and the only thing that is good for its own sake. One who is by this definition a hedonist need not, of course, maintain that pleasure is the only thing that is good, for other things are good insofar as they are productive of pleasure. But this is goodness in a different sense, being the goodness of a means rather than of an end. However, pleasure is, according to this philosophy, the only thing that is good as an end, or the only thing sought, not as a means to something else, but for its own sake.

J. S. MILL'S HEDONISM

The moral philosophy of John Stuart Mill is by this criterion a philosophy of hedonism. Mill called it utilitarianism, emphasizing the importance he attached to the practical consequences of actions, and also no doubt because of the odious connotations of the word *hedonism* in the minds of his contemporaries. It is, nevertheless, a doctrine of hedonism, as defined here.

For Mill did explicitly declare that pleasure is always good for its own sake, and that nothing else is such. For the most part, he regarded this as so obvious as to require no argument, and he accordingly referred to it as an "ultimate principle." It is, he thought, precisely what all men mean by calling something good; namely, that it is pleasant, or conducive to pleasure. Furthermore, it is the only thing that men universally desire for its own sake, and it must, therefore, be desirable.

From *Good and Evil* (Buffalo, N.Y.: Prometheus Books, 1984), pp. 88–101.

Many philosophers have wondered whether this last observation does not in fact amount to a philosophical argument, and if so, whether it is a valid one; but we need not go into that. Mill's basic starting point is that pleasure is by its nature good, and that it is the only thing that is good for its own sake.

Mill made two significant departures from the hedonism of the ancients, however. First, he declared that pleasure and human happiness are one and the same thing. To say that a man is *happy* is to say, and to say nothing more, than that he is experiencing pleasure; to say that he is *unhappy* is to say nothing more than that he is experiencing pain. This equation of pleasure and happiness seems harmless enough at first but, as we shall see, its philosophical consequences are great.

His second departure, the consequences of which were even greater, was to declare that pleasure is good, no matter whose pleasure it is. The pleasure of your neighbor, or even of the most distant stranger, has precisely the same value as a similar pleasure of your own, and that value is absolute and unqualified. He seems to have regarded this as axiomatic. If pleasure is good by its very nature, then its goodness does not depend on where it is, or by whom it is experienced.

THE GREATEST HAPPINESS PRINCIPLE

This claim enabled Mill to formulate a principle of *duty* that, as we have seen, was quite foreign to the philosophy of the Epicureans. If pleasure is alone good by nature, then it is every man's duty to maximize it and to minimize pain; and this means to increase to the utmost the total amount of pleasure *in the world* and to reduce to the utmost the total amount of pain. Mill formulated this by saying that it is a man's obligation to promote the greatest happiness for the greatest number of people; but here we must remember, of course, that by happiness he means pleasure. Thus, where the hedonism of the Epicureans was entirely self-regarding, Mill's hedonism was a thoroughgoing altruism. The Epicureans were mostly concerned with the question "What should I do in order to achieve for myself a life of goodness?" But Mill's question was an entirely different one: "What should I do in order to do my duty?" And his answer was perfectly straightforward: "I shall do my duty if I increase the total amount of pleasure in the world and reduce the total amount of pain." Every act can be tested by this principle. Every act one performs either does, in comparison with the other acts one might have performed instead, tend more to produce that result, or it does not. If it does, then the action is right, or in accordance with duty. If it does not, then it is in one degree or another wrong, or contrary to what is required by duty.

These are the fundamental principles of Mill's hedonism, and his own elaboration of them consisted of devising replies to all the objections he could contrive, and then recommending these principles as a guide to legislation. We can pretty much disregard all this, because it is the fundamental principles that concern us. There are, however, two objections he deals with that we should consider, as they throw considerable light on the basic principles.

DUTY AND MOTIVE

We are accustomed to taking into account a man's *motives* when bestowing praise or blame for his conduct—that is to say, when trying to decide whether he has succeeded or failed in doing his duty. The question is not, most people think, simply a question of what someone has done; we need also to know what moved him to do as he did, what he was trying to do, or, in short, what his motive was. Kant, of course, had made this perfectly explicit, declaring that the consequences of a man's behavior do not even enter the picture in assessing the moral quality of his actions. So long as an agent is guided by a dutiful motive, Kant declared, then his action is possessed of true moral worth, which shines forth, he said, like a jewel, by its own light. And this remains so, according to Kant, even in case the consequences of such conduct are perfectly dreadful in terms of human happiness. Similarly, Kant declared, one's actions are without such moral worth in case they are not prompted by the sense of duty, even though their fruits, in terms of human happiness, should turn out to be bountiful. What counts is *why* one acts as he does, and not, what he happens to produce by his action.

Now Mill appears to say the opposite: namely, that a man performs his duty, in case his actions foster happiness in all who are affected by them, whether this was what the man was trying to accomplish or not. If a man saves another from drowning, Mill said, then it does not matter, so far as the worth of his action is concerned, whether his motive was to relieve the distress of a fellow human being, or to be paid for his trouble. It is in either case the same action, with the same consequences, and it has therefore the same moral value. A consideration of the rescuer's motive can only be relevant to evaluating, not his action, but his character as a man, which is an entirely different matter. Pressed on this point, Mill eventually began drawing distinctions between motives and purposes, thus yielding to his critics what they seemed to demand without appearing to abandon his basic position, but it is doubtful whether he succeeded. Whether a man's action is dutiful must surely be a function either of his motive, or of the actual consequences of his action. One cannot have it both ways, because it is a fact, which no philosophical argument or elaboration of distinctions can banish, that we do not always accomplish what we try to accomplish, and sometimes, quite accidentally, we produce results that are far indeed from what we were attempting. The road to hell, it is said, is sometimes paved with good intentions, and to this we can add that the road to heaven is sometimes paved with bad ones.

Perhaps what Mill should have done was follow the example of the Epicureans and abandon altogether the idea of moral duty. The Epicureans said, in effect: Let us set about making ourselves as happy as possible. Had Epicurus been asked: Do you think *that* is your duty? he would surely have dismissed the question as having no relevance to his program. I am not, he would surely have said, trying to discover what is my moral duty; I am trying to make myself happy, and here is how I propose to accomplish that end. Now Mill could surely have done much the same thing. What he was plainly saying in effect, was this: Let us set about making the whole world as happy as possible. When asked, do you think *that* is your duty, he surely could have dismissed the question as irrelevant, as it quite plainly was. The concept of duty is derived from religion and law, neither of which rests on any foundation of hedonism. There was, therefore, no need whatever for Mill to try to show that his hedonism incorporated the very concept of duty that men had inherited from these sources. Here one can hardly help noting that the Epicureans saw things in a much clearer light than did Mill. They said: Let us make our lives pleasant. They then proceeded to show, in useful ways, how this might be done. Mill in effect said: Let us make a happier world. But instead of then proceeding to show, in useful ways, how this might be done, instead of setting forth any significant program for the reformation of society to bring about this result, he labored for page after page to convince his readers of what plainly is not so: that hedonism is what all men believe anyway, that it is the very basis of Judeo-Christian morality, the basis of law, and that it incorporates perfectly the traditional concepts of duty derived from these sources.

THE QUALITY OF PLEASURE

The other serious objection Mill considered was this: If pleasure is alone the supreme good, the only thing good as an end, does it not follow that one would be better off being a satisfied pig than a dissatisfied Socrates? What this question is meant to suggest, of course, is that if pleasure is the only thing good as an end, then it can hardly matter from what source one's pleasure is derived. So long as one is feeling pleasure, then he has attained the ideal state of existence, whatever other goods he may lack; and, conversely, if one is not feeling pleasure, and is in fact perhaps feeling pain, then he has failed to achieve anything worthwhile for himself, no matter what else he may have. To assert that we should try to increase, to the maximum possible, the total amount of pleasure in the world, seems to suggest that we should convert the world into one vast amusement park, disregarding all those fruits of civilized life that men prize and replacing them with cheap and simple feelings of pleasure.

The Epicureans faced this problem by noting that pleasures differ in numberless ways. Some are more durable than others, some less admixed with pain, and so on. On the basis of such considerations they rejected the Cyrenaic way of life, not as morally inferior, but simply as less pleasant in the long run. Mill, however, took the extraordinary tack of declaring that some pleasures are inherently *better* than others. Thus, the pleasures of literature, art, and those, in general, that the Greeks had called pleasures of the mind, were declared by Mill to be superior in their goodness to such bodily pleasures as pigs and other animals are presumably, together with men, capable of experiencing. The pleasure of some idle and pointless amusement, for example, might indeed be a pleasure, and might even be a fairly intense one for some persons, but it is much inferior in its quality of goodness to, say, the pleasures of literature, even though these latter might be more feebly felt. Mill even proposed a test by which one can discriminate between these higher and lower pleasures. Consult the man who has experienced both, he said, and it will invariably be found that such a man gives his preference to the higher pleasures, rejecting those that are base. It is doubtful whether Mill meant this as an actual empirical test, however, for if one consulted such a man, and was then surprised by his choice of a baser pleasure in preference to one of the pleasures of the mind, this would, I think, only prove to Mill that the man was not, after all, a good judge.

This view of Mill's is, in any case, extraordinary. To say that pleasure is the supreme good, and the only thing good for its own sake, that it is the only thing that lends value to anything else that is good, and then to declare that some pleasures are intrinsically *better* than others, is quite obviously to appeal to some standard of goodness other than pleasure, some standard by means of which even pleasures can be evaluated as better and worse. The claim is just incoherent. It would be no worse to declare that some yardsticks are longer than others. Clearly, if one were to say this, it would imply that there is some standard yardstick in terms of which others could be measured and declared longer or shorter. Of course this might very well be true; but in that case, one could hardly declare that the original yardsticks, now variable in length, were nevertheless an ultimate standard of length. The hedonist cannot have it both ways. Either pleasure is the standard of goodness, or it is not. If it is not, if something other than pleasure is good for its own sake, then of course the basic principle of hedonism is false.

But if it is, if pleasure is the only thing good for its own sake and is the standard by which other things are deemed good, as hedonism declares, then no pleasures can be inherently better than others. Pleasures can in this case only differ in quantity, some being more intense than others, or more lasting, and so on; they cannot differ in their quality of goodness. This point was made long before Mill ever wrote about pleasure, for in one of Plato's dialogues[1] Callicles suggests the same point; namely, that some pleasures are better than others. At that point, Socrates declares, quite aptly, that Callicles is treating him like a child! The fallacy here is so obvious that Socrates thought only a child could be hoodwinked by it.

THE PRESUPPOSITIONS OF HEDONISM

It is appropriate now to take a closer look at the basic presuppositions of hedonism. There have, of course, been many other hedonists besides the Cyrenaics, Epicureans, and Mill, but we need not consider any of them. The samples of hedonism we have before us are adequate for the present purpose, for I want to consider the basic presuppositions of *any* hedonistic philosophy. These are (1) that pleasure is always good for its own sake and pain always bad, and (2) that pleasure is the only thing good for its own sake and pain the only thing bad in the same way. Both claims are essential to any philosophy of hedonism. For if (1), for example, should be false—if pleasure should sometimes not be good for its own sake—then, contrary to the fundamental injunction of hedonism, it would not always be wise or reasonable to pursue it. And if (2) should be false—if things other than pleasure should sometimes be good for their own sakes—then the same will follow. For it will sometimes be wise to pursue things other than pleasure; namely, whatever other things are good for their own sakes.

It should be emphasized again here what pleasure, or anything else, being good for its own sake or in itself means. It means that it is good, not merely as a means to some end, but as an end in itself. Thus, concerning most of the things in our environment that we deem to be good, such as food, shelter, the various tools that we use, and so on, we can ask: What are they good *for?* This means: To what *end* are they useful as instruments or means? And in the case of most such things there is usually an obvious answer. Food, for example, is useful for nourishment, shelter for comfort and warmth, and so on. Such things, then, are good, not for their own sakes, or in themselves, but as means to certain ends that are good. If we ask concerning pleasure, however, what it is good *for,* then the question appears to be out of place. Pleasure, it is generally thought, is something good in itself, even if it is not good as a means to anything else.

But now let us ask whether pleasure is, in this sense, always good for its own sake and pain always bad. Suppose that, after a hard day's toiling in the fields, one showers off the dust of his labor, satisfies his hunger and thirst, and collapses into a good bed, his limbs aching with fatigue. Now the bed feels good, and the feeling of what has been wrought, in case it was considerable, is good too. And what about the aching limbs? Might not that very aching, together with the prospect of awakening refreshed, be good too? Is it not something that adds to the total felt goodness of the situation, something that one would, in these conditions, rather have than lack? In short, might not these very aches and pains be felt as good, in the same sense, for example, that the warmth of the bed felt good? If so, then pain is not, contrary to the hedonist's presupposition, always in its very nature something bad.

Here the temptation will be to say that what would normally be aches and pains, and therefore bad, are in these circumstances pleasant and, hence, good. But if one says that, then it is important to note that he is using "pleasant" not as a description of a particular kind of feeling, but as a term of appraisal for any feeling or experience that is liked, and "pain" for any feeling or experience one happens to dislike. The hedonist's presupposition will in that case rest only on a definition or words, and no longer express any fact at all. It is, however, with something that is alleged to be a fact that we are concerned: with whether it is a fact that feelings of pleasure are always good in themselves and feelings of pain always bad.

THE DOUBLE MEANINGS OF PLEASURE AND PAIN

To see more clearly what is at issue here, let us note that the words *pleasure* and *pain*, or *pleasant* and *painful*, each have a double meaning or use. This is, once it is recognized, particularly evident in Mill's philosophy. The plausibility of hedonism will then be found to rest entirely on this ambiguity. For hedonism purports to rest on a fact of experience: There is something that is always found to be good in itself, and something else that is always found to be bad in itself—these being pleasure and pain, respectively; and that, moreover, nothing else in the world is good in itself, and nothing else in the world is bad in itself. Insofar as this philosophy has any plausibility, however, it rests on nothing more than a conventional usage of words: the convention of applying the word pleasant to any experience or feeling (whatever it may be) that one finds to be good in itself, and unpleasant or painful to any experience or feeling that one finds to be bad in a similar way.

Thus, the word *pleasure* is sometimes used as a *name* for a certain familiar sensation or feeling, one that might be described as tingling, for example. Such a feeling can often be induced by mild stimulation of the skin surface, sometimes by certain cadences of music, and the like. It can sometimes be localized, that is, one can sometimes, although not always, say where it is being felt, such as on the back, around the ears, and so forth. Some parts of the body are more susceptible to the feeling than others, of course, and in those parts of the body that lack certain nerve structures, such as the lungs, it cannot be felt at all. Such a feeling has a beginning and a waning, so that one can sometimes say approximately how long it is felt—for about thirty seconds, or three minutes, for example.

Pain, similarly, is sometimes used as a *name* for a certain familiar sensation or feeling, a feeling that might be described as throbbing, or piercing. Such a feeling can of course be produced in numberless ways—by piercing the skin surface, wrenching this or that part of the body, and so on. The feeling can also often be localized—in the head, the back, the foot, the tooth, or whatever—and like the kindred feeling of pleasure, it waxes and wanes, so that one can sometimes say not only where, but for approximately how long, it is felt. In those parts of the body lacking pain receptors it cannot be felt at all, of course.

This, then, I shall refer to as *sense one* of the word pleasure, and similarly, *sense one* of the word pain. In this sense, the words pleasure and pain serve as *names* for definite feelings.

In what I shall now call the *second* sense, however, pleasure and pain, or more usually their cognates pleasant and painful, are more than nominal. Indeed, pleasant is in this second sense applied to any experience or state one happens to find good, whether it includes any feelings of pleasure, in sense one, or not. Painful, in a similar way, is applied to any experience or state one happens to dislike, whether or not it is painful (includes pain) in the first sense of the term. Thus, one can speak of such very diverse things as a refreshing walk, the reading of a book, a trip abroad, and, so on, as pleasant, in this sense, or of an awkward social situation, a reverse in one's finances, or a difficult day's work, as unpleasant or painful. These words are, in such contexts as these, merely *terms of appraisal.* They are not at all the *names* of anything, much less are they names of particular feelings. They are merely ways of saying, of the experiences in question, that they are liked, or that they are disliked. Other terms of appraisal, having their own nuances of meaning, serve just as well; such as enjoyable, agreeable, boring, and tedious, for example. The most *general* of the appraisal terms, however, are simply *good* and *bad.*

Now it is perfectly obvious that something might be pleasant (enjoyable, agreeable) in the second sense, without involving any *pleasure,* in the first sense, whatsoever. Similarly, something might be painful, in this second sense, without involving any feelings of pain. One might quite truly describe an entire day as pleasant, for instance, without suggesting that one was, throughout that day or even any considerable part of it, experiencing those feelings for which the word pleasure has a name. Indeed, it would be perfectly congruous to so describe such a day, even though it contained no such feelings or sensations at all. To describe a day as *pleasant* is only to appraise one's experiences of that day as liked, enjoyed, or experienced as *good*.

Now let us look again at the basic presuppositions of hedonism. The first is that pleasure is always good for its own sake, and pain is always bad. Is this true in the *first* sense of pleasure and pain, the sense in which these words serve as the names of certain feelings? It *may* be that it is, but this is by no means obvious. The ache in one's limbs after a day of successful toil that I described previously is pain in the first sense, for example; but it is not obvious that, in the circumstances described, it is also painful, in the second sense, and therefore bad. One might feel it as good.

Is this presupposition true, then, in the *second* sense of pleasure and pain? That is, is it true in the sense in which pleasant and painful are not descriptions of feelings, but are instead simply terms of appraisal? Are things that are in this sense pleasant always and invariably found to be good, and are things that are in this sense painful always found to be bad? Well of course they are, but only because this is a tautology, that is, a way of saying the same thing twice over. If calling something pleasant is, in this sense, simply a way of appraising it as good, and calling something painful is just another way of expressing one's dislike for it (and thus appraising it as bad), then it plainly tells us nothing to affirm that pleasant experiences are always good and painful ones bad. This is a necessary "truth," only because it is an empty one.

What, then, of the second hedonistic presupposition; namely, that pleasure is the *only* thing in the world that is good in itself, and pain the only thing that is bad?

Well, if we take pleasure and pain in their first sense, as the names of certain identifiable feelings, then this claim is obviously not true. Ever so many things, besides feelings of pleasure, are good in themselves—namely, absolutely all those things that various men and at various times and places *find* to be good for their own sakes, or, in another way of saying the same thing, find to be pleasant in the second sense. The experience of being loved, for example, and of loving, or the experience of seeing the sun set, or the feeling of achievement, and so on, *endlessly*. The things that are good in themselves, or for their own sakes, must indeed be numberless, for they include absolutely everything that any man ever likes for its own sake; that is, all the things that are ever found to be good and are thus prized, not as means to still other things, but as good in themselves. And one should be most careful, at this point, not to be tempted into thinking that because we have a common term of appraisal for such agreeable experiences—namely, the word pleasant—we must after all be talking about just one thing, *pleasure*. For insofar as *pleasure* is the name of just one sort of thing—a certain familiar kind of feeling or sensation—then it is not a term of appraisal, and what it names, even though it is doubtless something good, is assuredly not uniquely so. Most men, moreover, would unhesitatingly deem it not terribly good anyway, something of fairly trivial value in comparison with other things that are prized for their own sakes.

What, then, of pleasure, in the second sense? Is this uniquely good for its own sake? Of course it is, but only, again, because this is a tautology. To describe something as a pleasure, in this sense, is only to describe it as pleasant, which is in turn only a way of appraising it as good for its own sake. So of course we can say of anything that is good for its own sake that it is pleasant—but this is, unfortunately, not to say anything at all.

PLEASURE AND HAPPINESS

The confusion just noted, once it has been appreciated, becomes particularly evident in Mill's system. For Mill says at the outset that by pleasure and happiness he means exactly the same thing. Now clearly, insofar as pleasure is a *name* for a particular kind of feeling—the kind of feeling one experiences when the surface of his skin is lightly massaged, for instance—then happiness is not another name for the same thing. A man may be perfectly happy even though he is experiencing no such sensations or feelings at all, or even if he experiences them but rarely. They are no significant ingredient of happiness for most men. What, then, is happiness? Essentially it is a certain state, which the Greeks called *eudaimonia,* or well-being. Probably no definition of it could be given, but some sort of description is possible. A man is usually (not always) happy, for example, when, in addition to being in good health and relatively free to pursue his own goals, his interests are flourishing and the objectives he has set for himself show promise of realization. This is very general, vague, and still inadequate, because happiness, or human well-being, is a very grand, vague, and general idea, and the conditions of it for different men are quite variable. The happiness of an aboriginal Australian is remote indeed from the happiness of a modern European, having nothing in common except that they are referred to by the same word and are found agreeable to their possessors.

Is happiness, then, uniquely good for its own sake, as Mill maintains? Doubtless it is, but it should be apparent by now how empty a claim this is. It amounts to no more than saying that human well-being is uniquely good for men, or that it *is* human well-being, and that nothing else is such. This, of course, tells us nothing. But Mill attempts to make the claim look like a significant one by identifying happiness with *pleasure.* To the extent that the claim is thus made significant, however, it is also made false—for it is not true that pleasure, in this sense, is the only thing good for its own sake, and it is doubtful whether it is even invariably good. Mill thus weaves his whole moral philosophy around a presupposition that is true, just to the extent that it says nothing. To the extent that it does say something, it is quite plainly false.

NOTE

1. Plato, *Gorgias.* W. C. Helmbold, trans. (New York: Liberal Arts Press, 1952), p. 72.

17

The Governance of the Kingdom of Darkness
A Philosophical Fable

> "Wherein may be discerned the true essence of moral depravity, or that which really does, like a cesspool, corrupt whatever comes under its influence as containing within itself all evil and ugliness."
>
> —DIODORUS CRONUS

It is rare, so rare that no reliable way of coping with it has even yet been evolved, that the office of Prince of Darkness becomes vacant, and the awesome title of Satan must then be bestowed anew upon some candidate chosen from the denizens of Hell.

Lucifer, the first Ruler of Darkness, who was an imperious and exemplary Devil, held sway over the underworld for nearly fourteen thousand years, and it was widely supposed that his tenure of office would be everlasting. There was, therefore, great consternation and amazement in Hell when God, out of his infinite grace, suddenly and without forewarning extended salvation even to Lucifer, restored him to his place in the celestial hierarchy of the angels, and thereby created a vacuum at the summit of the ranks of Hell. Many had come to think that there can be only one supremely wicked being, and that this one's place in the scheme of things was as secure as that of evil itself; but these had to face up to the fact that, this one having departed, there was no longer even one, and a new Prince of Darkness would have to be found.

From *Southern Journal of Philosophy* 9 (1971): 113-118. Reprinted by permission of the publisher.

The first time this emergency was faced the method of popular election was hit upon as the best means of choice. It was thought that this would minimize bias and favoritism, in that the diverse prejudices of the damned would cancel each other out instead, as in fact happened, of augmenting each other. Of course, this was only rationalization, for the true reason for such an inept method of choice was the lack of any really clear criterion of moral depravity. Everyone supposed that this could be supplied by his neighbors.

The democratic method did, in any case, work singularly badly, for the hosts of the damned chose as their Prince one of their number whose wickedness could sometimes be viewed as positively endearing. He had, in his earthly life, been an uncommonly successful jewel thief, having stolen nearly two million dollars worth of gems and baubles from rich ladies without ever spending a day in jail, and before he finally went to Hell he was the most sought after criminal on the face of the globe.

It is needless to say that this fellow cut a very poor figure as Head Devil, and there were some who wondered whether he even belonged in Hell to begin with, in spite of his bad reputation on earth. On more than one occasion he was discovered doing things that bore unmistakable resemblance to virtuous action, and this evoked great uneasiness among his subjects. Thus he was seen tenderly assisting an unregenerate woman who had been nearly overcome by sulphur soon after arriving in Hell. She had borne a bastard child on earth and, dying in childbirth, had of course been banished to Hell. Now the Devil, in rescuing her from the brimstone fumes, claimed that he was only trying to ensure that she would survive to absorb all the pains that were in store for her; but this was not entirely believed. Outwardly, at least, his action had an unmistakable semblance of kindness—and there were other similar instances, which occasioned much misgiving.

This problem was solved, however, in the very manner in which it had been created in the first place; for this second Prince of Darkness was suddenly, like Lucifer, restored to the celestial hierarchy, through the infinite grace of the Almighty, almost before his reign could get started, he having then officially ruled only two hundred and fifty-six years.

To choose the successor to this inept Satan, and to minimize the likelihood of reproducing the embarrassments that his particular style had occasioned, a committee was chosen—or, rather, appointed itself, for there was no semblance of democratic procedure in the manner of its coming into being. This committee, composed of Belial, Beelzebub, and others of the most distinguished of the fallen angels, called itself the Council of Evil, and resolved to find someone who surpassed all others in genuine moral evil, applying this sole criterion with absolute rigor. The choice would be made, they declared, not on the basis of any specious claims, but only the single consideration of total moral depravity.

The field of candidates was eventually narrowed to six, of whom two were eliminated after only cursory consideration. One of these had been a consummate swindler, the other a corrupt politician, and the vices of neither seemed sufficiently distinctive to entitle their possessors to the greatest respect in Hell. Of the four remaining, one was finally chosen, and the wisdom of the choice has now been wholly vindicated for the moral evil of this Prince is so pure and undefiled by any goodness that not only does he still hold sway over Hell, after these four millenia, but his status continuously increases, attesting to the plenitude of his depravity.

The four finalists and their credentials were as follows.

The first candidate: Adama.

There was profound shock and shaking of heads when it was learned that one of the candidates under serious consideration was female, and would accordingly, if chosen, need to be called Princess of Darkness. Such an appellative seemed wholly inappropriate and even comic, the word "Princess" conjuring in the imagination qualities the very opposite of what could be associated with darkness and evil. Still, it was pointed out that throughout history far more evil had been wrought by women than men, that recognition of this was deserved, and that only arrogance and a jealousy of titles could blind men to the propriety of feminine rule. Such considerations seemed unanswerable, and so in view of what appeared to be the most obvious single qualification, Adama, a female candidate, gained considerable support.

Adama hardly resembled any popular conception of a devil, temptress, or other embodiment of evil. Dowdy in appearance and manner, she conveyed more the impression of a washerwoman. Nevertheless, she had the distinction of having destroyed more people than anyone who had ever walked on the face of the earth, having in her short lifetime caused the deaths of nearly nine-tenths of the inhabitants of two continents. She had, to be sure, never really intended anyone's death, but at the same time she made no effort to avoid spreading sickness and death wherever she went. For Adama, though seemingly in robust health herself, was the carrier of a plague which, once it gained the smallest foothold any place, at once spread like fire over dry weeds, engulfing whole nations. Adama knew this, and thus knew her role in the sorrow and death that spread itself over the land wherever she set foot, but others did not, and it was generally believed that the plagues to which Adama had such remarkable immunity were visited upon men by demons. Adama's knowledge of what she was doing produced in her no desire to limit her movement and thus reduce her threat to the general well-being, however. On the contrary, having all her life cared nothing for others, and having never cared whether any other person lived or died, she went about things exactly as she always had, according to her own convenience, grateful that she was herself spared the effects of the plague she so effectively distributed, but otherwise oblivious to her unusual condition. Thus when she decided to visit a relative she had never seen, she did not hesitate to take the simplest and shortest route to where this person lived, through the most densely populated area of the earth. The result was a staggering decimation of the population, only a few hundred besides Adama being miraculously spared; but she had expected as much, from her previous experience. It was not exactly what she had desired, but at the same time it was no personal loss to herself, as the extra day or two for the more roundabout journey would have been.

Adama finally died, was of course sent to Hell, and there her hopes were quickly kindled by the political developments already described. Murder, she pointed out, was everywhere considered the most flagitious of sins, and her claim to be supremely wicked thus appeared incontestable. Her opponents tried to draw metaphysical distinctions between murdering and causing to die, but these seemed too subtle to alter the overwhelming fact of Adama's monstrous achievement.

The second candidate: Bazel.

Bazel had during his life on earth been an executioner. Of course this was in itself no special distinction, for executioners arrive in Hell with such regularity and in such numbers that it is difficult to find any distinction for them at all. Bazel, however, was able to present himself as a rather special case. He had not merely, like most executioners, hanged men from time to time as a sideline to his proprietorship of a bar or trade as a plumber. Bazel had in the relatively brief span of just eleven years, four months and sixteen days managed to execute a staggering number of men, women and children, most of them the inhabitants of recently conquered territories. By his own reckoning he had processed 1,245,308 persons, and he felt certain the figure was accurate within a couple of hundred, plus or minus. This he had done by gassing them in airtight compounds. After only eighteen months of this rather demanding work he had devised ways of increasing his output by nearly thirty percent, without any significant increase in cost of materials, through a cleverly contrived method of packing the specimens into the compounds. Subsequent improvements over the years had enabled him nearly to double his output over the original two hundred or so per day. He had been diligent, too, for while he was obligated by his contract to work only eight hours a day plus a maximum of two hours overtime, at overtime pay, he seldom worked less than twelve in any one day, from devotion to his work, and on a few occasions he kept at it nearly twenty hours at a stretch, clearing away much accumulated backlog. At the conclusion of his tenth year of government service he received a special tribute, which amounted to a modest testimonial dinner and the awarding of a gold watch, inscribed with the record of his service to date. When he was finally dropped, as a result of military reversals abroad and political misfortunes at home, he was tolerably well-to-do, and a rough computation showed that he had averaged about eleven cents for each person dispatched, most of which he had managed to save. He spent his declining years comfortably in a foreign land, protected from his enemies who had never conceded the legitimacy of his vocation, and once granted an interview to a lifelong friend and journalist. In the interview he said, among other things, that he had never harbored any hatred or ill will toward any human being, had never so much as slapped a child or teased a cat, and had always been conscientious in the performance of such tasks as fell to him to perform. He was, as he looked back on things, sometimes astonished at what he had wrought, but he had not thought much of it at the time. He thought it illustrated how, with regular industry day by day, one can in a fair measure of time achieve a genuinely significant total result, and it seemed to him that this lesson was not being sufficiently imparted to the younger generation.

Armed with figures that not even the most decorated bomber pilots could hope to match, Bazel presented himself as candidate for the ruler of Hell. Adama's total figures were, he conceded, far higher, but he argued that her achievements were essentially accidental, resulting from biology rather than true character, whereas his were the product of determination, effort, and devotion to duty.

The third candidate: Calpon.

This candidate was at first unwilling to challenge the candidacy of Bazel, but he eventually convinced himself that he might in fact be the better qualified of the two. Bazel, he decided, was only parading figures to dazzle the Council of Evil and to cover up a considerable deficiency of true baseness. Bazel was, Calpon maintained, entirely motivated by the desires to please his employers and enhance his position in the community, motives which are perfectly commonplace and hardly entitle anyone to any distinction in the area of moral depravity. Bazel was in fact hardly more than a pest control officer, Calpon claimed, and went about his work in about the same way as any other, the single difference being in the species of pest he was hired to eradicate.

Calpon, too, was an executioner, though he had to pursue this calling on his own, in the face of much discouragement and without government support. Calpon belonged to a group of police officers in a small and corrupt country who had taken it upon themselves to do what they could, when off duty, to rid their society of the criminal element, as well as of beggars and similar undesirables. It was, they had found, of little use bringing criminals to justice by traditional means. More often than not they were freed, from lack of evidence against them, and just returned to their criminal pursuits—picking pockets, stealing, smuggling, and so on.

So Calpon and his associates—seven of them altogether—formed themselves into a death squad, and as soon as they heard of anyone being engaged in criminal activity, arranged to eliminate him. They first arrested him, and if no relative or other person inquired of his whereabouts in the next several weeks, and no attorney came forth to ask questions, they removed him from the jail, drove him to some desolate spot, and there disposed of him with knives or guns. Sometimes several were dealt with at once, occasionally as many as five or six. Calpon's role in this operation was somewhat unique, for he had no interest at all in combating crime. He belonged to the group simply because he happened to love the sight of blood, particularly blood flowing from wounds which he had inflicted. It gave him an intense pleasure, akin to but far greater than sexual excitation, he said, to see blood pour forth "like an opening rose." He thus came to be nicknamed "The Rose," and it was always he who was permitted to begin the work, either with gun or knife. He always selected a non-vital spot so he could watch the blood flow unhindered and as long as possible, becoming absorbed at these times in something of a trance. It was quite plainly the most intense joy he could experience. Once, when asked why he held such a hatred for criminals, he protested that he had no hatred for them at all. It was simply that he enjoyed the sight of human suffering, at close range, and that the animal slaughter houses in which he had found such pleasure as a boy had lost their charms for him. He enjoyed drawing blood from criminals, gypsies, beggars and other useless persons only because these happened to be the only people available for this purpose, at least without very great risk. Nor, he declared, did he kill for payment, for he had in fact never been paid for his work with the death squad, doing it all on his own time.

Thus did Calpon lay claim to the office of Prince, not because he had murdered in such staggering numbers as Bazel (he had in fact helped to kill only sixty-three persons) but because, unlike Bazel, he murdered for fun rather than as a means to an honest living.

The fourth candidate: Deprov.

It never occured to Deprov to compete for the office of Prince, nor did he ever understand why others had wanted to put his name before the Council of Evil. It must, he thought, be some malicious person's idea of a joke. Indeed, Deprov had never understood why he had found himself in Hell in the first place, and always insisted that there had been some ghastly mistake, some confusion of identities.

For Deprov had in fact led a perfectly law-abiding and blameless life, and when he had died, full of years, his record was as clean as when he was born. He had never so much as received a summons for a motor vehicle violation or a delinquent tax payment. He had a dreadful fear and respect for the police and all the forces of law, and felt a deep shame at the mere thought of his integrity being challenged in any way.

Deprov was, to be sure, cruel by nature, but this always expressed itself in acceptable ways within the framework of laws and conventional rules. He had never assaulted anyone in his life. He indulged his ever present cruelty only upon animals, and upon his fellow men only in permissible ways. Thus, when one day he came upon a beautiful young girl sitting in the park, looking disconsolate, he was struck with astonishment to discover that one entire side of her face, the side he had not approached and therefore not at first seen, was horribly discolored and disfigured, apparently from dreadful burns received long ago. Unnoticed, he took several instant pictures of her, from that side, and, with deep satisfaction spread across his face, presented all three to her at once, while she, dumbfounded, stared back at him in blank, unthinking horror. He had, he later said, only taken pictures, and had not tried to make anything seem different from what it really was, thus displaying a respect for truth. On another occasion, seeing the village drunk urinating in the public square, Deprov sought out this man's children and, finding them with numerous playmates on the swings on the playground, loudly announced to them their father's condition, and urged them to fetch their mother before he disgraced them still further. It was, he said, the most effective way of dealing with men of that sort, and children, as well as anyone else, are deserving of truth.

Deprov, along with his reverence for truth, had also a deep respect for law and morality, not only in the sense that he willingly and indeed eagerly guided his own steps within their straight and narrow path, but did whatever he could do to ensure that others did so as well. He regularly strolled about the town evenings, noting the comings and goings of his neighbors, and drawing such inferences as he could concerning their purposes. He was generally rewarded with at least some opportunity to correct large or small transgressions which, had it not been for him, might never have been detected at all. Thus when he found a dog whose owner, the village garbage collector, was well known to him, wandering about the town in violation of ordinance, he carefully amputated all the dog's toes. That dog, he reflected, would never walk again, and its owner would perhaps see that his animals were properly tethered or fenced after this. Again, when he discovered that the local barmaid (in fact a middle-aged divorcee) was spending every night, after work, in the rooming house quarters of the school janitor, who was a black man, he arranged to have the rooms raided by the police and a charge of adultery entered against both of them, and he arranged also for local newspaper coverage of the raid, for it seemed to him that everyone and especially the young would benefit from a dramatic arrest.

Deprov thus acquired a reputation as the sternest defender of law and morality in the county. After one of his more dramatic lessons on the futility of irregular behavior, administered to an ancient, toothless beggar who appeared in the streets one day, he was asked by the local doctor, who had known him for many years, why it was that he seemed to enjoy tormenting the lonely, the sick, and the brokenhearted. Deprov with real astonishment protested that he could never *enjoy* anything of the sort, and that, on the contrary, he had often foregone genuine pleasures and enjoyments in pressing his crusade for truth, law, and morality. A considerable part of his life, he accurately noted, was devoted to this, when he could, easily and without reproof, be spending his time in numberless entertainments and amusements, which he was as capable of enjoying as anyone.

It was thus mystifying to him that he, Deprov, should through some incredible misconception be represented as an *evil* man, when it was well known that he had spent his earthly life combating wickedness; and the more mystifying and astonishing when he viewed, with strenuously suppressed envy, the careers of Adama, Bazel, and Calpon, and their clear qualifications for Satanic governance. Yet certain friends who claimed to know him well thought it worthwhile to present his name along with a dossier of his achievements which, though filled mostly with trivia and the most banal of episodes, turned out to be the bulkiest dossier the Council of Evil had received.

18

The Virtue of Pride

We shall now illustrate, in a limited way, what we have called the ethics of aspiration, using *pride* as the example. We could consider different and doubtless more significant virtues, but this one is particularly appropriate because it is so neglected. In fact we have, for about two thousand years, been taught not even to regard it as a virtue, except perhaps in a very limited way. Pride is quite correctly perceived to be incompatible with the egalitarianism that we are so constantly admonished to uphold, as with the supposed virtue of humility that is so congenial to the devout mind and so foreign to the pagan temperament.

THE NATURE OF PRIDE

Pride is not a matter of manners or demeanor. One does not become proud simply by affecting certain behavior or projecting an impression that has been formed in the mind. It is a personal excellence much deeper than this. In fact it is the summation of most of the other virtues, since it presupposes them.

Pride is the justified love for oneself. The disqualification "justified" is crucial. Simpletons can love themselves and are, in fact, very apt to do so; but they are not proud, for there are no equalities of excellence to justify that love. They have not pride but mere conceit, which is something different altogether. Conceit is the simpleton's unwarranted sense of self-importance. Conceited persons thus imagine themselves as possessed of great worth, when in fact they have little or none; and that is why they are simple, as well as being very tiresome to others and of little worth in the eyes of those who are genuinely proud.

Genuinely proud people perceive themselves as better than others, and their pride is justified because their perception is correct. Thus they love themselves, not as children and ordinary people do, for these do not possess the kind of worth that justifies such self-esteem, but because they really are, in the classical sense of the term, good. Their virtues are not assimilated ones, nor do they consist merely in the kind of innocence that wins the approbation of others. Instead, they are their own in the truest sense: that they come from within themselves and win the approbation of the only judge who counts—oneself.

ARROGANCE, VANITY, AND EGOISM

Pride is not arrogance, and a proud person would never be overbearing towards others. While conceit is an attitude towards oneself, which in that respect resembles pride, arrogance is a way of behaving, a mannerism, and one that is profoundly offensive. One is arrogant only towards other persons. Arrogance cannot be exhibited in solitude, although conceit can—in vainglorious fantasy, for example, or at the other extreme, in solitary weeping.

Arrogance implies a belittling of opinions, conduct, or personal qualities of another person in an effort to draw attention to one's own presumed superiority. It is, therefore, most easily exhibited towards persons who stand in an inferior position, such as waiters or other servants, employees, clerks, and so on. Police officers, particularly those who are vulgar or otherwise lacking in personal excellence, are very prone to arrogance, for one's inferior position cannot be more manifest than in the presence of a police officer's gun. It is for this same reason that cowards, given suitable circumstances, are likely to be arrogant. Since the fault that cancels their personal worth, namely cowardice, is so grave and ineradicable, they attempt to compensate with arrogance and browbeating or, given the opportunity, outright cruelty.

Vanity and egoism, too, must be distinguished from pride, for they have little in common with it. Vanity is the delight people derive from praise or flattering allusions to themselves, from whatever source, and with respect to whatever things are alluded to, whether significant or not. Thus vain people delight in flattering comment from inferior persons, such as from children, or even from total strangers, whereas a truly proud person would be quite oblivious to this. Vain people can even be seen trying to elicit attention and admiring comment in public places, and from persons entirely unknown to them, by their loud and excessive laughter, for example, or their swaggering gait, or by their attire, or by the importance or beauty of their companions. Thus a man sometimes enjoys entering a restaurant with a beautiful companion on his arm, even though he may never have been there before and may know no one in the room. Similarly, a woman is sometimes pleased to draw looks, even from strangers, to her tasteful clothing. Such are familiar examples of vanity, and they could be multiplied at length. It is something to which every normal person is prone, for who can fail to be pleasantly aware of the admiring attention of others? A vain person, however, seeks that attention, sometimes going to great length to get it, while a proud person tries to ignore it, and would be ashamed to actually set about trying to elicit it. This would be especially true with respect to such things as clothing, or the influence one has over other people or external things, in other words, things having no connection with one's true nature or excellence.

Egoism is similar to vanity, though perhaps some distinctions between the two are useful. Egoism is a certain cast of mind, characterized by excessive absorption in oneself, to the extent that one's awareness of others is clouded. Vanity, as noted, is the delight evoked by the favorable attention of others, quite regardless of what qualities elicit such attention. Thus egoism may be more characteristic of men, and vanity of women, though of course such broad generalizations are not without many exceptions. Men do often tend to be absorbed in themselves to the detriment of their awareness of others, seeing these others as instruments to the pursuit of their own goals. This is perhaps an expression of the male concern for power and influence. Women, on the other hand, are sometimes more concerned to be "attractive," something which has very much to do with appearance. And the lesser self-absorption on the part of women may explain, to some extent at least, their sometimes greater awareness of the feelings of others; these others might include children and animals, and this awareness sometimes rises to genuine compassion. To be sure, men are also capable of this, but there seem to be differences of degree.

Neither vanity nor egoism is very compatible with genuine pride, even though no one can hope or pretend to be entirely without them. While vain people delight in others' admiration for things they *have*—possessions, for instance—proud people have little interest in the admiration of others except for what they *are;* and even that admiration must come only from such persons, always relatively few, who are themselves proud people, in the truest sense, and hence better. Thus, while no one would want to be poor, a proud person does not mind being erroneously thought to be poor. A person of excessive vanity or egoism, on the other hand, tries very hard to create the impression of affluence even when that is a false impression, something a proud person would not think of doing. Vain or self-centered persons live beyond their means, or spend what limited resources they have on things that will be seen by others—cars, house furnishings, clothing, and so on. Such persons thus try to compensate for their limitations as persons by augmenting those things that are external to themselves and their characters. One who is quite stupid, for example, tries to compensate with a showy car or house; or one who fears danger or dreads death tries to compensate with excessive but insincere affability. They try, in other words, to be *thought* good, in the original, nonmoral sense of that term, when in fact they are not.

PRIDE AND SELF-APPROBATION

Proud people are not much concerned with what others think of them and care nothing at all for the opinions of insignificant persons, but are instead concerned with what they think of themselves. Others know you for what you appear to be, which can be misleading, but you know yourself for what you are—at least, you are in a privileged position to. If it is you who are ignorant, or silly, or weak-willed, or fearful, or vain, then, however well you may succeed in concealing these faults from others, you cannot entirely conceal them from yourself unless you are very stupid. And for this reason proud people would not try to conceal themselves from themselves nor have any reason to, regardless of how little they care about the opinions of others. For proud people, as noted, are those who *justifiably* love themselves, that is, who have a high *and correct* opinion of their real worth. They therefore do not compare themselves with others with respect to things that are extraneous to themselves. For example, they do not compare their possessions with those of their neighbors or associates, or if they happen to be aware that what they own far exceeds what their neighbors own, they do not let on to this. Instead, they compare themselves only with the best. They are properly ashamed if others are wiser than they, or if others conduct their lives with better order and rationality, or if others have greater courage and self-discipline. Similarly, their envy is reserved, not for those who are praised by the multitude, for whatever reason, but for those whose honor is deserved and is bestowed only by the best.

Proud people do not bow to any others, except in such purely ceremonious ways as tipping their hats; nor are they deferential to persons of special status or rank, such as those holding high offices, or persons who are wealthy, or persons of a special and conspicuous class, such as priests—with the exception, once again, of purely ceremonious gestures of deference, such as the use of "sir" and "ma'am" in addressing them. The most conspicuous exception to these generalizations is old people who have grown wise with their years. Such persons are truly venerable, and pride is never compromised by treating them as such. The experience of years, quite by itself, may confer wisdom, and nothing is more deserving of honor than this; so it is not inappropriate that others, aspiring to wisdom, should bow to those who have won it.

THE MARKS OF PRIDE

Pride is seen in things both great and small. One of the greatest, for example, is the individual's response to acute danger, or his or her reaction to a life-threatening disease or to humiliation at the hands of enemies. One type of person bears such things with a natural, unpracticed fortitude and nobility, while, at the other extreme, some collapse into whimpering and self-pity. With respect to death, a proud person knows that even his or her own life is not worth clinging to at the cost of pride or honor; would never want it prolonged beyond the point where the virtues upon which pride rests have become debilitated; and would, for this reason, prefer to die ten years too soon than ten days too late.

And there are other great tests, such as one's reaction to the death of a son or daughter who was intelligent, and strong, and filled with promise of great achievement.

But such things as these are negative, being tests of strength in adversity. There are great positive tests as well: the power one displays in writing and speech, sensitivity to music and other things of great beauty, and perhaps above all else, one's own creative power. Whether you follow experience and reason to form your beliefs on either great or petty matters, or whether, on the other hand, you simply embrace whatever opinions answer to your fondest desires, this, as well as any other test, distinguishes a wise and proud person from a vain and foolish one. Thus people who are given to ideologies and faiths, that is, to large and untested claims that they find satisfying and reassuring, are not wise and cannot therefore be proud; for whatever love they may have for themselves can hardly be justified. On the other hand, those who accept even unpleasant facts because they are facts, or do not shrink from drawing appropriate inferences from what they observe, even when these facts or observations may run counter to everything they have been taught and everything they desperately hope is true, such persons are wise, whether learned or not, and have at least one correct basis for self-approbation. If, in addition, they are learned, then they have still another. And if, in addition to those qualities, they are creative, self-disciplined, and courageous, then they have still others; and there comes a point where external things which contribute nothing to those qualities are clearly seen by them to be worth very little, however much they may delight simple people.

But there are also, as noted, lesser marks of pride, easily recognized by other proud persons, though not understood by the meek and foolish. A proud person is, for example, serious, but not solemn, whereas a meek person's effort to be serious results only in a laughable solemnity. Such a person puts on a grave face and a reserved manner and imagines that he or she has become serious. Hearty laughter and the enjoyment of life are compatible with seriousnesss, which is positive and affirmative, but not with mere solemnity, which is negative and withdrawn. Again, a proud person is not garrulous and does not speak merely for the sake of "making conversation" or of hearing words flow. On matters not worthy of comment—such as weather, minor political issues, or things in the immediate surroundings—proud people normally say nothing at all. They do not mind long periods of dead silence, feel no embarrassment or anxiety at this, nor any need to break such silence with idle observations, except when silence would be interpreted as rudeness. Proud people delight in the company of other proud and worthwhile persons, and seek above all to discover and appreciate their strengths and virtues. Their awareness of those is not clouded by self-absorption, nor by any desire to project a good impression of themselves; for they know that their own excellences will be recognized by others of similar excellence and do not care if they are not seen by those who lack this.

One category of behavior which is sometimes erroneously associated with pride is the fastidious observance of what is called etiquette. Etiquette comprises the many rules of social intercourse, often petty in nature, which enable people to associate comfortably in special circumstances such as social gatherings. These rules are often important in preventing embarrassment and awkwardness, but they have almost nothing to do with pride and can sometimes even work against it. Thus, proud people are not ashamed to whistle in public places where such behavior is harmless though uncommon, nor do they mind wearing old or baggy clothing, for example, if that is their taste. Etiquette, by its very nature, encourages a kind of mindless conformity, whereas those who are proud conform their behavior to standards which are their own.

A proud person does not pretend to an insincere equality with others who are inferior, that is, who are meek, foolish, or silly. A person is not worthy of esteem just by the fact of being a person but, rather, by the fact of being a person of outstanding worth, which is something quite rare.

The Place of Externals

Among the lesser marks of pride are also those things that moralists once referred to as "externals," meaning by this all those things that are extraneous to what a person inherently is. Dress, for instance, is an external thing, as are one's reputation and standing in the popular mind, the praise or honors one receives from small-minded people, and so on.

Thus, with respect to dress, proud people do not ask what others expect of them, or how they wish them to look, and the least consideration in their minds is how *others* dress. They ask instead what will please themselves. It is compatible with perfect and beautiful pride never to wear a suit or necktie, to dress in baggy trousers and sweat shirt and cheap shoes. This description fits the appearance of one of the proudest persons of our century, Albert Einstein, whose almost superhuman virtues were combined with a boundless compassion and sweetness. But let it be added that affectation in dress, or the deliberate attempt to be outlandish and to attract the attention of others, is not pride but, as noted before, vanity. For again, the good opinion that one should seek is one's own, not others', and certainly not that of strangers.

PRIDE AND MORALITY

With respect to what is popularly called "morality," a proud person is in the best sense the creator of his or her own. Nothing is done *merely* because it is recommended and done by others. Rather, something is done because *he* or *she* sees it as worthy of being done, and especially because it is worthy of himself or herself. Thus a proud person would not injure or betray a friend, not because it would be "wrong," or would violate vulgar morality, but because it would be shameful. Nor would a proud person cheat or take dishonest advantage of anyone, again, not because it would be wrong, but because it would be incompatible with his or her own worth. To act otherwise would imply that there are external things that are of greater importance than one's own excellence, which would be totally inconsistent with pride. But perhaps the clearest indication of the ethics of pride is found in those situations for which popular morality has no clear rules. Consider, for example, the finding of things whose ownership is uncertain, or for which no owner can be determined at all. Thus, for example, if money or other valuables are found on the ground, a proud person does not hesitate to take them; but such a person could not be imagined seeing someone drop these things and then picking them up unless, of course, to restore them to the person who dropped them. The reason for such behavior does not rest upon any common notion of theft but on one's own clear notion of honor. But perhaps the best illustration of all is found in the opportunity to take money or other valuables from a corpse. These things, in the nature of the case, do not belong to anyone (assuming no surviving kin) and are thus, for all practical purposes, simply found. There is no clear rule of popular morality covering such a situation, for it is of rare occurrence, never occurring at all in the lives of most people. Yet a proud person would not have the slightest inclination to do such a thing, and for a reason that is overwhelming and conclusive, namely that such an act would be shameful. It is not shameful in the sense that we have been taught to regard it as such, for little has ever been said on such infrequent things. Rather, it is shameful in the true sense of the word, as being incompatible with one's own worth as a person, a worth that is possessed only by the proud. To be sure, this does leave humble persons with little incentive for personal honor, but that is not an untoward consequence, for such persons have little of this incentive anyway. They can be cajoled to decency by others, or compelled by laws and morality, but a genuinely proud person is cajoled to nothing at all by others, and is law-abiding and moral only as a condition of civilized life. Someone possessed of personal excellence requires more than morality for a life that is, in its true and original sense, good.

Such (in outline and with much omitted) is the virtue of pride. It is not the only virtue, nor even the highest, that being, without doubt, wisdom; but it is nevertheless, in the sense that was explained, a kind of summation of the virtues.

It is also a specimen of aspiration, which cannot be proved to be worth having. But in this area little can be proved anyway. We are dealing not with things that are true, in the usual sense, but with things that are good, in the philosophical sense. And as to the question whether this or any other virtue is worth having and worth giving a great deal to have, one has, of course, to find the answer within oneself. Conduct can sometimes be forced upon one, but virtue can only be discovered.

19

Happiness

Underlying all the moral philosophy of the ancients were two questions: What is happiness? And how is it attained? Those are the questions to which we now, finally, turn.

Happiness has to be the basic concern of all ethics, for if human beings had no capacity for it and for its opposite, there would be no point in reflecting about ethics at all. This was so obvious to the ancients that it seemed to them to need no defense. All these classical moralists justified their systems, finally, by claiming that the ideals they portrayed were the ingredients of a happy life. Even Plato felt the need to justify the austere lives of the guardians of his republic by claiming that they were, notwithstanding appearances, happy, and he recognized the suggestion that they were not as a possibly fatal criticism. The Stoics, too, in spite of their unbending rectitude and the severity of their principles, maintained that their ideal life of reason and self-denial was the only genuinely happy one.

The idea of happiness is no less essential to modern moral philosophy than to the ancient systems, even though it is now more apt to be taken for granted than treated as a difficult and profoundly important idea in its own right. The role of happiness in determining questions of moral right and wrong is generally acknowledged, but then attention is forthwith focused not on the nature of happiness, but upon the distinction of right and wrong. Still, no philosopher could consider his theories tenable if he were compelled to admit that the application of them to human affairs would inevitably promote misery. Even those who reject hedonism, and the various forms of utilitarianism, would find it hard to render their views plausible if they had to assume that

---

From *Ethics, Faith and Reason* (Englewood Cliffs, N.J.: Prentice-Hall, Inc., 1985), pp. 107–122.

human beings have no more capacity for happiness than unfeeling stones. However one approaches ethics—whether from the ancient standpoint of virtue, or the modern one of duty, or from any other—what one finally asserts has to be something that makes a difference and this, in the last analysis, must be a difference with respect to human happiness. Otherwise, what is said will be simply pointless.

THE NATURE OF HAPPINESS

However much the ancient schools differed in their various conceptions of happiness, they were agreed about its importance. Their word for it, *eudaimonia,* is not even adequately translatable into English. It usually comes out, in translation, as "happiness," but not without loss. Something like "fullfillment" would in some ways be better, but we shall stay with happiness, keeping in mind its shortcomings.

Eudaimonia means, literally, to be possessed of a good demon, and this conveys the idea of extreme good fortune on the part of its possessor. One possessed of *eudaimonia* was thought of by the ancients as blessed beyond measure, as having won something of supreme worth and, at the same time, something very elusive and hence rare. Just what it *is* was seldom clear, even in the minds of the greatest moralists, but there was no doubt at all of its importance and value. To discover the nature of this *eudaimonia* and the path to its attainment seemed to many great moralists of that age to be the main task of philosophy.

Most people seem to think they know what happiness is, which is unfortunate, for this prevents them from learning. One has no incentive to inquire into what one thinks one already knows. In fact, however, there seem to be few things more infected with error and false notions than people's ideas of happiness. It is very common for people, in their ill-considered quest for personal happiness, to spend their lives pursuing some specious ideal—such as the accumulation of wealth—and then, having succeeded, to miss the happiness erroneously identified with it. Of course people are reluctant to come to terms with their own illusions, and few who have wasted their lives are very willing to admit it even to themselves; but their failure is often quite obvious to others. We tend to be tolerant of error here, for its only victims are the possessors of it. Another person's dashed expectations seldom threaten our own. And we are therefore content to suppose that if someone seems to himself or herself to be happy, perhaps he or she really is happy after all. But one can see how shallow this is by asking whether one would really wish to *be* that other person. It is hard to see why not, if that other person is believed to be truly happy. But we know, in fact, that such persons are not; they only seem so to themselves, largely because they are unwilling to admit their own folly.

It was from reflections such as these that ancient moralists were fond of quoting Solon, to the effect that no man should be deemed happy until he is dead (for example, Aristotle, *Nicomachean Ethics,* Bk. 1, Ch. 10). This paradoxical remark seems to suggest the dead are more happy than the living, but that is not what is meant at all. The point is, rather, that the search for happiness is the task of a lifetime and that it can elude one, even at the last moment. And indeed, it does elude most persons, even those who thought they were on the track of it.

It will be best to begin, then, by citing a few of the things that are most commonly confused with happiness and seeing where they fail. Having cleared the way of false conceptions, we can hope to see, however imperfectly, what happiness really is and how it might be won.

HAPPINESS AND PLEASURE

It is very common for modern philosophers, and others too, to confuse happiness with pleasure. John Stuart Mill even declared them to be one and the same. Others make the same mistake, sometimes speaking as if happiness were something which, like pleasures, can come and go or be artificially induced or evoked by stimulation. The ancients rarely did this. They were partly protected from this error by having a word, *eudaimonia,* far richer in its connotations, than either of our words *happiness* or *pleasure.* The identification of happiness with pleasure would have sounded funny to them, whereas to us it may not.

The reason why modern philosophers are sometimes so eager to treat happiness and pleasure as the same is not hard to see. They want to think of happiness as something familiar, identifiable, and even measurable, rather than as something problematical or dubious. Pleasure, being an actual and common feeling, is certainly familiar and identifiable, and there seems to be no reason in principle why it should not be measurable. In short, the interest some moral philosophers have in the concept of pleasure is but a consequence of their predilection for empiricism. If, they think, ethics can be grounded in something plainly real and indisputable, then it ought to be possible to resolve the problems of ethics in a straightforward manner. This was certainly Mill's motive. He wanted to be able to define moral right and wrong (and hence duty) in terms of happiness and to identify happiness with pleasure, in order to remove questions of ethics from the realm of philosophical and religious polemic and to settle them beyond further controversy. And the motive of contemporary utilitarian philosophers is, at least in some cases, quite transparently similar. It has long been the hope of moral philosophers to be able to *prove* that certain things are right, certain things wrong, certain things dutiful, and it has seemed to some that basing the definitions of such normative terms on something non-normative, or factual and familiar to all, offers the best hope of being able to do that.

Familiar modes of discourse also suggest to some that pleasure and happiness might be equated. For example, being happy and being pleased seem, at one level, to be about the same. Someone who is happy with something—with his job, for instance—can also be described as pleased with it. And it is but a short step to equate being pleased with having feelings of pleasure.

Or again, it is perhaps quite impossible to imagine that someone might be happy while consistently and continuously exhibiting the symptoms of pain, or be thoroughly unhappy while continuously or repeatedly exhibiting the usual signs of pleasure. Thus do pleasure and happiness, or pain and unhappiness, seem clearly connected, not just causally, but logically. And it is not hard to suppose that the connection might be one of identity or, in other words, that happiness and pleasure might just be two words for one and the same thing.

In fact, however, happiness and pleasure have little in common other than that both are sought, and both are sometimes loosely referred to by the same vocabulary.

Pleasures, for example, can often be located in this or that part of the body. This is even more obvious in the case of pains. But one cannot speak of the happiness felt in his back when it is being massaged, or of the unhappiness in one's tooth or toe. Again, pleasures, like pains, come and go, and can be momentary; but one cannot momentarily be a happy person. One can momentarily exult or rejoice, to be sure, and while such states are typically ingredients of a happy existence, they are certainly not the same thing. Even persons who are quite plainly not happy can nevertheless feel occasional pleasures, just as those who are happy sometimes feel pain; and just as thoroughly unhappy people once in a while exult or rejoice, so do genuinely happy people sometimes feel dejection and frustration.

Again, pleasures sometimes arise from bad sources, just as pains sometimes arise from good ones; but one can hardly speak of genuine happiness as being rooted in evil or unhappiness growing from what is wholesome and good. There would, for example, be something incongruous in describing someone as achieving genuine and lasting happiness from the contemplation of suffering, though there are persons who apparently derive pleasure from such sources and from others as bad. And that reflection suggests another point of contrast, namely, that the term *happiness* is one of approbation, while pleasure is not, or at least not in the same way. Thus one can speak of happiness as an achievement, and admire those few people who manage to win it; but one hardly thinks of pleasures that way, not even those pleasures that are thought to be refined and even noble. It is at least moderately inspiring that someone, born to a wretched existence, should somehow die a happy person; but no comparable response is evoked by the thought of such a person dying with feelings of pleasure, even though this is, to be sure, preferable to its opposite. Happiness can even be thought of as the supreme good, as many philosophers have indeed described it; but it is hard to think of pleasures that way.

Furthermore, there are many different kinds of pleasures—the pleasures of eating, for instance, or of music, or of receiving praise. Pleasures are innumerable and varied. But there are not different kinds of happinesses, and indeed, even to use the word "happiness" in the plural is odd. No such oddness attaches to speaking of many pleasures. One is happy or he is not, or he is more or less so; but one cannot move from one happiness to another that is quite unlike it, as one sometimes moves from pleasure to pleasure.

And from that observation it can be noted that happiness and pleasure are really quite different kinds of things to begin with. Pleasures are, in the strictest sense, feelings, just as are pains; but happiness, and similarly unhappiness, are opposite states, not feelings. One can, to be sure, feel happy or unhappy—but not the way one feels a pleasure or pain. Feeling unhappy is feeling oneself to be in a certain general state. Pleasures and pains, on the other hand, are typically, and quite often literally, things felt—the pain of a toothache, for instance.

THE "HAPPINESS" OF LESSER BEINGS

Finally, it should be noted that children, idiots, barbarians, and even animals are perfectly capable of experiencing pleasure and pain, but none of these can become happy, in the sense in which the term is used here. One can, to be sure, speak correctly of a happy child, or a happy moron, but we need to attend carefully to what is being said in such cases. A happy child, for instance, is one who fares well *as a child,* or in other words, one for whom the benign conditions of well-being are met. These include affection, the sense of trust and security, loving discipline, and so on. Under such conditions a child can, indeed, be a *happy child,* in the sense of not being morose, disturbed, depressed, sullen, and so on, which is a perfectly clear sense of happiness. But the child is not happy in the sense that is important to philosophy, that is, in the sense of having achieved fulfillment or having been blessed with the highest personal good. This is the kind of happiness that can only be hoped for in time in the case of a child. The happiness of a happy child, though real and important, consists of little more than feeling good, a feeling that is rooted in certain salubrious conditions of life. It is a good, but it is not the great good that is the object of the moral life, the kind of good that normally takes the better part of a lifetime to attain.

The point is perhaps better made with the example of a happy moron. A person thus severely limited in those capacities that are so distinctively human can, like a child, feel happy. But that is about all his or her happiness is—a feeling. Such a person fares well, to be sure, but only as a moron, not as a person, in the full sense of the term. The point can be seen very readily if, contemplating a happy moron, one puts the matter to oneself this way: Happiness is the ultimate personal good, and this person is obviously happy. Would I not, then, be willing to be just like that moron, if I could thereby enjoy the same happiness? Of course the answer for any normal person is a resounding negative. This shows, not that happiness is not the ultimate personal good, but rather, that the happiness here illustrated is not the kind of happiness that a philosopher upholds as the highest good. Happiness, in this fuller sense, is much more than just a state of euphoria. It is the fulfillment of a person, as a person, and not as a child, or a moron, or whatever other limited person one might suggest.

PLEASURE AS AN INGREDIENT OF HAPPINESS

We can surely conclude, then, that happiness and pleasure are not the same, and that the concept of happiness, unlike that of pleasure, is a profound and difficult one.

Yet it would be rash to dismiss pleasure as having nothing to do with genuine happiness. It would be truer to say that pleasure, along with other things, is an ingredient of happiness, in the sense that no life that was utterly devoid of pleasures could ever be described as a fully happy one however estimable it might be otherwise.

Pleasure, then, should be included within that vast and heterogeneous assortment of things that the ancient moralists classed as *externals*. This apt term was applied to all things of value to one's life, which result from accident or good fortune, or are bestowed by others. What others bestow, they can also withhold, and similarly, one can be cursed by chance as readily as one can be blessed. Externals, in short, do not depend upon oneself, are largely or entirely beyond one's own control, and are for that very reason called externals.

And it is clear that persons cannot, for the most part, bestow pleasures upon themselves. They need other things and other persons as the source of them. This does not render them bad, but it does make them largely a matter of luck. They belong in a happy life but cannot be made the whole point of it. Genuine happiness, on the other hand, while it can be utterly ruined by chance—by dreaded illness, for example, or other disaster—nevertheless depends on oneself, in case it is ever won. Wisdom, or the choice of the right path to happiness, cannot guarantee that one will win it; but on the other hand, one is certain to miss it without that wisdom.

It would thus be as narrow to identify happiness with pleasure as to identify it with any other external good, such as property, honor, youth, beauty, or whatever. External goods are goods, and while a happy life cannot be devoid of them all, neither can any sum of them, however great, add up to such a life.

HAPPINESS AND POSSESSIONS

It would be unnecessary even to consider the identification of happiness with the accumulation of wealth were it not that shallow people, who are very numerous, tend to make precisely that identification. The pursuit of happiness is simply assumed by many to be the quest for possessions, and the "good life" is thought by the same persons to be a life of affluence.

The explanation for this, too, is not hard to find. Possessions, up to a certain minimum, are essential even to life. They are needed, beyond that point, for leisure; and while life is possible without leisure, happiness is not. There is, accordingly, a natural and wise inclination in everyone to possess things. If we add to this that all persons tend to be covetous and envious, then we have most of the explanation for the widespread greed for possessions, and of the identification of happiness with the feeding of that greed. Indeed, accumulation, and the display of wealth, sometimes become important mainly as a means to inciting envy.

It should, however, be obvious to any thinking person that happiness cannot possibly be found in the sheer accumulation of possessions, even when they are used to purchase great power, or when they are philanthropically used for the public good, as sometimes happens. Such purchase of power and bestowals of wealth sometimes mitigate the ugliness of the greed lying behind them, but these cannot add up to happiness in anyone. And if happiness is the great goal in life, as it surely is, then there are obscure, unknown people, of modest possessions, far more to be envied for what they have than even the very richest.

The pursuit of possessions beyond a certain point, far from constituting or even contributing to happiness, is an obstacle to it; for one has no chance of finding the right path to anything if he is resolutely determined to follow the wrong one, convinced that he is already doing things exactly right. The feeling of power that great wealth sometimes nourishes, and the envy that is incited in others, are both exhilarating, but neither can be regarded as an important ingredient of personal happiness. At best they add zest and challenge to one's life, effectively banishing boredom, but this is a poor substitute for happiness. Indeed the lover of possessions, who indulges that love to the exclusion of things more important, can be compared to the glutton, who indulges his love for food. For food, too, is necessary for life; but gluttony, far from constituting or even contributing to a good life, is utterly incompatible with it. To set that as one's ideal of life would be grotesque, and the clearest possible example of a wasted life. The successful pursuit of great wealth is no less grotesque and as certainly the waste of one's life. Most persons who would be repelled by gluttony, however, seem strangely blind to the comparison.

And this is really sad. For each of us does, indeed, have but one life to live, and if possible that life should be lived successfully. The chance of this happening is greatly diminished when the term *success* is applied to a kind of life which, from the standpoint of philosophy, is incompatible with success. That term should be reserved for the achievement of genuine happiness, and not for some popularly accepted illusion of happiness. If, to pursue the comparison once more, there were a race of people who exalted food without limit, indulged in gluttony, and envied corpulence as the mark of success in this pursuit, then we would say with certainty that theirs was a false and in fact disgusting ideal; nor would we change our judgment of them even if they declared with one voice that this was their happiness. The illusion of happiness is not happiness, nor is the feeling of happiness always a mark of possessing it.

HONOR, FAME, AND GLORY

The same can be said of many of the other goals people set for themselves, although some of these, such as the love of honor, come closer to the ideal. A person is sometimes honored for what he actually is, and if this is something that is noble, then that honor is well placed and its recipient is, to some extent, justified in believing that he has achieved something worthwhile. Still, such things as honor, fame, and glory, though certainly not despicable, do depend upon others and must therefore be classed as externals. One can seek honor, for example, and even honor that is deserved; but whether one gets it will always depend upon the perceptions and values and, sometimes, the caprices of others. One cannot bestow honors upon oneself. People tend, moreover, to honor and applaud their own benefactors, or sometimes even people who merely make them feel very good, such as charismatic clergy and the like, rather than honoring virtue for its own sake. What they give then resembles the price of a purchase more than a gift. Thus a victorious general is honored, rather than a losing one, even though the latter might in fact have displayed more resourcefulness and courage than the former. Similarly, a person may become rich at the expense of others, then be honored for charitably returning part of it to the very public that was exploited.

Moreover, people sometimes honor and even glorify things that are neither honorable nor glorious such as sheer power, even when it is selfishly used. Also, the masses of people are often eager to raise to great fame persons whose uniqueness is some mere eccentricity; this is sometimes true of popular entertainers, or something of very little worth, as in the case of prizefighters. People can, in fact, be swept off their feet by trifles and are willing to heap great honor and wealth upon the producers of such trifles, as in the case of professional athletes, who represent no group and no ideal other than by the outright sale of their skills.

Perhaps the fairest thing to say concerning such things as we have been considering—wealth, honor, glory, and the like—is that, like pleasure, they often contribute to happiness but never add up to it. Personal excellence or even heroism are often parts of a lasting happiness, and the recognition of such qualities by others often adds to that happiness. But the real reward of personal excellence, of the kind that leads one to do, perhaps with almost superhuman effort and resourcefulness, what no one else has ever done, is simply the possession of that excellence itself. To be uniquely able to create an extraordinary piece of music of great merit, or a poem, or a story, or a philosophical treatise, or a painting, or a building, or to accomplish any feat of great significance requiring genius or exemplary courage—all such abilities are gifts in themselves that are not much embellished by the gifts added by others. What one finds satisfying are things belonging to oneself rather than things added. At the same time, it would be unrealistic to treat the recognition or acclaim of others as worth nothing. What we should say is that such honor and acclaim are sometimes a part of one's happiness, possibly even a necessary part; but they can never constitute the sum and substance of it.

EUPHORIA, JOY, AND EXUBERANCE

It is, as we have noted, common to treat happiness as if it were a mere feeling, and even to confuse it with the feelings of pleasure. But while such feelings, and particularly the feelings of joy and exuberance, are often the expressions of a real inner happiness, they are not the same. They are too fleeting and superficial, and sometimes nothing more than the expressions of mood or of momentary satisfaction. And they are rarely chosen. Happiness, on the other hand, is an essential part of one's very existence, in the case of those lucky enough to possess it. While it is not gained simply by choice, as if nothing more were required in order to have it, it is nevertheless something chosen as contrasted with something accidental or thrust upon one.

WHAT HAPPINESS IS

The idea of happiness, we have suggested, contains the idea of fulfillment. It is also something of great and perhaps even ultimate value, and except when destroyed by accident or disaster, it is enduring. It is not something that comes and goes from one hour to the next. We have also said that it is a state of being and not a mere feeling.

It can be compared with something like health, to derive a useful analogy. For while there is such a thing as the feeling of health, no one imagines that health itself is no more than a feeling. To be healthy is to be in a certain state, the description of which we will consider shortly. And like happiness, it is very precious. Again like happiness, health is something that is normally lasting; one is not momentarily healthy. Nor, like happiness, are there different kinds of health. One either possesses it or does not. And for this reason the word "health" like the word "happiness" can only be used in the singular. Health, when one has it, is usually lost only through accident or disaster not through choice; so again, the comparison with happiness is apt.

The one way in which the analogy of health to happiness breaks down significantly is with respect to choice. Health is normal and natural; one can almost say, that one is normally born with it. It is something chosen and worked for only under unusual circumstances and then only in a limited way, as in the case of someone who has lost it and strives to recover it. Happiness, on the other hand, is certainly not a gift of nature; it is quite rare and is always the fruit of choice and effort exercised over a long period of time. Effort is needed to keep or regain health but not to win it in the first place, and in this respect it is quite unlike happiness.

Still, the analogy is useful, for health, like happiness, is a kind of fulfillment. And here it is very easy to see, in a general way, just what that fulfillment consists of. One is healthy when his body and all its parts function as they should. A diseased or unhealthy body is one that functions poorly. Similarly, a diseased or unhealthy heart, or lung, or whatever, is one whose function has been partially or wholly lost, so that a diseased heart and a malfunctioning one, for example, are exactly the same thing.

HAPPINESS AND THE CONCEPT OF FUNCTION

The point of making those seemingly banal observations about health is to bring out the important point that it is understood and defined entirely in terms of *function.* And since the analogy between happiness and health appears so very close, we seem justified in supposing that happiness, too, may be understandable in terms of function.

But function of what? If health consists simply of a properly functioning body, then what is happiness? The idea of happiness is obviously larger than that of health because, although this has not been noted before, the former presupposes the latter: A person can be healthy and lack happiness but not the other way around. Someone lacking health, however courageous or otherwise estimable he or she may be, cannot be fully happy, unless one of those rare individuals who combines great inner strength with extraordinary creative power—as will be explained shortly.

And this suggests that happiness is understandable as consisting of the proper functioning of a person as a whole. With this reflection it will be seen that we have come around full circle and back to the viewpoint of the ancient moralists who defined virtue in much the same way. We see, abstractly, the plausibility of the claim they so often made, that virtue and happiness are inseparable.

Let us now look a little more closely at happiness as thus conceived and then see whether this conception of it is borne out by actual experience.

The ancients quite rightly singled out the intellectual side of human nature as constituting our uniqueness. The exercise of this was, they thought, our proper function, and excellence in this exercise our special virtue. They called this part of our nature "reason"; but this meant for them simply the exercise of intelligence in discovering truth as well as in governing conduct. Socrates and Plato construed reason more narrowly, sometimes identifying it with dialectic, that is, with philosophical argumentation. Modern philosophers have, for the most part, unfortunately gone along with this narrower conception.

Let us, then, think of reason or intelligence in a broader sense, to include not merely the activity of reasoning (as exhibited for example in philosophy) but also observation and reflection and, above all, creative activity. This is, certainly, what distinguishes us from everything else. Human beings are, by virtue of their intelligence, capable of *creating* things that are novel, unique, sometimes of great value, and even sometimes, though rarely, of overwhelming value. One thinks, for example, of scientific theories or great works of art or literature, or profound philosophical treatises like Spinoza's *Ethics,* or the great and lasting music that emerges from the creative genius of one person. It is here, certainly, that we see what distinguishes us from all other living things and entitles us to think of ourselves as akin to the gods. Other creatures have no history and are virtually incapable of even the most trivial innovation or novelty. What was done by the generations that preceded them is done also by them in an endless repetition. But it is not so with human beings. Their works rise and fall, to be replaced by others that no one could have foreseen. Human beings, in a word, think, reflect, and *create*. It is no wonder that we are referred to in Scripture as having been created "in the image of God," for this has traditionally been thought of as the primary attribute of God, namely, that God is the *creator*.

Aristotle thought of the pursuit of knowledge as the human virtue par excellence. But it is significant that he thought of this, not merely as something passive, a mere absorption of things seen to be true, but rather as an activity. And it is the nature of intellectual activity that it is creative. To the extent that the mind is active, it is also creative, and this is true even in the sciences, and in such things as mathematics, where there is thought to be the least scope for novelty and innovation.

If we think of happiness as fulfillment, then it must consist of the fulfillment of ourselves as human beings, which means the exercise of our creative powers. For we are, among the creatures of the earth, the only ones possessed of such power. The idea of fulfillment is without meaning apart from the idea of function, however, and thus, as our bodies are fulfilled in health, so are our bodies and minds together fulfilled in creative activity. There are no real substitutes. The appearance of health, and the feelings associated with it, are often marks of that underlying state, but such things are not identical with it. The former can be present when the latter is not. And similarly, the appearance of happiness and the feeling of happiness are often marks of that precious state itself, but by no means to be confused with it. A person can appear happy and not be, and what is less readily understood, can feel happy and not be. Children, idiots, and animals, as we have seen, sometimes feel good, indeed, characteristically do; but they cannot possibly be happy in the true sense of the term. There simply is nothing more to be said of them with respect to their happiness than that they feel good.

Of course one might be tempted at this point to protest that if someone feels happy, what more can be wanted? Is it not quite enough to feel perfectly happy, without making much of the sources of that feeling? And why withhold the term *happiness* from anyone if that person is totally content with his own condition?

What more is wanted is, of course, the genuine thing. And one sees this readily enough if one imagines someone in whom the feelings of happiness are present, but the proper fulfillment of function is not, as again in the case of someone severely retarded. Whatever may be that person's feelings of self-satisfaction and joy, no one capable of a genuinely intelligent and creative life could ever trade it for this other. Feelings of joy complement and add to the happiness that most persons are capable of, but they can never replace it.

WHAT IS CREATIVITY?

When we think of creativity, we are apt to construe it narrowly, as the creation of things, sometimes even limiting it to things belonging to the arts. But this is arbitrary. Creative intelligence is exhibited by a dancer, by athletes, by a chess player, and indeed in virtually any activity guided by intelligence. In some respects the very paradigm of creative activity is the establishment of a brilliant position in a game of chess, even though what is created is of limited worth. Nor do such activities need to be the kind normally thought of as intellectual. For example, the exercise of skill in a profession, or in business, or even in such things as gardening and farming, or the rearing of a beautiful family, all such things are displays of creative intelligence. They can all be done badly or well and are always done *best* when done not by rule, rote, or imitation, but with successful originality. Nor is it hard to see that, in referring to such commonplace activities as these, at the same time we touch upon some of the greatest and most lasting sources of human happiness.

Consider, for example, something both commonplace and yet fairly unusual as begetting and rearing a beautiful family. There is, to be sure, nothing in the least creative about the mere begetting of children. It is something anyone can do. But to raise them and convert them to successful, that is, well-functioning, happy adults, requires great skill, intelligence, and creativity. We see this at once when we compare those who succeed at it with the many who do not. And now let us consider someone who has succeeded at this and ask what that person's happiness consists of, and how it compares with some of the specious substitutes for happiness that we have alluded to.

With respect to the first question, that is, what such a person's happiness consists of, we can easily see that it is not mere feeling. To be sure, the feelings of happiness are there, but they are based upon a state of being that is far more precious and enduring, namely, upon the lasting realization of what has been wrought. Feelings of reward, or of praise, or of envy in others, may be worth something; but if, for example, they rested upon nothing real, or upon actual error or misperception, then they would be worth very little. There would then be no real happiness behind them, but only the feelings of happiness. And with respect to the comparison of this person with someone whose happiness is perhaps spectacular but nonetheless specious, it is again not hard to see who is more blessed. Consider a man whose wealth far exceeds his needs and which has simply flowed to him without any creative effort on his part, as in the case of wealth that is inherited. This person cannot possibly have the happiness of even the most ordinary person who has created something valuable and lasting, even of a commonplace sort. To see this, you need only to get before your mind a clear image of both lives, and then ask not which one you envy, not which one is more honored by the masses of people, not which one shines with more glory, not which is filled with more feelings of exhilaration, but just simply: Which of these two persons is happier?

THE DEFEAT OF HAPPINESS

Happiness is often represented as something to be pursued, as something that might be conquered; and quite rightly, for this calls attention to the fact that it can also be lost, or that one might fail altogether to find it. It by no means flows automatically to those who wait for it, even when all the conditions for it are right. It must be chosen and sought.

Of course the clearest way in which it can be lost is by calamity, such as dreadful or life-destroying illness, and things of this nature, which either cannot be foreseen or cannot be warded off when they are foreseen. The Stoics maintained that even catastrophic setback or illness could not destroy one's happiness, but this was an extreme and unbelievable position. It is true that happiness cannot be conferred upon one, but it can certainly be taken away, and under some circumstances it is idle to speak of pursuing it.

The other ways in which one can fail to become happy are either: first, through ignorance of what happiness is, and hence an inability to distinguish genuine happiness from specious forms; or second, from lack of the creative intelligence necessary for its pursuit. We shall consider these in turn.

THE FAILURE FROM IGNORANCE

This has been dealt with incidentally. Thus, people who think happiness results from possession, for example, have no chance of becoming happy, for they go in the wrong direction. They may succeed in their pursuit of wealth, but having done that, they then find themselves using that wealth to pursue things equally specious, such as power over others or the envy of others, and other things totally unrelated to the kind of creative activity we have described; or else they find themselves going through the kinds of motions that have characterized their lives superfluously adding wealth to what they already have in great excess. The mere doing of things, perhaps on a large scale, achieves no more happiness than the mere defeat of boredom—for which, incidentally, most people appear quite willing to settle. Sheer boredom is indeed a baneful state. To escape it is, to some extent, a blessing though a negative one. Hence the incessant activity on the part of some—things done for no purpose beyond making more money; or travel undertaken for new sights and sounds passively absorbed; or projects pursued, sometimes on a grand scale, just to impress others; or things purchased for the same purpose. This is how many people live, escaping boredom, keeping busy, being preoccupied with something from one day to the next, giving little thought to life or to death. And this does achieve, for the moment, the banishment of boredom and loneliness; but that is as close to happiness as it gets. Meanwhile others who are wiser, having little of all this and almost never knowing boredom, go about life in their own way, creating from their own resources things original to themselves, quite unlike what others have done, things small, sometimes not small, sometimes even great and lasting, but every one of them something that is theirs and is the reflection of their own original power. Such people rejoice, perhaps unnoticed—and are happy.

THE WANT OF CREATIVE INTELLIGENCE

The second way to fail is through the sheer lack of what is needed to succeed. For if genuine happiness is found through the exercise of creative intelligence, then it is obvious that, without this, a person will have to be content with a specious kind of happiness, far less than the *eudaimonia* we have described. And many people, perhaps even most, are thus prevented.

Thus there are people whose every day is very much like the one just lived. They are essentially people without personal biographies except for the events which the mere passage of time thrusts upon them. In this they are like animals, each of whose lives is almost indistinguishable from others of its species, simply duplicating those of the generations before it. One sparrow does not differ from another. What it does, others have done and will do again, without creative improvement of any kind. Its life consists of what happens to it. And people who are like this have a similar uniformity. They do much as their neighbors do and as their parents have done, creating virtually no values of their own, but absorbing the values of those around them. Their lives are lived like clockwork, and thought, which should be the source of projects and ideals, is hardly more than a byproduct of what they are doing, an almost useless accompaniment like the ticking of a clock. You see these people everywhere, doing again today what they did yesterday, their ideas and feelings having about as little variation. And, it should be noted, such people are by the ordinary standards that prevail *quite happy*—that is, they are of good cheer, greet each sunrise with fresh anticipation, have friends, and spend much of their time exchanging empty remarks and pleasantries with others like them. They are, in a word, contented people who would declare with total sincerity, if asked, that they are perfectly happy, asking no more of the world than to escape those things, such as poverty or illness, which might threaten their contentment.

But we must not be misled by this. What such people have are certain feelings of happiness—feelings only. These are not bad, not even really illusory, but they do fall far short of the meaning of happiness the ancients tried to capture in the word *eudaimonia.* Such persons are not fulfilled but merely satisfied. They have a kind of contentment that is within the reach of anyone capable of suffering who luckily manages to escape suffering. What they have is not even distinctively personal or human. The measure of their happiness is nothing more than their lack of inclination to complain.

It is, to be sure, doubtful whether any normal person entirely fits this baneful description, but one can hardly fail to see that it expresses what is almost normal. Even the least creative among us are usually capable of something original, however innocuous it might be. But what is sad is that the kind of happiness that is within the reach only of human beings should be within the reach of so few of these. And what is sadder still is that those who have no clear idea of what happiness is, or worse, lack within themselves the resources to capture it, do not care. It is, in some ways, almost as if they had not even been born.

It is no wonder that the ancients thought of happiness as a blessing of almost divine worth, as something rare, and something that can be ascribed to someone only after he is dead.

Part Four

Love and Sex

Introduction

This section opens with Taylor's reflections on love's manifestation in friendship (*philia*), which rests on mutual affection among persons who share certain common interests and goals. He discusses the tripartite Aristotelian breakdown of friendship into its three varieties, namely, *philia* based on pleasure, *philia* based on utility or mutual advantage, and the highest form of friendship that is based on character or human excellence. Taylor finds such manifestations of love incomplete as *philia* remains in every instance self-regarding, and the friends quite literally alter egos.

While any type of *philia* is preferential (i.e., one is selective in choosing one's friends), it seems that a genuine friendship is also reciprocal. At its best, *philia* strives for an ideal relationship of "one soul in bodies twain." However, *philia's* whimsy surfaces when friendships turn cliquish, and the friends become a veritable coterie, closed off from the larger world of public or interpersonal relationships that the friends either neglect or act against. In short, friendship can lead to a type of secession or rebellion against the community-at-large. While genuine friendships do create a nexus of needs and expectations, they remain unconnected to any rules of obligation and correlative rights. Unlike passionate sexual love that is biochemically based, *philia* has a nonnatural quality about her, which, as C. S. Lewis has pointed out, offers no survival value but instead gives value to survival.

Taylor then turns to a discussion of *eros* or passionate sexual love. He notes that *eros* is not pursued because it is first judged good (it can often prove destructive), but rather judged good because it is blindly sought. Human beings seem to act on *eros* much like the salmon and herring that are driven to spawn, despite the obstacles, in the fresh water. *Eros* is an innate urge that goads us to act. But *eros* is also not the essence of love, for it often embodies no loving kindness and can prove shamefully ignoble.

Taylor depicts *eros* as a primitive force, a brute sexual passion, that when reciprocated in romantic sexual love strives to attain the ideal of "two souls in one body." Taylor, unlike some writers on romantic love, doesn't view an emotion like *eros* as an activity that involves a system of decisions in which the lovers project themselves into the world. Rather, for Taylor, the roles of lovers are more natural than conventional. *Eros* remains less of an art and more of a blind passion, a visceral reaction. In short, *eros* is a biological determinant and not a cultural artifice. However, even genuine, requited *eros* creates tensions between the shared private world of lovers, and the expectations and requirements of the public worlds. The lovers may affirm each other by attending to each other's needs, hopes, aspirations, and so on, but they often alienate others in the process. And like *philia, eros* can prove very fickle and ephemeral.

Instead, Taylor makes a case for "absolute love" that is unique to human beings. Here one rejoices in the sheer existence of things, both human and nonhuman. To be achieved, it must begin with a love of self that is not mere selfishness. This absolute love of being springs from the heart and cannot be rationally justified. It's a "joy of being," a "blessing," a gift of fortune or fate. It proves to be the "very nourishment of a life that is human." Taylor writes:

> It is, then, not primarily an incentive to actions, but a passional state, something that is to be possessed rather than used. It need not call upon one to *do* anything whatever, for it is instead the aspiration to *be* a certain kind of man, to exemplify an ideal of human nature that is found to be good, not primarily for what it does, but for what it is.

Being a passion, absolute love is not subject to or subsumable under rules of obligation. It cannot, as an emotion, be commanded, and when one otherwise so loves following a rule or injunction, the result is a merely simulated love. "A genuine act of charity is therefore not, as it is now generally thought to be, merely an act of giving; it is in its original sense an act that springs from love and is prompted by nothing else."

Unlike lesser forms of love that are tied to the fortunes of the world (e.g., *gratitude* at one's own fortune, *conjubilation* at that of others, or *compassion* directed toward the ill luck and suffering of others), absolute love is not so tied to the contingencies of existence. Absolute love is a blessing that one hopes to attain. It solicits us to be the sort of virtuous person that embodies human excellence. "The ultimate moral aspiration is simply this: To be a warm-hearted and loving human being."

Much as Christianity holds that *philia* and *eros* need to be transcended and transformed in *agape* (love of neighbor) and *caritas* (love of God), so, too, does Taylor—albeit nonreligiously and without any deontic requirement—attempt to transform and transcend *philia* and *eros* with his notion of "absolute love." In Plato's *Symposium,* love's dialectic unfolds when a person moves from the love of a particular individual's beauty or virtuous character, to a love for the beauty or virtue of other persons, and ultimately to love of Beauty and Virtue themselves. Less abstractly, but similarly ethereal, Taylor seems to move from the more particularist loves of *philia* and *eros* to the more elevated manifestation of love directed toward persons and the world in general.

An example of Taylor at his provocative, countercultural best can be found in his views on the ethics of having love affairs. By a love affair, Taylor means "an intense, passionate, and intimate relationship between a man and a woman, at least one of whom is married to, or cohabits in a marriage relationship with, someone else." Such a stipulative definition excludes platonic relationships, bisexual or homosexual relationships, as well as cohabitation relationships of unmarried people where there is no third person of the opposite sex involved in any passionate way.

While Taylor speaks of passionate love as "ultimate joy" and an incomparable good, he does not contend that love affairs are superior to genuine marriages. He is well aware of how destructive love affairs can prove to be. Paradoxically, Taylor intends his analysis to further human happiness and indeed to bolster the institution of marriage. He confesses that he is pro-family, not as a duty, but as a "blessing."

> . . . just as no war was ever prevented by people intoning "thou shall not kill," but only, instead, by understanding and removing the cause of war, so also no love affair was ever prevented by intoning "thou shall not commit adultery," but only instead by understanding and removing the causes of sexual infidelity.

Controversially, Taylor believes that as a general rule men and women differ in their basic needs, desires, and responses to matters of sex and love. Men, Taylor avers, are basically egotistical and polygamous; while women find their self-glorification in vanity. Taylor regards these gender differences as biologically based, and not the result of acculturation.

A man, Taylor writes, "by nature desires many sexual partners, and if custom or circumstances limit him to one, then his dreams and fantasies are filled with others." It isn't the case that men first reflect on their considerable fertility and then decide to be polygamous. Rather, their sexual passion "is simply the nonreflective expression of that fertility." By contrast, women tend to be vain, preening themselves in mirrors, often forming obsessive attachments to their hairstylists, ashamed when obese, and constantly seeking to be desirable and appreciated for their femininity and the recognition of their respective talents.

Those individuals who would downplay the basic differences that Taylor alleges between the sexes will have to grapple hard to counteract Taylor's thought experiment of the traveling businessmen dining in a motel dining room and how they would typically react to female enticement, versus a company of businesswomen similarly situated and their reaction to attempted male seduction. Taylor also tries to show how misunderstanding between the sexes often results from a gender-based view of sexuality being imposed on the other sex, as when men (women) read women (men) as men (women) would read themselves.

Since love and affection are great goods, and allowing that any rational ethic addresses itself to basic human needs, Taylor proposes an ethic of passionate love. Indeed, in his book *Having Love Affairs,* Taylor stipulates (nonoxymoronic) "moral rules for adulterous love."[1]

Taylor offers some insightful comments on the morbidity of many existing marriages. His depictions are sufficient to make one take seriously Shakespeare's aphorism "better well-hanged than ill wed." Of course, pillars of probity often point out the *positive* side of the bandied divorce figures, namely, that 50 percent of all marriages are intact. But, it would be rash to conclude that these intact marriages are all flourishing. As singer Tina Turner bluntly puts it, "What's love got to do with it?" Or, in a similar vein, the acerbic comedian Rodney Dangerfield who talks about married couples who sleep in different beds, take separate vacations, and do whatever it takes to make their marriages work. It seems that many married couples are not so much *sticking by* each other as they are *stuck* with each other. The real glue to their intact marriages is not love, but security, the caring of children, fears of beginning anew, accommodations with boredom, religious prohibition, worries about social ostracism, etc.

Taylor insightfully reminds us that love constitutes a marriage, and when that love is absent or moribund, so too is the marriage, appearances notwithstanding.

> Thus though a wife may be ever so dutiful, faultless, and virtuous in every skill required for the making of a home, if she lacks passion, then in a very real sense she already is without a husband, or he, at least, is without a wife. Similarly, a husband who is preoccupied with himself and his work, who is oblivious to the needs of his wife and insensitive to her vanities, who takes for granted her unique talents—whether they are significant or not—and who goes about his own business more or less as though she did not exist, has already withdrawn as a husband, except in name.[2]

In his analysis of marital fidelity, Taylor shows how the notion of *fidelity* originally meant constancy of love, but has now degenerated into a notion of sexual exclusiveness. Taylor boldly claims "it is perfectly possible for lovers, and for husbands and wives, to be faithful to each other even in spite of sexual nonexclusiveness." In short, genuine infidelity consists in the betrayal of the foundation of marriage, which is love. Taylor's case study of the marriage of Tony and Carmella is a powerful antidote to the prevalent moral and religious hypocrisy surrounding rules against cheating.

This section closes with Taylor's musings on the language of the eyes. Lovers not only look at each other, but look into each other as well. This process of eyeing each other is unlearned and often unconscious behavior. It is very difficult over time to "feign and dissimulate with the eyes" one's love or affection for another person. In fact, loveless glances can turn another person into an object. By contrast, loving eyes can make that other person a subject.

In short, Taylor is drawing our attention to the significance of nonverbal communication, especially among lovers and friends. Messages and thoughts are conveyed as much through bodily expression as they are by written or oral communication. Taylor's focus, however, is not on bodily language in general, where the human face alone has some forty-four muscles capable of yielding some seven thousand looks of fear, anger, sadness, joy, surprise, approval, anguish, and so on. Instead Taylor's focus is on the eyes alone as a vehicle of communication.

The nuances of bodily expression can often be just as complex as linguistic communication. Speaking of optic communication, Shakespeare in *Love's Labour's Lost* wrote: "For where is any author in the world, teaches such beauty as a woman's eye? Learning is but an adjunct to ourself." Taylor clearly agrees with the Bard and, moreover, would marvel at Shakespeare's apt comparison of the eyes to "Promethean fire; they are the books, the arts, the academes, that show, contain, and nourish all the world."

NOTES

1. In *Having Love Affairs* (Buffalo: Prometheus Books, 1982), Taylor formulates some twelve rules that, given his distaste for rules of obligation, seem to be practical guidelines for people involved in love affairs. All his "rules" are designed to reduce if not eliminate the destructive nature of the affair.

2. Ibid, p. 139.

20

Love and Friendship

In approaching this it is first essential to distinguish some of the various things that are often referred to as love but that have little or nothing in common other than a name. The considerable differences between them can perhaps be marked at the outset by giving them their classical names, as follows: (1) *Philia;* or mutual friendship; (2) *Eros, amor,* or the love of the sexes; (3) *Agapé, caritas,* or what might quite properly be called Christian love; and (4) *commiseratio, misericordia,* or what I have hitherto referred to as sympathy and compassion. . . .

It will be desirable first, however, to consider briefly the first two forms of love, *philia* and *eros,* to see how little they have in common with each other or with anything else, and to see what is their moral significance, if any.

PHILIA, OR FRIENDSHIP

Love, as it expresses itself in what I shall now refer to simply as friendship, is the mutual affection that sometimes arises between people well known to each other who share certain interests and pursuits. It hardly extends beyond men, although it can. A man might, for example, with some literal truth, describe his dog as a friend, insofar as the two might really share certain interests and pursuits, such as hunting, and sometimes cooperate in these. A genuine affection of this kind can arise between man and animal, although it is surely not common. No one could describe his relationship to a squirrel or a robin as friendship, without metaphor. To use the term in such a context would only be

---

From *Good and Evil* (Buffalo, N.Y.: Prometheus Books, 1984), pp. 223-239.

to express a kind of good will toward them, which is of course estimable, but it is not friendship.

Friendship requires for its existence two or more persons having common interests and pursuits and cooperating in their fulfillment; it also requires, of course, frequent association for a considerable time. This latter can perhaps be achieved to a limited extent without actual physical presence, but some personal interaction is quite plainly needed. It is for these reasons—the possession of common interests, cooperation, and frequent association—that no one could truly declare the entire world, or even any considerable part of it, to be his friend. One who is a "friend to man" is simply one who expresses good will to all. He cannot in any literal sense be a *friend* to all, without emptying the idea of its meaning.

FRIENDSHIP IN ARISTOTELIAN ETHICS

Aristotle's analysis of the various forms of love and friendship[1] and the values of each is probably the best to be found among the ancients, prior to the Gospels. This is not saying much, however, for the Greeks had a limited conception of love. Aristotle distinguished three different kinds of love: friendships based on pleasure, those based on utility or mutual advantage, and those based on character. He rated their significance in that order. The simplest friendships, those of pleasure, rest entirely on mutual enjoyment, and Aristotle quite correctly perceived that these are characteristic of children. Thus, when people seek each other out and form what all would recognize as friendship, and its sole foundation is the pleasure each finds in the other's company, as in the case of playmates, the friendship so formed is one of pleasure. It is, no doubt, an element in all friendship, but it can be the sole element. It is capable, quite by itself, of uniting people in friendship; but usually not, as Aristotle noted, in any lasting way. Resting entirely on the mutual pleasure that each derives from the company of the other and their common pleasurable pursuits, such friendship has nothing whatever to sustain it when the pleasure of the association has ceased. Friendship at this level is of course very common, not only among children, who are capable of no other kind, but among men. It is easily established and just as easily dissolved. Thus, two men, meeting for the first time and each discovering in the other a passionate devotion to fishing, have between them a very real basis for friendship. They can truly claim to be friends from the moment of that discovery. Nothing more is really required. But, in case that is the only thing uniting them, the friendship must certainly dissolve as soon as the fishing is over, or it can be kept alive only in anticipation of more.

Aristotle was doubtless right, then, in regarding this type of love as both the simplest and least valuable, although he was equally right in regarding it as a good. It is a genuine form of friendship, even though it is neither deep, strong, nor lasting. Somewhat more durable, although not otherwise different in kind, are those friendships based on utility. These arise between men having common purposes other than the pursuit of pleasure, such as partners in business or government, professional colleagues, and the like might enjoy. In such cases, each friend finds the other advantageous to himself in his pursuits, and thus there is formed a bond between them. A successful business partnership sometimes forms the basis of friendship of this kind. One might feel inclined to say that this is no genuine friendship at all, because it expresses no real love except the love of oneself and is plainly motivated by the anticipation of advantage to oneself; but in reply to this it should be insisted that friendship would be rare indeed, and life correspondingly harsh and dismal, if one were expected to love his friends more than himself and to abandon the concern for himself that is natural to all men. Far from being opposed to real friendship, an honest and unabashed love of oneself is a condition of loving anyone at all, as we shall see more clearly later on.

Aristotle's third kind of friendship is the more interesting, and he quite appropriately called it the love of the good, by which he meant the love of good men for each other. It is important to remember, however, that by a good man Aristotle did not mean primarily a morally upright man. He meant a superior man, one who excels in intelligence, sensitivity, and nobility of character. Friendships of this kind are based, not primarily on mutual pleasure or mutual advantage, but on the human excellences that each friend perceives in the other; that is to say, on the character of those united in friendship, using character in its laudatory sense. Putting it more plainly, one loves a friend of this kind for his own sake, for what he is. Aristotle inferred that inferior men cannot form this kind of friendship, because the requisites of character are lacking. They can be friends, in the sense that they derive pleasure and perhaps advantages from their association. They can even, on these bases, be firm, long-lasting, and loyal friends, and such friendship is by no means to be despised. They cannot, however, have between them the kind of friendship that rests on excellence and nobility of character, if such qualities do not exist in them. For the same reason, a man of this character cannot be a friend, in this sense, of persons inferior to himself, even though other things might unite them in a friendship that is perfectly genuine. Friendships of the good are within reach only of the good. Because, however, they are based on human excellence, that is, on character, and because this is not subject to change in men who possess it, this third form of friendship is the most lasting and can be destroyed only by death.

That is a superficial account of Aristotle's thought, but serves to lead us philosophically into the subject. Two things are now worth noting. The first is that Aristotle, like other moralists of his culture, never thought of love as anything but self-regarding. He simply assumes that a man loves himself first, and that friendships are for the enhancement of one's own life. The thought of self-sacrificial love is accordingly quite foreign to him. A true friend, he notes, will gladly give generously to his friend, but even this will be motivated by the love he has for himself. Aristotle observes that although his friend thus receives the benefit of the gift, the giver is enhancing his own pride and sense of worth, which is the greater of the two goods. The giver, therefore, is the one who comes off best after all. Love, in other words, is considered by Aristotle to be a blessing, rather than a virtue in the modern sense. He never speaks of actions prompted by love as duties, and there is no suggestion that one in any sense owes them to men as such. On the contrary, he explicitly denies that men far removed from each other in intellect or culture can be friends at all, in his third and highest sense. Aristotle is so far from questioning that friendship, even in its highest expression, rests on the natural love one has for himself that he describes a friend as an *alter ego*—literally, as another self.

The second thing to note is that Aristotle never confuses love with the sexual passion, or *eros,* and in this his thinking contrasts very sharply with contemporary ideas. Generally, when we think of love we think first of the love of the sexes; we are apt to suppose that this is simply a special and perhaps typical expression of love, differing from other forms of love and friendship only in its special basis. This, I think, would have moved Aristotle and his contemporaries to laughter. Sexual activity is an obvious source of pleasure and is also, manifestly, the means of perpetuating the species, but few of the ancients thought of it as having any essential connection with love and friendship.

EROS, OR THE LOVE OF THE SEXES

In this I think the ancients were basically right, and to see this we need to examine the sexual passion, as objectively as possible, to see what is its explanation and what connection it has, if any, with love and friendship and with good and evil.

The general conception most persons seem quite unthinkingly to have formed is something like this: Sexual union is a great good, an allurement that presents itself to the mind and the imagination; and, because it is thus viewed, one who is thus seized with this vision directs his will to the attainment of it. But this is to put the whole thing backward. The sexual embrace is not first seen as a great good and delight, and for that reason pursued; it is the reverse of this. That is, it is because it is keenly, and blindly, desired, that it is deemed a great good. The impulse and passion are what first make themselves felt and, in the younger portion of mankind, sometimes quite irresistably felt. Then, in response to this impulse, which lacks any intellectual direction whatever, that which is imagined as fulfilling it is deemed a great good. Men want to think otherwise, because they like to think they have reasons and even conscious reasons for pursuing the things they pursue. And what could the reason be, in the present case, other than the great goodness and delight of the thing sought? But this is to overlook what is in general true of all willing: the things men deem good are so considered because they are sought. They are not sought because they are first deemed good. Indeed, as we have seen, the good and evil of things generally is simply a consequence, and not a cause, of their promising fulfillment or threatening frustration of one's aims and purposes.

This becomes obvious, I think, if we consider the urge to sexual union as it finds expression in other creatures, and then note how unessential are the differences between these and ourselves. Certain fishes, such as the salmon and herring, for example, leave the salty oceans in vast numbers at a certain time of the year, seeking out the fresh waters where they spawn. This is nothing they would do ordinarily, for the environmental change, to which their bodily functions are so delicately attuned, is very great and abrupt. Evidently they are driven by a powerful force. This becomes more evident when we observe how they persevere against every obstacle, constantly exposing themselves to every danger, to sudden destruction among the rocks and in shallow waters, leaping against the powerful currents and high waterfalls, often persisting in this time after time, until one would suppose their energy and even their lives would long since have been spent in the effort. Finally, some of them do make it. Now then, after all this struggle, struggle against which no obstacle or danger can ever avail, and from which no force or danger can divert them, with what great good are they then rewarded? What allurement awaited them in the spawning beds, solicited from them such feats and exertions, and made it all so worthwhile? What actually happens is nothing more than this: the female fishes go about laying eggs, and the males follow behind to fertilize them, the two having no more concern for or contact with each other than is described here.

This is, of course, pretty much how the sexual urge expresses itself throughout nature, as anyone having any acquaintance with animals knows. It would be strange indeed if, coming to man, we were to find this picture suddenly *reversed*. What we do find is an impulse that is absolutely blind, at least from the point of view of that creature in whom it arises. From another point of view, it is of course not blind, for the function it actually serves is the perpetuation of the species. That this is no conscious or deliberate aim of other animals is perfectly obvious, for it would be laughable to suppose that one of these—one of the fishes just described, for example—framed in his mind the objective of producing others like himself and then embarked on the means he thought might lead to the goal. Nor is it just that such creatures lack the necessary wit to have purposes and plan the means to their attainment. It is more absurd than that. For if we could somehow imagine them endowed with the necessary intelligence, then we could not imagine them applying it in that fashion. What their intelligence or reason would tell them, if they had any, is that it is not worth it. Few animals show any interest in or concern for their young, once they have produced them, and in those that do, it persists only until the young are able to shift for themselves. Clearly, it was not hope of begetting these that lured them on. It was, instead, a blind urge that goaded them on, then produced this result. One might say that nature's great plan is thereby fulfilled, which would be rather poetic; but beneath the poetry there is, of course, a truth that could be expressed scientifically.

If one looks at eros in this way and considers that its human expression is not fundamentally different from its expression throughout nature, then many apparent mysteries begin to dissolve. They dissolve when one considers the blindness of eros, its incredible power, and its unfailing result, this latter being the perpetuation of the race—which is not, however, the end that is consciously sought even in the case of men, who can foresee it. We get inklings of its great power when we see what must give way before it. Prudence and good sense collapse almost at once, the moment an outlet for this demonic urge presents itself, even if but for a moment; it is no wonder, then, that heroic efforts are made, continuously and on every side, to cage and confine it. These take the form of conventions and attitudes of shame and modesty that are instilled in one from the tenderest age, and are woven so tightly that they often enable men and women to dwell in close proximity, day after day, without breaking them. All such efforts notwithstanding, however, we continuously see great careers brought to ruin, even thrones abandoned, and sometimes the interests of nations endangered by the insufficiency of such efforts, in the face of what they seek to restrain. This urge usurps a large part of the thinking of youth and infects all its emotions, day and night. No allusion to it fails to quicken immediate interest and, more often than not, to shove from the stage for the time being whatever other interests one has. No crime is so heinous that it has not been committed in response to this impulse, and no deed seems too heroic to attempt in response to the same. Thus does it become the central ingredient of most song, poetry, and story—and, oddly enough, of much humor. For most humor appears to result simply from this: someone, seemingly aware and knowing what he is up to, is nevertheless guided in his actions by things over which he has no control, and in such a way that he is carried to some absurd end that he could not really ever have intended. It is the surprise of this outcome, a surprise produced by the tension between planning and fate, that so often produces the inner tension that is expressed in laughter. Thus, the clown, apparently knowing what he is about, suddenly has something blow up in his face, precisely as a result of what he was so deliberately doing—and onlookers are bent over in laughter. The inebriate, similarly, plans his own motions, but is constantly foiled by a force he cannot control, presenting a ridiculous spectacle of thought versus force that culminates in a victory of force at the actor's expense. This is at the heart of much that presents itself to the mind as ridiculous, and it finds its purest and clearest expression in the sexual passion. For here we have, par excellence, the spectacle of an agent apparently planning and executing his own actions—deliberately, and often at great pains and expense of time, fortune, and effort—seemingly knowing what he is doing and why, yet all the time being entirely goaded from behind by a force that he never created and can now in no way abate or ignore. Like the clown, his labor carries him to a result that his mind or reason could never have chosen, and he is landed precisely in what all can at least dimly see as absurd. If one tries to divest the thing of its passional associations—so as to be blinded as little as possible—and brings clearly before his mind an actual image of the culmination and goal of the erotic drive, he can see that nothing could possibly be more totally absurd, nothing less likely as a candidate for a sane being's aspiration. It is without doubt our perception of this, of the unsurpassable ridiculousness in the image of sexual union, that prompts men everywhere to conceal it as nothing else on earth is concealed, and almost to pretend that it does not exist. It is not mere shame begotten by custom, for no mere custom could be so universally and tenaciously held—and in any case it is everywhere declared not to be shameful when certain conditions are met. It is, therefore, its inherent absurdity to the mind, together with its ineluctable appeal to the will, that has invested it with this feeling of embarrassment and shame that without fail leads lovers to places of darkness and concealment. What they do must never be seen, for it is so immensely absurd.

This is of course a large subject, and an intriguing one, about which much more could be said; but perhaps the brief and general description before us will suffice to answer the questions that now arise. Namely, is eros, or the sexual passion, an expression of love? What has it to do with love? And what is its moral significance?

Clearly, it is no form of love at all, beyond the fact that it happens to be called by that name, and it has almost nothing to do with love, in any sense in which this is of special moral significance. Eros, or the attraction of the sexes, is found in virtually everything that lives and appears to differ in men only in certain accidental details. Men, for example, are aware of this drive, can formulate and act on deliberate plans with respect to it, can to some degree at least understand it, and can foresee its consequences; but none of these things changes its essential nature. It is in us as irrational, blind, and unchosen as in any insect; it is something that is simply thrust on us by nature, we then to act out our response to it. The fact that we know what we are doing and are aware of what is going on does not change this in the least, for no more did any man ever choose *not* to be impelled by its urging, than did any ever choose to be so impelled. One could not aptly describe a pair of copulating grasshoppers, or mice, or dogs, as making *love;* they are simply copulating. The expression is no less inept when applied to people—except that here we feel some euphemism is needed, and this one serves.

Love, as a sentiment, expresses itself naturally in sympathetic kindness, even sometimes in a kind of identification of oneself with the thought, feelings, and aspirations of another. It is compatible with sexual passion, but it by no means rests on it nor, contrary to what so many would like to believe, does it find its highest expression there. This is made obvious by a number of things; for example, by the natural love of parents for their children, and by the fact that sentiments of genuine love and friendship can exist and sometimes persist through a lifetime among persons of either sex, wherein the erotic element is entirely absent. And on the other side, it is notorious that the sexual passion can be kindled by one for whom one cares nothing at all, and equally, that one may have a friend who is truly beloved who nevertheless stirs this passion not in the least. Looking at it from still another point of view, it is obvious to anyone having a knowledge of human affairs that genuine love, as St. Paul put it, "never fails"; that is to say, it is inseparable from loving kindness in action, and absolutely ennobles everything that it touches. The erotic passion, on the other hand, left to itself seldom succeeds, for it is a notoriously fertile source of folly, of madness, sometimes of human degradation, and very often of cruelty and unspeakable crime.

None of this is of course intended to deny that the two can dwell together; it is only meant to deny that they are one and the same, and even spring from a common source—all of which would probably be obvious if men did not insist on adorning in their own case whatever behavior they share with other animals. Certainly the adoration of lovers is increased by erotic fulfillment, and the latter is itself ennobled by loving sympathy, but an excursus on that theme belongs in manuals for lovers rather than in a philosophical treatise.[2]

ABSOLUTE LOVE

By this, which I shall also refer to as the love of man, I mean, not a love of which men are the special objects, but rather, the love of which men are alone capable. I shall try to convey some idea of what it is, and what it is not, to relate it to the moral life, and to enunciate an aspiration that this human capacity yields.

Men and men only have a capacity to rejoice in the sheer existence of things, first of all in their own existence, then in the existence of things around them, both human and nonhuman, animate and inanimate. It is a rejoicing that goes far beyond esthetic pleasure, encompassing things that are perfectly banal and without any esthetic significance, and far beyond the mere utility of things. Insofar as men are conative beings, with diverse desires and aims, both great and trivial, then they can, in the manner already described at length, divide things in the world into good and evil. But this in itself gives rise to no love of things, as I am now using the term. To love a thing is not merely to use it, except in a degraded sense of the term, and anyone can recognize an ineptness in speaking, as is so often done, of loving money, food, reputation, and such things as are merely useful in the fulfillment of aims. Behind this recognition is the perception of a rejoicing over things, not merely as they can be turned to advantage, but simply and solely in their existence.

The first such existence that fills the heart with love is one's own, and it cannot possibly be anything else. I have used the expression *the heart* to indicate that this love of being is entirely nondiscursive, nonintellectual, and nonrational, and although obviously no mindless being could possess it, it is at the same time nothing for which any reason or justification could be given. It is one's own being that is, thus, first loved; for if it is not, then nothing is ever loved at all. Self-love, by which is meant something far more than narrow self-interest, is an absolute precondition of loving anything, and one who is devoid of it is as deprived—indeed, as inhuman—as a vegetable or a machine. And such rejoicing must, if it is to exist at all, begin with one's own existence, because it is that which he first feels and in terms of which the existence of other things first becomes meaningful. Behind any view of the world there must be a viewer, but a man differs in this: he is himself the lens through which all the rest is seen. Thus, one who is filled with warmth in the sheer joy of his own being finds warmth in the world, whereas one who is bereft of this is automatically chilled, forsaken, and quite alone in the world.

This joy of being, which I have called the love of man, but which could with equal felicity be called love for the world, is nothing rare or esoteric, nothing that any learning or religion is needed to impart. It exists all around. We find it in children, who practically come into the world with it, and in them it is easily, almost casually, destroyed, often by the most innocent neglect. It usually survives as men grow older, although in very different degrees. In some it has been utterly suffocated, usually in their tender years and as often as not through sheer accident, whereas in others no suffering can diminish it and no fortune add to it. These latter go through to the day of their death bathed in the warmth of love that arose first in their own hearts, was at first absorbed in their own existence, and then for the rest of their years poured in on them as echoes are sent back to one from the hills of a valley. Such men fill others with awe, not because their lives are dramatic or even filled with achievement, but because we see in them intimations of what is divinely good. It is the crowning virtue of St. Francis, and of the numberless unknowns who have been exactly like him. At times it seems to shine with such brightness that men are willing to declare and believe, quite solemnly, that its possessors are gods, as in the case of Jesus or Gotama Buddha. This is however misleading if it suggests that such love is mysterious or even rare, for nothing could in fact be more distinctively human.

However narrow and superficial may have been the conception of love and friendship discoursed on by the ancient moralists, there is one particular in which they were undoubtedly right, and that was in viewing love as a blessing rather than thinking of it, as moralists since have tended to do, as a duty. The child is born with the capacity for it, but that capacity is either nourished or destroyed by forces over which he has no control; it is entirely at the mercy of others. Nothing which is so clearly a gift or deprivation of fortune can be represented as a duty. To say otherwise is as absurd as to declare it a man's duty to be born in the first place. It is not up to the child to be tenderly loved, but up to others; and failing this, he is damaged as severely and irreparably as if deprived of a limb. A line that is sometimes interjected by the clergyman into the ritual of marriage is therefore most fitting and reflects profound wisdom in every detail. He says, ". . . and may the love you will lavish on your children be returned to you a thousandfold." Here they are not exhorted to love children; it is simply taken for granted that they will. And such love is without grotesque exaggeration represented as a palpable substance, to be "lavished" on them; it is not merely a feeble inner prompting of appropriate actions, nor a mere precept to be borne in the mind and heeded from time to time as the occasion demands. And, finally, it is quite unabashedly recognized that it needs to come back, and the more the better—"a thousandfold." Such a wish is incomparably better than dozens of vows.

Physicians and nurses in childrens' hospitals well know the consequences to children who lack love, even at the very beginning of life, before the children can have any thoughts of it or know what is going on. Psychologists know, too, that such deprivation can seldom be redeemed. An infant so deprived is as surely starved as if denied food, and the consequences are hardly less horrible. In many ways they are more so, for it is the very spirit that is crippled, and it is seldom that it can ever be reached and healed again. A child thus damaged is divested of the most precious quality any man can possess, never to be restored. He cannot rejoice in his own being, can never love himself, is thus rendered incapable of loving anything else, and hence of ever becoming loved. It is a vicious and almost unbreakable circle that dooms its victim to be frozen out of the world forever.

The disease is well recognized in a children's ward, and its symptoms are quite clear and uniform. The infant, although it is fed, does not grow much. His nourishment is simply not assimilated, even though nothing is organically wrong. All development is profoundly retarded, and a blank, passive, unhappy look takes the place of what one expects to find in an infant. He is not apt to cry, but not apt to laugh either. His head droops, he appears to have little awareness of anything, even of his own hands or of moving objects around him, and he languishes into a state of inner nothingness. He looks sick, and remains in that passive, rather vegetative state, although there seems to be "nothing wrong" with him. The disease was at one time called marasmus, and it greatly puzzled medical science. It is now perfectly well known that its cause is simply deprivation of love. Interns and nurses are now directed to do what they can in supplying some semblance of the love such a child would normally receive from its mother, by holding it while it is fed and actions of this sort. Even such makeshift efforts as these produce visible improvement.[3]

In the face of such considerations as this we should not think of love as an ornament to human life, as something that brightens it and makes life more agreeable. We need to recognize that it is the very nourishment of a life that is human, from one's very first breath to his last. It is not something with which we, as men, should be exhorted to embellish our lives; it is something without which we cannot even be men. It requires more than the possession of arms and legs and the human form to be human, for corpses and statues have these; and it requires more than a body that is quickened and warm, for an animal has this. Aristotle thought that reason was what lifted men above the rest of nature, and this has become pretty much a part of our intellectual tradition; but it does not really seem possible that one can measure human goodness by this quality. Concerning a man who is rational, perhaps preeminently so, one can only say that he is, indeed, rational; but of one filled with love, of the kind I have been trying to describe—not love that is a mere sentiment of kindness, nor of the kind that rises no higher than a decent sense of justice—one can say that he is good and noble, and unfailingly so.

NOTES

1. *Nichomachean Ethics,* Books 8 and 9.

2. For a similar treatment of erotic love, see Schopenhauer, "On the Metaphysics of Sexual Love," in *The World As Will and Representation,* E. F. J. Payne, trans. (New York: Dover Publications, 1966). Vol. II.

3. See Ashley Montagu, *On Being Human* (New York: Hawthorn Books, 1966), Chap. 5.

21

The Love of Man

In my discussion of compassion I noted that actions generally are directed toward the weal or woe of some being, oneself or others, and this enables us to discern four general incentives to action: egoism, self-hatred, compassion, and malice. If we now consider, not the incentives to action, but simply the emotions or passions evoked in the mind by one's conception and regard for himself and other persons and things, then, by making similar broad classifications, we can discern a fairly rich variety of these. Some are easily recognized and named; others, although I think they can be recognized, are not easily named; and some, perhaps, do not even exist. Such a classification, which is by no means intended to be comprehensive or even accurate in detail, will be useful, I think, in bringing to the foreground the particular passion of love with which we are now concerned, and distinguishing it from other emotions with which it is easily confused.

SOME VARIETIES OF LOVE AND HATE AS PASSIONS

Let us begin, then, with two very general and familiar states of mind that I shall, for want of anything better, call elation and dejection. These rather banal terms will perhaps serve as well as any, by virtue of their etymology, to convey the ideas of being uplifted and of being cast down. What they stand for are in any case recognizable inner states, and probably correspond to what Spinoza had in mind when he spoke of the emotions associated with heightened and lowered vitality, which he thought were basic to all the other emotions. I make no such broad

---

claim as that, but these two states, once one grasps what they are, provide a basis for understanding certain passions of love and hatred and others that are similar to them, and that is all we need here.

By referring to such states as passions, I mean to convey the precise point that they are not states that one evokes in himself except in an indirect way and, thus, to contrast them with actions. One can *do* certain things, and what is thus done is an action, but emotions can only, in the strict sense, be "suffered." That is to say, they can be evoked within oneself either by one's own actions or by something else. One can, for example, move his limbs, voluntarily, or even pursue a certain train of thought, voluntarily; but one can in no similar way feel elation or dejection, or any other emotion involving these. It is for this reason that one could be commanded, for example, to swing his arms (an action) but could not intelligibly be commanded to love or hate (passions). The same point is expressed in a commonsense way by saying that, although what he does about something is sometimes up to one, how he feels about anything is never up to one.

Consider then, first, that elation or dejection can be felt in relation to the sufferings perceived, either in oneself or in others. Elation at the suffering of another, as such, is the feeling of *malice,* whereas dejection resulting from seeing such suffering is the feeling of *compassion.* If the dejection thus suffered is accompanied by the thought that one is himself the cause of such suffering, then it may be conjoined with the feeling of *guilt;* no doubt many actions that appear to arise from compassion are really prompted by guilt, and by the thought that by such action one might compensate for or remove that dejective feeling. If, on the other hand, the elation one feels at another's suffering is conjoined with the thought of oneself as the cause of it, then it is an elative (and of course perverse) feeling, not of guilt, but of *power.* When that thought is absent, such that the suffering is perceived as caused by something other than oneself, it is merely a feeling of superiority, of comparative good fortune. A fairly common example of this type of inner rejoicing is provided by those who find delight in gossiping, which arises from a combination of malice and self-love.

Dejection felt as a result of one's own suffering is, of course, exceedingly common; it is so common that it lacks any very precise and appropriate name other than simple dejection. If, however, one perceives such suffering in oneself as caused by another, the dejective feeling is one of *resentment;* whereas if it is perceived as caused by oneself it is perhaps best called mere *bitterness,* or sometimes (when deliberate) *self-hatred.* Elation at one's own suffering is uncommon, but perhaps not nonexistent. If such elation is accompanied by the thought that one is himself the cause of his own suffering, the elative feeling is perhaps that of *martyrdom;* whereas if one thinks instead that it is inflicted by others, then the elative feeling is one of *masochism,* which is quite rightly deemed a disease.

If we turn now to the basic emotions of elation and dejection resulting from good fortune in oneself and others, we can produce a similar array of specific kinds, many of them quite easily recognizable. Thus, if one is elated at the perception of another's fortune, which one has in no way produced, one's feeling is that of *conjubilation*, and this, as a feeling, is the precise obverse of the elative feeling of malice. If such elation results, however, from the thought of oneself as the cause of another's good fortune, then it is more likely to be simply the elation of *self-congratulation*, which is really elation at one's own good fortune or superiority and is not conjubilation at all. A fairly common example is being, and being known as, another's benefactor. Dejection at another's fortune, not brought about by oneself, is simply *envy;* whereas if it is perceived as having been produced by oneself, there is added the feeling of *bitterness* or *self-reproach.*

Elation at one's own good fortune is, like dejection at one's own suffering, so common that it lacks a good and appropriate name other than simply elation. When such fortune is thought of as produced by another, however, it is conjoined with the elative feeling of *gratitude;* whereas if it is thought of as having been produced by oneself, it is simply self-congratulation again, or rejoicing from one's double good fortune—the fortune produced, and the power within oneself to produce it. Dejection at one's own fortune is correspondingly rare, although perhaps not nonexistent. Such a dejective feeling would be one of *self-abasement* and similar to self-hatred.

ABSOLUTE LOVE AND HATRED

The foregoing analysis results from the various possible ways elation and dejection can be related to suffering and good fortune, both in oneself and in others, together with certain considerations as to the source of such suffering or fortune. Some of these elative and dejective emotions are without impropriety called love or hatred. All would recognize malice as a form of hatred, for example, and conjubilation as a form of love. It is also obvious, however, that such forms of love and hatred are all quite relative, having entirely to do with good and ill fortune. That is to say, they have to do with certain things that *happen* and thereby affect the will of this person or that. They are, thus, emotions that arise and pass, and are at the mercy of what happens to be going on in the world from one moment to the next. Love, as so conceived, is no ultimate blessing, nor hatred any ultimate affliction; both are mere passions that can shift with the wind.

One can, however, conceive a love and a hate that have to do, not with the rising and falling fortunes of men, but with existence itself, which is as ultimate as anything can be. Thus, elation that is felt, not just in relation to whatever passing blessing may have fallen into one's lap at that moment, but in relation to one's very existence, the elation of just being in the world, is what I have been calling *self-love*. Dejection arising from the same fact is obviously the clearest and most absolute form of *self-hatred*. Elation, on the other hand, at the existence of another thing—whether it is another person, a god, or the merest pebble or leaf—is what I mean by *absolute love*. And dejection, not merely at the sufferings or fortunes of another, but arising simply from the existence of that other, is manifestly the most perfect form that *hate* can assume.

The relationships of some of these passions to their sources, insofar as these latter are not brought about by oneself, are illustrated in the accompanying diagram.

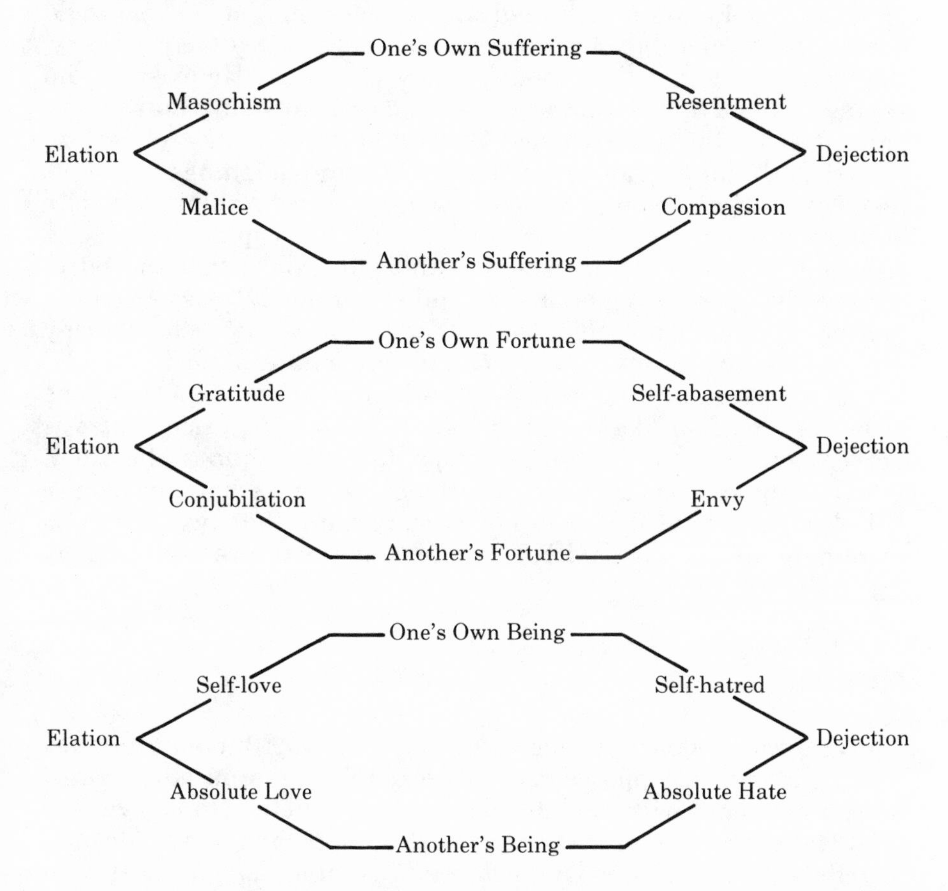

That such absolute love and hate are real is, I think, beyond doubt. There is nothing astonishing in the fact that a man should love his benefactor and hate his tormentor; such emotions represent little more than the attempt to keep oneself on course in the face of the changing tides of fortune. It is not absurd to suppose that even the higher animals may be capable of this. It is somewhat more astonishing that one should love his tormentor and hate his benefactor, but these are, nevertheless, sometimes real. It is also an obvious manifestation of the deepest love and hate that are possible. The ground of such love and hate can, therefore, only be the existence of the thing hated and loved. It is not merely what that being does to or for one, because it is loved or hated in spite of that. It is rather that there should be any such being at all. Thus when one considers the imperative of the Gospels, that one should love God with all one's heart, soul, and mind, one sees that something absolute is being called for. But it is just as clear that the injunction would be absolutely spoiled and contradicted if Jesus had then added something like this: "Because of the many blessings He bestows on you." *That* would be no absolute love, but only appreciation for good treatment. Clearly, the idea is just that God should be loved because He exists. I am saying that such love, and of course the corresponding hatred, can be evoked by the sheer existence of all sorts of things: of certain persons, for example, and even of certain inanimate things that have no power either to help or to hinder. This power of a thing to inspire both love and hate, just by existing, may also explain something else that at first seems mysterious and impossible: that these two apparently opposite emotions are often strangely close together, almost as though intermingled. But many have noted how easily an absolute love seems to turn to an absolute hate, almost casually, and many men can find examples in their own lives. The emotions of lovers are often like this, and such that only the briefest step is needed, and not a long series of steps, to convert one to the other. It is but the existence of one and the same thing that can inspire either passion; and it should not be surprising that two things so seemingly different should be so alike, when both are explained by the same fact.

POSSESSIVE LOVE

I have already said that absolute love, or what I have also called the love of man, as opposed to the various relative forms adumbrated here, must begin with oneself and cannot possibly begin anywhere else. There is nothing novel or odd in this claim, and one needs only to reflect on what his own existence is to him, as compared with everything else, to see that this had to be so. One would never be tempted to think otherwise, except for certain debased moral ideals whose authors, in their zeal for loving all of mankind, have tended to treat such love as mere altruism and service to others and thus to disregard the fact that one is himself a man. Spinoza has perhaps declared more forceably than anyone the necessity of first loving oneself as a condition of loving anything at all; but even when the rule of Christianity says you must love your neighbors it immediately adds, "*as yourself.*"

Such self-love, it should be clear by now, is not what one would ordinarily think of as selfishness; indeed, it is the other way around. A selfish person, in the ordinary sense, is precisely one who to whatever degree he is selfish does *not* love himself. Selfishness in this sense is self-serving behavior, and the selfish man is accordingly one who, *not* loving his own existence and being to that extent discontent with himself, seeks to add all sorts of things to himself precisely in order to make up what to him seems a deficiency. It is largely from this that the boundless love of possessions arises. It represents a vain and futile attempt to compensate for what seems lacking in one's own being, and thus bring oneself up to a level comparable to the goodness one finds, and sometimes bitterly rues, in others. I refer to it as vain and futile because, being so motivated it can obviously never succeed. It is not surprising, therefore, that such self-hatred, whether great or small, is a fertile source of envy, spite, and hatred. Self-love, on the other hand, which is an agreeable total satisfaction with one's own being, has no need of self-serving, and can never be a source of hatred toward anything. It is, on the contrary, the first step toward love for the sheer existence of all sorts of things.

But it is only the first step. Love can stop at that point, at love of oneself, and in that case everything else one loves he loves only for his own sake, not theirs. This is the essence of possessive love, and it is not uncommon in husbands and wives whose love for each other, and even for their children, has not gone beyond that. I mention these two relationships, conjugal and parental, because they constitute something of a test case, usually presenting the clearest and closest opportunity one can ever have for stepping beyond himself. Some persons do, nonetheless, think of their spouses and children first of all as ornaments to themselves, the wife drawing her inner satisfaction from the achievements of the man in whose eyes she has found favor, the husband relishing the physical beauty and talents of his wife, and both prizing the achievements of their children as though they were somehow their own. Such possessive love easily extends to other things, of course, particularly to things of beauty with which one can surround himself and call his own; and while such love of possession can, as already suggested, express a certain degree of self-hatred, it can also be the expression of self-love that has failed to get beyond itself. As self-love it is not to be despised or berated; indeed, all love for other things must begin there.

It nevertheless falls far short of the ideal of human nature that now begins to emerge.

LOVE AS A DUTY

Kant saw perfectly the incompatibility of love and duty. To the extent that one is prompted by love to render assistance to others, or to do anything else, then to that extent, Kant noted, he is *not* being prompted to do it by the incentive of duty. His motivation clearly lies in his own feelings and inclinations; he is merely doing what he wants to do; and although this might indeed be precisely what duty would bid him to do if he did not love, it is nevertheless not a dutiful act. Kant, accordingly, dismissed such actions as being without genuine moral worth and referred to feelings of love as pathological. A similar claim had been made by the Stoics of antiquity, who endeavored to rid their lives of all passions and hearken only to reason and the sense of duty. Thus Epictetus advised that, in case one should come upon a friend sitting in the gutter who is groaning and wailing from the misfortunes that have befallen him, one should try to comfort him in whatever ways duty suggests, even to the extent of groaning with him, if necessary. However, Epictetus immediately added, "Be careful that you do not groan inwardly too." Feelings of love and compassion, just because they are passions and, hence, not within our power or control, are thus claimed to be unsuitable incentives to action. Only the sense of duty provides this.

This seems a strange and grotesquely perverse turn for the thinking of a moralist, and it is astonishing how many have been impressed by it, and even inspired.[1] The insight is certainly correct, that love and duty do not mix as incentives to action, and that love, as a feeling, cannot be commanded. It is, as I have noted, a passion and not an action, and therefore it cannot be evoked or banished at will. But from none of this does it follow that the passion of love is without moral significance, *unless* one simply presupposes a morality of duty. Another inference is perfectly possible, and it is this: Love is a passion that cannot be commanded, and hence cannot be represented as a duty, but because it is, nevertheless, a virtue and the noblest incentive to action, then, to that extent, the concept of duty has no place in the moral life. Kant, with perfect consistency, could have developed his insight in that direction. The insight that love, as a feeling, is incompatible with the incentive of duty, is plainly correct. In the light of it one can expunge feelings of love from theoretical ethics, or one can expunge the incentive of duty. Kant took the former course, and I take the latter.

And why, anyway, should it seem so obvious to so many that the concept of duty is inseparable from ethical thought? It plays no significant role in some of the most inspiring moral philosophy that history provides. Duty, in any abstract and uniquely moral sense, hardly entered the thinking of the Greeks; one can read Plato and Aristotle without finding it, and without missing it. Good and evil were what concerned them, and it was in terms of good and evil, rather than in terms of dutiful conduct, that they interpreted virtue and vice. Spinoza's philosophy provides another example—a system that is fatalistic throughout, in which the idea of performance of duty hardly makes an appearance, but the idea of finding the supreme good is everything. And this is, surely, a proper aim of moral philosophy—*not* to discover one's duty, so that one may *perform* it, but rather to find the greatest good, so that one may hope to *attain* it.

Having a duty, as I pointed out earlier, involves the idea of *owing* something, and is in fact one and the same notion. It implies having some kind of *debt*. To whom, then, do we owe any actions? Well, obviously we owe them to whomever we have contracted to perform them. Later this idea was extended to include the idea of owing them to the state, inasmuch as they are prescribed by the laws. The idea was then extended still further, to include owing certain actions to God because they are demanded in the Scriptures. But what, now, if we lift this concept of duty even from the theological context, in which it still preserves a meaning, and speak of actions that are owed—that is, actions that it is our duty to perform—but not owed *to* any person or thing? This is the extension that Kant has tried to give the idea, and at that point the idea becomes completely empty. It maintains its powerful grip, though, mostly because of the conditioning that religion has had on our culture. The idea of goodness has suffered no such preemption of meaning, and it is still very worthy of being the central and noblest concern of philosophy.

LOVE AS A BLESSING

It has been altogether too common to represent love as a social virtue and recommend it as an incentive to action because of its fruits and the agreeableness it adds to social life. We need another emphasis, and that I try to effect by representing love as a blessing. By this I mean that it is a good to be attained, but not a thing to be used. Calling it a blessing is inept, as it suggests themes of devotional literature rather than philosophy; but I do not know what else to call it. Perhaps it should simply be called the greatest good.

I have indicated the possibility of the passion of love beginning with oneself and then extending beyond, first, no doubt, to other persons, but not ending with them or including all men, which seems quite impossible. Such things are loved, not for what they can do, but for exactly the same reason one loves himself; namely, because they are there. It extends to things both trivial and great and need not even make much of a distinction between these, because the existence of things is not something that admits of degrees. Thus one can love, in the sense I am suggesting, not only another person, but a sunset, a flock of migrating geese, and even the pebbles and insects at one's feet. I call this the love of man, not because it is exclusively directed toward men, but because men are alone capable of it. It is, then, not primarily an incentive to actions, but a passional state, something that is to be possessed rather then used. It need not call upon one to *do* anything whatever, for it is instead the aspiration to *be* a certain kind of man, to exemplify an ideal of human nature that is found to be good, not primarily for what it does, but for what it is. To look at it otherwise—to think of its worth, for example, solely in terms of what it produces in conduct—is to take a utilitarian, almost commercial view of the matter and to risk missing its goodness entirely.

What, then, is so good about it? Now to ask that question is, it seems to me, to miss the point. It is like asking what is so good about a sunset, when after all it yields so little light. The goodness of something cannot be shown, it can only be found.

Earlier I tried to show that good and evil are relative to needs, purposes, and desires, that the goodness of a thing consists of its being sought, and evil, of its being shunned. It is nevertheless possible, although it seems at first to contradict this, to pursue what is not good, and shun what is not evil; for it is perfectly possible to find that something that has been pursued and won is not after all satisfying, or that something that has been avoided but nevertheless thrust upon one is, after all, satisfying of the purposes and desires he in fact has. The truth of this is what is at the heart of Socrates' claim, so misleadingly expressed, that one cannot voluntarily and knowingly pursue what is evil. The goodness of the ideal I have portrayed therefore consists simply in this and cannot be anything else: It entirely fulfills the need that men, as men and not as animals, naturally have, and this remains true even for those who may not know it. But this is a truth that can only be said. To be shown, there must be eyes that can see it.

MORAL RULES AND ASPIRATIONS

Moral philosophy, at least since the rise of Christianity, has for the most part been concerned with imperatives, commands, rules, or principles, all of which are essentially the same. The reason for this is obvious; namely, that it has been considered the task of moral philosophy, largely under the influence of religion as it was conditioned by Roman law, to specify what *actions* men should perform. The normal way to express this is by a rule.

Imperatives and commands are one and the same; namely, expressions of what some man or men must do in compliance with the will of another. "Remember the Sabbath day and keep it holy," for example, is a command representing in Scripture the will of God. Such commands may be positive, as this is, or negative, as in the case of prohibitions. In either case, however, it is actions that are enjoined or prohibited.

Rules are simply commands or expressions of the will of another that are continuously binding. Thus, the command "Come forward," addressed to a particular man or group, is no rule, although it is a command; whereas "Thou shall not steal" is a command that is a rule. Like other commands, therefore, rules enjoin and prohibit actions.

Moral rules and principles, as they are elaborated by moral philosophy, are entirely general, inasmuch as they are supposed to apply to all rational men. They differ from other commands, rules, and laws in one very significant respect: they are not represented as expressing the will of any author or commander. They are instead supposed to be expressions of the will of him who is commanded, provided he is rational. Thus, if a man understands why he should, for example, try to promote the greatest happiness of the greatest number, which is a moral rule, then he presumably will, in obedience to his reason, impose that rule on himself. No other commander is needed.

I have already raised doubts concerning the intelligibility of a command that issues from no commander and is thus assumed to express no will except that of him to whom it is meant to apply. I have also maintained that no moral rules are really binding, because they all admit of exceptions that are made on some basis other than rules themselves. Any moral rule of the form "always act such that . . ." is entirely canceled by acceptance of a single dictum having the same content but asserting "In *this* case do not act such that . . .," and I have argued that, in the case of every such moral rule, there is such a dictum. There is, then, no need to reintroduce any of those doubts concerning the legitimacy and value of moral rules.

What does need to be emphasized, however, is that moral rules or imperatives, like any others, are rules of *action*. Like laws, commands of Scripture, or any other imperatives and rules, they have to do with what men are supposed to do and to refrain from doing. And this obviously presupposes that the things men are, by such rules, supposed to do or refrain from are things they *can* do or refrain from; or in other words, that they are actions.

From this it can be seen that the foregoing reflections on the beatitude of love and the incentive of compassion can give rise to no moral rules whatsoever. Love and compassion are passions, not actions, are therefore subject to no rule or command, and can in no way be represented in terms of duties or moral obligations. This is in any case obvious just from consideration of any moral rule that might appear to have such a content. If, for example, one is commanded to love his neighbor, then the love that is commanded cannot be any passion or feeling; it can only be a command to act toward one's neighbor as one acts who does love his neighbor. Love, as a feeling, cannot be commanded, even by God, simply because it is not up to anyone at any given moment how he feels about his neighbor or anything else. Regardless of how he may feel, however, he can be commanded to treat his neighbor in certain ways, or in other words, to act in the manner enjoined.

Hence, one could never represent it as a moral rule that one should act from compassion, and the claim I have made, that compassion is a uniquely moral incentive, gives rise to no moral rule whatever. For one to act from compassion, his action must really be prompted by compassion. But this is a feeling or state of mind, not subject even to one's own will, and so not subject to any other. It can, therefore, be subject to no command. One can, indeed, command one to act as a compassionate person would act, and one could even try to make of this a moral rule, because such a command or rule reaches only to the act and not to its incentive. But such actions are no longer acts of compassion and are, in fact, acts of hypocrisy. A compassionate act, as so conceived, is only an act that is intended to resemble a real act of compassion and does not in any way require the presence of the one thing that would make it genuine.

Sometimes, partly perhaps in response to the felt need for rules and commands, and for exhorting men to desirable actions, words that once referred solely to passions come instead to apply only to actions. The word *charity* is an instance of this, for this word is derived from *caritas,* which is the Latin for *agapé*, or religious love. A genuine act of charity is therefore not, as it is now generally thought to be, merely an act of giving; it is in its original sense an act that springs from love and is prompted by nothing else. And, clearly, there can be no such thing as giving *to* charity; one can only give *from* charity, in its true sense. Because, however, this too is a passion and not something that can be commanded, men have generally settled for the imitation, which is just the external act, and something that can be enjoined. This has become so complete that even the word has nearly lost its original sense.

LOVE AS INSPIRATION

Taking such things as this into account, many moralists, such as Kant and even Mill, have tended to treat the passions as of secondary importance to moral philosophy. Men can be instructed about what they should do, or what their actions must be in order to be dutiful, but no one can presume to dictate how men should feel. But here, I suggest, moral philosophy has simply taken the wrong turn. Instead of aiming at the elaboration of moral rules, which has been notoriously unsuccessful from the start, moral philosophy should aim at the presentation of moral aspirations, which do extend to the passions and to the inner man. Moral rules—as contrasted with positive laws and other conventions that need have no moral content and can be justified on purely practical grounds—are already sufficiently dubious, even if there were agreement concerning which ones should be honored. When taken in dead earnest they can become a source of untold mischief, even enabling men to spread suffering around them and providing what appears as an excuse for so doing—or even better than an excuse, something that one can really believe is a moral justification. And in any case men are surely capable of something better than going about from one day to the next busying themselves doing all sorts of things in accordance with moral principles and rules, and congratulating themselves that they have, just by virtue of this, attained morally significant lives. One of Socrates' claims was surely true: It is the inner man that matters, for what a man is is infinitely more important than what he from time to time does. No mere rule of morality, however strenuous and noble, is going to reverse the relative worth of these two things.

The passion of love, as I have described it, has two sides, a negative and a positive one. Negatively, it expresses itself in compassion for suffering. Positively, it is the absolute love for the existence of persons and things, of oneself and others. This yields no rule of morality, but what of an ultimate or final moral aspiration? Clearly it points to this, and I express it in the most banal and unpretentious way I can, in order that its transparently simply meaning cannot be lost, and to foil any temptation to make war on it with dialectical reason. The ultimate moral aspiration is simply this: *To be a warm-hearted and loving human being.* I call this an *ultimate* aspiration because no question of *why* can be asked concerning it, without misunderstanding it. It is not deemed good on account of any beneficial deeds that it prompts, or because of its usefulness to men; nor is it fulfilled by anything that one merely does. It invites one to *be* rather than commanding him to *do,* and yet it cannot fail to ennoble whatever one does. There is in this simple aspiration no rationalization, no requirement to measure the consequences of one's deeds against some goodness outside of himself, no reasoning upon one's incentives to see if they are consistent, no rule or principle whatever. It commands nothing, and so requires no commander either within oneself or without. It simply invites, and replaces moral sanction, which is negative, with solicitation, which is not. Its solicitation is to be a kind of person that the nature of absolute love shows to be supremely good.

But is not such an aspiration just a moral principle all over again, something one is expected somehow to fulfill? Not at all, for it is very likely that no man really can, and very certain that no man can do so at will. In this it resembles, but by no means pretends to be the same, as an aspiration enunciated by Jesus—namely, the aspiration to be *perfect,* like God. Clearly this is not a command, much less a moral rule, because it in no way says what to do, but only what to be, and what it exhorts one to be is something impossible.

NOTE

1. Thus Gilbert Murray, commenting on the Stoic devotion to duty and indifference to consequences, said that "this view is so sublime and so stirring that at times it almost deadens one's power of criticism." *Stoic, Christian and Humanist* (London: Allen & Unwin, Ltd., 1940), p. 109.

22

The Ethics of Having Love Affairs

"Women are not men's equals in anything except responsibility. We are not their inferiors, either, or even their superiors. We are quite simply different races."

—PHYLLIS McGINLEY

A love affair is defined for our purposes as an intense, passionate, and intimate relationship between a man and a woman, at least one of whom is married to, or cohabits in a marriage relationship with, someone else. By defining a love affair in this somewhat restricted way I am, therefore, excluding from consideration so-called "platonic" relationships, which may be intense but not intimate, as well as homosexual relationships, which involve all sorts of questions that will not occupy us here.

My definition also excludes from the class of "love affairs" the mere cohabitation of unmarried people, where neither is married to, or has any marriage relationship with, someone else.

Love affairs are dangerous and often destructive, particularly for married people. They risk not only the deep injury of eventual rejection, but the destruction of homes and damage to children. Even unmarried people, such as those in college, sometimes scrupulously avoid sexual intimacies, usually on moral or religious principles, and there is no doubt that they thereby avoid certain risks. Passionate love is strong, and sometimes explosive in its effects.

People who value safety, orderliness, and a certain predictability in their lives—expecially married people of this temperament—are probably wise to avoid temptation and hold firmly to accepted values, drawing

From *Having Love Affairs* (Buffalo, N.Y.: Prometheus Books, 1982), pp. 17, 47–55.

comfort from a socially approved pre-marital virginity and then monogamous marriage.

At the same time, no one should assume that everyone ought to avoid love affairs, or that even married people should necessarily abstain. Dangerous as love affairs may be, no one would suggest that they are without joy. In fact, the vehemence with which they are condemned from some quarters is indicative of how absolutely exhilarating they can be.

Nor should love affairs be thought of as casual and light-hearted, mere games that are easily entered into and just as easily abandoned. This idea, common to popular journalism, is closer to fantasy than fact. The idea that love affairs add spice to marriage, or that an affair can be a tonic to revive a faltering marriage, is simply naive. Love affairs are deadly serious, and the popular references to "playing around" are merely intended to belittle them by distortion. Perhaps life would be simpler if sex were not serious business. Certainly human relations would be easier and we would be spared a great deal of misery. But that is not how we were made. The most powerful passions in life cannot be made trivial.

In this realm we are where every person must decide for himself and accept his own responsibility. No one can tell another person what is and is not permissible with respect to whom he or she will love, and when or where, or under what conditions. No clergyman can make that decision for you, nor can any moralist, teacher, parent, or functionary. It is your decision and yours alone, to which you need answer to no one but yourself. Nor can such a decision be made by one partner in a marriage for the other; for to pass the choice to someone else—anyone else—is not to act correctly, but simply not to act at all. It is to relinquish all responsibility for one's decisons and actions with respect to the choice in question.

However inadvisable it may be to seek love outside the conventional restraints, the *right* to do so is about as clear as any right can be. For we are here dealing with what is ultimately personal and private, with that realm into which no one else can step without trespassing. Everyone has a right to be in anyone's arms he chooses. Other people can think what they like and do as they like with their own lives and loves, but they cannot decide for you. Only you can do that.

I am therefore not going to consider the morality or immorality of adultery, simply because no morality or immorality exists there to consider. I shall instead consider the ethical, and to some extent the purely practical, questions that emerge from love affairs. These relationships are dangerous and often destructive, but do they have to be? They are not going to cease just because someone plucks a supposedly moral prohibition from the thin air. Given that people do fall in love, and not always in ways which others consider permissible, we want to minimize the danger and destructiveness of doing so. The problem is just this simple. The answers, however, are less simple.

It is a paradox of human psychology that sexual passion underlies the deepest and tenderest affection as well as the most hideous form of assault, namely, rape; that it is the basis of both beauty and pornography, virtue and vice, of that which is ennobling, as well as that which is totally corrupting of a person's heart, mind, and feelings. It is because of this limitless power for both good and evil that the expression of sexual passion is everywhere hedged with rules, the most common being: "Thou shalt not." Very few of even the most natural expressions of this passion are actually condoned; many, where enforcement is possible, are positively forbidden. Indeed, the only completely acceptable indulgence of sexual love is normal coitus within marriage, a rule that construes "normal" in the narrowest fashion, and "marriage" as mere legality.

In civilized society this is everywhere recognized as absurd, yet hardly anyone wants to say so. That rules are needed for the control of so dreadful a force is obvious; however, nothing but hypocrisy is served by mere lip service. Even worse, when the single rule "Thou shalt not" is so generally disregarded in practice, and people become involved in affairs for which no other rule has been laid down, then, suddenly, *anything* is permitted. Deceptions, lies, and the use of the most terrible psychological weapons at one's disposal are given free reign, often with the most incredibly devastating consequences. Even the law condones the viciousness of such a total breakdown of human relationships, considering that when the basic prohibition has been breached then every decent consideration may be jettisoned with it. Spying is encouraged, even the introduction into divorce proceedings of clandestine photographs, and, in general, the debasement of everything that is warm and tender and good in human relationships—all this in the name of the law. Persons whose moral bent is extremely narrow will survey the destruction and roundly iterate the purely negative but hallowed rule "Thou shalt not," thinking that this is going to salvage something worthwhile. The hypocrisy and ugliness is compounded when persons of small imagination, in whom the love of life burns dimly, secretly yearn for the gratuitous affection of a truly passionate love affair. Despairing of finding it, they unctiously intone for the rest of humanity the mean and niggardly command "Thou shalt not."

Monogamous love was never the deliverance of nature. It was the invention of frightened human beings, motivated originally by no better motive than the selfish regard for ownership; adultery was originally thought of, in our religious tradition, as a violation of a man's (not a woman's) property. "*My* wife" had exactly the connotation as "*my* chattel"; it still does, the moment the ownership expressed by "my" appears to any husband to have been violated. The "my" of "my husband," on the other hand, is less an expression of a property relation than it is an expression of subordination and deference, as in the case of "my master." It is for this reason that the idea of a cuckolded husband is easily understood, but no one ever speaks of a cuckolded wife. If a wife is discovered in an adulterous relationship, then her husband is thought to have been put upon, and made a fool of—cuckolded, in the archaic but apt vocabulary of our ancestors. The wife of a husband thus discovered is, on the other hand, merely pitied. Her security and her home have been unsettled, but not her ownership of a person, for this was never thought to exist for her in the first place.

There is certainly no longer any need to pretend that this expresses an acceptable, or even a genuinely civilized, morality. If love and affection are good—and they are, indeed, the ultimate good, exceeding wealth, honor, and everything else in the joy they bring to their possessor—then the free expression of passionate love cannot be bad, except in effects. And, to be sure, these effects can be so horribly bad, so totally destructive of everything good, that it is no wonder people still find a kind of elemental wisdom in simply restricting passionate love to the formal relationship of marriage.

The answer, then, does not lie simply in abandoning the traditional restrictions. If these restrictions are to be abandoned, as they should be, then some protection is needed against the evils that they were originally designed to avert. What is needed is the guidance offered by some kind of rules. These rules will be, for those who are fond of paradoxical expressions, the moral rules for adulterous love—an expression that raises smiles only because it sounds like the introduction of rules into that which has already been made wrong by ancient commandment. Let us say, then, that we need guidelines for the expression of passionate love, the rule of prohibition having been abandoned once and for all. Or better, we shall not say "Thou shalt not," but rather, "Thou shalt love, freely, honestly, tenderly, joyously, generously, and unselfishly." But all this needs to be spelled out, otherwise it sounds like a mere slogan.

No ethic ever emerges in a vacuum. Every ethic, though it may be represented as the deliverance of God, is in fact a response to human needs. That moral rules are intoned with solemnity, and deviations from them regarded with frowns and ostracism, testifies to the depth of the needs which those rules protect and not to their exalted origin. For their origin is in the needs themselves, a humble beginning, but most certainly a real one. Of course it follows from this that moral rules which no longer help to fulfill human needs are rules that do not deserve any intelligent person's allegiance. Timid moralists and clergymen who have themselves become so acculturated to ancient ways and conventional rules as to make them the basis of their own emotional security recoil against such suggestions, with fear and sometimes anger; but they have nothing with which to oppose them, except the tireless and solemn iteration of the rules themselves, as though the mere repetition of some slogan were a confirmation of its truth and wisdom.

This is written with the conviction of the unrivaled goodness of passionate love, in which the greatest fulfillments anyone can find are sometimes possible. Indeed, genuine and intense happiness probably has no other source except, perhaps, in the ecstasies of religion. Those who seek fulfillment elsewhere—in fame, power, wealth, or whatever—find nothing but substitutes for real happiness. Some people do, for example, find power in high positions, but it is a poor substitute for the warmth of genuine affection that is sometimes found in the arms of a lover. Similarly, some attain fame, but it, too, is a poor second to the actual understanding of the heart and mind that is achieved by lovers. Convinced of the helplessness and misery of mankind, the famed defense attorney Clarence Darrow concluded one of his extensive litanies about the wretchedness of life with the declaration that no genuine happiness exists anywhere—but then added, in parentheses, as if by grudging afterthought, "except within the warmth of the family circle." Cold and calculating, and steeped in the pessimism and cynicism that his life and career had fostered, even Darrow felt forced to concede this one possibility of happiness. It was a source that was withheld from him. His own marriage had ended in ruin, and he almost never alluded to it.

The happiness that is sometimes within the reach of lovers is by no means automatic, however. It is almost banal to point this out, for who but the romantic and sentimental is unaware that lovers expose themselves far more to misery than joy? All persons suffer—some more, some less—from illness, accident, loss, humiliation, and so on. But there is something especially poignant and seemingly unnecessary in the sufferings of lovers. They *ought* to be happy, so why are they so miserable? We like to imagine that it is some sort of mistake, that an adjustment here or there will restore everything, and sometimes, even, that a few well-spoken words or a renewed declaration of love will put everything back as it should be. Yet, in fact, the misery of those whose love is dead, particularly those still married, is profound and virtually immovable. Hardly anything is so heavy with sadness as a household in which the warmth of love has been replaced by a stolid acceptance of something else, whose whole value consists in the fact that it is less bad than the possibilities exposed by abandoning it. If you find yourself in such a household, you see the lines of sorrow that have replaced the glow of love in faces of former lovers. Here and there are half-completed projects, once started with zeal, and now pursued perfunctorily, often in the vain hope that someday things will get better, someday the kind of days once lived will return again. Children come and go with sullenness, for while they are not participants in the crumbling love their parents once felt, they nevertheless pick up the sense of something lost. They feel insecure and no verbal assurances can convince them that all is well. They know otherwise. A garden goes to weeds and projects in the shop or yard are left half finished; friends come and go as before, but only momentarily divert the sad participants in this unhappy allegiance. There is worse suffering than this, certainly. In fact, this kind of dead but still existing marriage is closer to the norm than we would like to admit. Most marriages limp, even those that are not crippled or moribund. Those that are vibrant are rare. But the kind of pall that settles over a dying marriage has a poignancy and sadness of its own, partly because of the hopes that seem so needlessly unfulfilled, and partly because the bitterness of it all seems so irrevocable. It is the kind of suffering that accompanies repeated hope in the face of utter hopelessness.

It is partly from a perception of the immense goodness, and the immense evil, that lovers can create, and partly, of course, for the protection of children, that civilized peoples everywhere have hedged the institution of marriage—and, to a lesser extent, unmarried love—with rules, prohibitions, laws, taboos, and customs which have ritualized marriage and erected obstacles to its termination. The home, it is thought, must by all means be preserved; and having no other means of keeping it intact, societies have resorted to rules and ceremony. Needless to say, this does not work. A society can, to be sure, render the legal dissolution of a marriage impossible, as has been done in some countries; but all this has ever achieved is the preservation of the thinnest outward appearance. A church can, of course, with much solemnity, formalize the state of matrimony, even declare it incorruptible and indissoluble; but this, too, only creates the outward appearance. Marriage itself can in no way be created by any priest or servant of the state. It cannot be preserved by them nor by any other power of heaven or earth, except in appearance. Nor can it really be terminated by them; they can at best only recognize what has already ended. Marriage is entirely the work of those who enter into it. Its successes, and rewards of rejoicing, the warmth and fulfillment it gives, are theirs alone. Its failure, and the inner desolation this produces, are theirs too. The rest of the world can look on, but only they will have the blessings if they succeed, and the anguish if they do not.

Of course this implies that marriage, being the creation of two persons, can be made ethical or moral by them alone. No priest, no political functionary, no state, no church, no rules, and no laws can confer moral rightness on this relationship, nor can any of these make that relationship morally wrong. Only lovers can do these things. It is lovers who make a marriage. No priest makes it. It is lovers, or former lovers, who destroy a marriage. No court dissolves it. Really, all a church or court can do is to confer outward legality on a state of affairs that the individuals involved have already established.

This truly goes to the heart of the matter, so far as morality is concerned. For there is a popular conception to the very contrary; that is, it is widely thought, even regarded as obvious, that *only* an authorized functionary of the church or government, a clergyman or judge, can make the relationship of lovers ethical, and indeed, that marriage between lovers is the very creation of such persons or the rituals they perform. People become married, it is thought, at a stroke, by the ceremonious pronouncement of words and the signing of documents, as though there were no more to it than this. Of course that formality is required for the *legality* of a marriage relationship. This is a truism. But to suppose it to be required for the *morality* or even the existence of that relationship is a naive, even vulgar confusion of genuine morality with law. Not all that the law requires measures up to any significant moral standard, nor does everything that is forbidden by law violate morality. If it were otherwise, then the merest infractions of parking regulations, or unintentional tax delinquencies, would be violations of morality, while, on the other hand, the total and casual disregard of human suffering, which is permitted by law, would violate no moral requirement. What is required or forbidden by law is often but not always the same as what is required or forbidden by morality. To suppose that the deepest and most precious feelings of which human beings are capable—the very feelings that are the basis not only of all social life, but life itself, the feelings of love and passion between the sexes—can be significantly influenced by any outsiders at all, or that any outsider can confer either morality or immorality upon them, is to suppose what is plainly absurd. Worse than that, it is to try to chuck onto the shoulders of some functionary a responsibility that no person can possibly relinquish, namely, the responsibility of lovers to create their own marriage. They will not accomplish this through the approval of others nor the approval of their church nor even through the approval of the whole of mankind, who are forever outside that relationship and all its implications.

There is, therefore, absolutely nothing wrong or immoral in the marriage relationships so commonly established between young people, especially those entered into at college, and society as a whole is gradually coming to realize this. Persons involved in such extra-legal relationships should make no attempt to conceal them, and if this outrages their parents, then it is actually the parents who ought to be ashamed, rather than their children. The legality of a marriage relationship adds nothing whatever to its morality, and the absence of such legality takes nothing away from it. All that legality does is to suggest a greater permanence, being considered the expression of a stronger commitment on the part of the partners; but it by no means guarantees this. And it has nothing to do with the rightness or wrongness of the relationship.

The marriage relationships of students are in most ways not essentially different from the marriages of their parents. The motivations for them are similar, and their patterns are much the same. They differ mainly in that they are less public, depending upon parental attitudes, and there are usually no outsiders filling the roles of in-laws.

What leads college men and women to take up living together is not the desire for sex, as some outsiders sometimes suppose, for most campuses are already perfectly free with respect to sexual relationships. It is by no means necessary for students to live together in order to sleep together, for they can do that any time they wish. Just like marriage itself, the marriage relationship severely restricts the sexual freedom of its partners, for each is then accountable to the other in a way he would not otherwise be. Secrecy, too, becomes more difficult, since the whereabouts of each partner is apt to be known to the other or can, at least, be inquired about.

The primary motivation students have for entering into a marriage relationship is security. It is a word students almost invariably use when asked why they want to live together, usually in secrecy from their parents. However, the security of such a primary friendship is often purchased at the cost of many less important but more numerous relationships. The following, for example, is more or less typical:

> The reason Bob and I moved in together was for emotional security. I wanted to go back to our room and know he would always be there, and that's how he felt, too. It was going back to someplace that meant something, not just to a place to sleep and study and a roommate I hadn't even chosen. Even if we had a fight, I knew he would come back, because that was home.
>
> One night when Bob was hours late coming home I nearly went crazy. He was supposed to be back at ten-thirty, and it was nearly one in the morning when he walked in. He hadn't even phoned or anything. I didn't care where he was, and I didn't think he was with another girl or anything like that, but I felt neglected and abandoned when he didn't let me know, and then finally walked in just as if nothing in the world was wrong, and wondered what I was upset about. He had only been out with some friends, and that was perfectly okay, but he could have let me know.

To this account of an experience that is familiar to many wives, the student added the following, which is not so familiar to people long married:

> The relationship lasted less than two years. We're still friends, but we don't live together. We found we had cut out all our other friends, without intending to. They all thought they had been put in second place, and I can see why. Seeing that the two of us were completely wrapped up in each other and never went any place except together, they just looked to other people when they wanted to go to a movie or a concert or anything. And I also think they were sometimes jealous. They knew we liked

each other better than we would ever like them. Of course if everyone in college were living with a lover, then it would be different, but that isn't the way it is.

Accounts such as this, so banal and so typical of married life, do raise the question as to whether the presence or absence of legality in a marriage relationship has anything more than symbolic significance, and a fairly trivial significance at that.

In any case, in what follows I shall treat extra-legal marriage relationships as marriages, since the problems arising in them are essentially the same as the conventional marriages; and when I speak of "husbands" or "wives," what is said can usually be understood to apply to the partners in these relationships as well as to legally united couples. The main differences between the two, so far as this discussion is concerned, are that nonlegal marriage relationships are usually (though not always) less stable or lasting, and they seldom involve children. Most important of all, these marriage relationships will never be treated as *love affairs*. This expression will be reserved for intense and passionate relationships between men and women, at least one of whom is already married to, or in a marriage relationship with, someone else.

The idea that the relationship of lovers is made morally acceptable only by formal legality has created an amazing number of perversions. They result from the supposition that people are "really married" if they have been legally joined, but not *really* married otherwise, a notion that sometimes seems almost impossible to dislodge. Even clergymen, whose concerns are normally thought to transcend those of police officers and magistrates, fall victim to this strange notion—partly, perhaps, because the law has given them the role of bestowing legality on that relationship, and they do not wish to see their power undermined.

Thus two persons, once married lovers and still not divorced, can become the bitterest of enemies, living apart and in a state of warfare, contending for children or property, each relishing the thought of the other's annihilation. Yet, if the male member of this wretched pair should, for example, force himself upon the other, in most jurisdictions he cannot be accused of rape. He is, after all, her husband. On the other hand, if either member of this pair should find genuine tenderness and warmth in another's arms, then this would be widely regarded as perhaps understandable and forgivable, but not really quite right—they are, after all, not married. Here the minimal requirements of law are taken as the final and ultimate standard of morality, with the smallest minds and the narrowest attitudes made the measure for all. But alas, it is generally true that the noblest ideals of ethics rapidly deteriorate into sheer pettiness and hair-splitting distinctions at the hands of the vulgar who compound life's absurdities by presenting themselves as bound by the "highest," or that is to say, narrowest, standards. Indeed, such people have become so blinded by the complex web of convention ruling their lives and thoughts that they are unable to recognize a genuinely noble ideal when they see one. For the ideal of genuine love, recognized as ultimate by the world's religions and the most inspired philosophies, they substitute peer approval, even the approval of strangers. This they represent as the straight and narrow path of morality, and here they are supported by the law-abiding and the clergy. Nothing that is in fact *narrow* is worth the allegiance of anyone except those who are themselves narrow of mind and feeling.

The rightness of marriage lies in its goodness. Since this goodness is, or at least sometimes can be, immense, then the relationship of married lovers is indeed filled with moral significance. What is needed, however, is a new morality of marriage, not just a reiteration of the old and often petty legalisms that do nothing for marriage and little even for the appearance of it.

23

Fidelity

"Those who are faithful know only the trivial side of love; it is the faithless who know love's tragedies."

—OSCAR WILDE

There is a tendency among human beings to convert things that are truly good and noble into something else, some counterfeit of the original, and then, quite forgetting the nobel thing they began with, to treat the imitation as that which is good, even calling it by the same name as the original.

Patriotism is an example of this. In its original sense, patriotism is the love for one's country; and if we think of such love in its true sense, as resting upon the perception of the beauty and goodness of one's country, its institutions, and history, then it is surely in every sense a good and inspiring thing. But, over time, this originally noble idea has been doubly corrupted. The love that is embodied in it has been reduced to a kind of blind and mindless allegiance, and the object of such love has become no longer one's beautiful country, but the *symbols* of that country, such as the flag or, worse yet, the instruments and weapons of war. Thus a patriot is now thought of as someone who, without thought, displays the flag of his country here and there and who can be counted on to support war and the preparations for war. Quite obviously, this is not genuine patriotism, but a counterfeit so skillfully done that virtually everyone is gulled into accepting it as the real thing.

Another example is religion, which originally stood for the love for God. Conceived in this sense, it can hardly be doubted that it, too, is

From *Having Love Affairs* (Buffalo, N.Y.: Prometheus Books, 1982), pp. 57–62.

a noble and inspiring thing, assuming (as some of course would not) that it rests upon a true perception of the goodness of God. At the hands of human beings, however, religion has come to mean a devotion, often mindless and blind, to the *symbols* of religion, and to certain practices that have come to be associated with religion. Sometimes, in fact, it tends to deteriorate into a devotion to an *institution,* namely the church, and to the officials who administer the affairs of the church—a bishop or pope, for example—even when devotion of this kind is condemned as idolatrous. The corruption of religion becomes so complete that the counterfeit reduces the original almost to nothing, and millions of devotees imagine themselves actually to be religious, even deeply so, when in fact their devotion to the mere symbols of religion has made it impossible for them to be truly religious at all, in the original sense of the term. Thus they deceive themselves, their devotion to a counterfeit rendering them no longer capable of recognizing, or even of forming a very clear idea of, a genuine devotion to God. Nor, of course, do they deceive only themselves. If we see someone whose thoughts are much preoccupied with his church, who spends much of his life ritualistically observing the practices fostered by his church, and who venerates its priests or other officials, then it is difficult *not* to think of him as "religious." But this only shows how totally distorted the idea has become in the minds of most people.

The very same can be said of marital fidelity. Originally, fidelity meant faithfulness, which translates into constancy of love when we are speaking of the love between men and women. But like patriotism, religion, and other noble things, fidelity has been corrupted and replaced by a counterfeit. Fidelity in a marriage relationship has been reduced to mere sexual exclusiveness and, what is worse, this is thought of as more important than the constancy of love itself. Thus people see no contradiction in saying of some wife, for example, that even though she long since stopped loving her husband, she at least remained "faithful," in spite of the numerous infidelities on his part.

There are innumerable ways lovers can break faith with each other having nothing whatever to do with sexual inconstancy; and, equally important, from the standpoint of ethics, it is perfectly possible for lovers, and for husbands and wives, to be faithful to each other even in spite of sexual nonexclusiveness. People sometimes find this hard to understand, but that is only because they have forgotten what fidelity actually means and have, in their own minds, substituted another, less important, conception of it.

These points will be illustrated as we go along, but first, a few more general things need to be said.

The purpose of what follows is to set forth, not a comprehensive ethic of marriage, but only the ethical principles and guidelines that should govern a part of that relationship, namely, that pertaining to sexual fidelity. Suddenly, with the introduction of that term, we find ourselves involved with some large misconceptions.

The first, and probably the most dangerous, of these is that the ethic unique to marriage is completely exhausted by the concept of fidelity, or in other words, that morality in marriage requires the sexual exclusivity of its partners. Other rules and guidelines, it is supposed, are of a purely practical nature, some of which are of great importance, but none of them are considered strictly moral. This mean and trivial standard gives married lovers one primary rule: Thou shalt not commit adultery. The notion is cultivated in married couples that, so long as they heed this rule, the basic requirement of morality, at least so far as marriage is concerned, has been met; if the rule is ever broken, then morality has been violated. It is thought to be that simple. Adultery is, for example, the only ground that is universally considered sufficient for divorce. And here, accordingly, we begin to see why the goodness and well-being that marriage promises are so rarely found; namely, that the ethic governing it is so grossly oversimplified.

The second misconception has to do with the concept of fidelity. Infidelity is everywhere treated as though it were simply synonymous with adultery, illustrating once more the vulgarization of the ethic which seems everywhere to accompany its ritualization. Some persons look upon the wedding band as a kind of "no trespassing" sign, and upon the marriage certificate as a type of permit or license to make love, a right which must then have been lacking until conferred by that document! Yet, as we have already noted, the real and literal meaning of fidelity is *faithfulness;* and what thinking person could imagine that there is only one way in which someone can fail to keep faith with another? Faithfulness is a state of one's heart and mind. It is not the mere outward conformity to rules. There are countless ways that it can fail which have nothing whatever to do with sexual intimacy nor, indeed, with outside persons. It can be fulfilled in various ways as well, even in spite of sexual nonexclusiveness, though this is sometimes more difficult to see.

To illustrate this, imagine a man who has long been married to one person, a man who has never lapsed from the rule of strict sexual constancy, nor has he ever appeared to, and who could never be suspected of this by anyone with the slightest knowledge of his character. This man, we shall imagine, assumes without doubt the rightness of his behavior, is scornful of anyone whose standards are less strict, would not permit a violation of this rule by anyone under his own roof, and would consider no circumstances to mitigate the breach of it. So far, so good; he is, it would seem to most persons, a faithful husband.

But now let us add to the picture that this same man, being of a passive nature and having somewhat of an aversion to sex, has never yielded to temptations for the simple reason that he has had no temptations placed before him. His intimacy with his own wife is perfunctory, infrequent, dutiful, and quite devoid of joy for himself or his spouse. They are, in fact, essentially strangers to each other's feelings. In this light, the nobility of his austere ethic begins to appear less impressive, does it not?

But we are not finished with our description. Let us add to the foregoing that these two persons appear to the world as hard workers, but still quite poor. He works monotonously as a sales clerk in a declining drug store, we can suppose, while she adds what she can to the family's resources by putting in long hours assisting in the local public library. Appearances are misleading, however, for behind this facade of meager resources there are, unbeknown to anyone but the husband, and scrupulously kept secret from his wife, eight savings accounts, which have been built up over the years, each in his name only, and none containing less than thirty thousand dollars. At every opportunity—sometimes by shrewd dealing, often by sheer penuriousness, and always by the most dedicated selfishness—the husband squirrels away more savings, so that by this time the total, augmented by interest compounded over the years, adds up to a most impressive sum.

Has the rule of good faith been breached?

But to continue the description: We now suppose that the long-suffering wife of this dreary marriage is stricken, let us say, with cancer, and undergoes a radical mastectomy as the only hope of saving her life. Whereupon whatever small affection her husband ever had for her evaporates completely. He turns sullen, distant, and only dimly aware of his wife's presence, finding all the comfort for his life in those growing and secret savings accounts. He never thinks of sexual infidelity, and congratulates himself for this, as well as for other things, such as his thrift.

Finally, let us suppose that his wife has always been a poet of considerable creative power, whose creations have never received the attention they deserve, least of all her husband's, he being only dimly aware that they even exist. Yet they are finally seen and sincerely praised by another sensitive soul having the qualities of mind necessary to appreciate them, and through his encouragement, we shall imagine, she is finally able to have a sense of meaningfulness in her life, hitherto found only meagerly in the lonely creation of poetic beauty. This same newfound friend is, moreover, oblivious to the scars of her illness; he cares only for her, and, unlike her husband, his love is sincere, impulsive, passionate, imaginative, and as frequent as conditions allow.

We could expand this story, but the point of it is abundantly clear by now. It is found in answering the question: *Who has been faithless to whom?* In that answer one finds not only the essential meaning of infidelity, which is a betrayal of the promise to love, but also, by contrast, the true meaning of fidelity.

There is no need to point out that the kind of faithlessness just illustrated has its counterparts in the real world. In fact, its essential elements are found in virtually every marriage, perhaps less exaggerated here and there, but nevertheless present. How many husbands, for instance, see no breach of faith in keeping their incomes secret from their wives, precisely as a means of control? It is astonishing how this type of marital infidelity sometimes evokes no real condemnation, not even from the church, whose sense of fidelity one would expect to be most acute.

Consider, for example, this true account:

> My Uncle Tony came to this country from Italy in the twenties, with a young wife, my Aunt Carmella, but very few material goods. He found jobs in motion picture theaters, which were just getting started, and which were then called "photo plays" and, eventually, "movies." Of course sound films, or "talkies," had not yet been invented.
>
> My uncle and aunt were poor but, nevertheless, they saved enough to move to the Catskills. Eventually, Uncle Tony had saved enough to buy a movie theater of his own. This was very lucky for him, because theaters were among the very few businesses that flourished through the long depression that started at about that time. In fact my uncle prospered and bought more theaters, finally owning a string of six. Still, he and Aunt Carmella lived as frugally as ever. They lived all their lives in the same simple house he had bought when they moved up from the city, and she either made all her own clothes, or bought cheap dresses. She was a simple, uneducated, and devoted wife who never had any idea of her husband's prosperity.
>
> When Uncle Tony died, it was learned that he had left his entire fortune to Our Lady of of Mount Carmel Church, except for a couple thousand dollars he left to each of his two brothers. There was about a million dollars in his estate, which was a very great deal of money in those days. Aunt Carmella was stunned. She received nothing at all except the house she was living in. She spent her last years, after her husband died, impoverished and wretched. Uncle Tony, everyone thought, had simply tried to buy his way into heaven.

Although the abomination just described caused a great deal of comment among relatives, there is no record of its having been condemned by the church, in spite of the fact that a more perfect example of marital infidelity, in its true sense, would be hard to find. But worse than this, had it been discovered that this same man, or for that matter his wife, had just once been intimately involved with any third person, then *this* perhaps trifling situation would have been singled out, by the church and others, as an act of infidelity, quite deserving of strong moral condemnation. This is, to be sure, the usual way of moral rules. Starting out from a clear perception of genuine evil, they eventually degenerate to mere triviality, while evil flourishes as before, with about the same buoyancy as ever.

The ethical principles governing a marriage are thought to be expressed in the vows enunciated by the partners involved. These are typically administered by a clergyman, intoned usually under solemn circumstances and in the presence of witnesses, every effort being made to ensure that they are taken with the utmost seriousness.

A love affair, on the other hand, is generally thought to be governed by no moral princples whatever. If either of the partners is married, then the affair itself is considered to be a violation of a basic moral prohibition and of the vows that have been taken. "Thou shalt not" is thought to be the sole ethical rule applied to this relationship. Since the love affair is considered to be wrong in and of itself, there can be no acceptable rules for it.

Yet love affairs do exist, and they always have. Moral condemnation has never prevented them, and it never will, particularly since those who pursue them do not always feel particularly guilty. Nor does society resolutely condemn them. If neither partner is married, then there is usually no condemnation at all. Less than a decade ago unmarried persons who sought the privacy of a motel ran the risk of arrest, and were viewed with suspicion if no luggage accompanied them. Now, most large motel chains have special day rates, and no well-mannered room clerk would presume to ask why a room would be wanted then.

But more important, love affairs are sometimes, and in fact usually, profoundly serious relationships. Indeed, they can be life shattering, and it is no wonder, for we are here dealing with the passions that lie at the very basis of life. No true love affair could ever be forgotten. It is doubtful whether anyone could ever live through another day without his thoughts returning to those unbelievable hours, now long past and never to be revived, except in his memory. Love affairs are not casual. Those who treat them as such are merely trying to camouflage other feelings, such as guilt in the case of participants, or rejection in the case of those who feel abandoned. Thus a wife will sometimes refer to her husband's behavior as "playing around," trying to diminish the significance of what would otherwise be viewed as a profound rejection of herself. Or a man will sometimes allude to his own affairs as if they were casual diversions, or "dalliances," as they are sometimes called, thereby appearing to reduce both their significance and his own feelings of guilt. One cannot really feel too bad about a mere game.

Yet, in truth, these relationships are not mere games, or at least not usually. Lives are wrecked by them, just as, sometimes, otherwise tortured lives are redeemed because of them. Therefore, what is needed is an *ethic* for love affairs, an ethic that goes beyond the shallow and self-defeating "Thou shalt not." Love affairs should be taken with the same seriousness as marriage. Instead of pretending that they do not exist, which is plainly false and hypocritical, or pretending that something so common ought not to exist, which is ethically naive, we should set before us some guiding principles, some dos and don'ts, that begin with the love relationship itself and then seek, instead of simply abolishing or diminishing it, to minimize its power to cause damage and destruction, thus increasing its power to yield fulfillment to those involved.

24

Male and Female

"Woman wants monogamy
Man delights in novelty"

—DOROTHY PARKER

It is not uncommon to find sex treated as though it were merely a source of pleasure, almost a form of entertainment. Thus people are likely to be thought of as pleasure seekers, and sexual activity is then thought of as differing from other pleasant activities mainly in its intensity. Looking at the matter this way, one can indeed wonder why people would choose not to be monogamous, since there is no very clear reason why sex with one person should be significantly more pleasant than with another. One should be enough. Sometimes when one's wife or husband is discovered to have had an affair the painful reaction is expressed in the question "What is wrong with me?" or "Am I not enough?" as though the whole thing were a mere quest for pleasure—pleasure which, it was thought, was already available at home.

Such a view is so superficial as to be essentially false; and, in addition to this, it so trivializes human nature and sexuality as to be a debasement of both. Sexual intercourse and the activities that normally accompany it are of course pleasant, but that is not why they are sought; and human beings do sometimes seek pleasures, but that is no real explanation for their behavior. The impulse to sexual intimacy expresses one of the deepest yearnings of any person, which goes beyond even the yearning to love and be loved. What sensitive and thoughtful people seek in their lives is not pleasure, but fulfillment and an inner sense of worth as persons. Even these characterizations are superficial, but they provide

---

From *Having Love Affairs* (Buffalo, N.Y.: Prometheus Books, 1982), pp 69-83.

a far better foundation for the understanding of the love of the sexes than the gross oversimplification expressed in the idea of pleasure.

When someone is discovered—whether by a wife, a husband, or a lover—to be involved in an affair with someone else, the first reaction is likely to be shame and guilt, not unlike the feelings of an adolescent discovered masturbating. These feelings are as groundless in the one case as in the other; and worse than this, someone with such a sense of guilt usually has ways of expressing these feelings which seem appropriate enough to himself, but which are in fact frightfully damaging. The guilt and shame are made worse still when, as is often the case, they are combined with other strong and negative emotions, such as self-pity.

The reactions of men and women thus discovered are likely to be quite different, though not necessarily so. Thus a husband is apt to react with fervent declarations of love, not for his wife, but for the third person, declarations that are deeply felt and even, perhaps, accompanied by tears. He does not see that, even though his love may be real, his declaration of it, to the very last person on earth who should hear it, is no more than an attempt to mitigate his feelings of guilt. It is without a doubt the most inept and ill-considered behavior he could possibly display. What he should do is feel no guilt at all; and, if he does, he should either keep still, or pour his feelings into the ear of someone he can absolutely trust to keep his mouth shut.

What lies behind the feelings of guilt is quite simple. We all have been taught that adultery is wrong. Many believe it, in spite of the fact that there is no more basis for this than its iteration from one generation to another. Feelings are hard to shake off, even long after they are recognized to be groundless. The feeling that sexual infidelity is wrong is a perfect example of this. Human beings were not created by nature to be monogamous. On the contrary, monogamous love violates the natural feelings people have. A man who claims that monogamous love expresses not merely his own moral standard, which is common enough, or the norm required by his church, which is also common, but that it expresses his own feelings and inclinations, is either a hypocrite or is quite devoid of feelings in this area. A man, by nature, desires many sexual partners, and if custom or circumstances limit him to one, then his dreams and fantasies are filled with others. Hence the male preoccupation with the females he encounters: the constant flirting with waitresses, with female employees, with whomever he can view as subordinate or somehow beholden to him and thus, possibly, available. Most such behavior is inept, often childish and repellent, especially in the eyes of women, and it is almost never successful. But it cannot be said that it is not natural. What is unnatural is the cultural conditioning, the purely man-made rule of monogamy, which gives rise to this bizarre and pathetic behavior. Thus a man will unabashedly flirt with some waitress who is a perfect stranger to him, and who he knows is almost certainly destined to remain one. Even this knowledge does not extinguish his hope. The man can take this brief flirtation at face value, that is, as the expression of genuinely felt desire; whereas, on the woman's part, it is really an act, and even perceived as such, expressing no more than the hope of a good tip. And this is what it culminates in, an absurdly large tip, carrying the very simple message that the giver of it is every bit as glorious a man as he wishes to be thought. It is a small trip for the ego, a poor consolation for the ego trip that is really wanted and so vainly sought, and it is dearly purchased, not just in terms of coin, but in terms of the foolishness that the giver displays. But the price is never begrudged. The tip, indeed, is meant mostly to offset the otherwise inescapable image of the fool, and it does this, more or less, by being a large one.

However proper a man may appear—staunchly reserved in manner, speech, dress, and bearing—however scrupulously he may submit to the most refined demands of society with respect to his habits and appearance, totally succumbing to convention, there nevertheless is, or once was, a completely polygamous being behind that facade. By nature he is capable of siring a hundred or more children a year, and nature, which seems sometimes to have no other goal than the proliferation of her creatures, has given him the impulses consonant with that power. Though inwardly proud of their power, men are not taught to be proud of the desires that accompany it. Women are likely to think of them as "animals" on account of these quite unselective desires, as though the stiff and contrived civilized man was somehow nobler. Good he may be by conventional standards, but that monogamous man is not the expression of his true nature. It should be no mystery why men revert to such silliness in the presence of younger women, why in groups, as at conventions, far from the security of their wives, the childishness of each man reinforces that of the others, until before long an assemblage of respectable men, once reserved and innocuous, seems miraculously converted to a kindergarten. It is as though the sun's rising depended, in their minds, upon seeing, even if at a distance and for a brief moment, a young woman undress.

Sometimes the repressive force of society does succeed in producing what seems to be a monogamous man; in other words, a man who can sincerely say that he has no lively interest in "other" women, one who no longer dreams and fantasizes on these themes. It is even the misguided wish of some women that their own husbands or lovers should be so repressed. But such a man is also apt to be one in whom the sexual impulse itself has begun to fade. He has become an unimaginative and perfunctory lover, if still a lover at all, and frequently one whose energy has been directed to other outlets, as they are so aptly called. Thus, finding no longer any overwhelming enchantment in sex, he seeks his ego fulfillments in his business or profession, spending long hours at this and, quite often, with stunning success. Thus professors, whose teaching may require their presence on a campus only two or three days a week, sometimes spend each long day there, and even vie for committee work, sometimes only to escape the galling atmosphere of their home life. Their apparent dedication may be real enough, but its source not always entirely understood. Other men find outlets in hobbies—long fishing trips, endless hours in their gardens, or whatnot.

Society looks upon this type of man with approval, either for his industry or for his devotion to utterly harmless pursuits; but underneath it all is likely to be a very unimaginative and boring person. The following account suggests the serious impact this could have on a marriage:

> My marriage was perfect, from every standpoint except mine. Jack was kind, loved animals and children, loved his home, and was a wonderful gardener. He would spend hours in his garden or working around the house. No one in his family ever wanted for anything, and bills were always paid.
>
> Then what was wrong? He was boring. In the evening after supper he would just fall asleep, and he never did anything more exciting than work in his garden. He never gave me any gifts, even on my birthdays, unless someone told him to. We raised our children, but through all those years sex was a nothing, as far as I was concerned, and I don't think it ever meant much to him either.
>
> Then I met Norman, who was just the opposite, and had a love affair with him that lasted over ten years. Norman praised me, taught me the real estate business, gave me self-confidence, and encouraged me to take the regular training courses in real estate, which I did, and I became very successful at it. He would send me cards and gifts even when there was no occasion to, and as for sex, he taught me everything I know about it, and it was wonderful. There was really only one thing wrong with him, and that is, that for all those ten years he led me to think he was going to get a divorce, and he never did, and never intended to. Finally, when his wife had learned about us, I went to see her, assured her that I never wanted anything to do with her husband again, and I meant it. For a long time I hated him deeply, I'm not quite sure why. Now when I see him we say hello, and maybe chat, and that's it. There's nothing left.

It may seem to be driving the point home a bit too hard to say that, after having learned of his wife's affair, the husband described above committed suicide by turning a shotgun against himself in his garden; but it is true.

The suppression of the polygamous impulse in a man is, in any case, bought at a great price. Deep inside he is likely to think of no sweeter joy than a genuine love affair, for which he has ruefully abandoned hope. Any such man, whatever may be his worldly glory, is really pitiable.

When, some years ago, ago, an enterprising man set up booths near the campus of a university in a large city, and hired female students to pose nude in them for the benefit of persons having a passion for photography who might want to take pictures, men came with their cameras. These were mainly for the sake of appearances, however, like the empty luggage lovers used to take with them to motels. All they really wanted to do was look. And, as it turned out, one of the constant patrons of these booths was a vice president of one of the greatest corporations in the world. He had every conventional blessing, but needed still the greatest blessing of them all, and by this pathetic act came as close as he could to getting it.

Nature and human convention not only fail to coincide, in this realm, they are in clear conflict with each other. Nature summons a man to one thing, while custom demands another; and it is not at all clear why nature should stand condemned. Cultures may create their own prohibitions and induce men to heed them, but these are never going to eradicate the deepest expressions of our human nature. A clergyman may extract from a bridegroom the promise to forsake all others, but he cannot be induced to forsake his own feelings. The power of custom, and the general approval that goes with it, is, to be sure, sometimes astonishing. By it people can be made to do almost anything. They can be forced to bow down daily and pray, to doff their caps and bow to persons high born, to leap to their feet in the presence of royal persons, to conceal their bodies on pain of mortification, or allow themselves to be blown to bits for their country, even to cling to a totally meaningless existence rather than expose themselves to taunts and ridicule. In the same way, custom can secure a uniform declaration that monogamous love alone is good, even that it is ordained by nature, which it most certainly is not. People can be made to believe this, associate it with the greatest approval, and reserve the deepest condemnation for departures from it. Thus a man who has never departed from the exclusive attachment to his own wife, and has perhaps not even permitted himself to think of doing so, is likely to congratulate himself inwardly, to feel that he has somehow lived up to some worthwhile ideal. No one can say why this is so, other than to point to the fact that it bears the stamp of religion and custom. Sometimes this strange custom is carried to an absurd length, as when it is suggested that ideally, a person should experience no intimate love for anyone even *prior* to marriage. This was once thought obvious. It no longer is. But it is also not yet seen to be utterly absurd. Thus one can still proclaim this as a moral precept, and while his declaration may be met with skepticism, usually he will not be greeted with laughter. Such is the power of custom, even customs that have been largely abandoned in practice. There are actually persons who feel a certain moral approbation for those few species of animals, such as pigeons and elephants, who mate once for life, as though even these were somehow heeding a precept of morality.

This conflict between the demands of nature and the demands of custom would be of little interest to anyone except philosophers if it were not for the fact that it generates negative emotions, particularly guilt and, to a lesser extent, jealousy. These are terrible not only in themselves, in that they are painful to their possessors, but even more terrible in their destructive power. The power of jealousy to destroy precious human relationships is well known. The similar power of guilt is not always so obvious.

There are two extreme views of female sexuality, both very simple, and each as absurd as the other. One is that sexual activity is pleasant, that men and women alike seek pleasure, are equally capable of receiving it from this source, and that therefore any differences in the expression of their respective sexual impulses must be due simply to the effect of cultural conditioning. The implication of this is that once such cultural conditioning is overcome, the feelings of men and women, and the behavior arising from such feelings, will be about the same. This view is sometimes implied in the remarks of feminists. More often, however, they interpret its denial as little more than another expression of male chauvinism. Persons who think like this are likely to maintain that the only natural differences between men and women are the obvious anatomical ones and that, inwardly, the sexes are the same. Some, indeed, quite illogically interpret the denial of this as rejecting a natural equality among males and females.

The extreme opposite view, which is now happily less often heard, is that it is a man's natural role to initiate, dominate, and command, while a woman's role is to follow, to submit, and to obey. The ramifications of this basic idea—which not very long ago was considered quite obvious even to educated women—were exceedingly numerous and penetrated just about every area of social life. Thus, women did not, and many still do not, see any absence of balance in the thought that it is a man's place to provide, and a woman's to make a home. Until recently, the head of a household could only be male, and a homemaker could only be female. Sexual intercourse was naturally initiated by a man, and only very indirectly, if at all, by a woman. In fact, for an unmarried woman to initiate sex with a man was thought to mark her as cheap, whereas no such stigma has ever been attached to men for that reason. Again, men alone were, and indeed still are, thought capable of rape, or of forced sex. It is exceedingly difficult to think of any woman importuning a total stranger for sex except from some ulterior motive, as in the case of prostitutes.

Much of this conception of respective sexual roles has persisted, of course, and not all of it is absurd. What is absurd is the idea that there is some sort of natural master-servant relationship between men and women. It is certainly false to insist that men and women are by nature just alike, except for obvious anatomical differences, and that all other differences in their thoughts and feelings are the product of cultural conditioning. But it is equally false that there is a natural difference between them which implies a subordinate relationship of women to men.

To get a clearer view of this we should begin by noting that, while a man can, except for the restrictions imposed by convention, easily sire over a hundred children a year, and has every natural impulse to do so, a woman can usually bear only one. It is she, moreover, who will for a considerable time carry and then give birth to that one child. This is a fundamental and incontestable difference between men and women. It seems to underlie both male and female sexuality and sheds far more light on the basic ways men and women feel about each other and act towards one another than any considerations of cultural conditioning. In fact, much of what various cultures nourish and enforce seems to have its roots, not in the thin air of pointless and arbitrary practice, but in the overwhelmingly important and unalterable differences just noted.

The constancy of a woman's feelings towards a man becomes, at least for the time being, quite fixed from the moment she marries him. Provided she has no misgivings concerning the wisdom and rightness of the step she has taken, then she also has little sexual attraction to other men, or at least none that she would be likely to act upon. This fidelity is deep and sincere, wrought not by custom and teaching, which are easily circumvented, but by her own nature. Consciously or otherwise—and it is probably true that she gives little thought to it—her deep interest is the security of the home that has thus been established, which means, the security of herself and the child who will eventually be borne. Thus a woman who, immediately after marriage, should find herself sexually attracted to every suitable man who crossed her path, would quite rightly wonder whether she was really ready for marriage. Others would put the same interpretation on her behavior. Nor does this merely mean, as some would have it, that she had perhaps not yet come to appreciate what was expected of her. To depart from conventional ways is one thing. To reject one's most natural feelings is very different.

A man, on the other hand, just recently married, has little such inner urge to fidelity, but the very opposite. Faithful he may be, but in his case, unlike that of his wife, this is maintained out of respect for the vows he has made, and his sincerely felt devotion to her. Whatever profession he may make to the contrary, the husband considers monogamy to be a restraint and a limitation; and it is no less a limitation if freely undertaken out of concern for something else he prizes, such as his own reputation, especially in the eyes of his wife.

The general rule that women tend to be monogamous while men are polygamous also applies to marriage relationships formed in college, but not, of course, without exception. In such relationships it is usually the female partner who genuinely and constantly cares for the man she lives with, who assumes the responsibility for birth control, who feels the greater sense of commitment, and who expects to be cared for. It is the female who waits, sometimes frantically, for the male to return after having been unaccountably gone and long overdue. Very often she will be the one to leave him, if the departure is intended to be permanent, but seldom otherwise. Many college men have ruefully described to me how their girls simply left them, once and for all. It was, on the other hand, almost invariably the men who had, as their girls usually described it, "slept" with someone else with no thought at all of ending the existing relationship. This account is characteristic of a man in such a situation:

> Joan was studying music in New York, and I only got to be with her on weekends. During the week away from her I sometimes slept with other girls, but not very often, and it didn't mean anything. One night I took Jan, who was singing at the Holiday Inn, home with me, and after we had had sex I told her she had to go home. She was outraged, but I hadn't agreed to anything more than that, and I just didn't want her there all night. Besides, Joan would be phoning in the morning, and I didn't want to have to lie to her. I didn't see that I had any obligation to let Jan stay all night, so even though she protested and said she absolutely wasn't going to leave like that in the middle of the night, I made her go.

Oddly enough, it never occurred to this man that the way in which he treated his casual friend was extremely shabby. He insisted that he had been honest with her, and supposed that he had thereby met any requirements of ethics.

Of course comparable behavior on the part of women is not unheard of; indeed, some of the college women who shared their experiences with me had had a bewildering succession of casual sexual relationships. It was, however, quite uncommon for such women to have other lovers while being totally involved in a marriage relationship, whereas it was exceedingly common for men to do so—repeatedly.

It is in the light of this basic difference that many things concerning the relations of the sexes become clear, far more so than they would by trying, as is usually done, to account for every difference in terms of cultural conditioning. For example, regardless of her opinions concerning men, sex, and liberation, a newly and happily married woman is unlikely to be interested in casual sex with a total stranger. That sort of interest can usually be aroused only in women who have long since become disenchanted with their husbands or lovers and with their own conditions, women who feel they have been cheated out of something meaningful in their lives. Even these women are rarely roused to ardor by a man they know almost nothing about. On the contrary, they are likely to need assurance that their partner does in some sense at least care for or respect them, and that he is inspired by more than the mere thought of sexual gratification.

A man, on the other hand, is roused by the mere presence of any female of apparent buoyant health and appearance, particularly if she is young, or at least younger than himself. And he is prepared to satisfy this passion the moment an opportunity arises. The casualness of a sexual liaison with an utter stranger is no inhibition to a man; on the contrary, it is usually a strong incitement to his ego. The presence of a new bride, who perhaps embodies every quality he would want in a partner and who, in addition, adores him as much as he does her, appears to make no difference at all. What is necessary is that she be far away, and this stranger close at hand and available.

No one would pretend that the description just given applies without qualification or exception to every man. Nor does the description given of a woman's basic reactions apply universally. Both descriptions are oversimplified. Nevertheless, they express the basic truth.

It is not unusual, for example, to find the dining-room of a motor inn filled almost entirely with men, traveling on business, dining and talking with each other, their minds on work-related matters, and the conversations innocuous. They seem, and in fact they are, the models of probity and reserve. But if anyone imagines that this scene casts doubt upon the above descriptions, then he need only imagine that into this setting—one of ordinary, conventional men by themselves and lodged at an inn far from home—there should suddenly appear numerous young women, engagingly dressed, and distributed among these male patrons with ostentatious overtures of friendship and hints of availability. How many of these men would still find each other's company more engrossing than that of their new companions, whose very names might still be unknown to them? How many would resist the solicitations to sex? Some would, of course, but it is absurd to suppose that this sudden alteration of the scene would not evoke a profound difference in the feelings of these men. Desires of unbelievable force would be unleashed.

To further clarify this point, we need only to exercise our imaginations once more, this time by reversing things a bit. Imagine that these guests at the motor inn are all women—conventional, middle class, and mostly married—who are far from their homes and dining together, there being no men in sight at all except, perhaps, a busboy or two. Suppose as well that into this setting there should suddenly appear numerous men, who distribute themselves among the female guests and, with only the most perfunctory introductions or explanations, make overtures of friendship and invitations to have sex. It is not hard to imagine all of these women departing, in more or less acute discomfort, while it would be quite hard to imagine them rushing into bed.

One can, if he likes, set this down to acculturation, but that would be naive. Set it down instead to a man's naturally immense fertility, in comparison to that of a woman, and to the accompanying primitive desires nature has given him. If acted upon, these desires—which no man creates himself and which are controlled only with effort—would require numerous sexual partners. A woman's basic desire, on the other hand, is usually not to have a great multiplicity of lovers, since a dozen men can make her no more pregnant than one. Her need is to beget and subsequently to nourish the one child at a time of which she is capable. For this she needs only one lover; but her need for him, and likewise her child's need for him, continues for years and even decades. None of that is compatible, so far as her feelings are concerned, with casual sex, which can only be self-defeating.

Although admittedly oversimplified, it must be stressed that the foregoing analyses are not intended to suggest that rationales underlying the behavior of men and women are conscious or deliberate. They probably never are. But neither, for that matter, are the sexual impulses themselves. We find ourselves impelled by these desires, without ever having selected them. Similarly, we find their manifestations unselected and far below the level of conscious, much less rational, choice. They are indeed neither rational nor irrational, nor, probably, are they morally significant, considered in themselves, though life would certainly be poorer, almost to the point of emptiness, without them.

Moreover, it must not be objected that the analyses have no qualifications or exceptions. The most characteristic exceptions are themselves instructive.

Thus, it is certainly true that not all men are polygamous. But those who are not are usually older men, long married, who have found ways to direct their sexual energies towards more acceptable goals, such as wealth, position, or professional recognition. Similarly, married women do sometimes invite casual sex, but these are usually women with grown children, women who feel neglected by or have lost interest in their husbands, and who, very often, feel denied the more interesting experiences of life. Many are simply bored with their domestic existence. What they seek is not just sex, but attention and an appreciation of themselves. It is apparent to any such women that their "womanness" is something deeply appreciated by men, something that can become an avenue to the appreciation of themselves as persons.

Each sex sometimes falls into curious and foolish errors by seeing the behavior of the other through its own eyes or, in other words, by supposing that sexual attraction expresses itself in much the same way regardless of one's gender. Thus, for example, a recently married woman is apt to feel shocked and hurt upon discovering that her husband's need to flit from flower to flower continues unabated. She mistakenly interprets it as a rejection of herself in favor of others. Still, it is severely condemned by society, and a recently married man is himself made to feel shame at overt and wholehearted flirtation, which, until a short while ago, he could have indulged to his heart's content. Therefore, men do conceal their passions, particularly from their wives or lovers, not only out of fear of hurting them but to escape a learned feeling of guilt. These feelings have most certainly been inculcated; no man by nature feels the least guilty about the most unabashed flirtation provided it can be concealed. Monogamous marriage was not instituted by nature but by society, and while it places rigid controls upon a man's public behavior, it modifies his inner life very little. Even if his feelings cannot be expressed in their most natural way, due to social restraints and customs, they will nevertheless find expression—in unabashed flirtation and pursuit if no one is watching, or otherwise in lurid fantasy. This is the primary reason why the casual conversations of married men sometimes seem so preoccupied with sex when these men are not in the company of women. This talk is an opportunity to express their fantasies and, quite pathetically, it is likely to be the only overt expression available to them. Young unmarried men, whose lives are quite free and polygamous, observe this behavior on the part of older men, this conversation and leering; they note with disgust the kind of humor and joke that moves older men to great laughter. It all seems so childish to them, which in a sense it is, for it certainly is not the behavior one expects from men of responsibility who cut significant figures in the world of business and the professions. Nevertheless, it is precisely the type of behavior one would expect from men of normal—that is to say, polygamous—sexuality, who long ago found themselves locked into monogamous marriage and have been closely watched most of the time. One has to remember that without vivid fantasy such men would, in a very significant psychological sense, cease to be men. When these fantasies have no hope of duplication in the real world, what on earth should we expect? It may be of little importance what young and unmarried men may sometimes think of the behavior of men who have been married for a long time, but it is of real practical importance that these men be understood by their wives. For these women to interpret their husbands' behavior and feelings as a rejection of themselves is grossly unfair and tends to undermine the genuine and total devotion their husbands do feel for them. What is involved here is not rejection, but rather, a man's realization of who he is.

A mistake made on the other side—a misunderstanding by men of the feelings and behavior of women—is even more common, quite stupid, and inexcusable. This mistake rests upon the supposition that women derive pleasure from sex just as men do, which is true, and that therefore, even taking into consideration the inhibitions created in some women by acculturation, they can be expected to have similar desires for sex, even casual sex. In other words, men project their own basic sexuality onto women, explaining differences as the product of cultural conditioning. Then it is supposed that all they need to do is identify those women who "do," and those who "don't," which is as artificial as any distinction ever could be.

Thus a man, upon learning that a woman he knows has been involved in a love affair, is likely to direct special attention to her and even, sometimes out of the blue and on the spur of the moment, "proposition" her, that is, more or less obliquely suggest sexual intercourse. This absolutely never succeeds, and the suggestion itself is received with shocked astonishment. For example:

> One thing I had to put up with after my affair with Louise was discovered was the constant moralizing of one of my partners. This man is a stiff Presbyterian who would never dream of the slightest deviation from morality. I don't think he would rake his yard without making sure he looked all right to any passer-by. Needless to say, he expressed grave doubts about my fitness to continue in the partnership.
>
> But then a strange thing happened. The annual conference was held in Philadelphia that year. I didn't go, but all my partners did, and Louise was there too. And do you know what this partner did? He propositioned her!

The same incredible misconception is expressed in this experience:

> I was involved with Lila, a lab assistant, less than half my age and hardly out of high school. One thing that was interesting was the way she came to be treated by other men when they learned about us. They all just assumed that she was fair game. They thought that if she would go to bed with me, then chances were she would go to bed with anyone. That was really incredibly stupid to anyone who actually knew Lila, who was a very quiet and proper girl and not at all easy to get to know. But lonely men thought they could just walk up to her any time and start talking. Sometimes they began with some sort of remark about me—how I was married, comments about my age, that sort of thing—and then right away they would begin to boast about themselves, as if to invite comparison. Sometimes one of them would hang around where he knew she could be found, and as soon as she came by, just start walking along with her, uninvited. She didn't appreciate it at all, and in fact sort of liked some of these men, as friends, until they started acting that way. Mostly she was disgusted, and didn't understand it at all. I did.

The experiences expressed above illustrate a kind of impulsiveness and preoccupation with sex which, while very characteristic of men, is not characteristic of most women. Indeed, it is exceedingly rare for a woman to respond positively to a suggestion for casual sex, with the occasional exception of women who are embittered at their lovers or husbands or who are similarly disillusioned with their personal lives. Certainly there is no significant distinction between women who will respond positively and those who will not. Just as men are much the same in their sexuality (that is, polygamous), so are women much the same (that is, *not* polygamous). A woman's needs are significantly different from a man's, and one does not even begin to appreciate what these are by supposing that women seek sexual pleasure. They seek a far more significant fulfillment than this—and so, for that matter, do men. But men and women seek different things from each other, of which a great deal more will be said later.

That psychological orientations differ significantly between males and females with respect to passionate love seems beyond question. In fact, it would probably never be questioned if it did not seem to some, quite erroneously, to imply a subordinate status for women. Of course it has no such implications at all. But what has been widely doubted is that these are natural differences. Here it is claimed that they are, and that they are partly rooted in the totally different capacities of men and women with respect to siring and bearing children. The sexuality of men and women appears to be an almost metaphysical expression of these biological differences. That is to say, a man's responses are precisely what one should expect in the light of his capacities, and the same can be said of a woman's responses. These are characterized as "metaphysical" in order to avoid an otherwise inevitable misunderstanding. No man ever consciously reflects upon his immense fertility, and then decides to be polygamous. There is no thought or reflection about it at all; his sexuality is simply the nonreflective expression of that fertility. Similarly, no woman reflects much upon her vastly more limited fertility, amounting to the occasional production of a single egg in contrast to a man's daily production of a million seeds; nor does she decide in the light of this that her need is for a single and more or less permanent lover. The need is, again, simply the natural and unformulated expression of a basic biological fact.

These factors have influenced, in numerous ways, our fundamental conceptions of masculine and feminine nature, many of trivial significance but nevertheless revealing, and others more telling.

It has already been noted, for example, that women are never thought to perpetrate a rape, and any man who made such an accusation would not be believed. Nor would his claim become any more credible if it happened to be the case that he was slight of strength and build and therefore relatively defenseless in comparison with his alleged Amazon assailant. Relative strength has nothing to do with it. The accusation is absurd in the light of what anyone perceives as natural female sexuality, in contrast to that of a man. No one would doubt that a man of slight stature might be capable of raping someone twice as strong as himself, since all that is involved is a certain difficulty, not a basic absurdity.

Again, when the concept of a "home wrecker" is employed one usually envisions a female. No doubt this is partly due to the different roles society has tried to assign to men and women, and to sexual stereotypes that are hard to dislodge, but not entirely so. A man can, indeed, destroy a marriage by seducing another man's wife, but this is usually not how marriages are destroyed by third persons. A young mother whose husband is strong, resourceful, and a devoted spouse and father, is an unpromising target for seduction by an outside male, no matter what he may have to offer. She already has everything of importance to her that he could provide. On the other hand, a woman long married whose children are grown and whose life seems to her somewhat empty, easily yields to a man who offers her, not primarily sexual pleasure, but rather appreciation of herself and her worth as a person. This is true even when there is no deficiency whatever in the sexual capacities of her husband. To a woman, sex is likely to be considered quite incidental in a love affair; not something withheld, to be sure, but at the same time something of secondary importance. An outside man, in short, does not destroy a home, though he may take advantage of its already weakened condition. Its actual destruction is much more likely to be wrought by the jealousy of the cuckolded husband, who feels belittled and inadequate, as well as deprived of something he thought was his.

A female home wrecker, on the other hand, is sometimes quite properly so-called—and this is said not in order to apply a different standard of conduct to women than to men, but rather to exhibit, once again, a basic difference in male and female sexuality. Thus, simply by the solicitations of sex, an outside woman can win over a devoted husband and father who until then had felt no deprivation whatsoever in his domestic life. His life need not be in any sense empty in order for this to happen; on the contrary, it can be one of rich fulfillment. Nor need his wife assume that she in any way compares badly with her rival. It may be as obvious to her as to anyone that the very opposite is true. Here, the appeal to a man's sexual nature—to his basic polygamy—is sometimes quite enough. It is for this reason that a woman, but not a man, can be aptly called a home wrecker, a term intended not so much as an adverse reflection on her as it is an indication of a man's vulnerability to the feminine blandishments. It is somehow supposed that everyone should know this, and that women, accordingly, ought not to exploit this male weakness thereby placing in jeopardy some other woman's home, a situation made even more precarious if there are children involved.

Other common notions bear out the same thesis concerning the natural differences between the sexes. Though a given man, for example, may have had many more sexual partners than a given woman, he is seldom referred to as promiscuous. Only a woman is usually so described. The reason is quite obvious; namely, that such behavior is thought to be more or less characteristic of a man, and hence no real fault, but uncharacteristic of a woman and not in keeping with her basic nature. Undoubtedly, the judgmental element in such assessments is unfair to women, but the distinctions involved nevertheless rest upon a correct perception. The same is true with respect to the idea of a "call girl." A male is in fact seldom referred to by the corresponding term gigolo, and very few men fill such a role—the role, namely, of providing casual sex to total strangers for payment. The idea of a "call boy" is inherently ridiculous because little demand for it exists, whereas the demand for women is so intense as to create the role itself even when this conflicts not only with clearly defined ideas of morality, but with the criminal law as well. Men are by nature intensely polygamous, and this is concealed only by a veneer of convention. Women are not, and no modification of convention will make them so.

25

The Language of the Eyes

> "Why does the lover hang with complete abandonment on the eyes of his chosen one, and is ready to make every sacrifice for her? Because it is his immortal part that longs after her; while it is only his mortal part that desires everything else."
>
> —ARTHUR SCHOPENHAUER

There is one fairly subtle characteristic of both men and women who are prone to love affairs. Since it is rarely noticed and, to my knowledge it has never been specifically pointed out by anyone else, it should be well worth describing here.

Quite simply, the characteristic is that these people *look* into the faces of others, and into the faces of each other. This behavior on the part of a woman, when directed towards strangers, is sometimes regarded as flirtation, though in fact it is not really noticed much, because it is usually subtle and normally unconscious on her part. It is less often thought of that way when observed in men. In any case, it is probably the surest, and at the same time the least noticed, mark of true love, simply because it is unfeigned and seldom even conscious. For someone to look at you, to look into your face, with animation and interest, when you are speaking, for example, or even when you are not, and when there is really nothing to be looking *for*—this is one of the most utterly disarming and totally genuine signs of devotion that any person can display.

If you point your camera at two lovers, you are likely to find, when the snapshot comes back, that one of them is looking appreciatively into the face of the other, or indeed, sometimes both are; though normally

---

From *Having Love Affaairs* (Buffalo, N.Y.: Prometheus Books, 1982), pp. 119–124.

people look in the direction of the camera when exhorted to pose for informal photography. This mannerism is not, of course, confined to partners of love affairs, but is sometimes—though alas! rarely—discovered in married persons, even occasionally those who have been married many years. It is, far more than words, gifts, kisses, or other learned behavior, the token of love *par excellence,* precisely because it is unlearned, usually unintentional, and even unconscious.

It is also quite overwhelming in its effects, which are often far out of proportion to a cause so seemingly trifling. This is is especially noticeable when glances are exchanged between partners. Consider, for example, this specimen of a fairly commonplace experience:

> The day I arrived to start my new job at the university, I walked into the departmental office and the secretary looked up at me as if overjoyed at the sight of this total stranger, before I had even said hello. We had lunch the next day, and before long were having lunch together every time I was on campus. She learned, the second time we had lunch, that I already had a wife. Maybe that's why it was never much of a love affair, but we're still good friends, and I think we like each other more than either of us wants to admit. She just doesn't want another woman's husband, and I don't want her telling me so.

Or this one:

> If you ask about the very beginning of that friendship, it was when we started out in line to board the plane. I was walking ahead of Joan, whom I'd never seen, and I held the door open so it wouldn't just go shut in her face. She looked at me in astonishment, as if I had done the nicest thing in the world, though I would have done the same no matter who was behind me; so would anyone else. I sat down next to her; she told me about the gay holiday she had just been having in Boston with her dentist husband; but forty minutes later, by the time we landed in Rochester, she had told me all about her love affairs and her problems at home. We got in her car, she took me to her house for lunch, then to my office, and we were good friends, the very first day.

Or finally this:

> I remember seeing a woman, over fifty years ago, from a taxicab. She was standing there; the cab was stopped for a traffic light, and during that entire brief time we stared into each other's eyes. I would have gotten out if my mother had not been in the cab with me, because that lovely woman and I virtually fell in love in those couple of minutes. The way we gazed into each other's eyes said everything that needed to be said. I remember it vividly, after these several decades.

None of these accounts is of much interest, so far as their content is concerned, but a philosopher can scarcely fail to note that in each case a significant chain of events began, or might have begun, with nothing more than a look exchanged between two strangers. I suspect that most love affairs, perhaps nearly all of them, begin in no other way.

One of the persons I interviewed, still in her twenties and divorced, had known a staggering number of lovers. The accounts she gave, over the course of our several talks, were mind-boggling, and somehow scarcely seemed to fit the demure manner and beauty of the person before me. I realized that she was uncommonly attractive and subtly flirtatious, but at first I did not quite see how I had come to this conclusion. Before long I realized that her face radiated pleasure every time she looked at me, which was often. Each time we parted, even though our talk had been candid and reserved, she would invariably steal one last smiling glance over her shoulder. I believe she responds exactly that way to every man who crosses her path. On the night preceding our first interview she had received profound declarations of love, by telephone from the other side of the continent, from a man she had met less than a week before. Her whole life was like that. This drove home to me the power of the eyes, of simply looking at someone; for quite some time, I was not even aware that she did this, though I was quite conscious of the fact that I liked her and felt comfortable in her presence.

The power of the eyes, whether merely to quicken interest in the case of strangers or to convey profound feelings in the case of lovers, is partly due to the fact that such expressiveness is not deliberate. It is quite unconsciously and therefore quite honestly given as a sign of genuine love, and is, equally unconsciously, interpreted as such, at least tentatively. Therefore, its message is likely to overwhelm every other feeling or doubt, and to supersede every explicit avowal. Precisely because little actual thought is given, beyond bare and almost subliminal awareness, to the fact that someone who is cared for very much is looking, perhaps even gazing, into one's face, for this very reason no defense is erected against it. The message "I love you" goes straight to the heart and feelings, and comes directly from an identical source, without thought, and hence without doubt and guarded response. Such behavior is, moreover, in no way unnatural or rude, so long as it is a look of friendship or even enchantment, and not one of curious scrutiny. Hence, such looking can sometimes, in the case of lovers, become excessive to the point of becoming starry-eyed, without making the person who is the object of it self-conscious or uncomfortable. It has this latter dampening effect only when it passes from looking to scrutinizing, at which point the person being examined begins to have precisely the feeling no lover can abide, namely, that of being a mere object or thing.

On the other side of this phenomenon, you can feel no more total rejection as a person, nor one against which you are so helpless to protest, than to find that someone lacks even enough interest in you to bestow a look. It is, quite literally, an expression of your total worthlessness in his eyes. To be in the company, perhaps the sole company, of someone who treats you this way for any considerable time is to experience an acute discomfort and ineradicable resentment, even though perhaps no unfriendly word is spoken and no overt gesture of hostility is ever made. One would rather be confronted with actual verbal abuse, to which at least a response can be made, than to be treated as worth less even than that.

One man I spoke with, for example, had had only one love affair in his life, and that one had not been very successful. He was a man in his thirties who had never married, who had involuntarily spent his nights alone, and who desperately craved the company of women. Nor was there at first any apparent reason why he should have to endure loneliness, for he was attractive and had a flourishing, even sometimes glamorous career as a photographer. Yet on the one occasion when I saw him in the company of a woman I noticed that every time she spoke he looked down at his hands or at the table, any place except directly into her face. This mannerism was, I am sure, the result of shyness, and not due to a lack of interest, yet its negative effect was decisive. The language of the eyes was simply one he could not speak, even ineptly. Whether or not this is what isolated him in his loneliness, it surely was a contributing factor.

A simple experiment of the imagination, however, will easily convince us of this power that the eyes possess. Suppose, for example, that you are at a social gathering—perhaps at dinner—and you find yourself seated next to an attractive stranger who directs not a single glance at you throughout the entire evening. He (she) converses, responds to your questions, shows no lack of awareness of your presence—but your eyes never meet. Now imagine the very same situation, with the single difference that this person is constantly looking your way; and even though he (she) perhaps says nothing to you in the whole course of the evening, you can hardly look in that direction without finding those eyes already upon you.

Which of the two would you approach after dinner? Which might you subsequently telephone or write to? Which, indeed, can you imagine yourself falling in love with?

There is no more perfect measure of the emotions than the eyes. The most subtle modifications of feeling are recorded there, in changes so slight that the most sensitive camera or artist could hardly capture them; yet they are recorded instantly and unambiguously in the mind of a beholder, often without any conscious awareness of the message he has received, which was probably transmitted in the same unconscious manner. Even dog owners soon learn to read the silent language of their pet's eyes, detecting every shift of feeling—fear, anxiety, adoration, hunger, discomfort, whatever. This also accounts for the discomfort one feels when in the presence of a complete stranger whose eyes are obscured by dark glasses. A whole and rich area of communication is thereby cut off, creating deep uncertainty. We have learned to depend on it, most of all to know just how we stand in the attitudes and feelings of others, for we know that these signals are far more reliable than words. Hence it is into another person's eyes—and not, for example, into his mouth—that we normally and almost instinctively look, in case we look at him at all, for we have long since learned the subtle but unambiguous language they speak. Words can be uttered without meaning, but it is quite impossible to feign and dissimulate with the eyes, for one can never check to see what has just been said. You see your own eyes only when you are staring into a mirror—precisely when you *cannot* dissimulate, for then you have no one but yourself to lie to.

The power of the eyes is rarely appreciated except by such persons as hypnotists. That is why most of us so easily and nonreflectively believe what is conveyed through another person's eyes. If a professor finds that an attractive or even moderately attractive student has her eyes fixed upon him most of the time, perhaps with a hint of deep interest or admiration, then he will hardly fail to glance her way each time he fancies that he has expressed some interesting insight, or combined his words rather well, or in some way managed to look good, just to see how his performance has registered there. He may be totally unaware of this, and not even clearly aware of her apparent fascination with him, but any teacher with the least capacity for self-appraisal can test it out for himself. In fact experiments have been conducted to confirm it. Thus it has been arranged, without the professor's knowledge, that the students on one side of his classroom will exhibit interest and attention whenever he happens to be on that side of the room, and exhibit indifference or boredom whenever he is not. After a few class meetings it is found that the professor is almost always on the side of the room first referred to, but has no idea why. If asked to explain his predilection for that side of the room, he responds, sincerely, that he just happens to prefer it, or that there is more light on that side, or something equally naive.

It is because the eyes are honest that most of us fall victim to their power. But the power itself is wielded sincerely and benignly, except in rare and almost aberrant cases. In fact, it is hard to use that power malevolently or to exploit, just because dissimulation is so nearly impossible. You really do not harm a person by telling him that you despise him, if that is the truth—or at least, you harm him far less than you would if you told him the opposite, which you cannot do with your eyes, if that is not so. And you certainly do not harm the person by telling him that you love him, if you speak the truth, and if it is your eyes unmistakably conveying this to him. Nor is there much danger that exploitative people might fancy that they have here an instrument for controlling others for whom they have no sincere affection. For not only is it difficult to lie by this means—especially over any period of time—but there is, in addition, an almost unavoidable and sometimes profound effect upon the gazer himself. In other words, to look appreciatively into the face and eyes of another person is, in truth, to gain an awareness not only of that person's beauty, which is sometimes not apparent with a casual glance, but to become aware also of that person's mind and soul; that is to say, of the thoughts and feelings underneath. It is quite hard not to love someone in the presence of such perception as this and, what will by now be even more clear, such love is almost sure to be reciprocated twice over. Surely this is precisely how the whole of mankind would have been created had we been the work of gods who were poets, and not merely gods.

Part Five

Metaphysical Matters

Introduction

Taylor is perhaps best known in the philosophical community for his defense of fatalism, the view that whatever happens is unavoidable. Human beings are prone to various self-deceptive ploys to avoid reflection on our respective fates, believing instead that our dignity as persons rests on our freedom of will. Taylor maintains this is all a conceit, with the result that we erroneously conflate blessings with achievements, and misfortunes with mistakes. Paradoxically, Taylor asserts that fatalism offers its own consolations, ridding us of such notions as moral responsibility and praise and blame.

Fatalism need not rest on any theological presupposition, although traditionally many religious people, believing in divine omniscience, have thought this belief cancels out their human freedom. Conversely, many people who locate the essence of human dignity in our ability to choose freely have often adopted a nontheistic stance for reasons not unsimilar to those of the religious fatalist, namely, that if there were an omniscient deity who (by definition) knew everything, then freedom is an illusion, as humans are all puppets on a divine string. Since such a scenario would cause havoc to our human dignity, secular humanists believe the presupposition of divine omniscience must be rejected, if human freedom is to be affirmed.

Taylor, for illustrative purposes, presents an imaginative story of Osmo, whom a scribe (on revelation from God) has written about in book form. A dusty copy of the biography of Osmo is discovered in an Indiana library by a twenty-six-year-old high school teacher named Osmo. The book is written in the present tense, but arranged chronologically, with a chapter for each year of Osmo's life. An understandably excited Osmo is shocked to find only true descriptions of his own life up to chapter 26. Osmo is even more terrified to learn that the book has but 29 chapters, and that he is described as dying in a plane crash in the last chapter, at the age of 29.

The elaborate narrative account of Osmo's biography, all perfectly accurate, shows how truth doesn't vary by the mere passage of time. True statements about future events have the same content as those about the past, except for the temporal variables involved. Taylor is inviting the reader to place himself or herself in Osmo's shoes, to imagine that these biographical facts in the book are about the reader's life, and to see if the reader can then resist fatalism. To reply that statements about the future cannot be true until the events that make them true actually occur would be met by Taylor with the response that this point has parity with the equally absurd claim that statements about the past cease to be true after the events that made them true are no longer happening.

If fatalism is true (as Taylor alleges), then should we be idle spectators in the world? Taylor leaves the answer up to us (and, of course, even that decision isn't really avoidable). Granted we do not know our fate, unlike Osmo, but destined, Taylor believes, we truly are.

In "How to Bury the Mind-Body Problem," Taylor boldly asserts that the distinction between the mind and the body is a "philosophical fabrication." Philosophers have for centuries wrestled with the question whether a person is more than the sum of his or her material parts. Some philosophers have answered affirmatively and located *true* selfhood in the disembodied mind, discarnate personality, or soul. Some have even spoken of the person as a primitive notion, the subject of both physical and mentalistic predication.

Taylor seeks to exorcise this ghostlike, nonphysical self and claims that there are no minds, nor any distinctly mental states or events. He points out that philosophical argument cannot prove the existence or nonexistence of anything, provided the description or definition of the thing in question is consistent. What one can do, as in the case of the alleged existence of minds or souls, is point out that they are not discoverable by any empirical inquiry and attempt to show the falsity of the presuppositions that gave rise to such beliefs.

The basic presupposition behind dualism or mentalism is that matter cannot think. Accordingly, states of consciousness (e.g., thinking, choosing, believing, feeling, etc.) are held to be not reducible to physical states or events, and hence not explained by the language of the natural sciences.

Contrary to the position of mentalism, which holds a person is equatable with a mind, Taylor claims that any argument for this view is equally a good argument for materialism, which identifies a person with a body. Appeals to ordinary language usage that speak only of minds performing certain activities can be countered by similar idioms where it would be absurd to speak of minds performing certain actions.

For instance, we speak of a person running five miles, engaging in aerobic exercise, weighing 180 pounds, being six feet tall, taking a shower, and so on, and it would be folly to substitute *mind* for *person* here.

Taylor claims that the same being that engages in mentalistic activities also engages in physical activities. There aren't two entities in some sort of mysterious union here. There are just the visible, palpable bodies of human beings. And, while it does seem undeniable that such mental states as thoughts, sensations, beliefs, images, etc., exist, it is more accurate to say that human beings think, sense, believe, imagine, etc. And it is redundant and misleading to say, for example, that people think thoughts, sense sensations, or feel feelings.

Philosophers who speak of the mind as the animating principle of life are speaking metaphorically. Life is not some separate thing that animates matter. Human beings are terribly complex and intricate bodies evidencing living and thinking matter. "If," Taylor notes, "there is a difficulty in comprehending how a body can do such things (e.g., exhibit intellectual abilities), there is surely no less difficulty in seeing how something which is not a body can do them any better."

In short, Taylor wants to show that just as it is arbitrary to regard *life* as something that animate beings possess and inanimate ones lack, so, too, it is equally arbitrary and absurd to claim that the possession of minds or souls marks the difference between things that think and those that do not think. Granted a person has a mind, but this does not mean that there is some independently existing thing, called a mind, that that person possesses. Rather, it means that the person is intelligent and can do certain things that machines and the like cannot do. The terms *life* and *mind* are not nouns that stand for independent things. Rather, they are terms of classification, separating the living from the nonliving, the thinking from the nonthinking.

In his delightfully sardonic essay "De Anima," Taylor creates the fable of Walter's Amoebiary. Walter keeps an amoebiary and seeks to determine the lineage of his amoebae so that he might more effectively influence the breeding of future amoebae. Of course, amoebae reproduce by splitting into two. Naturally the inevitable metaphysical question arises: which is the parent and which is the offspring? Walter's various attempts to formulate an answer to this query by various criteria of marking, size, behavioral traits, etc., all seemed to fail.

After much consternation, Walter realized that his problem of identifying an amoeba was a pseudoproblem, because he had previously overlooked the essential metaphysical aspects of the problem. He came to realize that amoebae lacked souls, and only souls are what uniquely characterize entities as distinct individuals. Of course, Taylor is here being facetious, his point being that the concept of a mind or soul is metaphysically useless. The moral of Taylor's little joke is that if it is difficult to differentiate amoebae, which are material creatures, it is even more difficult (indeed absurd) to attempt to individuate souls.

Taylor thinks that much of what passes for metaphysical analysis in academic circles is the result of polarized thinking. Polarity always places things into two exclusive categories: either this or not this. Unfortunately, this imposed pattern of categorization is sometimes mistaken, because reality is not so neat and tidy as to accommodate such a pattern of thought. There are many either/or choices where there is no correct answer to the problem at hand, other than ad hoc, practical solutions mandated by law, morality, religion, or conventional social practice. Even a statement seemingly as cut and dried as "either the couple is married or not" is clouded by such conditions as trial separations, divorce filings, open marriage, etc. At times, we have to settle for neithers or boths, or "some of each."

Taylor, inspired by his reflections on Zen Buddhism, argues that many putative solutions to metaphysical problems are really philosophic inventions based on the "predilections, needs, and prejudices of their inventors." Such "solutions" are not, despite appearances, declarations of fact. Some of these "solutions" may be better than others, but the mark of their worth is the practical and the useful.

Of course, we very much want our truths to be precise and definitive. But often reality doesn't warrant such exactitude. Ironically, Taylor seems to raise some doubts about his own views on fatalism, resting as that philosophical position does on the polarized supposition of excluded middle that actions or events are either unavoidable or not.

Taylor believes in a notion of relative (or nonstrict) identity over time for objects and persons. In short, he believes that existence admits of degrees. Consider some object, such as a tree, which exists now but which at some past time did not exist. It would be rash to conclude that there must be an exact moment at which that tree came into existence. Rather, he suggests, between the tree's existence and nonexistence, the tree was in the process of coming into existence, and in that interval of time, the tree partially existed and partially didn't exist.

Moreover, Taylor is not even prepared to accept the polarized alternative that a person is either dead or alive. The real answer here may well be a both/and, in which situation calling a person "partly alive" or "partly dead" doesn't entail that the person is either alive or dead. Death (perishing), like birth (coming into being), is a gradual process, and it is illusory to seek an empirically exact death moment or birth moment. That is, just as we realize that flowers, for example, gradually come into existence and gradually perish, so, too, we need to realize that persons also gradually come into existence and finally perish. In neither process is there anything sudden or instantaneous.

Taylor also addresses the complicated matter of brain transplant operations (a thought-experiment philosophers dearly love to reflect on), where two persons, Brown and Robinson, with quite different psychological and physical characteristics, are imagined to have their brains surgically interchanged. While postoperatively they both retain their respective, outward physical appearances, they think and act quite differently than before the surgery. A number of puzzling philosophical questions involving personal identity immediately arise, such as: Is Brown still Brown? Is Robinson still Robinson? Or is Brown now Robinson and Robinson now Brown? Or do we have post-operatively two new persons, Bronson and Rowan? Taylor says it is a mistake to polarize our eventual answers to such complicated personal identity questions into an either/or pattern. The persons in question are not either Brown or Robinson, Taylor says, but part of each.

26

Fate

We are all, at certain moments of pain, threat, or bereavement, apt to entertain the idea of fatalism, the thought that what is happening at a particular moment is unavoidable, that we are powerless to prevent it. Sometimes we find ourselves in circumstances not of our own making, in which our very being and destinies are so thoroughly anchored that the thought of fatalism can be quite overwhelming, and sometimes consoling. One feels that whatever then happens, however good or ill, will be what those circumstances yield, and we are helpless. Soldiers, it is said, are sometimes possessed by such thoughts. Perhaps everyone would feel more inclined to them if they paused once in a while to think of how little they ever had to do with bringing themselves to wherever they have arrived in life, how much of their fortunes and destinies were decided for them by sheer circumstance, and how the entire course of their lives is often set, once and for all, by the most trivial incidents, which they did not produce and could not even have foreseen. If we are free to work on our destinies at all, which is doubtful, we have freedom that is at best exercised within exceedingly narrow paths. All the important things—when we are born, of what parents, into what culture, whether we are loved or rejected, whether we are male or female, our temperament, our intelligence or stupidity, indeed everything that makes for the bulk of our happiness and misery—all these are decided for us by the most casual and indifferent circumstances, by sheer coincidences, chance encounters, and seemingly insignificant fortuities. One can see this in retrospect if he searches, but few search. The fate that has given us our very being has given us also our pride and conceit, and has thereby formed us so that, being human, we congratulate ourselves on our bless-

---

From *Metaphysics,* 3d ed. (Englewood Cliffs, N.J.: Prentice-Hall, 1983), pp. 51–62.

ings, which we call our achievements; blame the world for our blunders, which we call our misfortunes; and scarcely give a thought to that impersonal fate that arbitrarily dispenses both.

FATALISM AND DETERMINISM

Determinism, it will be recalled, is the theory that all events are rendered unavoidable by their causes. The attempt is sometimes made to distinguish this from fatalism by saying that, according to the fatalist, certain events are going to happen *no matter what,* or in other words, regardless of causes. But this is enormously contrived. It would be hard to find in the whole history of thought a single fatalist, on that conception of it.

Fatalism is the belief that whatever happens is unavoidable. That is the clearest expression of the doctrine, and it provides the basis of the attitude of calm acceptance that the fatalist is thought, quite correctly, to embody. One who endorses the claim of universal causation, then, and the theory of the causal determination of all human behavior, is a kind of fatalist—or at least he should be, if he is consistent. For that theory, as we have seen, once it is clearly spelled out and not hedged about with unresolved "ifs," does entail that whatever happens is rendered inevitable by the causal conditions preceding it, and is therefore unavoidable. One can indeed think of verbal formulas for distinguishing the two theories, but if we think of a fatalist as one who has a certain attitude, we find it to be the attitude that a thoroughgoing determinist should, in consistency, assume. That some philosophical determinists are not fatalists does not so much illustrate a great difference between fatalism and determinism but rather the humiliation to one's pride that a fatalist position can deliver, and the comfort that can sometimes be found in evasion.

FATALISM WITH RESPECT TO THE FUTURE AND THE PAST

A fatalist, then, is someone who believes that whatever happens is and always was unavoidable. He thinks it is not up to him what will happen a thousand years hence, next year, tomorrow, or the very next moment. Of course he does not pretend always to *know* what is going to happen. Hence, he might try sometimes to read signs and portents, as meteorologists and astrologers do, or to contemplate the effects upon him of the various things that might, for all he knows, be fated to occur. But he does not suppose that whatever happens could ever have really been avoidable.

A fatalist thus thinks of the future in the way we all think of the past, for everyone is a fatalist as he looks *back* on things. To a large extent we know what has happened—some of it we can even remember—whereas the future is still obscure to us, and we are therefore tempted to imbue it, in our imagination, with all sorts of "possibilities." The fatalist resists this temptation, knowing that mere ignorance can hardly give rise to any genuine possibility in things. He thinks of both past and future "under the aspect of eternity," the way God is supposed to view them. We all think of the past this way, as something settled and fixed, to be taken for what it is. We are never in the least tempted to try to modify it. It is not in the least up to us what happened last year, yesterday, or even a moment ago, any more than are the motions of the heavens or the political developments in Tibet. If we are not fatalists, then we might think that past things once *were* up to us, to bring about or prevent, as long as they were still future, but this expresses our attitude toward the future, not the past.

Such is surely our conception of the whole past, whether near or remote. But the consistent fatalist thinks of the future in the same way. We say of past things that they are no longer within our power. The fatalist says they never were.

THE SOURCES OF FATALISM

A fatalistic way of thinking most often arises from theological ideas, or from what are generally thought to be certain presuppositions of science and logic. Thus, if God is really all-knowing and all-powerful, it is not hard to suppose that He has arranged for everything to happen just as it is going to happen, that He already knows every detail of the whole future course of the world, and there is nothing left for you and me to do except watch things unfold, in the here or the hereafter. But without bringing God into the picture, it is not hard to suppose, as we have seen, that everything that happens is wholly determined by what went before it, and hence that whatever happens at any future time is the only thing that can then happen, given what precedes it. Or even disregarding that, it seems natural to suppose that there is a body of truth concerning what the future holds, just as there is such truth concerning what is contained in the past, whether or not it is known to any person or even to God, and hence, that everything asserted in that body of truth will assuredly happen, in the fullness of time, precisely as it is described therein.

No one needs to be convinced that fatalism is the only proper way to view the past. That it is also the proper way to view the future is less obvious, due in part, perhaps, to our vastly greater ignorance of what the future holds. The consequences of holding such fatalism are obviously momentous. To say nothing of the consolation of fatalism, which enables a person to view all things as they arise with the same undisturbed mind with which he contemplates even the most revolting of history's horrors, the fatalist teaching also relieves one of all tendency towards both blame and approbation of others and of both guilt and conceit in himself. It promises that a perfect understanding is possible and removes the temptation to view things in terms of human wickedness and moral responsibility. This thought alone, once firmly grasped, yields a sublime acceptance of all that life and nature offer, whether to oneself or one's fellows; and although it thereby reduces one's pride, it simultaneously enhances the feelings, opens the heart, and expands the understanding.

DIVINE OMNISCIENCE

Suppose for the moment, just for the purpose of this discussion, that God exists and is omniscient. To say that God is omniscient means that He knows everything that is true. He cannot, of course, know that which is false. Concerning any falsehood, an omniscient being can know that it is false; but then it is a truth that is known, namely, the truth that the thing in question *is* a falsehood. So if it is false that the moon is a cube, then God can, like you or me, know that this is false; but He cannot know the falsehood itself, that the moon is a cube.

Thus, if God is omniscient He knows, as you probably do, the date of your birth. He also knows, as you may not, the hour of your birth. Furthermore, God knows, as you assuredly do not, the date of your conception—for there is such a truth, and we are supposing that God knows every truth. Moreover, He knows, as you surely do not, the date of your death, and the circumstances thereof—whether at that moment, known already to Him, you die as the result of accident, a fatal malady, suicide, murder, whatever. And, still assuming God exists and knows everything, He knows whether any ant walked across my desk last night, and if so, what ant it was, where it came from, how long it was on the desk, how it came to be there, and so on, to every truth about this insect that there is. Similarly, of course, He knows when some ant will again appear on my desk, if ever. He knows the number of hairs on my head, notes the fall of every sparrow, knows why it fell, and why it was going to fall. These are simply a few of the consequences of the omniscience that we are for the moment assuming. A more precise way of expressing all this is to say that God knows, concerning any statement whatever that anyone could formulate, that it is true, in case it is, and otherwise, that it is false. And let us suppose that God, at some time or other, or perhaps from time to time, vouchsafes some of his knowledge to people, or perhaps to certain chosen persons. Thus prophets arise, proclaiming the coming of certain events, and things do then happen as they have foretold. Of course it is not surprising that they should, on the supposition we are making; namely, that the foreknowledge of these things comes from God, who is omniscient.

THE STORY OF OSMO

Now, then, let us make one further supposition, which will get us squarely into the philosophical issue these ideas are intended to introduce. Let us suppose that God has revealed a particular set of facts to a chosen scribe who, believing (correctly) that they came from God, wrote them all down. The facts in question then turned out to be all the more or less significant episodes in the life of some perfectly ordinary man named Osmo. Osmo was entirely unknown to the scribe, and in fact to just about everyone, but there was no doubt concerning whom all these facts were about, for the very first thing received by the scribe from God, was: "He of whom I speak is called Osmo." When the revelations reached a fairly voluminous bulk and appeared to be completed, the scribe arranged them in chronological order and assembled them into a book. He at first gave it the title *The Life of Osmo, as Given by God,* but thinking that people would take this to be some sort of joke, he dropped the reference to God.

The book was published but attracted no attention whatsoever, because it appeared to be nothing more than a record of the dull life of a very plain man named Osmo. The scribe wondered, in fact, why God had chosen to convey such a mass of seemingly pointless trivia.

The book eventually found its way into various libraries, where it gathered dust until one day a high school teacher in Indiana, who rejoiced under the name of Osmo, saw a copy on the shelf. The title caught his eye. Curiously picking it up and blowing the dust off, he was thunderstruck by the opening sentence: "Osmo is born in Mercy Hospital in Auburn, Indiana, on June 6, 1942, of Finnish parentage, and after nearly losing his life from an attack of pneumonia at the age of five, he is enrolled in the St. James school there." Osmo turned pale. The book nearly fell from his hands. He thumbed back in excitement to discover who had written it. Nothing was given of its authorship nor, for that matter, of its publisher. His questions of the librarian produced no further information, he being as ignorant as Osmo of how the book came to be there.

So Osmo, with the book pressed tightly under his arm, dashed across the street for some coffee, thinking to compose himself and then examine this book with care. Meanwhile he glanced at a few more of its opening remarks, at the things said there about his difficulties with his younger sister, how he was slow in learning to read, of the summer on Mackinac Island, and so on. His emotions now somewhat quieted, Osmo began a close reading. He noted that everything was expressed in the present tense, the way newspaper headlines are written. For example, the text read, "Osmo is born in Mercy Hospital," instead of saying he *was* born there, and is recorded that he quarrels with his sister, is a slow student, is fitted with dental braces at age eight, and so on, all in the journalistic present tense. But the text itself made quite clear approximately when all these various things happened, for everything was in chronological order, and in any case each year of its subject's life constituted a separate chapter and was so titled—"Osmo's Seventh Year," "Osmo's Eighth Year," and so on through the book.

Osmo became absolutely engrossed, to the extent that he forgot his original astonishment, bordering on panic, and for a while even lost his curiosity concerning authorship. He sat drinking coffee and reliving his childhood, much of which he had all but forgotten until the memories were revived by the book now before him. He had almost forgotten about the kitten, for example, and had entirely forgotten its name, until he read, in the chapter called "Osmo's Seventh Year," this observation: "Sobbing, Osmo takes Fluffy, now quite dead, to the garden, and buries her next to the rose bush." Ah yes! And then there was Louise, who sat next to him in the eighth grade—it was all right there. And how he got caught smoking one day. And how he felt when his father died. On and on. Osmo became so absorbed that he quite forgot the business of the day, until it occurred to him to turn to Chapter 26, to see what might be said there, he having just recently turned twenty-six. He had no sooner done so than his panic returned, for lo! what the book said was *true!* That it rains on his birthday for example, that his wife fails to give him the binoculars he had hinted he would like, that he receives a raise in salary shortly thereafter, and so on. Now how in God's name, Osmo pondered, could anyone know that apparently before it had happened? For these were quite recent events, and the book had dust on it. Quickly moving on, Osmo came to this: "Sitting and reading in the coffee shop across from the library, Osmo, perspiring copiously, entirely forgets, until it is too late, that he is supposed to collect his wife at the hairdresser's at four." Oh my god! He had forgotten all about that. Yanking out his watch, Osmo discovered that it was nearly five o'clock—too late. She would be on her way home by now, and in a very sour mood.

Osmo's anguish at this discovery was nothing, though, compared with what the rest of the day held for him. He poured more coffee, and it now occurred to him to check the number of chapters in this amazing book: only twenty-nine! But surely, he thought, that doesn't mean anything. How anyone could have gotten all this stuff down so far was puzzling enough, to be sure, but no one on God's earth could possibly know in advance how long this or that person is going to live. (Only God could know that sort of thing, Osmo reflected.) So he read along; though not without considerable uneasiness and even depression, for the remaining three chapters were on the whole discouraging. He thought he had gotten that ulcer under control, for example. And he didn't see any reason to suppose his job was going to turn out that badly, or that he was really going to break a leg skiing; after all, he could just give up skiing. But then the book took on a terribly dismal note. It said: "And Osmo, having taken Northwest flight 569 from O'Hare, perishes when the aircraft crashes on the runway at Fort Wayne, with considerable loss of life, a tragedy rendered the far more calamitous by the fact that Osmo had neglected to renew his life insurance before the expiration of the grace period." And that was all. That was the end of the book.

So *that's* why it had only twenty-nine chapters. Some idiot thought he was going to get killed in a plane crash. But, Osmo thought, he just wouldn't get on that plane. And this would also remind him to keep his insurance in force.

(About three years later our hero, having boarded a flight for St. Paul, went berserk when the pilot announced they were going to land at Fort Wayne instead. According to one of the flight attendants, he tried to hijack the aircraft and divert it to another airfield. The Civil Aeronautics Board cited the resulting disruptions as contributing to the crash that followed as the plane tried to land.)

FOUR QUESTIONS

Osmo's extraordinary circumstances led him to embrace the doctrine of fatalism. Not quite completely, perhaps, for there he was, right up to the end, trying vainly to buck his fate—trying, in effect, to make a fool of God, though he did not know this, because he had no idea of the book's source. Still, he had the overwhelming evidence of his whole past life to make him think that everything was going to work out exactly as described in the book. It always had. It was, in fact, precisely this conviction that terrified him so.

But now let us ask these questions, in order to make Osmo's experiences more relevant to our own. First, why did he become, or nearly become, a fatalist? Second, just what did his fatalism amount to? Third, was his belief justified in terms of the evidence he had? And finally, is that belief justified in terms of the evidence *we* have—or in other words, should we be fatalists too?

This last, of course, is the important metaphysical question, but we have to approach it through the others.

Why did Osmo become a fatalist? Osmo became a fatalist because there existed a set of true statements about the details of his life, both past and future, and he came to know what some of these statements were and to believe them, including many concerning his future. That is the whole of it.

No theological ideas entered into his conviction, nor any presuppositions about causal determinism, the coercion of his actions by causes, or anything of this sort. The foundations of Osmo's fatalism were entirely in logic and epistemology, having to do only with truth and knowledge. Ideas about God did not enter in, for he never suspected that God was the ultimate source of those statements. And at no point did he think God was *making* him do what he did. All he was concerned about was that someone seemed somehow to *know* what he had done and was going to do.

What, then, did Osmo believe? He did not, it should be noted, believe that certain things were going to happen to him *no matter what.* That does not express a logically coherent belief. He did not think he was in danger of perishing in an airplane crash even in case he did not get into any airplane, for example, or that he was going to break his leg skiing, whether he went skiing or not. No one believes what he considers to be plainly impossible. If anyone believes that a given event is going to happen, he does not doubt that those things necessary for its occurrence are going to happen too. The expression "no matter what," by means of which some philosophers have sought an easy and even childish refutation of fatalism, is accordingly highly inappropriate in any description of the fatalist conviction.

Osmo's fatalism was simply the realization that the things described in the book were unavoidable.

Of course we are all fatalists in this sense about some things, and the metaphysical question is whether this familiar attitude should not be extended to everything. We know the sun will rise tomorrow, for example, and there is nothing we can do about it. Each of us knows he is sooner or later going to die, too, and there is nothing to be done about that either. We normally do not know just when, of course, but it is mercifully so! For otherwise we would sit simply checking off the days as they passed, with growing despair, like a man condemned to the gallows and knowing the hour set for his execution. The tides ebb and flow, and heavens revolve, the seasons follow in order, generations arise and pass, and no one speaks of taking preventive measures. With respect to those things each of us recognizes as beyond his control, we are of necessity fatalists.

The question of fatalism is simply: Of all the things that happen in the world, which, if any, are avoidable? And the philosophical fatalist replies: None of them. They never were. Some of them only seemed so.

Was Osmo's fatalism justified? Of course it was. When he could sit right there and read a true description of those parts of his life that had not yet been lived, it would be idle to suggest to him that his future might, nonetheless, contain alternative possibilities. The only doubts Osmo had were whether those statements could really be true. But here he had the proof of his own experience, as one by one they were tested.

Whenever he tried to prevent what was set forth, he of course failed. Such failure, over and over, of even the most herculean efforts, with never a single success, must surely suggest, sooner or later, that he was *destined* to fail. Even to the end, when Osmo tried so desperately to save himself from the destruction described in the book, his effort was totally in vain—as he should have realized it was going to be had he really known that what was said there was true. No power in heaven or earth can render false a statement that is true. It has never been done, and never will be.

Is the doctrine of fatalism, then, true? This amounts to asking whether our circumstances are significantly different from Osmo's. Of course we cannot read our own biographies the way he could. Only people who become famous ever have their lives recorded, and even so, it is always in retrospect. This is unfortunate. It is too bad that someone with sufficient knowledge—God, for example—cannot set down the lives of great men in advance, so that their achievements can be appreciated better by their contemporaries, and indeed, by their predecessors—their parents, for instance. But mortals do not have the requisite knowledge, and if there are any gods who do, they seem to keep it to themselves.

None of this matters, as far as our own fatalism is concerned. For the important thing to note is that, of the two considerations that explain Osmo's fatalism, only one of them was philosophically relevant, and that one applies to us no less than to him. The two considerations were: (1) there existed a set of true statements about his life, both past and future, and (2) he came to know what those statements were and to believe them. Now the second of these two considerations explains why, as a matter of psychological fact, Osmo became fatalistic, but it has nothing to do with the validity of that point of view. Its validity is assured by (1) alone. It was not the fact that the statements happened to be written down that rendered the things they described unavoidable; that had nothing to do with it at all. Nor was it the fact that, because they had been written, Osmo could read them. His reading them and coming to believe them likewise had nothing to do with the inevitability of what they described. This was ensured simply by there being such a set of statements, whether written or not, whether read by anyone or not, and whether or not known to be true. All that is required is that they should *be* true.

Each of us has but one possible past, described by that totality of statements about us in the past tense, each of which happens to be true. No one ever thinks of rearranging things there; it is simply accepted as given. But so also, each of us has but one possible future, described by that totality of statements about oneself in the future tense, each of which happens to be true. The sum of these constitutes one's biography. Part of it has been lived. The main outlines of it can still be seen, in retrospect, though most of its details are obscure. The other part has not been lived, though it most assuredly is going to be, in exact accordance with that set of statements just referred to. Some of its outlines can already be seen, in prospect, but it is on the whole more obscure than the part belonging to the past. We have at best only premonitory glimpses of it. It is no doubt for this reason that not all of this part, the part that awaits us, is perceived as given, and people do sometimes speak absurdly of altering it—as though what the future holds, as identified by any true statement in the future tense, might after all *not* hold.

Osmo's biography was all expressed in the present tense because all that mattered was that the things referred to were real events, it did not matter to what part of time they belonged. His past consisted of those things that preceded his reading of the book, and he simply accepted it as given. He was not tempted to revise what was said there, for he was sure it was true. But it took the book to make him realize that his future was also something given. It was equally pointless for him to try to revise what was said there, for it, too, was true. As the past contains what has happened, the future contains what will happen, and neither contains, in addition to these things, various other things that did not and will not happen.

Of course we know relatively little of what the future contains. Some things we know. We know the sun will go on rising and setting, for example, that taxes will be levied and wars will rage, that people will continue to be callous and greedy, and that people will be murdered and robbed. It is only the details that remain to be discovered. But the same is true of the past; it is only a matter of degree. When I meet a total stranger, I do not know, and will probably never know, what his past has been, beyond certain obvious things—that he had a mother, and things of this sort. I know nothing of the particulars of that vast realm of fact that is unique to his past. And the same for his future, with only this difference—that *all* people are strangers to me as far as their futures are concerned, and here I am even a stranger to myself.

Yet there is one thing I know concerning any stranger's past and the past of everything under the sun; namely, that whatever it might hold, there is nothing anyone can do about it now. What has happened cannot be undone. The mere fact that it has happened guarantees this.

And so it is, by the same token, of the future of everything under the sun. Whatever the future might hold, there is nothing anyone can do about it now. What will happen cannot be altered. The mere fact that it is going to happen guarantees this.

THE LAW OF EXCLUDED MIDDLE

The presupposition of fatalism is therefore nothing but the commonest presupposition of all logic and inqiury; namely, that there is such a thing as truth, and that this has nothing at all to do with the passage of time. Nothing *becomes* true or *ceases* to be true; whatever is truth at all simply *is* true.

It comes to the same thing, and is perhaps more precise, to say that every meaningful statement, whether about oneself or anything else, is either true or else it is false; that is, its denial is true. There is no middle ground. The principle is thus appropriately called *the law of excluded middle.* It has nothing to do with what tense a statement happens to express, nor with the question for whether anyone, man or god, happens to know whether it is true or false.

Thus no one knows whether there was an ant on my desk last night, and no one ever will. But we do know that either this statement is true or else its denial is true—there is no third alternative. If we say it *might* be true, we mean only that we do not happen to know. Similarly, no one knows whether or not there is going to be an ant there tonight, but we know that either it will or else it will not be there.

In a similar way we can distinguish two mutually exclusive but exhaustive classes of statements about any person; namely, the class of all those that are true, and the class of all that are false. There are no others in addition to these. Included in each are statements never asserted or even considered by anyone, but such that, if anyone were to formulate one of them, it would either be a true statement or else a false one.

Consider, then, that class of statements about some particular person—you, let us suppose—each of which happens to be true. Their totality constitutes your biography. One combination of such statements describes the time, place, and circumstances of your birth. Another combination describes the time, place, and circumstances of your death. Others describe in detail the rises and falls of your fortunes, your achievements and failures, your joys and sorrows—absolutely everything that is true of you.

Some of these things you have already experienced, others await you. But the entire biography is there. It is not written, and probably never will be; but it is nevertheless there, all of it. If, like Osmo, you had some way of discovering those statements in advance, then like him you could hardly help becoming a fatalist. But foreknowledge of the truth would not create any truth, nor invest your philosophy with truth, nor add anything to the philosophical foundations of the fatalism that would then be so apparent to you. It would only serve to make it apparent.

OBJECTIONS

This thought, and the sense of its force, have tormented and frightened people from the beginning, and thinkers whose pride sometimes exceeds their acumen and their reverence for truth have attempted every means imaginable to demolish it. There are few articles of faith upon which virtually everyone can agree, but one of them is certainly the belief in their cherished free will. Any argument in opposition to the doctrine of fate, however feeble, is immediately and uncritically embraced, as though the refutation of fatalism required only the denial of it, supported by reasons that would hardly do credit to a child. It will be worthwhile, therefore, to look briefly at some of the arguments most commonly heard.

1. One can neither foresee the future nor prove that there is any god, or even if there is, that he could know in advance the free actions of men.

   The reply to this is that it is irrelevant. The thesis of fatalism rests on no theory of divination and on no theology. These ideas were introduced only illustratively.

2. True statements are not the causes of anything. Statements only entail; they do not cause, and hence threaten no man's freedom.

   But this, too, is irrelvant, for the claim here denied is not one that has been made.

3. The whole argument just conflates fact and necessity into one and the same thing, treating as unavoidable that which is merely true. The fact that a given thing is going to happen implies only that it is *going* to happen, not that it *has* to. Someone might still be able to prevent it—though of course no one will. For example, President Kennedy was murdered. This means it was true that he was going to be murdered. But it does not mean his death at that time and place was unavoidable. Someone *could* have rendered that statement false; though of course no one did.

   That is probably the commonest "refutation" of fatalism ever offered. But how strong is the claim that something *can* be done, when in fact it never *has* been done in the whole history of the universe, in spite, sometimes, of the most strenuous efforts? No one has ever rendered false a statement that was true, however hard some have tried. When an attempt, perhaps a heroic attempt, is made to avoid a given calamity, and the thing in question happens anyway, at just the moment and in just the way it was going to happen, we have reason to doubt that it could have been avoided. And in fact great effort was made to save President Kennedy, for example, from the destruction toward which he was heading on that fatal day, a whole legion of bodyguards having no other mission. And it failed. True, we can say that *if* more strenuous precautions had been taken, the event would not have happened. But to this we must add *true,* they were not taken, and hence *true,* they were not going to be taken—and we have on our hands again a true statement of the kind that no man has ever had the slightest degree of success in rendering false.

4. The fatalist argument just rests on a "confusion of modalities." The fact that something is true entails only that its denial is false, not that its denial is impossible. All that is impossible is that both should be true, or both false. Thus, if the president is going to be murdered, it is certainly false that he is not—but not impossible. What is impossible is that he will be both murdered and spared.

   Here again we have only a distracting irrelevancy, similar to the point just made. The fatalist argument has nothing to do with impossibility in those senses familiar to logic. It has to do with unavoidability. It is, in other words, concerned with human abilities. The fact that a statement is true does not, to be sure, entail that it is necessary, nor do all false statements express impossibilities. Nonetheless, no one is able to avoid what is truly described, however contingently, in any statement, nor to bring about what is thus falsely described. Nor can anyone convert the one to the other, making suddenly true that which was false, or vice versa. It has never been done, and it never will be. It would be a conceit indeed for someone now to suggest that he, alone among men, might be able to accomplish that feat. This inability goes far beyond the obvious impossibility of making something both true and false at once. No metaphysics turns on that simple point.

5. Perhaps it would be best, then, to discard the presupposition underlying the whole fatalist philosophy; namely, the idea that statements are true in advance of the things they describe. The future is the realm of possibilities, concerning any of which we should neither say it is true that it will happen, nor that it is false.

   But, in reply, this desperate move is nothing but arbitrary fiction, resorted to for no other reason than to be rid of the detested doctrine of fatalism. What is at issue here is the very law of excluded middle, which, it is suggested, we shall be allowed to affirm only up to that point at which it threatens something dear. We shall permit it to hold for one part of time, but suddenly retract it in speaking of another, even though the future is continuously being converted to the past through sheer temporal passage.

   Most surely, if the statement made now, that President Kennedy has been murdered, is a true one, then the prediction, made before the event, that he was going to be murdered, was true too. The two statements have exactly the same content, and are in fact one and the same statement, except for the variation of tense. The fact that this statement is more easily known in retrospect than in prospect casts no doubt on its truth but only illustrates a familiar fact of epistemology. A prediction, to be sure, must await fulfillment, but it does not thereupon for the first time acquire its truth. Indeed, had it not been true from the start, it could not have been fulfilled, nor its author congratulated later for having it right. Fulfillment is nothing but the occurrence of what is correctly predicted.

   The law of excluded middle is not like a blank check into which we can write whatever values we please, according to our preferences.

> We can no more make ourselves metaphysically free and masters of our destinies by adding qualifications to this law than a poor person can make himself rich just by adding figures to his bankbook. That law pronounces every meaningful statement true, or, if not true, then false. It leaves no handy peg between these two on which one may hang his beloved freedom of will for safekeeping, nor does it say anything whatever about time.

Every single philosophical argument against the teaching of fatalism rests upon the assumption that we are free to pursue and realize various alternative future possibilities—the very thing, of course, that is at issue. When some of these possibilities have become realized and moved on into the past, the supposed alternative possibilities usually appear to have been less real than they had seemed; but this somehow does not destroy the fond notion that they were there. Metaphysics and logic are weak indeed in the face of an opinion nourished by invincible pride, and most people would sooner lose their very souls than be divested of that dignity that they imagine rests upon their freedom of will.

INVINCIBLE FATE

We shall say, therefore, of whatever happens that it was going to be that way. And this is a comfort, both in fortune and in adversity. We shall say of him who turns out bad and mean that he was going to; of him who turns out happy and blessed that he was going to; neither praising nor berating fortune, crying over what has been, lamenting what was going to be, or passing moral judgments.

Shall we, then, sit idly by, passively observing the changing scene without participation, never testing our strength and our goodness, having no hand in what happens, or in making things come out as they should? This is a question for which each will find his own answer. Some people do little or nothing with their lives and might as well never have lived, they make such a waste of it. Others do much, and the lives of a few even shine like the stars. But we knew this before we ever began talking about fate. In time we will all know of which sort we were destined to be.

27

How to Bury the Mind-Body Problem

The mind-body problem, in all its variants, is a philosophical fabrication resting on no genuine data at all. It has arisen from certain presuppositions about matter and human nature familiar to philosophy from the time of the Pythagoreans, presuppositions which have persisted just to the extent that they have been left unexamined. And they have not been questioned very much simply because they are so familiar.

There are vexing, unsolved problems of psychology and problems of mental health, but there are no mind-body problems. And there are problems of "philosophical psychology," as they are sometimes called today—problems of perception, sensation, the analysis of deliberation, of purposeful behavior, and so on—but there are no mind-body problems.

The reason why there are no mind-body problems is the most straightforward imaginable: It is because there are no such things as *minds* in the first place. There being no minds, there are in strictness no mental states or events; there are only certain familiar states, capacities, and abilities which are conventionally but misleadingly called "mental." They are so called partly in deference to certain philosophical presuppositions and partly as a reflection of our lack of understanding of them, that is, of our ignorance.

Men and women are not minds, nor do they "have" minds. It is not merely that they do not "have" minds the way they have arms and legs; they do not have minds in any proper sense at all. And just as no man or woman has or ever has had any mind, so also are cats, dogs, frogs, vegetables, and the rest of living creation without minds—though philosophers of the highest rank, such as Aristotle, have felt driven to say that all living things, vegetables included, must have souls (else how

From *American Philosophical Quarterly* 6 (1969): 136–143. Reprinted by permission of the publisher.

could they be *living* things?) just as others of similar eminence, like Descartes, have thought that men must have minds, else how could they be *thinking* things? Today, when philosophers talk about mind-body problems, and advance various claims concerning the possible relationships between "mental" and "physical" states and events, they are, of course, talking about men. But they might as well be talking about frogs, because the presuppositions that give rise to these theories apply to other animals as well as to men.

PHILOSOPHICAL ARGUMENTS FOR THE EXISTENCE OR NONEXISTENCE OF THINGS

There cannot be any philosophical argument proving that something does or does not exist, so long as the description or definition of it is self-consistent. Thus there cannot be a philosophical argument proving that men do or do not, as some medieval thinkers believed, have an indestructible bone in their bodies. One can only say that such a bone has never been found (which is not a philosophical argument) and then exhibit the groundlessness or falsity of the presuppositions that gave rise to the belief in the first place. (In this case it was certain presuppositions concerning the requirements of the resurrection of the body.) Similarly, there can be no philosophical argument proving that men do or do not have souls, spirits, or minds, or that there are not *sui generis* mental states or events, assuming that these can be described in a self-consistent way. One can only note that such things have never been found in any man, living or dead, and then exhibit the arbitrariness and apparent falsity of the presuppositions that give rise to these opinions in the first place. Now of course, as far as *finding* them goes, many philosophers claim to find them all the time, *within themselves*. They are alleged to be *private* things, deeply hidden, discernible only by their possessors. All they really "find," however, are the most commonplace facts about themselves that are perfectly well known to anyone who knows anything at all—but of this, more later.

THE GRAND PRESUPPOSITION OF THE MIND-BODY PROBLEM

What I must do now, then, is consider the presupposition that has given birth to the so-called mind-body problem, and show that there is nothing in it at all that anyone needs to believe; that, on the contrary, we have good evidence that it is false.

The presupposition can be tersely expressed by saying: *Matter cannot think*. That is the way a Cartesian would put it, but philosophers now spell it out a little better. Thus we are apt to be told that thinking, choosing, deliberating, reasoning, perceiving, and even feeling are not concepts of physics and chemistry, so that these terms have no application to bodies. Since, however, men do think, choose, deliberate, reason, perceive, and feel, it follows that men are not "mere bodies." They are instead minds or souls or, as it is more common to say today, "selves" or "persons," and such terms as "is thinking," "is choosing," "is perceiving," etc., are not physical or bodily but *personal* predications. A man may be in one clear sense a physical object, having arms and legs and so on, but a person is not just that visible and palpable object; there is more to a self or person than this. For it is the self or person that thinks, chooses, deliberates, feels, and so on, and not his body or some part of it.

Again—and this is really only another way of expressing the same presupposition—we are apt to be told that thoughts, choices, reasons, feelings, etc., are not physical things. It makes no sense to ask how large a thought is, whether it is soluble in alcohol, and so on. Yet these things do exist—any man can be aware of them, "within himself." Hence, that "self" within which such things occur must be something more than or other than the body. It must be just the totality of all those nonphysical ("mental") things, but in any case it is mental in nature, so a self or person is not the same thing as his body.

Or again, in case one boggles at calling thoughts, feelings, and the like "things," at least (it is said) no one can deny that they are events or states. But they are not events or states that occur or obtain in the laboratories of physicists and chemists—except in the sense that they sometimes occur in physicists and chemists themselves, who sometimes happen to be in laboratories. No one could ever truly represent whatever might be happening in a test tube or vacuum tube as the transpiring of a thought or feeling. These things just do not—indeed obviously could not—happen in test tubes or vacuum tubes, because they are not the *kind* of event involving changes of matter. They are a kind of "mental" event. And since these things do, obviously, happen in men, then things happen in men which are nonphysical, "mental," in nature. And so on.

"SELVES" OR "PERSONS" AS MINDS AND BODIES

The word "self" and the plural "selves" are fairly common items of contemporary philosophical vocabulary. These words never occur outside of philosophy, except as suffixes to personal pronouns, but in philosophical contexts they are sometimes taken to denote rather extraordinary things. Selves are, indeed about the strangest inhabitants of nature that one can imagine—except that, as sometimes described in philosophy, they are not even imaginable in the first place, being quite nonphysical. You cannot poke a self with a stick; the nearest you can come to that is to poke his body. The self that has that body is not supposed to be quite the same thing as his body—that is a (mere) physical object, a possible subject matter for physics and chemistry. *That* is not what thinks, reasons, deliberates, and so on: it is the self that does things like this.

At the same time, selves are never doubted to be the same things as *persons* and persons are thought to be the same things as people, as men. And there is no doubt at all that men are visible, palpable objects, having arms and legs and so on: that they are, in short, physical objects. So the thing becomes highly ambiguous. We do not, in contexts in which it would seem silly or embarrassing to do so, have to say that selves (men) are spirit beings (minds) which in some sense or other happen to "have" bodies. Clearly men are visible and palpable things, that is, are bodies. We can say that all right. But at the same time we need not say—indeed, *must* not say—that men are just (mere) bodies. There is, after all, a difference between a man's body, and that which thinks, perceives, feels, deliberates, and so on; and those are things that men (selves) do, not things that bodies do. Or, again, there is, after all, a difference between bodily predicates (weighs 160 pounds, falls, is warm) and personal predicates (chooses, believes, loves his country, etc.). The former can be predicated of a man's body, just like any other body, but it would "make no sense" to predicate the latter of any (mere) body, and hence of any man's body. They are only predicated of persons. So even though selves are persons and persons are men and men are visible, palpable beings, we must not think that they are just nothing but physical beings. They are physical bodies with minds or, as some would prefer, minds with physical bodies, or, as most writers on this subject want to say, they are somehow *both*.

So the "mental" is discriminated from the (merely) "physical," and the mind-body problem emerges at once. What is the *connection* between them? What is the relationship between men's minds and their bodies? or between mental and physical events? or between personal and physical predicates? Anyone who raises this question—for these all amount to one and the same question—can see at once that it is going to be extremely difficult to answer. And this means that it is capable of nourishing a vast amount of philosophy. It has, in fact, kept philosophers on scattered continents busy for hundreds of years, and even today claims much of the time of philosophical faculties and their proteges. It seems a conceit to undertake to put an end to all this, but that is what I propose now to do.

MENTALISM AND MATERIALISM

Consider the following two theses:

I. A person is not something that has, possesses, utilizes, or contains a mind. That is, a person is not one thing and his mind another thing. A person or self and his mind are one and the same thing.

II. A person is not something that has, possesses, utilizes, or occupies a body. That is, a person is not one thing and his body another thing. A person or self and his body are one and the same thing.

We can call these two theses "mentalism" and "materialism" respectively, since the first asserts that men are minds and not bodies, and the second that they are bodies and not minds.

Now the first thing to note about these two rather crudely stated theses is that both of them cannot be true, since each asserts what the other denies. They could, of course, both be false, since a person might be identical neither with his body nor with his mind (though it is hard to think of any other candidate for the title of "person"), or a person might somehow be identical with the two of them at once. These two simple theses are, nevertheless, a good starting point for discussion, and I am going to maintain that (II), the materialist thesis, is absolutely true.

Philosophers have tended to regard (I), or some more sophisticated version of it, as correct, and to dismiss (II) as unworthy of consideration. In fact, however—and it is hard to see how this could have been so generally overlooked—*any* philosophical argument in favor of (I) against (II) is just as good an argument for (II) against (I). This I shall illustrate shortly.

In the meantime, let us give what is due to the humble fact that there are considerations drawn from common sense, indeed from the common knowledge of mankind, which favor, without proving, (II). It is common knowledge that there are such things as human bodies, that there are men and women in the world. There is also one such body which everyone customarily, and without the least suggestion of absurdity, refers to as himself; he sees himself in the mirror, dresses himself, scratches himself, and so on. This is known, absolutely as well as anything can be known, and if any man were to profess doubt about it—if he doubted, for example, that there are such physical objects in the world as men and women, and therefore doubted the reality of his own body—then that man would have to be considered *totally* ignorant. For there is nothing more obvious than this. A man would be ignorant indeed if he did not know that there are such things as the sun, moon, earth, rivers, and lakes. I have never met anyone so ignorant as that. But a man who did not even know that there are men and women in the world and that he—his body—was one of them, would be totally ignorant.

Now there is no such common knowledge of the existence of minds or souls. No one has ever found such a thing, anywhere. Belief in such things rests either on religious persuasion or on philosophical arguments, sometimes on nothing but the connotations of familiar words. Such beliefs are opinions, easily doubted, and nothing that anyone knows. If a man denies that such things exist, as many have, then he exhibits no ignorance; he expresses only skepticism or doubt concerning certain religious or philosophical presuppositions or arguments.

If, accordingly, we are seeking some sort of thing with which to identify persons, then this is a *prima facie* consideration in favor of identifying them with their bodies, with things we know to be real, rather than with things postulated to suit the requirements of philosophical arguments or religious faith. This does not prove that men are nothing but bodies, of course, but it is enough to show that, since we know there are such things as persons, and we know there are such things as men (living human bodies), we had better regard these as the very same things *unless* there are some facts which would prohibit our doing so. And I shall maintain that there are no such facts. There are only philosophical arguments, not one of which proves anything.

The Arguments for Mentalism

I shall now consider the arguments I know, already adumbrated, in favor of what I have called mentalism. Of course, not all philosophers who take seriously the mind-body problem subscribe to this simple thesis as I have formulated it, but the more sophisticated versions can be considered as we go along, and it will be seen that the arguments for these are equally inconclusive.

The First Argument

There are certain predicates that undoubtedly apply to persons, but not to their bodies. Persons and their bodies cannot, therefore, be the same. One can sometimes truly say of a person, for example, that he is intelligent, sentimental, that he loves his country, believes in God, holds strange theories on the doctrine of universals, and so on. But it would sound very odd—indeed, not even make sense—to assert any such things of any such physical object whatever and hence of any man's body. It would at best be a confusion of categories to say that a certain man's *body* loves its country, for example.

Reply

If the foregoing is considered a good argument for the nonidentity of persons and bodies, then the following is obviously just as good an argument for not identifying them with their minds: There are certain predicates that undoubtedly apply to persons, but not to their minds. A person and his mind cannot, therefore, be the same. One can sometimes truly say of a person, for example, that he is walking, ran into a post, is feverish, or that he fell down. But it would sound very odd—indeed, not even make sense—to assert such things of any mind whatever. It would at best be a confusion of categories to say, for instance, that a certain man's *mind* ran into a post.

Considerations such as these have led many philosophers to affirm that a person or the "true self" is neither a mind, nor a body. Hence, a person must be (a) something else altogether or, as some would prefer to say, the term "person" must express a "primitive" concept of (b) both mind and body; i.e., a person must be something having both mental and physical properties.

The former of these alternatives is simply evasive. Persons are real beings, so there must be existing things which are persons. If when we bump into a man we are not bumping into a person, and if at the same time we are not referring to a person when we say of someone that he is thinking, then it is quite impossible to see what is left to fill the role of a person. The word "person" may indeed be a primitive one, but this, I think, only means that such arguments as the two just cited are equally good and equally bad.

The second alternative, that persons are beings having both mental and physical properties, is obviously only as good as the claim that there are such things as "mental properties" to begin with. Indeed, it is not even that good, for just as a physical property can be nothing but a property of a physical thing, i.e., a body, so also a mental property can be nothing but the property of a mental thing, i.e., a mind. For something to count as a physical property of something it is sufficient, and necessary, that the thing in question be a physical object. By the same token, for something to count as a mental property it is sufficient, and necessary, that it be the property that some mind possesses. Any property whatsoever that can be duly claimed to be the property of some body, animate or inanimate, is a physical property; the assertion that some body possesses a nonphysical property is simply a contradiction. This second alternative, that persons are beings possessing both physical and mental properties, therefore amounts to saying that a person is at one and the same time *two* utterly different things—a body with its physical properties and a mind with its mental properties. These are not supposed to be two things in the same sense that a family, for instance, is a plurality of beings consisting of husband, wife, and perhaps one or more children, but two wholly disparate kinds of beings having, as Descartes put it, nothing in common. Now this is no resolution of the antithesis between what I have called mentalism and materialism. It is only a reformulation of that issue. For now we can surely ask: Which of these two is the person, the true self? The body which has a mind, or the mind which has a body? And we are then back where we started.

The Second Argument

This argument consists of pointing out the rather remarkable things that a person can do but which, it is alleged, no physical object, of whatever complexity, can do, from which it of course follows that a person is not a physical object and hence is not identical with his own body. A person, for example, can reason, deliberate about ends and means, plan for the future, draw inferences from evidence, speculate, and so on. No physical objects do such things, and even complicated machines can at best only simulate these activities. Indeed, it would not even make sense to say that a man's body was, for example, speculating on the outcome of an election, though this would not be an absurd description of some person. A person, therefore, is not the same thing as his body, and can only be described in terms of certain concepts of mind.

Reply

This argument is not very different from the first; it only substitutes activities for properties which are baptized "mental." And one reply to it is the same as to the first argument; namely, that since persons often do things that no mind could do—for instance, they run races, go fishing, raise families, and so on—then it follows that persons are not minds.

A far better reply, however, and one that is not so question-begging as it looks, is to note that since men do reason, deliberate, plan, speculate, draw inferences, run races, go fishing, raise families, and so on, and since the men that do all such things are the visible, palpable beings that we see around us all the time, then it follows that *some* physical objects—namely, men—do all these things. All are, accordingly, the activities of physical objects: they are not activities divided between a physical object, the visible man, on the one hand, and some visible thing, his mind, on the other.

Consider the statement: "I saw George yesterday; he was trying to figure out the best way to get from Albany to Montpelier." Now this statement obviously refers, in a normal context, to a person, and it is perfectly clear that the name "George" and the pronoun "he" refer to *one and the same* being, that person. And what they both refer to is something that was seen, a certain man's body; they do not refer to some unseen thing, of which that body is some sort of visible manifestation. If that were so, then the statement would not really be true. And in any case, it would be embarrassingly silly to suppose that a more accurate rendition of the thought expressed in this statement might be:

"I saw George's body yesterday. His mind was trying to figure out how to get (how to get what?) from Albany to Montpelier." It is, accordingly, one and the same thing which (a) is seen and (b) figures and plans, and that thing is undoubtedly the physical object George. Now if conventions incline us to describe figuring out something as a "mental' activity, then we shall have to say that some purely physical objects—namely, living men—engage in mental activities. But this is simply misleading, if not contradictory, for it suggests that we are ascribing to a physical object an activity of something that is not physical, but mental. It would, therefore, be far better to say that some physical objects, namely, men or persons, sometimes perform physical activities such as figuring and planning which are quite unlike those we are accustomed to finding in certain other physical objects such as machines and the like.

The Third Argument

This argument, the commonest of all, is to the effect that while there may or may not be such things as "minds" (whatever that might mean), there are indisputably certain nonphysical things which are quite properly called "mental," as anyone can verify within himself. Indeed, it is sometimes claimed that nothing, not even the reality of our own bodies, is as certain as the existence of these mental things, which are perceived "directly."

Reply

What are here referred to as mental entities are, of course, such things as thoughts, mental images, after-images, sensations, feelings, and so on. Pains are frequently mentioned in this context, being, presumably, things whose existence no one would question. Having got to this point, then, the next step, of course, is to speculate on the connection between these mental things and certain "physical" states of the body. They evidently are not the same, and yet it is hard to see what the connection could be. Speculation also extends to such questions as whether two or more men might have "the same" pain, or why it is impossible that they should in view of the fact that they can hold common possession of ordinary "physical" things like clocks and books. Again, curiosity is aroused by the fact that a mental image, for instance, seems to have color, and yet it somehow can be perceived only by one person, its owner. Again, images sometimes seem to have shape—enough so that a perceiver can distinguish one from another, for instance—and yet no assignable size. Here, really, is a gold mine for philosophical speculation, and such speculations have filled, as they still fill, volumes.

Now surely there is a *better* way to express all that is known to be true in all this, and it is a way that does not even permit these odd theories to get started. What we know is true, and we all know is true, is that men think, sense, imagine, feel, etc. It is sheer redundancy to say that men think things called "thoughts," sense things called "sensations," imagine "images," and feel "feelings." There are no such things. And to say there are no such things is *not* to deny that men think, sense, imagine, and feel.

What, for instance, does it mean to say a man feels a pain in his foot? Absolutely nothing, except that his foot hurts. But this hurting, what sort of thing is it? It is not a thing at all; not a thing felt, and certainly not a mental thing that is felt *in his foot*. It is a state, and in no sense a state of his mind, but a straightforward state of his foot. But can that be a *physical* state? Well, it is assuredly a state of his foot, and that is a physical object; there is nothing else—no spirit foot, no spirit being, no spirit mind—that it can be a state of. Why, then, cannot other people have that same state? Why cannot other people feel the same pain I feel in my foot? And if it is a physical state, why cannot we open the foot and *see* it there? Or make some straightforward test of its presence in another man's foot?

To ask questions like these is just not to understand what is meant by describing an object as being in a certain state. Consider a piece of molten lead. Now this molten state, what sort of thing is it? The answer is that it is not a thing at all; it is a state or condition of a thing. Is it a physical state? Well, it is a state of the lead, and that is a physical object; there is nothing else for it to be a state of. Why, then, cannot another piece of lead have the same state? Why cannot something else have the molten state of this piece of lead? Of course something else can, in the only meaningful sense that can be attached to such a question; that is, another piece of lead, or some things which are not lead, can melt the same way this piece of lead melted. To ask why another piece of lead cannot have the molten state of this piece of lead is, of course, unintelligible, unless it is interpreted the way just suggested, in which case the answer is that it can. But similarly, to ask why another man cannot have the pain that this man is feeling is also unintelligible, unless construed as the question why other men cannot suffer pain, in which case this presupposition is wrong—they can. And if the piece of lead's being melted is a "physical" state, why can we not separate the lead into drops and see that state? Simply because it is a state of the lead, and not some other thing contained in the lead. Indeed, to separate it into drops *is* to see, not its meltedness (there is no such thing), but that it is melted—that is just the test. We do not have to *ask* the lead whether it is melted, and rely upon its testimony; we can tell by its behavior. And in the same way we can sometimes—admittedly not always—see that a man is suffering, without having to ask him. That we sometimes go wrong here does not result from the fact that his suffering is something quite hidden within him, which he alone can find and then report; there is nothing hidden, and nothing for him to find. Still, there is a straightforward way of testing whether a piece of lead is melted, and there is no similarly straightforward way of testing whether a man's foot hurts—he may only be pretending it does. Does this indicate that there might be a pain, which he has found in his foot but might conceal, as he might conceal the contents of his wallet? Surely not; it shows only that men, unlike pieces of lead, are capable of dissimulating. No philosophy was needed to unearth that commonplace fact. It is easier to test for the presence of some states or properties than others, and this is true not only of the states of men's bodies, but of everything under the sun. But things that are hard to establish do not, just by virtue of that, warrant the title of "mental."

Similar remarks can be made about images, which are frequent candidates for the role of mental entities. When queried about their mental imagery, people often will describe it in colorful detail and even with pride, not unlike the regard one might have for a precious gem accessible only to himself. It turns out, though, that all one thereby describes is his power of imagination, which is, of course, sometimes quite great. To say that one has a lively imagination, even great powers of imagination, does not mean that he can create with his mind, *ex nihilo,* things called "images" and composed of some mental, nonphysical, spiritual material. There is no material that is nonmaterial, and there are no images composed of this or anything else—except, of course, those physical objects (pictures, etc.) visible to anyone who can see, which are rightly called images of things. When someone sees something, there is (i) the man who sees and (ii) the thing seen; for instance, some building or scene. There is not, between these, a third thing called appearance of what is seen; philosophers are pretty much agreed on this. But similarly, when someone *imagines* something or, as it is misleadingly put, "forms an image" of it, there is (i) the man who imagines and (ii) sometimes, but not always, something that he imagines; for instance, some building or scene, which might or might not be real. There is not, between these, a third thing called the image of what is imagined. There is just the imagining of the thing in question. And to say that a man is imagining something is to say what he is doing, or perhaps to refer to some state he is in; it is not to refer to some inner thing that he creates and, while it lasts, exclusively possesses.

It is enough, it seems to me, to point this out; that is, to point out that we can say all we want to say about one's powers of imagination without ever introducing the substantive "an image." Philosophy is robbed of nothing by the disposal of these, and there is absolutely no fact about human nature which requires us to affirm their existence. But if one does insist upon the reality of mental images, and professes, for instance, to find them right in his own mind by introspecting—and it is astonishing how eager students of philosophy seem to be to make this claim—then we can ask some very embarrassing questions. Suppose, for instance, one professes to be able to form a very clear image of, say, the campus library—he can bring it before his mind, hold it there, perhaps even turn it bottom side up, and banish it at will. We ask him, then, to hold it before his mind and count the number of steps in the image, the number of windows, the number and disposition of pigeons on the roof, and so on. He could do these things if he had a photograph of the thing before him. But he cannot do them with the image, in spite of the fact that it is supposed to be right there "before his mind," easily and "directly" inspectable. He can tell how many steps there are only if he has sometime counted the steps on the building itself (or in a photograph of it) and now *remembers*—but that is not counting the steps in the image. Or he can *imagine* that it has, say, 30 steps, and then *say* "30"—but that is not counting anything either; it is only a performance. The image he professes to "have" there, so clearly and with such detail, does not even exist. He claims to have produced in his mind an image of the library; but all he has actually done is imagine the library.

What, then, is imagining something? Is it an activity, a state, or what? It does not really matter here how we answer that; it is only *not* the producing of an entity called a "mental image." Let us suppose for this context, then, that to be imagining something is to be in a certain *state*. Is it, then, a *physical* state? Well, it is a state of a man, just as drunkenness, sleep, perspiration, obesity, etc., are sometimes states of this man or that. What is meant by asking whether these are "physical" states, other than asking whether they are states of a physical object? What shall we say of being in a state of sleep, for instance? It is the state of a man, and a man is a physical—that is, a visible and palpable—being. You cannot poke a man's state of imagining something with a stick; all you can do is poke him. That is true. But you cannot poke his somnolence with a stick either. There is nothing to poke; there is only the man sleeping, or the man imagining, or the man becoming drunk, or whatever.

How, then, can a man, if he is nothing but a (mere) physical object, be in such a state as this, that is, of imagining something? If he is only a body and can do this, why cannot sticks and stones be in such a state, for are they not bodies too? The answer is: for just the same reason that sticks and stones cannot be drunken, asleep, perspiring, obese, or hungry; namely, that they are sticks and stones and not men. The reason is not that they lack minds. Even if they had them, they still could not be drunken, asleep, perspiring, obese, or hungry, for they would still be sticks and stones and not men.

The Fourth (and Last) Argument

It is fairly common for people, including philosophers, to say that they can perfectly well imagine surviving the death of their bodies, which would be quite impossible for anyone who supposed that he and his body were one and the same thing. Admittedly no one knows whether there is any survival of death, but it is at least not necessarily false. The doctrine of metempsychosis, for example, though there may be no reason for believing it, cannot be shown to be impossible just on philosophical grounds. It would be impossible, however, if a person and his body were identical, and so would any other form of survival. We know the fate of the body: dust. If I am the same as my body, then it is logically impossible that I should not share that fate.

Reply

All this argument shows is that not everyone, perhaps even no one, *knows* that he and his body are one and the same thing. It does not in the least show that, in fact, they are not. Some things, like the Evening Star and the Morning Star, which some are accustomed to thinking of and describing as different things, nevertheless do turn out to be the same.

Suppose a god were to promise me a life after death—promising, perhaps, to have me (the very person that I am) reborn elsewhere with a different body. Now such a promise might quicken a real hope in me, provided I am capable (as everyone is) of thinking of myself as being something different from my body. But the fact that I can think such a distinction does not show that there is one, and in case there is not—in case I happen to be identical with my body—then of course no god could fulfill such a promise. Consider this analogy: If an enemy of our country did not know that Albany is (the same thing as) the capital of New York, then he might be very interested in a proposal to bomb the one but to spare the other. It would nevertheless be a proposal that no one could carry out. The fact that someone who is ignorant of this identity can entertain the possibility of its being carried out does not show that it is possible; it shows only that he does not know that it is not.

THE SOUL AS LIFE AND THE SOUL AS THOUGHT

It is useful in concluding, I think, to compare the philosophical conception of the mind with what was once the philosophical conception of life. It was once pretty much taken for granted that men and other animals *possess* something which inanimate things lack, namely, life, and that it is *because* they possess this that they can do all sorts of things that inanimate things cannot do, such as move themselves, assimilate nourishment, reproduce their kind, and so on. Aristotle classified the souls of living things according to the abilities they imparted to their owners, and thought that even vegetables had souls. Indeed, an animal's *life* and *soul* were generally thought to be one and the same thing. The very word "animal" has its origin in this belief. Socrates, according to Plato, was even able to convince himself of his own immortality on the basis of this notion, for, he thought, it is only because he has a life or soul to begin with that he is a living man, then it is idle to fear the death of that very soul. Life seemed to him identical with his soul, but accidental to his body, indeed, even foreign to such a thing of clay. A similar model was at work in Descartes' philosophy when he declared that the soul could never stop thinking. Thought seemed to him identical with his soul, but positively foreign to his body.

Now of course, we still talk of life that way, but we no longer take such common modes of speech as descriptive of any reality. We speak of a man "losing" his life, of a man "taking" another's life, of the "gift" of life, and even of the "breath" of life which God is supposed to infuse into an otherwise *lifeless* body. But these are plainly metaphors. No one supposes that a man or animal moves, assimilates nourishment, reproduces, and so on *because* it is possessed of life. We no longer think of life as something added to an animal body, some separable thing that quickens matter. To distinguish something as a living animal is only to call attention to the very complicated way the matter of its body is organized and to a large class of capacities which result from such organization. A living body is simply one in which certain processes, some of them frightfully complex and ill understood, take place. A living body, in short, differs from a nonliving one, not in what it possesses, but in what it does, and these are facts about it that can be verified in a straightforward way.

I have been urging a similar way of speaking of the mind: not as something mysteriously *embodied* here and there, and something that is supposed to *account* for the more or less intelligent behavior of certain beings. A being capable of more or less intelligent thought and action differs from one lacking such capacities, not in something it possesses, but precisely in what it does. And this, incidentally, explains why a man tends to regard it as a deep insult to be told that he has no mind. It is not because he is thus divested in our eyes of some possession dearly prized, but rather, because such a remark is quite rightly taken to mean that he lacks certain important and distinctively human abilities and capacities. If a man is assured that his possession of certain more or less intellectual abilities is in no way in question, he feels divested of nothing upon learning that among his parts or possessions there is none that is properly denoted "a mind."

DOES MATTER THINK?

Probably every philosopher has felt more or less acutely at one time or another a profound puzzlement in the idea of (mere) matter doing those various things rightly ascribable only to persons. How, it is wondered, can a body think, deliberate, imagine things, figure and plan, and so on?

There is really no proper source of bafflement, however. No one can say, *a priori,* what the highly organized material systems of one's body are or are not capable of. It was once thought incredible that matter, unquickened by any soul, could be alive, for matter seemed to inquirers to be inert or lifeless by its very nature. Yet we see around us all the time specimens of living matter—in the merest insects, for instance—so philosophical prejudice has had to yield to the fact. Similarly, I submit, we see around us all the time specimens of thinking matter; that is, material beings which deliberate, imagine, plan, and so on. For men do in fact do these things, and when we see a man, we are seeing a material being—a dreadfully complex and highly organized one, to be sure, but no less a visible and palpable object for that. In any case, the seeming mystery or incredibility that may attach to the idea of matter exercising intellectual capacities, is hardly dissolved by postulating something *else* to exercise those capacities. If there is a difficulty in comprehending how a body can do such things, there is surely no less difficulty in seeing how something which is not a body can do them any better.

28

De Anima

Some philosophers say that each of us has, or indeed *is,* a personal self, ego or soul, related some way or other to his body and to the rest of the world. Just what those relationships are is much debated; but it is considered beyond doubt that there is at the very center of things this self or ego. Such, at least, is the teaching of a long and respectable philosophical tradition. It is said that this personal self came into being at a certain moment in time, and that, alas, it is going to perish at some approaching moment of time, never to exist again in the whole of eternity. Theologians say it arose as a result of God's creating it and that, if certain of God's expectations are lived up to, it can hope to go right on existing forever in some place specially reserved for it.

Other philosophers say that there is no such thing at all, that a man is nothing more than his body and that his ultimate fate, therefore, is simply the fate of his body, which is known to be dust and ashes. This teaching has the advantage of simplicity and seems generally more scientific, but since it is rather depressing, it is not so widely held.

Both schools of thought seem agreed in this, however: that a man is a finite being, distinct from everything that is not himself; that he came into being at a certain more or less identifiable moment; and that, apart from the hope nourished by religion, he is going to perish at some future moment not yet known.

Both points of view are basically mistaken on that point, though it is not easy to demonstrate this through philosophical arguments. That should be no cause for embarrassment, for philosophers have never proved anything about this, one way or another, anyway. Each imagines that he has, and dismisses those of a contrary opinion as too dense

---

From *With Heart and Mind* (New York: St. Martin's Press, 1973), pp. 122–133.

to follow his demonstrations, but in fact all any philosopher has ever done here is to arrange his presuppositions and prejudices in an orderly way, then step back and say, "Behold what I have proved."

Nor is it easy to show in any other way what is wrong here. Proofs seem to accomplish nothing, except to stimulate controversy. Nothing can be counted on, but we might have some luck with

WALTER'S AMOEBIARY: A PHILOSOPHICAL FABLE

Walter had an engrossing interest in microscopy, but this eventually evolved into an interest in microorganisms and, more particularly, amoebae, not merely as subjects of microscopic study, but for their own sakes. That is, he grew fond of them, studied sympathetically their individual traits and personalities, and in time got to the point of spending hours upon hours in their company. Of course he gave them names: Alice, Henry, and so on. The choice of the name was in no way guided by the sex of its possessor, for amoebae are not distinguishable by sex, but this did not matter. Walter found it natural and easy to think of Alice as female, for instance, Henry as male, and so on, considering that an amoeba's name was a perfectly reliable guide in determining whether to refer to a given animal as *he* or *she*.

From the many hours he spent with them, Walter eventually came to know his animals with astonishing understanding. He could pick out Alice at once, for example, knew the circumstances of her birth and something of her achievements, frustrations, and failures. When any amoeba seemed sluggish or ill, he felt genuine concern, and when one perished, it was for Walter not just the loss of something easily replaced. The amoebae, to be sure, showed little reciprocation for this devotion and in fact exhibited no more fidelity to their owner than does a cat, but this made no difference to Walter.

It was a harmless little hobby until Walter decided to breed the tiny animals, with a view to improving the strain, and this led him almost to the madhouse. Amoebae multiply rather quickly, but Walter's problems did not arise from this. They were instead metaphysical. They were perfectly straightforward questions, the answers to which he needed for his records, and while those answers lay right under his nose, he somehow could not find them. He became more obsessed with metaphysics than with his amoebae. He was beginning to think himself deficient in intellect, but this was unjustified, for, as he eventually discovered, the questions that plagued him were questions that could not arise.

His frustrations arose in the following way. The breeder of any stock needs to know its ancestry. This would at first seem to be utterly simple for the amoeba breeder, for an amoeba has only one parent. Instead, then, of the usual family histories, with their numberless branches and ramifications, which in a few generations baffle all comprehension, the amoeba breeder would need only a simple linear record of successive parents and offspring. The breed would be improved by encouraging those with the desired traits to multiply and by inhibiting the rest. It all seemed utterly simple. There would be no need at all to pair off prospective parents and then hope for the best, meanwhile becoming mired in the complexities of bisexual genetics.

But then arose the first problem. The amoeba reproduces simply by splitting in two. So if Henry thus divides himself, the question arises, which of the two resulting amoebae is really Henry and which is his offspring? Walter at first answered that in what seemed a perfectly straightforward, unarbitrary way. The parent, he thought, would be the larger of the two; and the offspring the smaller. In fact it was usually quite obvious when he was on hand to witness the birth, for the offspring first appeared as a tiny bud on the parent, gradually grew larger, and then split off. There was then no problem.

But then Walter got to wondering: Why do I record the small bud as breaking off from the larger one to become its offspring, instead of thinking of the large bud as breaking away from the smaller one to become *its* offspring? Is identity a mere function of size? How do I know, to begin with, that a small bud appears on the parent amoeba? Perhaps the parent amoeba withdraws into a small bud and leaves behind the larger remains, its offspring; the parent then eventually recovers its original size and resembles its offspring. How would I ever know, in case that actually happened? How do I know it does not happen every time? So perhaps my records are all backwards, exhibiting a total confusion between parents and offspring?

Walter lost many hours and quite a bit of sleep too, pondering this question, until he hit upon a technique whereby he could, he thought, unfailingly identify any one of his animals, once and for all. He would tag them, he decided. So he developed a technique for imprinting minute but indelible colored spots on them, which could be combined in various configurations. With each animal so marked, he could then know for certain just which amoeba was before him, by checking its markings. Being thus able to distinguish any amoeba from any other, he could thereby distinguish it from any offspring, including its own. He found this particularly useful in those cases of an amoeba's reproducing by dividing itself through the middle, resulting in two animals of the same size. Had it not been for the markings, it would have been utterly impossible to tell which was the offspring, which the original. With the marking system, Walter had only to check to see which animal bore the identifying mark. That would be the parent; and the other, the offspring. He particularly rejoiced at having this system when several times he found that the offspring was in fact the larger of the two divisions, for it was in these cases the bud which bore the identifying marks. This of course confirmed his earlier fear that the larger part might sometimes be the bud that breaks off from the smaller original, so that in truth the larger of the two is the offspring and the smaller one is the parent.

This was all fine, and Walter felt entirely secure in the accuracy of his records and pedigrees, until one day a strange thing happened. One of his amoebae gave birth, but retained only half of the identifying marking, passing the other half to its offspring. Walter found himself totally unable to tell which was which. Without knowing which was the parent, his record of lineage, with respect to that particular family of amoebae, had come to a dead end, to his dismay.

At first he thought he had minimized the chance of this ever happening again, by making the markings so tiny that it would be very unlikely that they would be divided in any fission of their bearers. But then there arose the following question, which suggested to Walter that the entire system of markings might be unreliable. What if, he thought, a parent amoeba, in shedding some and perhaps even most of its substance to give rise to a totally new individual, should at the same time shed its identifying mark, so that the very mark which was supposed to identify the parent should now be sported by its offspring? Would that not throw the records into a confusion which would be metaphysically impossible to clarify?

For quite a while Walter tried to banish this doubt by insisting that, since marks had been introduced as the very criteria of identity, no question could arise of one amoeba's transmitting its marks to another. The amoeba bearing the marks criterially distinctive of Henry, for example, would have to *be* Henry. It is by those very marks, after all, that we pick Henry out in the first place. To speak of another amoeba as having Henry's marks is to speak unintelligibly.

But like so much that passes for incisive philosophical thinking, this was soon seen to be an arbitrary fiction, from the most elementary consideration. For clearly, if one could regard a given animal as that one upon which a certain mark was bestowed, making its identity entirely a function of this, then one could by the same logic regard a given animal as one upon which a certain name is bestowed. Thus, Henry would be whichever animal one called "Henry," and that would be the end of the matter. But surely such a solution to the problem would be worthy only of children and the most dull-witted philosophers. Our common sense tells us that there would be nothing under the sun to prevent one from flushing Henry down a drain and henceforth calling another amoeba by that name. No animal's continuing identity is ensured by a resolution to continue applying its name. But as an animal can shed its name, so also it can shed its markings—and with that obvious reflection Walter found himself back where he had begun, and on the brink of madness.

After such frustrations, Walter finally destroyed all his records, convinced they must be filled with errors. He tried other systems, but with no better luck. He had long since noted, for example, that his different amoebae displayed different personality traits, different preferences and habits, though all these were of course rather simple. When observing his amoebiary he could quite reliably distinguish one from another by these traits of character, and had in fact been partly guided by these observations in bestowing individual names in the first place. So for a time he used distinctive character traits as his guide, deciding which amoeba was Henry, which Alice, and so on, simply by how they behaved. It was not difficult, once he got to know them sufficiently well. But then one of the amoebae split, and each of the two resulting animals exhibited the character traits of the original to about the same degree. So again it was impossible to tell which was the pre-existing parent and which the offspring just come into being. It was equally impossible to regard both as having been there from the start, and just as impossible to say that each had arisen with the coming into being of the other. In fact it was impossible to say anything that had any sense to it.

If amoebae only had fingers, Walter thought, so that one could make fingerprints. But were not the distinctive marks the equivalent of fingerprints? And they did not do much good. Or if only one could communicate with amoebae at even the most rudimentary level. That would settle any doubts. If there are two similar dogs, for example, and one wants to know which is Rover, one needs only to say "Rover" and see which dog picks up his ears. But then, what if an amoeba named Henry divided into two, and each half responded to the name Henry?

Walter finally gave up the whole enterprise of records, pedigrees and family histories, deciding that any resolution of the problems they presented would be achieved only by metaphysicians. He went back to enjoying his pets for their own sakes, inspired by thoughts of the grandeur of even the lowliest of God's creatures, and he tried to banish metaphysical puzzles from his mind. Some of the old problems did from time to time unsettle his peace and trouble his sleep, but he resisted fairly well any temptation to try solving them.

In time the truth of things did finally dawn on Walter, however not in the sense that any of his problems were solved, but rather, that he realized there had never been any problems there to begin with. They were all just problems that could never arise in the first place.

This enlightenment began when Walter started receiving instruction in metaphysical thinking. One of the first things he learned was that all men have souls. This is what makes them persons. If they did not have souls, they would be nothing but bodies, in principle no different from amoebae. More complicated, to be sure, but otherwise of the same order of being. Philosophers refer to this inner soul as the *self*.

Since it is what thinks, it is also called the *mind.* Amoebae do not think, because they do not have any minds to think with. It is also this soul which gives men their dignity. That is why amoebae have no dignity. They lack the necessary souls. All this was of course very clear, and Walter began seeing everything in a new and much better light.

What was particularly significant for Walter, of course, was that it is on the basis of the inner self that it makes sense to distinguish one person from another in the first place. This distinction has to begin with the distinction between the self and what is not the self, which of course brings us right back again to the soul. When someone refers to *himself,* he is really referring (though he may not realize it) to his self. He as much as says so. That is, he is not referring to his body, which is only a gross physical thing, continuously changing into other things, continuously arising and perishing. He is referring to his *self.* Therefore this must be something that is not physical. It is related somehow or other to the body, no doubt. It possesses and commands the body, for example. Thus when the self commands the arm to rise, the arm does rise, and in a similar way (readily understood in one's own case) it commands the tongue to speak, instructs it in what it should say and so on. It (the self) retains its unalterable identity throughout all the changes transpiring around it in the world at large and particularly in that part of the outside world that the self refers to as its body.

The birth of the body is therefore not the origination of the person, for everyone knows that the body does not spring into being at birth. It existed before then, as part of another body. Indeed, it has always existed, mingled with other things, like the self itself. The person begins when there comes into being a brand new self, or what theologians appropriately call the soul, and philosophers, the mind, the ego, or simply the self. Without such minds or souls, there would only be the corporeal realm, where everything is constantly changing, where nothing is ever created or utterly perishes and where all distinctions between things are relative, as they are in the case of amoebae. In the world considered solely as corporeal, there could be no absolute distinctions between one self and another, for in such a world there would be no selves to distinguish. Hence, in such a world there could be no ultimate distinction between me and thee, mine and thine, for there would not even be the most fundamental and precious of all distinctions, that between oneself and everything else.

Walter saw, of course, that such distinctions as these, so obvious to one who has mastered the fundamentals of metaphysics, do not apply at the level of amoebae. Amoebae are not possessed of egos, selves, or souls. *That,* Walter perceived, must be why the distinction between parent and offspring was so elusive. It must be a distinction which at that level does not exist. There one finds only life assuming successive forms, wherein nothing is really born and nothing really dies—unlike that which is discovered, through metaphysics, at the higher personal level.

All this enabled Walter to see pretty clear what had gone wrong with his attempts to keep records of amoeban ancestry. If his amoebae had possessed souls, as we do, there would have been no difficulty whatsoever. He would only have needed to keep track of souls and to record the relations of the different souls to each other.

Punch line:

"Then," thought Walter, "everything would have been straightforward, perfectly simple, and above all, of course, clear."

29

Polarity

There is a common way of thinking that we can call *polarization,* and that appears to be the source of much metaphysics. It consists of dividing things into two exclusive categories, and then supposing that if something under consideration does not belong to one of them, then it must belong in the other. "Either/or" is the pattern of such thought, and because it is usually clear, rigorous, and incisive, it is also often regarded by philosophers as uniquely rational. Not surprisingly, it is presupposed in logic texts, in which we are told, on the first page, that every proposition is *either* true *or* false—and the abstract science of logic proceeds from there. Legal reasoning is also sometimes polarized, for the skill of an attorney or judge in defending a point of view is likely to rest upon his ability to lead his audience down the path he wants them to take by foreclosing, one after another, every bypath. "Guilty or innocent," "taxable or exempt," "lawful or unlawful," "sane or insane" are the kinds of choices he offers, with no opportunity to reject both or to accept a mixture.

Philosophers have cultivated polarized thought since the time of Socrates, who was the master of it. Thus Socrates characteristically gave his opponent a choice between two answers and, one of them being accepted, another choice immediately arose, giving rise to still another, until the opponent found himself face to face with some conclusion, usually a highly implausible one, that he could not back away from, every path of retreat having been closed off by the choices already made. And Socrates would then represent this strange conclusion as something not known before, which had been "learned" by this dialectical procedure.

From *Metaphysics,* 3d ed. (Englewood Cliffs, N.J.: Prentice-Hall, 1983), pp. 106–118.

Polarized thinking is not, however, the invention of philosophers. It is very common, almost natural, to anyone who thinks at all. For example, it is quite common for people to suppose that if a given action—killing one person to save another, for example—is not "wrong," then it must be "right," at least in the sense of being allowable. It is not considered possible that it might be both. Or again, it seems like common sense to say that a given person must be either married or unmarried—"You can't have it both ways"; or that someone either is in, say, Wisconsin, or he is not in Wisconsin—"You can't be two places at once"; or that at a given date and place it either rained, or it did not rain—and so on.

Of course, such thinking has great practical value. It is in fact required for the most common choices we make. People are often much bothered by the "morality" of their actions, for instance, and need some way to categorize them with respect to rightness or wrongness; hence the avid search for "ethical principles" that will somehow enable them to do this. Similarly, someone might be most eager to know whether some person of interest to him is "married" or not; much can depend on it. And it could be crucial to a prosecuting attorney whether someone he has charged with a crime was or was not in Wisconsin at a given time.

And, let it be said at once, things usually *can* be at least roughly categorized in these ways. For example, there usually is a definite answer, yes or no, to the question whether a given person is, say, in Wisconsin at a given moment. Note, however, that the crucial words in these two sentences are *usually* and *roughly*. The principle of polarity would have us use, instead, the words *always* and *exactly* in order to make our classifications sharp and precise. But, we are suggesting here, such sharpness and precision are sometimes bought at the expense of truth, for reality is far too loose a mixture of things to admit of such absolute distinctions. And sometimes, both in our practical affairs and in our philosophy, we are led into serious errors, which are fervently embraced just because they seem so clearly to have been proved.

THE EXCEPTIONABILITY OF POLARIZATIONS

Consider what would seem to be an obvious instance where the "either/or" pattern would fit without exception—for example, the statement that either it rained at a given place and time, or it did not. And let the place be Chicago, on some specific date—July 4, 1982, let us say. Now if it rained all over Chicago that day, then it assuredly rained then in Chicago. But what if it was a beautiful, fair day—except for a brief shower in some corner of that city. Did it rain in Chicago? The temptation is to say yes—for if there was any rain at all, then strictly speaking we have to say it rained. But suppose that on an exceptionally clear day a few raindrops fell in some remote corner of Chicago. Was the weather forecaster wrong who said the day before that it would be clear? Here we are tempted to say that, "strictly speaking," he was not quite right, but that practically speaking he was. But suppose there is but a single raindrop in my yard, along with others nearby. Did it rain in Chicago? Did it rain in my yard? In my entire yard? Or only in part of it? Or only in this or that square inch of it? Or only at the spot where the drop fell? Or what?

One should resist the temptation to figure out (by drawing more distinctions) the same answers to these odd questions. There is no right answer. Either "yes" or "no" is as good an answer as the other. And the only thing odd about such questions is that there would seldom be any practical point in raising them. When questions of this sort arise in philosophy, however, then it does not matter whether there is any practical point in raising them, for philosophy does not pretend to be practical.

Consider the question whether, at a given moment, a certain person was or was not in Wisconsin. In most cases, of course, there will be a definite answer. But what of a passenger in an airplane flying over a corner of Wisconsin? Would he be wrong if, some years later, he said he had never visited Wisconsin? Here the temptation is to say that, "strictly speaking," he would be mistaken, since we must include the space above Wisconsin within its geographical limits. But must we? How much space? Shall we say that astronauts, thousands of miles above earth, are nevertheless still passing through Wisconsin? And what does "above" mean here? How shall we determine what is "above" the earth and what "below" it? Surely we have here crossed over into nonsense. Nor will it help to go in the other direction, insisting that, "strictly speaking," one is in Wisconsin only if he is on the *terra firma* of that state—for in that case people would depart Wisconsin by the simple act of getting onto elevators. Nor should we split hairs by adding "or upon structures resting upon that *terra firma*," for someone who falls from a tree whose roots are planted in Wisconsin does not suddenly leave, and then as suddenly reenter, Wisconsin.

The point then is that with respect to such "either/or" choices, there are no right answers to be *found,* they can only be *invented,* and this is invariably done with an eye to practical consequences. But then you have to be careful not to view this invention, this "sharpening up" of a concept, as it is sometimes misleadingly described, as enabling you to express the truth more accurately than before. On the contrary, it distorts the truth by making reality appear to your mind to be more neat and tidy than it is.

PROBLEMS OF POPULAR METAPHYSICS

The danger just alluded to—that of producing "either/or" choices where "neither" or "both" would be a clearer approximation to truth, and of thus defining terms more precisely than the realities they are supposed to fit—sometimes produces inferences and "conclusions" that can have far-reaching effects. The danger is made more insidious by the illusion that one has "shown" something to be true that is not really true at all, often in areas where there simply is no actual truth to be shown.

For example, you sometimes find people, even educated people, trying to discern the borderline between life and death. Is someone whose heart and pulse are strong and normal, but whose brain has irreversibly ceased to function, still alive? What is the seat of life: the heart? or the brain? Questions like these, following the "either/or" pattern, invite answers, and there is an almost irresistible temptation to try to find them. Philosophy teachers sometimes engage their students in discussions of this kind, because they are invariably lively ones that "get the students thinking." It is seldom made clear that such thinking is in the nature of the case certain to end in failure. Sometimes, however, metaphysical wisdom begins not with finding an answer to a metaphysical question but with the realization that no answer exists, even, sometimes, to a question that is perfectly clear and precise.

Of course, answers to such questions can always be invented, and indeed they always are. But as with all inventions, they differ according to the predilections, needs, and prejudices of their inventors. In the realm of metaphysics the competing inventors of answers then fall to wrangling over which answer is the "true" one, quite failing to realize that no one has discovered any truth at all. The answers are in fact nothing but rival fabrications.

Here man is, indeed, the measure of things, in precisely the sense Protagoras meant. Rival answers to questions of this nature can all be declared to be true, which is but another way of saying that none is objectively true. But as Protagoras insisted, some answers are nevertheless *better* than others; better, that is, in terms of their consequences. So the answer one produces to such a question as that concerning the beginning or ending of life is going to be a function of what he wants to get out of that answer; or in other words, what its consequences will be. Declaring that a person's life ends when his heart finally stops will have decidedly different consequences from saying that it ends with the cessation of brain function. In the latter case, for instance, but not in the former, you can remove someone's healthy, pulsating heart, for whatever purpose—e.g., to give it to someone else who needs it. You choose between answers by first deciding, consciously or otherwise, which consequences you like better. And there can be nothing wrong with this, for there simply is no other basis for choice.

Thus if you think about it, you can see that the correct answer in such cases as this does not fit the "either/or" pattern at all, but rather a pattern we can express as "some of each." For example, a person whose brain is forever dead but whose heart and other vital processes are normal is not quite dead, but neither is he quite alive; he is, *strictly speaking,* partly each. And here you have to resist the impulse to say, "But how can he be both dead and alive?" for that is only to betray a mindless dedication to the "either/or" thought pattern. It does not promote rigorous and precise thinking, but the very opposite. Nor should one be tempted to say that if anyone is partly still alive, then he is, after all, still living, and therefore, alive; for from the point of view of logic, it would be exactly as good to say that, if someone is partly dead—for instance, if his brain is dead, or any other part of him, such as a foot or a finger or indeed a hair on his head, then he is, after all, already *dead*—which is of course absurd. It is, moreover, well known that many of the body's cells are still living quite some time after death, by every traditional criterion, has set in; but no one is going to insist that someone is still "alive" just because a few cells in the hair follicles or fingernails are still multiplying.

The point then is that the transition from life to death, like most natural transitions, is a gradual one, and that no *borderline* between the two exists. Borderlines can be invented, of course, but they cannot be found, for they are not there.

COMING INTO BEING

The same will be true, of course, with respect to coming into existence. We tend to assume that any given thing either exists, or it does not, and that there can thus be no gradual transition into that state; but that is only because we long ago became the victims of polarized thought. Thus each of us is apt to suppose that, since he now exists, but at some past time (*e.g.,* one hundred years ago) did not, then there must have been some moment between then and now when he came into existence. Traditionally that time has been fixed as the moment of birth, but the relative arbitrariness of this is apparent to everyone. There is, for example, no *moment* of birth; birth is itself a process that takes time. But more important, existence obviously precedes birth which is nothing more than the passage, not into existence, but into the light of day.

Having noted this, one is then invited to work back to some imagined "moment" at which existence itself began. But existence of *what?* An ovum? a zygote? bonded genetic material? fused nuclei? life? a blastula? an embryo? a person? what?

And the next thing to note is, whichever of these one selects, *its* coming into existence is also a process, and not something that is achieved in a "moment." The beginnings of a particular ovum, for example, are nebulous and in no sense located at a point in time. The same is true of the formation of a human zygote, the various stages of which involve numerous complex and time-consuming processes on the parts of both male and female gametes, even after these have become more or less united and before their nuclei have become fused. This fusion of parent nuclei is in turn an unbelievably complex process that takes place over time, without discernible time of commencement or completion, nor is the genetic material of these nuclei bonded in a single instantaneous, or even very brief, time. The same can be said about the origins of the blastula, embryo, or any other stage of development that has received a biological name. The initial division of the fertilized ovum, which can perhaps be considered some sort of beginning of an organism, takes thirty-six hours, and not for another twenty-eight hours are there as many as four cells. And as for personhood, or life, these words obviously denote no *things* at all. Being a person is a quality with which some things, namely human beings, are invested, according to conventional criteria. So the question whether, for example, a tadpole, or a horse, or a zygote, "has" that quality is nothing more than the question whether we have found it useful, for legal or other purposes, to regard it that way. We have found no reason to treat tadpoles or horses as persons. Perhaps if one of them began using language intelligibly, or exhibited a potential to do so, then we would; perhaps we would not. Nor have human spermatazoans ever been treated as persons, nor human ova. Perhaps they are too numerous, or too small, but more likely, there would just be no point in so regarding them. The human zygote, however, in spite of its minuteness, *is* called a "person" by some, usually for theological reasons, though most people consider this absurd. Whether it is "really" a person or not is, of course, a metaphysical question, and one that has no answer, being a perfect expression of polarized thinking in an area where such thinking is certain to produce nonsense. For anyone to declare an undifferentiated human zygote to be a "person" is thus only to express a preference or choice, often one that has been guided by moral or religious presuppositions. It cannot, in the nature of the case, be a declaration of fact.

Still, one wants to say, I exist, and there was a time past when I did not. I must, therefore, whether instantly or otherwise, at some time have come into existence, and the solicitation seems overwhelming to find that time. Nor is it just a matter of metaphysical curiosity. Questions of religion and morality do seem to turn upon it. Even politicians find themselves drawn into the question of when "life" begins, and indeed, feelings on this strange question can be so intense as to ruin political careers.

What people actually seek in the pursuit of such questions is some dramatic or at least recognizable *event* in one's history that can be regarded as "the beginning" of life, or personhood, or humanity, or whatever. The trouble is, of course, that one's history is filled with more or less dramatic events that seem to mark beginnings of some sort, yet no such event seems to serve any better than some other as the beginning of life.

Thus, my awakening this morning was a beginning, more or less dramatic—but not the beginning of *me,* since I remembered yesterday, and many days before that. So likewise was my birth a beginning, a fairly dramatic one, but for reasons already considered, it was not the beginning of *me* (except for certain purposes of law and custom, such as assigning me an age). *I* was there, in the womb, waiting to be born, before this happened. Of course, having pushed back to this point, virtually everyone then pushes back still farther, to some minute and unwitnessed event, vaguely described in such expressions as "the moment of conception," and there are persons who will solemnly declare, as if enunciating some kind of fact, even as a fact of biology, that this is an absolute beginning. But it obviously is not, for there is, again, no such "moment"—conception is a profoundly complex process that takes time—and furthermore, the elements that enter into that process were already living prior to then. From the standpoint of metaphysics, the "moment" of conception is no better choice for marking the passage into existence than the "moment" of birth. It only is earlier, less familiar, and hence more mysterious and more obscure.

Of course, one can simply abandon consideration of fact altogether, which is what usually happens with questions like this, and say, for example, quite arbitrarily, that God infuses a soul into a human ovum at some moment—usually, again, the "moment" of conception, converting it to a "person." But there is obviously no way of checking this, nor indeed, even knowing what one would be checking for. What kind of observation would count as either confirming or disconfirming it? What, indeed, does such a declaration even mean? It clearly arises, not from anything anyone knows or even believes, but simply from theological presupposition, or more often, from purely moral presuppositions. And in this case, of course, it is the theology or morality that is determining what is to be regarded as "fact," and not facts that are producing theological or moral inferences. Thus persons who, for whatever reason, happen to have an aversion to abortion are very likely to prefer one kind of description, whereas those who have no such aversion will prefer another, then the two sides will argue *as if* they were disputing certain facts—indeed, certain facts of biology—whereas they are only expressing their divergent and sometimes strong feelings about rival policies. And metaphysics, which is here invoked to resolve such a dispute, can obviously do nothing—except, of course, exacerbate it, by falsely appearing to provide a metaphysical foundation in support of one set of feelings or the other.

There are other familiar transitions of a more or less meaningful kind in which no one is ever tempted to seek out the "moment" of such transition, because no religious or moral feelings require it. When does a child become an adolescent? or an adolescent an adult? And on what day does one pass into middle age? It is easy to see that, in spite of the fact that such transitions occur, there is no real time at which they begin or end. Often, when human needs require it, we *invent* such times. For example, an adolescent is declared suddenly to turn to an adult on his twenty-first birthday, sometimes his eighteenth. But everyone recognizes this as conventional. We *need* a date, for legal purposes. So we *declare* one, and we give it the force of law. But we do not find one. The same is quite obviously true with respect to the question: When did I become a person? Metaphysically, the answer to this is: I am a person; once I was not; hence I became a person—but there is no *time* at which this was accomplished. It occurred gradually, over a considerable time, and had no real beginning or ending. And the same line of thinking applies to such questions as: when did I begin to exist? When did I become human? and so on.

Of course, we would like our truths to be sharper, more incisive, more exact than that. But metaphysically, one has to see that, sharp or not, that is the *exact* truth, and anything more sharp and definite is *not* going to be exact.

POLARITY AND TRADITIONAL METAPHYSICS

Of course that is just one of the innumerable ways one can get bogged down philosophically by polarized thinking. The history of philosophy abounds with such illustrations. Indeed, it is probably no exaggeration to say that metaphysics has, from the beginning of philosophy, drawn more nourishment from this unfortunate source than from the mysterious and perplexing world itself.

Very early in the history of western philosophy, for example, Parmenides was driven to the outrageous metaphysical conclusion that there is no such thing as becoming or passing away, and hence, no change anywhere. What appears to us as motion and change must be simply illusion. Behind this incredible proposition lay a perfect example of polarization; namely, his supposition that, if something were to change, then something that *is* would cease to be, or in other words, become what is *not,* and that what is *not* would perforce come to *be.* His conclusion seemed to him inevitable, just because he allowed himself no choice of answers besides those offered within this "either/or" framework. His disciple Zeno, of Elea, arrived at similar conclusions by adhering to the same "rigorous" pattern of thought. Thus, for example, Zeno argued that anything that exists, in case it consists of parts, must be infinitely large, because (and here is the polarization) each such part either has some size, or it does not. But if each such part has size, then so also does each part of *it*—for example, each of its two halves; and each part of these, in turn, has size too, and so on, *ad infinitum*. You can never conceive of a part so small as to be without size, and hence without parts. Therefore, anything composed of parts is composed of infinitely many of them, each having some size, so the thing in question will be infinitely large. The only alternative to this (so Zeno thought) would be for it to have no size at all, and hence to be utterly nonexistent, this result following from the supposition that its "parts" have no size. Everything is therefore either infinitely large or infinitely small, filling the whole of space or none of it, or in other words, being identical with everything, or with nothing. Strange as this conclusion is, it can be quite rigorously deduced from the premises Zeno began with, together with his restriction of answers to just two possibilities.

Nor do metaphysicians seem to have learned of the pitfalls of polarized thinking with the passage of the centuries. It is quite common to find them, even now, earnestly engaged in disputation over issues having no other source. How much of the issue of fatalism, for example, rests upon the supposition that every declarative assertion must be either true or false? How often is it considered possible that some such assertions might be a bit of both, or perhaps neither? Why is it thought that the world must fit so exactly our neat and precise descriptions? Similarly, how much of the celebrated problem of free will turns on the supposition that everything that happens either is, or is not, causally determined? Why are these two choices thought to exhaust the possibilities?

BEING AND NON-BEING AS EXCLUSIVE CATEGORIES

Still another area of metaphysics, and a very large one, that appears particularly susceptible to polarized thought is that which deals with questions of existence. Anything whatever, it would seem, either exists, or it does not—there can be no middle ground between these possibilities. Thus, the moon exists, as does the city of Paris, the Statue of Liberty, and the 101st person appointed to the U.S. Supreme Court. The satellite of our moon, on the other hand, does not exist at all, nor does any unicorn, nor any daughter of the 101st Supreme Court Justice, since all her children are male. Nor, it would seem, would it make sense to speak of any of these things as *partially* existing, or as belonging to some existential realm between being and nonbeing. The moon, for instance, cannot partially exist and partially not. Existence is something it simply has, and something its satellite lacks.

There are, to be sure, some things that have a dubious kind of existence, if any at all—numbers, for example, or abstract things such as justice, or fictional beings such as Hamlet, or entities such as the average taxpayer. These things have properties, about which one can discourse intelligibly, but metaphysicians can dispute whether they really exist.

That, however, does not concern us here, for we can simply limit ourselves to physical objects, to things that, in case they are real, can be located in space and seen—things like the Statue of Liberty, for instance. And concerning any of these, at least, we seem safe in saying that it either does exist, or it does not. No such thing has a merely partial existence.

Yet in spite of the seeming obviousness of this, and what would seem to be the unquestionable applicability of polarity here, it does have a consequence that is certainly *not* obvious and that seems, in fact, quite absurd; namely, that every existing object which at any time in history did not exist has sprung suddenly into existence at some moment of time. This seems to follow from the supposition that it at one time did not exist, then at a later time did, and that there can be no gradual transition from the one state to the other, during which it only partially exists.

This certainly does not seem in any sense true of such things as we have been considering. The Statue of Liberty, for instance, did not at some instant come into being all at once; yet it does exist, and there was a time when it did not.

Then what shall we say? The truth seems to be expressed best this way: that there was a time past when there was no Statue of Liberty at all; that there was a subsequent time, *e.g.*, yesterday, when it entirely existed; and that between those two times there was a considerable interval of time during which it was in the process of coming into existence; and further, that throughout that interval, it partially existed, and partially did not.

Now if that description is correct—and it does seem to be exactly correct—then polarity, as applied to questions of existence, is *not* correct. For existence appears to admit of degrees, like everything else.

Of course the temptation here is to break the thing in question down into parts and to say that the existence of each of these, at least, does not admit of degrees. But this, too, is apparently false. The head of that statue, for instance, came into existence quite gradually, as did the statue itself. And so with any other part. Of course its most minute parts—the atoms, perhaps, of which it is composed, in case there are such things—may *always* have existed, but that is not relevant. We are here dealing with only things that at one time did not exist, and we are saying that their existence is something they can acquire quite gradually, in spite of what our habits of polarized thinking may incline us to regard as obvious.

THE PROBLEM OF PERSONAL IDENTITY OVER TIME

There is one metaphysical problem that seems to have resulted almost entirely from polarization, and that is the celebrated problem of personal identity. A part of that problem can be expressed in the following way: Am I the same person as that infant upon whom my mother bestowed my name? Or have I perhaps become someone else? This latter suggestion, the way it is put, seems so plainly dubious that philosophers are inclined to treat the alternative—that I am still the very same person—as axiomatic.

Generalizing the question, we may note that everyone, over the course of his life, undergoes great changes, some of them so radical that he seems finally to have lost his identity with his earlier self. He passes from infancy to old age, the two stages bearing almost no similarity to each other. In the course of this his body sometimes undergoes total renewal, such that none of the cells of the infant body are still possessed by that adult who, nevertheless, still considers himself as being in some sense "the same person" as the infant of years ago. The teeth, it is said, do not undergo such renewal, so that some of these, or parts of them, might in the strictest sense remain the same throughout one's lifetime. But of course, one sometimes loses all one's teeth, and has them replaced with false ones, so that even this continuity is destroyed.

Suppose, then, I pick out a certain child of several decades ago and say of him, "That is I," meaning that the child alluded to (me, as an infant) and the person alluding to him (me again, now as an adult) are one and the same person. I might pick out the child by a snapshot, for example ("That's me, on my mother's lap"), or by a document ("Here's my birth certificate—the person it says was born at that time and place to those parents is me"), or in numerous other ways.

Now clearly, this identification does seem in some sense sometimes correct. There is some sense in which I am one and the same person as *one* of the infants shown in an old photograph, sitting on my mother's knee, and not at all the same as the other infant on the other knee, that being my twin brother. And yet, my body may not have a single cell or molecule in common with *either* of those infants. So in what sense am I nevertheless the same person as one of them, and not the same as the other?

It cannot be, of course, that I have the same properties, for I do not, or, to the slight extent that I do, then I share those same properties with the infant on the other knee, my brother. I have the property of being male, for instance, and so do both of those infants. I have the property of having a certain person as my mother—but again, so do both of those infants. And many, virtually all, of my present properties are shared by *neither* of those infants—I am bearded for example, and weigh more than 100 pounds, and so on, unlike either of those infants, to *one* of which I nevertheless claim to be identical, and from the other of which I claim to be a totally different person.

What connects me with the one and not the other?

The answer is contained in the statement that I am *the same person* as the one but not the other. But what does that mean?

Metaphysicians, or at least a great many of them, have supposed it to mean that there is a strict identity in something, namely, a person, over the course of time. But since no such identity holds with respect to his body over the course of time—for the body is constantly being changed and renewed, no particle of it remaining indefinitely—then the person who is possessed of such identity must be something *other* than the physical or biological body. I am one thing, it is thought, that remains *the same* thing through time, and my body is something else, which becomes something quite different over the course of time, becoming, eventually, entirely or totally different from the body I once identified as "mine."

And this reflection, of course, at once gives rise to a great number of theories as to just what that person—a being *within* a body, as it would seem—actually is. Some imagine it to be the mind or soul. And it has even been seriously maintained that this *person,* which retains its strict identity through time, is nothing other than some invisibly minute particle of matter located, presumably, somewhere in the brain.

But clearly such bizarre theories, which provide endless delight to metaphysicians and their students, do not arise from any observations of people. No one has ever *seen* a person, on such metaphysical accounts as these; we see only the ever-changing bodies in which their persons are housed. This is, of course, why such theories are considered metaphysical in the first place. They arise from metaphysical reflection and in no way lend themselves either to confirmation or refutation by any actual observations.

But what *is* the character of the thought that produces such metaphysics? It is, plainly, polarized thought. It is assumed that a person either is one and the same as his former self, or else totally different, and since he cannot be totally different, we have to say he is one and the same.

But we do not have to think that way. Instead we can say that a person undergoes constant change and renewal over the course of time, such that he is in some respects the same today as he was yesterday and in some respects different, that over the course of sufficient time he undergoes a total renewal such that he shares no cell or particle with a former self long since past, but that he is nevertheless *the same person* in this relative sense, that he *grew out of* that former person. This is exactly the sense in which a butterfly, for example, is the same insect as the caterpillar from which it evolved, or the oak tree is the same plant as the tiny shoot that emerged from a certain acorn. The sameness is relative, but it is entirely sufficient for every claim we need to make about the identity of persons over time, whether the claims be moral, legal, or whatever. Thus: I am the same as *one* of the infants pictured sitting on my mother's knee in a very old photograph, but a different person from the other infant shown there, who is my twin brother. This means that, while no part or particle of my body is shared with either infant, and while I share as many common properties with the one as with the other, there is nevertheless a relationship that I have to one, and not to the other, quite well expressed by my saying that I grew out of the infant on the left knee, not the one on the right.

IDENTITY OVER TIME AND SPACE

Perhaps the easiest way to understand the identity of a person over a length of time is to compare it with the identity of a rope over a length of space.

Thus, think of a rope of considerable length, composed of individual fibers, none of which is as long as the rope itself. No fiber, accordingly, reaches from one end of the rope to the other. We can even suppose that the longest fiber in the rope is but a small fraction of the length of the rope. Hence the successive segments of the rope will consist of fibers, some of which extend into adjoining segments, overlapping fibers there, and some of which do not, and all of the fibers at either end of the rope will be different from those at the other end. Still, it is all one rope. If each of us pulls on a different end of it in a tug of war, we are assuredly pulling on the same rope. There is no need at all to assume some single fiber to continue unbroken through the length of the rope in order to ensure this identity. And we can say that each segment is continuous with or "emerges from" every anterior segment in a way similar to that in which a person is continuous with or "grows out of" every earlier chronological segment of his past. And to make the analogy complete, we can suppose that the length of rope we are considering arose in the following way: that from two previously existing ropes two fibers broke away and became entwined with each other to form a minute strand, then more strands became added to this, making it longer and larger until it grew into a complete length of rope in its own right. This illustrates the manner in which a rope might arise from two parent ropes and yet be an individual rope distinct from them and, by perfect analogy, the way in which a person derives his existence from his parents, and yet acquires an individual identity of his own, distinct from theirs, that persists through time.

ANOTHER IDENTITY PROBLEM

Metaphysicians sometimes concoct puzzles of identity, putting into them the very ingredients that seem to preclude solution. For example, it is well known that some human parts, tissues, and organs can be exchanged between people. It is not hard to transplant a hair from one person to another, for instance, and blood from one person can be transfused to another with relative ease. Kidneys, likewise, are sometimes transferred, and more recently, hearts and lungs. Suppose, then, that as a result of greatly improved techniques of neurosurgery, the brains of two persons—Mr. Brown and Mr. Robinson, let us call them—get exchanged, Brown ending up with Robinson's brain, and vice-versa. Now further suppose that, after recovery from this rather radical surgical procedure, Brown—or the man who *looks* like Brown—goes home to Robinson's house and family, remembers all the things Robinson remembered, recognizes the people there as his wife and children, goes to Robinson's office and resumes the rather demanding and specialized work that Robinson had always done there so well, and so on. And make the same sort of assumptions about Robinson—that he (or what everyone supposes is he) emerges from the surgery with all of Brown's memories and associations, thinks that Brown's wife and children are his family, and so on.

Which one is really Brown, and which is really Robinson?

The trouble with this question is the way it is put, for it offers only two choices. Either this person who looks like Robinson but acts like Brown is Robinson, or he is Brown. And similarly for that person, who looks like Brown but acts like Robinson. It is simply assumed that the answer will have to be *one or the other.*

But there is no reason for us to accept this polarized and exclusive "either/or" presupposition. The "problem" simply disappears as a problem when we say that each of the persons emerging from this procedure is part Robinson, part Brown; that neither is, strictly speaking, either Brown *or* Robinson. The identity of either person over time has simply been abruptly destroyed by so radical a change as this, and we can no longer really say, of the persons we end up with, which grew out of Robinson, which out of Brown. Either claim would be as good as the other.

What we would have in such a case would not differ, metaphysically, from what we would have in the case of two cars whose parts were interchanged. If the tires of one are put on the other, we do not hesitate to say that it is still the same car, just as, in the case of a person, we think of him as preserving his identity even if he receives someone else's kidney, or even his heart. But if we purchased a car and then went back to the dealer to get it, only to learn that its engine had been replaced with another, we could certainly raise the question whether it was the same car. And if two cars, a Ford and a Plymouth, had their engines exchanged, and we then raised the question, which is the Ford, and which is the Plymouth, surely the correct answer would be: neither. Each car is part Ford, part Plymouth.

And in just exactly that way we should say, of our two men whose brains get swapped, that each is part Brown, part Robinson, this being the *whole* answer to the question. And if anyone were to press on and ask, but who is *really* Brown there, and who is really Robinson? then he would *not* be expressing clear and precise metaphysical thinking at all. He would be displaying polarized thinking and exhibiting not a deeper sense of the problem but rather a failure to grasp it at all.

POLARIZATION AND COMMON SENSE

Metaphysical bewilderment sometimes results from our seeing clearly enough how things are but being unable to describe what we see. Thus everyone understands his relationship to that particular infant from which he developed, as well as he understands his relationship to his own mother. The problem lies simply in describing that relationship. Similarly, we easily see the result of exchanging, in imagination, two persons' brains as easily as we see the results of exchanging the engines of two cars. It is only a matter of describing what has happened, and the result. And the reason it is a problem is that we apply an "either/or" pattern, which works in most cases, to cases where that pattern does not fit. The result is metaphysics—not the kind of metaphysics that is a part of philosophical wisdom, but rather, the metaphysics of disputation, hair-splitting, and paradox, so dearly loved by some. The solutions to non-problems can only be non-solutions, however; and as these non-problems are sometimes the creations of our own thinking, the way through them is not through more of the same kind of thinking but rather through a revision of thought patterns themselves.